# FIXERS

# FIXERS

A NOVEL

## MICHAEL M. THOMAS

 MELVILLE HOUSE
BROOKLYN • LONDON

**FIXERS**

Copyright © 2016 by Michael M. Thomas

First Melville House Printing: January 2016

Melville House Publishing    8 Blackstock Mews
46 John Street   and   Islington
Brooklyn, NY 11201    London N4 2BT

mhpbooks.com   facebook.com/mhpbooks   @melvillehouse

Library of Congress Cataloging-in-Publication Data
Names: Thomas, Michael M., author.
Title: Fixers : a novel of Wall Street and Washington / Michael M.
  Thomas.
Description: First edition. | Brooklyn : Melville House, [2016]
Identifiers: LCCN 2015044867 (print) | LCCN 2015048974 (ebook)
  | ISBN 9781612194981 (hardcover) | ISBN 9781612194998 (ebook)
Subjects: LCSH: Global Financial Crisis, 2008–2009—Fiction. |
  Banks and banking—Corrupt practices—United States—Fiction. |
  Political corruption—United States—Fiction. | Rich people—
  United States—Fiction. | Political fiction. | BISAC: FICTION /
  Political.
Classification: LCC PS3570.H574 F59 2016 (print) | LCC PS3570.
H574 (ebook) | DDC 813/.54—dc23
LC record available at http://lccn.loc.gov/2015044867

Designed by Marina Drukman

Printed in the United States of America
10  9  8  7  6  5  4  3  2  1

This is a work of fiction. The principal characters, those with
speaking parts, are wholly creatures of the author's imagination
and invention. The transactions and situations in which
they are involved, however, are matters of historical record.

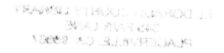

For Tamara—with love, gratitude, and so much else

*The law doth punish man or woman*
*That steals the goose from off the common,*
*But lets the greater felon loose*
*That steals the common from the goose.*
—seventeenth-century English rhyme

# PART ONE

# THE SECRET DIARY
# OF CHAUNCEY SUYDAM
# 2007–2010

## Excerpts

Gibbon records in his autobiography that the idea of writing *The Decline and Fall of the Roman Empire* came to him while listening to "the bare-footed friars singing in the Temple of Jupiter."

My own authorial epiphany, the spur to keep a diary that will be a firsthand account of a potentially nation-changing scam that I have been asked to carry out, came twelve hours ago as I stood on the corner of Madison Avenue and 76th Street and watched a multimillionaire investment banker climb into a $75,000 Mercedes SUV to be driven north to his twenty-acre Connecticut estate, where he'll spend the weekend hammering away at a collection of museum-quality harpsichords. That's about as far from barefooted as you can get.

The man's name is Leon Mankoff. My former CIA boss and mentor and a current consulting client, he's the CEO of Struthers Strauss (henceforth referred to by its trading symbol: STST), the giant investment bank and globe-bestriding power in the world of high finance. A firm admired, envied, feared, and hated by its competitors, adored by its clients and people. I'm no special fan of Wall Street myself—but if "the Street" didn't generate the kind of wealth that underwrites the philanthropies I advise on, I wouldn't have a job.

To jump ahead, let me tell you where I'll be going with this. This morning, in the course of a coffee-shop breakfast, Mankoff asked me to fix next year's presidential election.

That make your jaw drop, Gentle Reader? It should. It certainly did mine. As I thought when he described what he had in mind, "Jesus, man! You're talking about the biggest goddamn bait-and-switch in history!"

The better part of an hour later, after he'd gone into some

detail about what he has in mind, as I watched his car pull away, it occurred to me that if I go along with Mankoff's plan, I'll have the opportunity not only to be at the center of a defining moment in the history of American politics, but to furnish future historians with an accurate insider transcript of what was said, what got done, and why.

I think the future will value such an account. The great story of our time, according to many observers, has been the takeover of Washington by Big Money, namely Wall Street, and the other private-sector "Bigs": Big Pharma, Big Transportation, Big Realty, and the like. The record I intend to keep, if I accept Mankoff's commission—and there's still some heavy thinking I have to do about *that*—should shed new and penetrating light on how the power game is played.

The exercise of power in America today is almost entirely an insider's game that completely shuts out 99.9 percent of the population, which is never made truly privy to the backstage dealings that decide matters of great pith and moment—which in this great, shining republic generally run to the issue of who is to get what and for how much, with the bulk of the money coming from the full faith and credit of the American taxpayer. We groundlings are never told what was actually, exactly said and agreed, as opposed to what *They*—with a capital T—and their stooges in the media tell us. You might say I intend to bridge the gap between the true facts of the matter and what the public will have been told.

People argue that untrained palates profit little from knowing how the sausage gets made, and presumably this is true of both pork and politics (no pun intended, although I recognize that today the two are one and the same). I disagree. In my book, knowledge is life, ignorance is death, and if you doubt that, just check out America's politics in this year of Our Lord 2007. I think of myself as apolitical, with a diffidence born of contempt, but I flatter myself that I have some sense of what's going on and going down in this great nation—certainly enough to conclude that if the United States and what it theoretically has stood for is destined to perish from this earth, the prejudice-driven, media-assisted ignorance of its citizens will have been a principal cause no less than the opportunism, hypocrisy, and venality of our corporate chiefs and elected representatives.

If I go ahead, I will do my damnedest to set down only what I believe to be absolutely necessary to my reader's understanding, although I may permit myself the odd splash of characterization, or local or historical color.

So this will be my gift to history: fifty years from now, historians will have an accurate record of one of the most astounding political capers in U.S. history—provided I pull it off, as I think I can. I should also say that keeping this diary and ultimately making it available to history offsets certain moral qualms I have about the job.

While I obviously have in mind such immortal diarists as Pepys, Herzen, or my special favorite, George Templeton Strong, a man about New York at the time of the Civil War, it feels more natural to me to use the first-person narrative tone and style and address the reader directly: hence "Gentle Reader," as I shall call her or him into whose hands this journal may someday pass. I think I express myself best if I write in the same voice in which I'd tell this story to a friend over lunch.

Now: let us begin.

It all started last night, around 11:45 p.m. I was falling asleep over my bedtime reading and about to turn out the light when my phone buzzed. I recognized the number on the caller ID. It was Mankoff's private number.

This surprised me. I've known Mankoff for thirty-seven years;

I worked directly for him for a good part of a decade, and never but never—except on one occasion when a foreign-exchange maneuver in Bolivia went the wrong way and we had to backtrack and start damage control at warp speed—have I known him to call outside office hours, notwithstanding that STST prides itself as being a 24/7/365 hive of activity, holidays included. The only thing Mankoff and I have on our plate right now is a proposal for a named chair in Baroque Performance at Indiana U.'s famous music school, which hardly warrants a midnight call.

"I have a job for you, Chauncey," Mankoff said when I answered. "Like the old days. Can you meet me tomorrow at Three Guys, seven a.m.?"

Seven in the morning! On a Saturday! Anyone else, I'd object. But as I've said, Mankoff and I have a long-lasting relationship, and he's been very helpful to me in building my consulting business as well as providing a nice office at a very decent rent. "The old days?" Our CIA fun and games? Had to be. "Sure," I said. "For you, anything. Want to give me a hint?"

"Bank of West Congo," he said, then added, "with a bit of that Partagas operation of yours thrown in," and hung up. Mankoff's not much for small talk.

Bank of West Congo was a coup he and I had pulled off not long before he left Langley for Wall Street. A $40 million (real money back then) politics-cum-finance chain-jerk that in 1986 destabilized a big chunk of Africa and secured all sorts of lucrative mineral and mining rights for people who Washington thought would help the cause of democracy, as it was then defined by certain friends of then-President Reagan who liked buying underdeveloped countries' natural resources cheap. In such operations, "democracy" is synonymous with "Chevron" or "Shell" or "Total."

Looking back, however, I have to say that those friends, compared to today's Clinton-Bush greedheads, seem positively socialist. West

Congo had been a hugely effective sting, and great fun in the bargain, especially because we managed in the process to eviscerate a couple of Swiss private banks that were playing the long game on the other side. Of course our "clients" turned out to be complete crooks, but you can't have everything, and the caper itself was flawlessly executed.

I was surprised and yet I wasn't that he knew about "Partagas" (named after the Cuban cigars), a Havana knockoff of Iran-Contra that I managed the year after Mankoff left Langley, involving some expropriated sugar properties and a phony transfer of title via Honduras, with $5 million ending up in a bank in Liechtenstein. Once CIA, always CIA: we old Langley types keep up with whatever's doing at our alma mater. Even today, some fifteen years after I left the agency, I consider myself reasonably state-of-the-art in certain tricks and games when it comes to moving money covertly.

Anyway, mention of the old days got the old juices stirring. I could hardly wait to hear what was on Mankoff's mind.

Mankoff's choice of venue, Three Guys, is an upmarket coffee shop/restaurant on Madison Avenue across from the Carlyle Hotel, where Mankoff and his wife Grace are camping out at $2,500 a night while their six-bedroom duplex around the corner off Fifth Avenue is being done over by the decorator of the moment. That's Grace's domain; when it comes to lifestyle, Mankoff may dress the part and have the accessories the world expects of a man in his position, but basically he's plain vanilla. He'd live in a yurt, provided there was room for a harpsichord or two.

The Three Guys coffee shop is Mankoff's preferred setting for breakfast meetings. It's been around forever; he's been going there for probably twenty years—since he and Grace first moved into the neighborhood. Smaller shots than he like the bowing and scraping over juice cleanses and egg-white omelets at the Regency or the Mark, but Mankoff isn't one to show off in public. For him breakfast is about getting business done, not meet and greet.

I set the alarm for 6:00 a.m., called my car service and told them to pick me up at 6:40. I live in a loft in Tribeca, just off Vesey Street. Although I had an uptown upbringing, I prefer living downtown. "Tribeca" still has a pleasantly bohemian ring, even if the name no longer fits the neighborhood, which has been gentrified beyond recognition, and when the weather's nice, I can stroll home from my office in Midtown in an easy hour.

As I fell asleep, I found myself wondering what exactly Mankoff wanted to talk about. He definitely had his game voice on. "The old days," was what he'd said. Hmmm. Should I get up extra-early and iron the old cloak and polish up the dagger? I wondered. Well, tomorrow would come soon enough. I soon gave up speculating and drifted off.

At this point, a bit of background is in order.

My name is Chauncey Arlington Suydam III. I'm forty-six years old, about to turn forty-seven (DOB March 22, 1960). As you can guess from my name, I'm white, single, WASP to the core. I was born and raised on Manhattan's Upper East Side; educated at the Buckley School on East 74th Street, class of 1973, then Groton '77, then Yale '81: always a year young for my grade.

I'm what people of my parents' generation used to describe as "a confirmed bachelor," usually to describe homosexual friends, but don't take the fact that I've never married as some kind of evidence that I'm gay. To put it frankly, the calculations that go into the marriage algorithm leave me puzzled and hesitant. I've come close to marrying three times—but either I or the ladies backed off, the last instance being four years ago when the object of my ravishment decided I wasn't as rich as she needed me to be. I might also say this: my status has kept me out of the arms of a certain kind of woman who prowls Manhattan and other glitter spots in search of well-off early-middle-aged married men needing psychological help with their midlife crises and willing to pay handsomely for it.

When I look at the emotional carnage these entanglements leave behind, I'm even more determined to go it alone.

I can't complain that I lack for companionship, male or female. I'm an undemanding friend, who doesn't wear out his welcome or extort confidences, and people seem pleased to have me around. My acquaintanceship is organized in circles more wide than deep; some go back to very early days, to grade school and dancing school; there are a number from Groton, but surprisingly few from Yale (last year I went to my twenty-fifth reunion; it was awful! Everyone showing off how rich they've become). What is disconcerting about New York life is the way people drop in and out of each other's lives, sometimes as the result of a quarrel, more often as the consequence of a change in material circumstances. Why relative wealth should make that much of a difference to warm friendships of long standing baffles me—but nowadays it seems to. I'm often approached by friends on whom Mammon has turned a cold eye and beseeched to explain "why so-and-so has exiled me from his life." The only answer I have for that is that given the way money is made today, given the sort of people who seem most adept at making it, given the inescapable conclusion that money has been allowed to suffocate most other sources of human satisfaction, I'm not surprised that people disburse their "disposable" affections in terms of relative net worth.

The "III" in my name isn't an affectation but a form of salute to tradition and my father. It has never occurred to me to drop the roman numerals; in the world in which I was raised such incidentals counted for something, and perhaps it's the best monument I can leave in place to a father I adored and to whom I owe so much. My father was "Chauncey Two," Chauncey Arlington Suydam II, Senior Vice-President and Chief Investment Officer at the old Stuyvesant Fidelity Trust (now an unhappy part of Merrill

9

Lynch), so I naturally became known as "Chauncey Three." Never for a second have I felt diminished.

Perhaps this is the place to deliver a short testimonial to the man who brought me up by himself (with a governess and housekeeper-cook), my mother having dumped us when I was eight and run off with one of those lockjaw-mouthed, inherited-money assholes who the next year killed them both when he flew his Learjet into a mountain outside Sun Valley.

My father, whom I called "Pop," was a species now defunct; what in his day were called "gentlemen sportsmen," a term that denoted not only how well you executed certain athletic maneuvers—drop shot off the back wall, twenty-foot curling downhill putt, fox-trot with an ungainly debutante or bride's mother, wet fly under a salmon's nose—but how you conducted yourself in business and in life in general.

Of course, Pop's palmy days were back when Wall Street was different from the money- and people-grinding machine it is now. The phrase "24/7" hadn't been coined. One finished one's working day by 6:00 p.m. at the latest—the "day" including (if he didn't take one of his clientele of widows and trustees to lunch) a midday or early afternoon game of squash or court tennis at the Racquet Club or at the River Club. After work, one looked in at one's club for a drink, although Pop was an attentive father, unlike many WASP parents. He was always home in time for dinner with me at 7:00 p.m. (or, if he had a date, to sit with me and my governess while we ate). We spent time together. At least once or twice every autumn we'd drive up to New Haven for a Yale football game; I lived for those outings. On vacation Sunday nights, he'd take me to Rangers games. We saw a lot of plays together. My old man was a good sport and a good guy. Men and women liked him equally well. I like to think I resemble him.

The man I'd be meeting at Three Guys, Leon Simon Mankoff,

is spun from different social cloth. I don't think he's ever played a round of golf. He lives for work and the harpsichord. In my view, and I'm certainly not alone, he's an authentic Wall Street genius. I think my opinion's worth something, even though I only worked (technically) on the Street for two years after I left the Agency, at a Washington-based hedge fund (hated it—but let's get to that later), where I learned to talk the talk, even if I couldn't make myself walk the walk. I know what CDOs are, and the rest of the derivatives stew that has become Wall Street's favorite entrée, and because a significant portion of my consulting work is with Wall Street people, I've more or less kept up with the latest forms of witchcraft and financial prestidigitation. This isn't to say that you could plunk me down at a trading slot at STST and I'd end the day with my book up $50 million, but I can hold up my end of the conversation with the people who do—although I now and then confuse "fiscal policy" and "monetary policy."

More important, I've seen Wall Street up close, personal and plain, and I think I get the picture. The key to Wall Street is that these people really don't give a damn about what anyone other than peers and competitors think and their accountants and law-yers tell them. They'll claim that they do, for public consumption, or when they feel the hot breath of pending regulation, but take it from me: I've been around them for almost thirty years, watching them talking the talk and walking the walk, and apart from the 1 percent of the 1 percent, they don't give a screw about the rest of mankind. That said, you also need to consider that they've man-aged to work things out so that what they do, overpaid though it may be, has become essential to the working of the world. Life runs on fossil fuels and credit. And Wall Street's the guy at the credit pump, sporting $5,000 pinstripes instead of coveralls with a nametag.

I do confess to a casual interest in Wall Street history, mainly because it was kind of a hobby of my father's. His generation appears to have been one of the last to whom times past really mattered, and he passed that perspective on to me: he and my teachers at Buckley, Groton, and Yale, not to mention the goings-on in the tomb. My old man left me a whole library on high finance that I dip into now and then: the biographies of famous financiers, mostly, or old books like Charles Francis and Henry Adams's *Chapters of Erie*, about the fight for control of the Erie Railroad in the late 1860s. Read that and you'll quickly conclude that the effect and influence of Big Bad Money has changed very little in the intervening century and a half. Some of it is actually funny: I'll bet you don't know that the author of one of the earliest treatises on American banking had the singularly appropriate name of "Gouge."

One of the things that fascinates me about the Street today is how little its high flyers seem to know about the history of their business. A guy I know at Lehman tells me that since the firm has been taken over by a bunch of lowlifes, not one in a hundred people there knows or cares who Robert Lehman was or how far back in American history the firm goes and where it began life (1857, Montgomery, Alabama). Come to think about it, why should they? That was *then*, and everybody knows that *now* is where the bucks are. Perhaps this is why the Street's so prone to these boom-bust cycles when everyone seems to forget the past and make the same mistakes that crashed the markets a decade or so earlier (don't worry, I'm not going to quote Santayana).

Now: Mankoff. How best to sum up the guy? There's a place in Scott Fitzgerald's unfinished novel *The Last Tycoon*, where he describes his protagonist, Monroe Stahr, as one of the few men in Hollywood capable of keeping "the whole equation of movies in his head." Substitute "Wall Street" for "movies," and that's Leon Mankoff—at least as far I understand how Wall Street works. And

I should add that with Mankoff, it's his gut as well as his intellect that rules. His feel for the interactions of human nature helps him read markets as profitably as anything his computer jockeys' algorithms tell him.

Mankoff's a round dozen years older than I am. We're both sons of Old Eli, which is where we first encountered each other, although not as undergraduates: Mankoff was Yale class of '69 (graduated when he was twenty), summa cum laude in Mathematics and Economics, a dozen years before I graduated magna cum laude in English and Art History. What really links us is Skull & Bones.

I dare say I'm the sort you think of when people say "Skull & Bones": a button-down, "white shoe" type right out of *Stover at Yale*, a fourth generation Skull & Bones legacy. To the tomb born, as it were. But Mankoff is also a well-recognized Bones type: the campus unknown of whom people remark year after year, when the *Yale Daily News* publishes the list of secret society acceptances the morning after Tap Day, "Who the hell is that guy and how the hell did he get tapped for Bones?" Take it from me: every Bones delegation includes one or more "that guy" (or today, "that girl"). It's what gives the Russell Trust Association (Skull & Bones' legal designation) its flair and energy year after year. It isn't all legacies and connections.

At my Bones initiation in the spring of 1980 when my delegation formally took over from its predecessor, Mankoff was one of a selected group of alumni invited to be present to make sure all went off according to prescribed ritual and voodoo. What I didn't know at the time was that he was talent-spotting for the CIA, where he'd been tasked to set up a section specializing in economic warfare and destabilization.

We hit it off immediately. Mainly, I guess because we're both curious to the point of obsession. Everything interests us and prompts us to check it out: facts, rumors, news stories. We need to know the hows and whys of life. That way, we both figure, we have a leg up when it comes to controlling the whos and whens. We read, we listen, we notice; we chew things over, we continuously ask questions of others and ourselves, we do research, we value experience.

After I graduated *from* Yale (my old man would have killed me if I'd ever said "graduated Yale"), I spent a year at NYU's Institute of Fine Arts working on a master's in art history. I had a vague idea of making museum work my life's calling, but I wasn't committed. I attended a couple of the summer get-togethers Bones holds on this island it owns in Maine, and I ran into Mankoff there, and at reunion gatherings in the tomb on High Street. We found ourselves to be kindred spirits in a number of ways, and in the late spring of 1982 he recruited me to come to work at the CIA, just like in the movie *The Good Shepherd*.

The timing was propitious. The day on which I reported for duty at the agency was August 17, 1982, which was also the day a hundred-point pop in the stock market would mark the end of a decade that had subjected the country to Watergate, the Vietnam humiliation, and OPEC inflation, that saw a 17 percent prime rate and 11 percent unemployment, and signaled the beginning of the Age of Milken and all that has flowed therefrom for better or worse. A wealth manager I work with in Chicago, a trustee of that fair city's splendid Lyric Opera, compares that glorious Thursday in August 1982 to the incredible moment in *Fidelio* when the prisoners emerge from Stygian gloom into sunlight and sing a hugely moving, uplifting chorus.

For the next ten years, Mankoff and I flourished as a team. Basically our job was to sling economic and financial monkey wrenches into vulnerable central banks; to make the cold war markets hot for collectivist economies and hostile kleptocracies. We had a good, productive time together, and I learned all about the craft of moving large amounts of money around in ways that left no foot- or fingerprints. I also picked up a lot about human motivation and corruptibility.

During that time, I came to a significant conclusion about my native land. It's this. The Pledge of Allegiance that I was made to memorize at grade school includes the phrase "one nation under God." It was at Langley that I learned that, in practical terms, the deity meant isn't the God of Moses or Jesus or Mohammed, it's Mammon. That's a theme I'll be surprised if I don't return to in the course of this account.

In 1992, our partnership, which I was beginning to think of as "legendary," ended when Mankoff quit the Agency for STST, recruited by a former partner who was serving as a deputy secretary of defense in the Bush I administration. He offered me the chance to come along with him, but I declined. My old man was on Wall Street, and if I joined STST I'd be competing with him, at least remotely. I'd seen, from the example of certain school and college friends, what that could do to even the tightest father-son relationships, so I passed. I treasured my relationship with my father and was loath to take even the tiniest risk of screwing it up for money.

Agency life without Mankoff and his sharp instincts quickly palled, and in 1993, I put aside my finer feelings and allowed myself to be recruited by a Washington hedge fund that specialized in trading on overseas political intelligence. That's where I learned the buzzwords and how the sexiest games were played. It's also where, within the space of a year, I came to conclude that Wall Street work wasn't for me. It wasn't only that the work was boring—a deal is a deal is a deal, after all, and except for the sums and units of account, one trade pretty much resembles another—it was the people. My old man always said that if you don't like what you're doing, or who you're doing it with, sooner or later you're not going to be very good at it. I realized that to succeed, I would have to become like these people. I would have to partake of their greed, share their unconcern for the general welfare, adopt their lack of conscience—and that I couldn't do.

Fortunately, relief/rescue was at hand. Through a museum connection I got a job in a family office in San Francisco, running its $50-million arts philanthropies. They were deep into the entire spectrum of San Francisco culture, from the Opera House to the de Young Museum, and often partnered with other big money, which let me widen my acquaintance in that world.

I turned out to be pretty adept at mediating between the people with the money and the people who wanted it, as long as the money was going to projects I believed in, and in 2004, emboldened by the urgings of a number of people I'd worked with, I decided to go out on my own as an independent operator in the broad field of art and cultural philanthropy. Thus, Maecenas Associates. I suppose my clients think of me as a consultant, but I think of myself as a cultural investment banker; I conjure up projects—lecture series, art exhibitions, a Shakespeare opera series I'm just starting to think through—and make them happen: find the right venue, the right participants and resources, the money. For which I get paid hand-some but not exorbitant fees and retainers—unlike Wall Street.

When I started the business, I had Mankoff targeted as a client and he was among the first to sign on, not only because he liked and trusted me, but also—I reckoned—because he figured that it made sense to give STST's cultural proxy to a guy who looks like he's just stepped out of a Louis Auchincloss novel. A lot of people are turned off by STST's public image as a sharp-elbowed, take-no-prisoners, rip-their-face-off, eat-what-you-kill outfit; I might help ameliorate that impression. Whatever his reasoning, there's no doubt in my mind that without Mankoff's initial sponsorship, I wouldn't be where I fancy I am today.

And where that is consists of roughly fifty accounts, mainly family offices running between $250 million and $3 billion in assets, with a scattering of carefully winnowed hedge-fund types (none of these is private equity, of which—knowing what I know—I don't wholly approve, but what is it they say about beggars' freedom of choice?) and rich individuals, a Scandinavian sovereign fund's U.S. arts-exchange offshoot, and—finally—Mankoff/STST, my only "true" Wall Street client. My work consists of vetting and authenticating proposals and pitches and negotiating the "buyers' side" of the projects. I work with my clients' financial advisers to make sure the funding fits their portfolio standards and that everyone has a clear understanding of their commitment. I try to avoid client conflicts. I'm famously closemouthed; in my business, you hear things, and my policy is to let it be someone else who spills the secrets of the pillow or the family dining table. I also take on the occasional pro bono job where I feel I owe a favor, or it will be especially good for my image.

It's not all blue skies and robin redbreast, though. The trouble with my work is that you have to be where the money is, and right now we're going through an era where the *really* big money every museum and educational institution is chasing after belongs to a pretty sorry bunch of people: Arabs, Russians, twenty-year-old tech geniuses who were too busy coding to learn which fork to use, let alone what Socrates or Beethoven have meant to the world, or that it's gauche to light a cigar with a 500-euro note, as I heard some Russians were doing a few years back in Saint-Tropez.

I occupy space at a sweetheart annual rent in a small office building on 63rd Street between Lexington and Third Avenues that came with an STST acquisition before Mankoff got there, and that the firm has never gotten around to using for its own purposes. The exception is a suite of grace-and-favor offices down the hall on my floor that STST makes available to a few retired partners.

I've nicknamed this space "San Calisto" after the sixteenth-century palazzo in Rome where the Vatican houses its elderly cardinals. About this, more anon.

Although STST is technically my client, I work almost exclusively with Mankoff. I'm grateful for this, because it protects me from the perception that I'm readily available to advance the social aspirations of the wives of certain higher-ups and their clients, such as prestigious trustee boards, superior *placement* at a particularly desirable gala, even restaurant reservations. I know, for example, that Ludmilla Rosenweis, wife of Mankoff's #2, Rich Rosenweis, is pushing her husband hard to take a bigger role in the firm's arts benefactions, a role she clearly believes she can slipstream into a more prominent position in Manhattan society.

My work with STST can be varied. It isn't all program underwriting and endowments. Right now, for instance, Mankoff has sought my advice concerning the artist to be commissioned to do a huge painting for the lobby of the STST Global Headquarters building that they'll be moving into next year. Like its predecessors, the lobby murals at places like LaGuardia Airport and Rockefeller Center, it's supposed to reflect wealth, technology, power, energy, soaring modernity—the blessings of capitalism. STST's own Sistine Chapel ceiling, you might say. To my mind, the ideal artist to fulfill this commission in terms of sheer visual excitement would have been Jackson Pollock, and I'd have loved to see what Basquiat would have done with that space, but they're both dead. The competition is hot and heavy-handed, and the jury's still out. At least three of Manhattan's most prestigious art galleries—I'm not naming names, but if you know the art scene, you can make an educated guess—have offered me under-the-table bribes to swing the job to one of their house artists. They seemed surprised and chagrined to learn that I'm not in the "pay to play" business, as many in my line of work are.

While I would never say as much to Mankoff, I have to admit to a certain discomfort at the subsidy of nearly a half-billion dollars that Mankoff and Rich Rosenweis exacted from New York City by threatening to build STST's new global headquarters across the Hudson in New Jersey. That is a lot of money, if you translate it into teachers' salaries, or infrastructural improvements, or health-care assets, or poor kids' school meals, or fixing up public housing.

I know from my Maecenas work that the rich always threaten to take their money elsewhere if they don't get what they want. Frankly, I think it's all a big bluff. What's the point of having all that money if you can't live where you want, do business where you want? Restaurants you want to eat in, where there are servitors and sycophants to bow and scrape, where there are the sort of people you think your money qualifies you to hang out with, where there's what the immortal F. Scott calls the consoling proximity of other millionaires? But the bluff is never called. It's other side that always folds, the side playing with taxpayers' dollars. And why not? It isn't their money; more importantly, when the time comes to leave public service, quote unquote, favors get returned in the form of lucrative Wall Street employment.

Let me make clear how I personally think about money. Think about it morally, if you will. It's a tricky part of my business and frequently requires fairly agile rhetorical footwork.

Frankly, I keep my thoughts on the subject of wealth and its concomitants to myself. Perhaps that's a bit cowardly, but I have a living to make. We live in an age that worships money and has forced it into every crack and cranny of existence. Nothing is examined, nothing is evaluated, nothing is thought about without attention being devoted to its pecuniary aspects. Professionally, I respect money; I appreciate what it can make happen; 99 percent of my work at one stage or another involves wealthy people, and I have to take into account *their* attitudes toward *their* money, which tend on the whole to be pretty worshipful and not always attractive.

But I will never become rich, because I lack that love of money that is essential to attaining or maintaining great wealth. In the chapels of my soul, I have built no altars to Mammon. When asked by someone I trust with my confidences whether I wish I were as rich as so-and-so, I usually answer, "Not really—because then I would have to *be* so-and-so," and leave it at that.

I can say fairly that my business is a success. Between family offices, wealth managers, sovereign funds, humongous overseas investors, and nonfinancial corporations, there's more business out there than was ever dreamt of in my initial philosophy. Take my two Russian clients, who until Putin came in had a net worth of zero and are now worth billions. People tend to be snotty about them, but you have to put yourself in their brand-new bespoke driving shoes. How would you handle it if on Tuesday you were scrabbling for crusts in the dumpsters of Moscow and on Thursday, thanks to your friend Vladimir, you controlled all the phosphate in Russia and were booking a suite at the Ritz in Paris and leafing through books of yacht designs and Gulfstream configurations. The adjustment must be traumatic, like PTSD.

My clients don't complain about my fees: a monthy retainer cancelable on ninety days' notice, plus an hourly charge of $300 an hour for me, less than that for my senior associates. I employ roughly a dozen people. I give them their heads, pretty much, and pay them decently, usually with a nice bonus. School and college taught me to be a team player, with morale and leadership the captain's responsibility.

I do well enough. This year on the basis of projects in hand and my existing client base I may bring down a half-million dollars-plus to the annual bottom line after paying myself $450K for personal living and taxes. That's plenty for me. "Sniff at" money on Wall Street, I know, but very good pay for work I enjoy and that gratifies me, that allows me to see marvelous things and meet interesting people. If I do say so myself, the key to my success has been skillful management of the social aspects of the business: I'll play the extra man when I absolutely have to, and I'm not averse to the odd cruise in the Baltic or Mediterranean on a client's yacht, but I don't overdo it. My female associates are extremely attractive, but I keep my pen out of the company inkwell. I've had a couple of clients and clients' wives make passes at me that would have to be classified as more than tentative; usually these can be dealt with without becoming deal-breakers, but when it's been clear that's not the case, the deal has been broken. Oh, yes, one other thing: I don't stage or attend parties in stores.

Which doesn't mean my work doesn't have its social draw-backs. I have to go to more charity benefits and awards ceremonies than any right-minded person totally in control of his or her pro-fessional destiny would put up with. Friends aware of this used to ask, "How can you—how can these people—suffer each other's company night after night after night? Always the same faces in the *Times* Styles section?" You have to understand about the rich, especially those with newer money: it's only in the company of people like themselves that they feel secure.

All in all, my life is pretty much my own, which is a pretty high standard for a business like mine. I was brought up to know who I am and where I came from and what the good life properly lived looks like, mostly if not entirely thanks to my old man, so I have no need for the trappings of self-validation that so many of my clients crave. My household overhead is limited to myself and a twice-weekly housekeeper; if I entertain, I bring in a caterer.

If I ever find Ms. or Miss Right, that may require some upward budgetary adjustment, but no luck so far—and by now I'm so habituated to living alone, with every element just so, it may be too late. Still, you never know, do you?

But enough about Chauncey. Let's get back to Mankoff. You need to know more about him.

After the CIA, he hit the ground running at STST and never looked back, a star from day one. Imagine Mozart being recruited to the Juilliard faculty to teach composition and you'll get the idea. Within a month of starting at STST he'd found his true calling: risk management, which seemed closest to the kind of work he'd starred in at Langley. Within six weeks, he'd persuaded the senior partners to let him set up an independent risk evaluation department to ensure that STST avoided a repeat of 1987, when its huge bet on something called "portfolio insurance" blew up.

His breakout year was 1998, when the foreign-exchange trading desk at STST ignored his red flags and lost $250 million in the collapse of Long-Term Capital Management. Even so, if it hadn't been for Mankoff and his finger-in-the-wind risk calculations, the firm's loss could have run into the billions, and he was delegated to represent the firm at the LTCM bailout negotiations.

The reports that came back of the imagination and authority with which he handled himself only added to the glow. In 1999, when it was clear that the capital the firm needed could no longer be supplied by the partners' personal fortunes, Mankoff did the planning that took STST public in the year 2000. Two years after that, following the 2001 dot-com bust when, largely thanks to him, STST missed the worst of the Street-gutting calamities like Enron, WorldCom, and Global Crossing, he became head boy. He was only fifty-five at the time, the youngest person ever to run STST.

LTCM was merely the most glaring among several theory-based busts that Mankoff would spot before they happened. One reason that Mankoff had quit the CIA was that the agency was shifting

22

from operations to analysis, which is another way of saying from practice to theory, from what they call "humint," as in "human intelligence"—spies in dark corners whispering secrets observed or gleaned firsthand—to serried ranks of MBAs in cubicles staring at computer screens with half their minds fixed on tonight's blind date and where to eat in Georgetown. The same was happening on Wall Street, as it turned out, with the ascendancy of the "quants," or quantitative analysts, and computer-driven mathematical formulas taking over from human judgment based on instinct, common sense, and experience with occasional lashings of fair dealing.

As Mankoff is fond of pointing out, the mathematical fun and games that the Street's quants revel in—these are people who show up at industry get-togethers wearing T-shirts that say "Algorithm Terrorist"—tend to be true and accurate in proportion to their initial utility. In other words, to the early bird fall whatever worms there may be. But then, once everyone starts using a certain formula, it gets absorbed into the problem it was devised to solve or elucidate and becomes a self-referential, back-looping integral part of the phenomenon it's supposed to measure externally and objectively. Synecdoche turned inside out, you might call it. At least, that's what I think happens. I think it's what George Soros means by "reflexivity."

Under Mankoff's leadership, STST has moved from strength to strength. The price of the stock has more than tripled—from around $60 when he took over to close to $200 at yesterday's close. Three years from now, in 2010, people are saying the stock could sell at $500. Why not? To the world, for better or worse, STST represents Capitalism Triumphant.

Now let's move to what transpired at Three Guys this morning.

I got to the restaurant precisely on time. With me, punctuality rules. Mankoff was already in his usual booth, tucked off to the left behind the front door, with an egg-white omelet, sausage, and toast teed up in front of him. How he stays as skinny as he does is a mystery. I slid in across from him and ordered a macchiato (Three Guys is now *that* kind of coffee shop), grapefruit juice, and a dry English muffin, then looked at him expectantly.

"Here's the story," he said. "Basically, I'm worried about the political and financial situation. Something needs to be done."

"And that something includes me, right?"

He nodded.

"So what do you have in mind?"

"I want you to fix next year's presidential election for me," he said matter-of-factly.

After I picked myself off the floor, he spelled out his game plan. He thinks there's going to be a huge implosion in the financial markets sometime before the election. The portents are already there. Add this to the mess in Iraq, and the GOP's dead. Whoever the Democratic candidate is—and at this point it looks like Hillary Clinton—will go after Wall Street the way FDR did in 1932: with a lynch-mob agenda calling for both prosecution and reform. There will be a hue and cry for a pushback of the deregulation that has made the past decade the fattest in the Street's history. "Reregulation" will be the rallying cry.

Mankoff has devised a scheme to sabotage any such effort. He wants me to execute it, using tradecraft I acquired during my time at the CIA. I said I'd need to think it over.

I'll explain all this in further detail, but right now I have to go to an old friend's birthday dance at the Stuyvesant Club and when I get home I'm sure I won't be in any shape or disposition to do the chapter-and-verse bit about Mankoff's plan.

Let me just close by saying that as I listened to Mankoff elucidate the whys and wherefores of his grand design I was reminded of a famous episode in the annals of Wall Street, starring J. Pierpont Morgan—who is to Wall Street what Babe Ruth is to Cooperstown—and Theodore Roosevelt, one of our most admired presidents. It occurred in 1902, when Morgan got crossways with Washington on some dubious financing scheme. He sent the following message to President Theodore Roosevelt: "If we have done anything wrong, send your man to my man and they will fix it up."

I am to be Mankoff's "man." More anon.

OK: last night was a riotous evening, as expected, but I couldn't tear my mind away from my meeting with Mankoff. Who could?

Back to Three Guys.

According to Mankoff, the admission last week by the world's third-largest bank that they're taking a big write-down on their mortgage assets signals the beginning of real trouble. Mankoff reads this as the first of a series of discrete blips that are going to compound into something the size of that giant stone ball that chases Harrison Ford through the jungle in the first *Indiana Jones* movie. Unlike in the film, however, the ball's going to catch up and Wall Street is going to get crushed.

To summarize Mankoff's take in a very few words: a number of factors are in the process of coalescing into a perfect storm. These include Greenspan's (and now Bernanke's) free-money policies at the Federal Reserve, which are straight-out pandering to Wall Street; a decline in the housing market bordering on collapse; and the utter corruption of Washington that has followed the massive rollback of regulation that took place under Clinton. Wall Street has been allowed to totally blow through any commonsensical— forget prudent—risk parameters. The big banks have been allowed to become too enormous and complicated to manage. To summarize: Mankoff foresees a huge chain-reaction shit storm breaking over the collective head of Wall Street and the other financial markets, spilling over into the general economy of making, doing, and serving. He's predicting every kind of computer-driven financial calamity you can think of: credit freeze, bank insolvencies, a foreclosure pandemic, a liquidity crisis, accounting scandals, balance sheet implosions, a few big firms driven to the wall, total breakdown of trust between institutions, all adding up to something on the order of the 1929 bust—only bigger and more violent thanks to the bubble-inflating technology the Street depends on.

As Mankoff tells it, what's going to send the markets crashing is basically theme-and-variations on the cardinal sin of finance: borrowing short to lend long with the collateral being recirculated so that sometimes you have the same billion-dollar stack of Treasuries pledged to secure four or five entirely discrete billion-dollar loans involving different sets of lenders and borrowers. This is what Mankoff calls "chain-letter collateralization," where the same security is pledged serially: A borrows from B, securing the loan with derivative X, a third-party contract to make B whole if A goes belly-up; B turns around and uses X to collateralize a loan from C, which B then uses to fund its loan to A—and so on and so on, back and forth and in circles.

The Great Deregulation of the Clinton years, the repeal of Glass-Steagall, the untethering of derivatives, etc., etc., was literally like yanking open the lid of Pandora's box. Every malign and mischievous imp of finance burst free and began to work its evil spells. Access to unlimited short-term credit, thanks to the Fed flooding the market with crisp new greenbacks, gave essentially second-rate firms like Bear Stearns and Lehman Brothers the wherewithal to compete against the big banks, which up to then had huge reserves of federally insured deposits to finance their lending.

Specifically, according to Mankoff, the credit markets have put themselves terribly at risk. The world economy runs on two principal fuels: fossil (as in gas/oil/coal) and credit. Shut either down and you're looking at economic catastrophe, and it can happen virtually overnight. Wall Street got a taste of how that feels back in the seventies, when OPEC tightened the oil flow. The old boys at San Calisto still shake their heads at how bad it got in 1973 and '74.

And not only Wall Street. The American Way was predicated on a high level of cheap creature comforts. The privations of World War II were in the distant past, fodder for the reminiscences of old men. The word "rationing," barely uttered for three decades, was once again a common usage, as lines began to form at 4:00 a.m. at gas pumps. Everything suddenly seemed inside out. The country went on year-round daylight saving time. That the same thing might happen now to the worldwide flow of money and credit seems unthinkable. But the way Mankoff spells it out, it seems not only possible, but likely.

There's other stuff that makes Mankoff's gloomy picture even more dire. He thinks the Street's going to drown in the viscous alphabet soup of "securitizations"—pools of credit instruments known as MBS, CDS, CDO, CLO, and whatever—that has been brewed in the past ten years. Deals have gotten so complicated that the parties to them often don't have a clear picture of what they've bought or sold, especially when you add derivatives to the volatile mix. Mankoff thinks derivatives—options that are often generically called "swaps," even though many are custom-tailored to fit the components of a trade—will make everything worse. He's not alone: the multibillionaire Merlin Gerrett, easily America's best-beloved capitalist, calls derivatives the financial equivalent of thermonuclear bombs.

So what are derivatives—or "swaps," as they're often generically called? All that you and I need to know, Gentle Reader, is that they're contracts between two or more "counterparties" that are supposed to protect price and value on one side, with the other side assuming the risk for a nice fee. Say I take a position of $50 million ABC bonds. My next step is to find someone who'll make me whole on that $50 million should prices decline. I want to limit my risk, so I need to seek out someone who, for a price, will insure me against loss. We do a deal, then what usually happens next nowadays is that the person from whom I bought protection goes and buys protection on the protection he sold me. And so on and so on, round and around and up and down, until you're looking at a pyramid of offsets and make-wholes balanced precariously upside down on its tip. You can imagine what happens if my original $50 million position craters. Crash!

From what I've heard, a key element of these swaps deals is that they're designed to make it difficult to figure out exactly who's obligated to whom, under what circumstances, and for how much. Mankoff says a ton of swaps-backed loans have been made to cities, towns, and educational establishments with the assurance that they're buying safety when, depending on the way interest rates move, they could be taking on a lethal degree of risk. These borrowers have no idea of what their potential liability might be if the markets experience a serious sell-off and chain letter turns into chain reaction.

The big problem, according to Mankoff, is that it used to be that the collateral supporting the overnight loans that the banks use to finance their term lending and other operations was good as gold: U.S. Treasury bills and notes, sometimes gold itself. Lenders could cash in that collateral instantly if they had to. But in the frenzy of the last few years, these overnight loans have come to be supported by collateral that incorporates many more degrees of risk than Treasuries. Mortgage-backed paper, auto loans, credit card receivables, stuff like that. Security a lender can't "realize on" by snapping his fingers. Stuff that could lose 10 percent, 20 percent of its value overnight, maybe more, maybe to the point where no one will bid for it or lend against it.

He let me digest that, then added, "And that doesn't cover the worst part."

"Which is?"

"God help us if this credit crisis goes retail."

"What do you mean, 'retail'?"

"All the debt individuals have taken on to bridge the gap between the money they make and the cost of what they think they're entitled to: more luxurious houses in better neighborhoods, flashier cars, Ivy League educations for the kids, bigger flat screens, vacations in the south of France. How much consumer debt do you think is out there?"

I shook my head. I couldn't begin to.

"Try fourteen trillion dollars. A lot of it owed by people living pretty close to the bone."

"Ouch!"

"If there's a recession, millions of people are going to come up short. There'll be foreclosures and repossessions, and that's how revolutions get started."

"Or movements to penalize foolish lenders."

He nodded. "Quite right. There'll be pressure on Washington to force creditors to take haircuts."

"Makes sense to me." I instinctively root for the little guy. Mankoff doesn't. I knew who he was *really* worrying about: creditors' creditors. I thought about adding something to the effect that with Congress and regulators in the Street's pocket, there couldn't be much to worry about—but decided to keep my trap shut.

"Worst case," Mankoff said, "we could see a repeat of the savings-and-loan mess of the eighties, only carried out to about the tenth power." He reminded me that when the savings-and-loan industry blew up in the late eighties, just about the time that Mankoff and I were putting the blocks to the Bank of West Congo, the American Taxpayer, who would be obliged to put up $125 bil-lion to ultimately fix the mess, called for the blood of the people responsible and Washington granted his wish. Names were named; the manacles were brought out; federal and state prosecutions succeeded in sending a bunch of big-name S&L executives to jail. You probably remember photos of one Charles Keating, friend of presidents and a man of influence, doing the perp walk. A thousand S&L executives, some say, ended up doing time.

This time could be worse, Mankoff says. A lot of the top executives on the Street have knowingly or unknowingly signed off on various forms of transactions that walk, talk, and smell like fraud, he told me. He's concerned that he hasn't been as vigilant as he might have been with respect to what Rosenweis's regiment of traders may have gotten up to. Worst case, if the Feds get serious and go strictly by the book, they could bring criminal charges against many of the million-dollar earners on the Street.

I thought about asking him about a series of trades that STST's been doing with a major hedge fund, bespoke transactions that sound distinctly dodgy to my untutored sense of straight and crooked, but I'm not sure I'm supposed to know about them, so I keep silent. I'll tell you about them in due course.

Anyway, what worries Mankoff is that Washington, which, thanks to the utter corruption of Congress and the regulatory agencies that will have been Wall Street's equal in precipitating the coming crisis, will try to cover its ass by attacking the Street with new legislation and regulation. Wouldn't be the first time a guilty party turned on his coconspirators to save his own skin. There will be calls for punitive retribution, and people may go to jail, but what he really fears are reformist policies and programs that widely heeded "progressive" pundits like the Nobel economists Krugman and Stiglitz will have a hand in shaping. The thirst for reform will be sharpened by the massive financial inequality that is now an acknowledged fact of the U.S. economy. There will be calls for legislative reaction that will take Wall Street back to the New Deal regulatory structure that the Street has spent millions to dismantle over the past fifteen years.

"You mean like bringing back Glass-Steagall?" I asked. I swear he paled at my mere mention of the New Deal's cornerstone bank reform—which separated deposit banking from investment banking and trading, and has protected the country from high-rollers and usurers in marble halls since 1933.

"Precisely. And much worse. If there has to be a government bailout of outfits like Citi—Chuck Prince hasn't got the slightest idea of what his people have been up to—and I don't see any way around it, Washington may end up nationalizing a number of the banks. We can't let that happen. Wall Street is essential to the American way of life."

I nodded. I was brought up to believe that while freedom is wonderful, one needn't exploit all its loopholes. "In other words," I said, "you don't want another Pecora."

"Precisely." Even seventy-odd years after the fact, the name "Pecora" still makes Wall Streeters grimace. Ferdinand Pecora was the special prosecutor FDR forced on the Senate Banking Committee in 1933 to go after "the malefactors of great wealth" responsible for the 1929 Crash. When Pecora got through with the big boys—Morgan, Chase, and First City (predecessor of today's Citi)—a couple of famous bankers were in jail, others had been forced to pay up, and Wall Street was smothered in disgrace and mockery. When my old man went to work at the bank, my grandfather gave him a copy of Pecora's book, *Wall Street Under Oath*; it's still on my shelves—though I can't say I've read it.

Mankoff plans to batten down the hatches at STST. "We're going to put ourselves in position to come out on the other side of the mess in a stronger position than anyone else—except maybe Dimon, who has all those insured deposits to back him up."

Jamie Dimon is the CEO of JP Morgan Chase (JPMC), regarded in most quarters as the best-run of the big banks and a ferocious rival to STST. The media routinely run his and Mankoff's photographs side by side, as the two reigning powers in high finance. Dimon is Mankoff's virtual opposite: youthful and athletic, looks good in a yellow tie, says stuff that the media laps up but that I know drives Mankoff batshit. When it comes to brains and banking sense, my money'd be on Mankoff, but ours is an era when image is all. Or at least 90 percent. And Dimon's certainly no lightweight.

The conversation now turned to politics. Mankoff expects the financial crisis—and there's no other word for it—to erupt sometime next year, probably late next summer. "At that point, the GOP will be dead," he said. "The Democrats could nominate a cow and the animal would win."

"Which at the moment looks like a bovine named Hillary, correct?"

"Exactly," Mankoff replied. "And that we can't let happen. Which is where you come in."

Now this surprised me. Up to now, it's been known that Mankoff has supported the presidential hopes of the junior senator from New York. He's attended a few dinners and lunches that have gotten into the papers; he's probably dropped off a couple of decent-sized checks. Apparently he's had a major rethink.

I'm not so hot on Mrs. Clinton myself; there's too much steel in her for a gentle soul like me, her ambition's too transparent and too flagrant. She reminds me of practically every Wellesley girl I've ever been involved with: that frightening self-confidence, that certainty of being born to rule. Slam bam, thank you ma'am, and then she's out of bed to discover radium, run GM, or rewrite the Constitution. She must be a tiger to live with; her husband, even when he was president, has exhibited many of the characteristics I've come to associate with truly oppressed "great men": mainly an inability to keep it in his pants, as if philandering is some kind of proof to his mirror that he's still the head of his household, no matter what it looks like to the world outside. My old man always said that was the case with JFK.

Mrs. Clinton is way out in front of all the other would-be

Democratic nominees when it comes to war chest, state caucuses, and party delegates locked up, all that goes into winning her party's nomination.

"I thought you were supporting her," I said. "I thought she's supposed to be the Street's bitch. Weren't you at that big fundraiser a couple of weeks ago?"

"I was. Strictly to have a look. I kicked in my statutory $3,800 just to stay in the hand. But the closer I listened, the more I had second thoughts. There's something about her I just don't trust. She's almost *too* political."

I knew what he meant. This is a woman known for, shall we say, a certain moral flexibility. The country's still trying to figure out where she stands on the mess in Iraq. And like most really ambitious politicians, she has a long memory. A very long memory. No slight, whether intended or unintended, goes unremembered.

What Mankoff's heard is that she secretly hates Wall Street for persuading her husband to dump her elaborate health-care scheme on the grounds that it would be a budget-killer, an episode that left her looking like a complete fool. On top of that, there's the obscene wealth garnered by the Street in the wake of the deregulatory bill of goods pushed on her husband by former Treasury Secretary Robert Rubin and his principal stooges, Harley Winters, the big-shot economist, and former Fed Chairman Alan Greenspan. With the rich getting richer while the middle-class goes nowhere (just check out the wage statistics), there's a political opportunity too juicy to pass up. If there's a crisis for which Wall Street can be blamed, she'll blame Wall Street and call out the tumbrels of reregulation. That the bulk of the deregulation occurred on her husband's watch and with his support won't affect her campaign rhetoric. Politicians like her live strictly in and of the moment. They put aside their deepest long-range yearnings—with the Clintons that's obviously money—for near-term tactical advantage.

Right now, she's making nice with the Street, and the Street's making nice back, but what bothers Mankoff is that her inner circle—the Wall Streeters closest to her, people like Roger Altman, Alan Patricof, and Steven Rattner—aren't really Wall Street souls. They make it plain that they consider themselves to be of a higher order of moral and intellectual being. They're the sort "who pound the pulpit with the same hand they use to endorse the check," as a friend of mine puts it.

Mankoff then got to the crux of the matter. If a crisis comes, Mankoff told me, it's likely to be so big that only Uncle Sam will have pockets deep enough to stave off total calamity. The Street's going to want—it's going to need—a big dollop of the people's full faith and credit to bail itself out, a process unlikely to win the approval of an electorate howling for Wall Street blood. And there'll be Mrs. Clinton: Joan of Arc in a pantsuit instead of chain mail.

So Hillary Clinton has got to be headed off. Capitol Hill is pretty well bought and paid for, no worries there, but wherever one turns one sees what some call "regulatory capture," which is Stockholm Syndrome in reverse—in this case, the captors submit to their victims. The SEC and public-private finance schemes like Fannie Mae and its siblings are run by people who've stood by and let Wall Street have its way while they polish their CVs in anticipation of lucrative private-sector employment. Still, the picture isn't complete without the White House.

Now, you and I might, out of innocence or resignation, argue that those who caused the damage should pay for at least a significant part of it, but that's not the way the Street thinks. This may not sound fair, but "fair" is one of those words—like "right," "wrong," and "conscience"—that are not to be found in the Official Wall Street Lexicon. Say any of those words to your average "big-swinging-dick" trader and they look at you like you're speaking Swahili. The same goes for certain phrases that were integral to the moral vocabulary of my father's generation—notions like "civic responsibility" and "public spirit" that are now as extinct as the passenger pigeon.

When I say this, don't take me for one of those knee-jerk anti–Wall Street types (*accent aigu* on the "jerk," as a friend puts it). It's just the lay of the land. Take Mankoff, for example. You have to admire the guy for his brains and his "Street smarts," but I'm under no illusions about his overall moral depths. He may know about Bach and Scarlatti, and others may consider this a virtue, but at bottom he's simply a culturally and intellectually dressed-up version of the Wall Street breed, not a representative of a wholly other philosophical or ethical species who finds himself on an alien planet and must make the best of it.

Pragmatism is his middle name, profit and capital preservation are his vocation. To have risen as high as he has requires a soul and mind attuned to the Street's values—or lack of them. Does he have a conscience? I couldn't tell you, not even after thirty years. "Conscience" is about feelings for other people, it's about God and country and civic duty and the Golden Rule, stuff like that—values and systems of belief in which someone like me was marinated beginning in the cradle and survive even now, when I'm obliged to confront the way the real world works. You should see the looks I get from younger friends who work at STST when I tell them I was educated to be a good loser. In their catechism, losing is a mortal sin.

"OK," I said, "so you think Mrs. Clinton could be a problem. How do you stop her?"

Mankoff smiled. "What do you think about this guy from Illinois?" he asked me.

The politician to whom Mankoff made reference is an Illinois Democrat who just last week announced a run for the White House in 2008. He did so on the steps of the Illinois state capitol in Springfield, where Lincoln declared his candidacy in 1860. From now on, I'll refer to him simply as "OG": "Our Guy."

OG vaulted into national prominence at the 2004 Democratic Convention when he gave a real stem-winder of a keynote speech that unleashed a tidal wave of adulatory, rock star-type enthusiasm and springboarded him into the Senate, where he's a bit over two years into his first term. Now he thinks he's ready for the White House.

Has he got the chops? His résumé is very impressive, at least on paper. Columbia University, Harvard Law, editor of the *Law Review.* He's worked for IBM and a couple of think tanks, been a law professor, a community organizer, and an Illinois state senator; seasoned political experts talk about him as if he walks on water, but I've been around long enough to know that while a big-deal résumé can help get you the job you're after, it's no guarantee of performance. Look at George H. W. Bush or Herbert Hoover.

But performance, as it turns out, isn't what Mankoff is looking for. All he cares about is how OG stacks up as a candidate.

I shrugged. "I'm not sure what I think about him. I know people whose opinions I value have been impressed when they met him."

"Do you think the race issue will matter?" he asked. OG is half black.

I shrugged again. "Might, might not." What do I know?

"Would it affect the way you vote?"

"Of course not." And it wouldn't.

"Here's where I come out right now," I said. "The guy gives dynamite podium. I thought that keynote speech in 2004 was great; it certainly established him as a player. But since he's been in Washington, what's he done, really? He could turn out to be another Mario Cuomo, a one-speech wonder, as my old man used to say. Plus there was that big-time flip-flop on Iraq."

Mankoff responded with a shrug of his own, a "so what?" gesture he really ought to patent. "I've looked pretty hard at this guy," he told me. "I think he's the kind of person most people will vote for on faith, without asking the hard questions, because he looks good and sounds good and after eight years of Bush-Cheney, people are desperate for a chance in White House style. Plus, I think there's still enough idealism left in this country to be a force." He pronounced "idealism" in a way that said he doesn't put much stock—literally—in the concept.

"OK," I replied. "Whatever you may think of the guy, what you're really trying to figure out is: how can he get past Hillary?"

Mankoff nodded, then said exactly what I expected him to say. "I think it can be made to happen. Provided he gets his hands on enough money now."

I could see where this had to be going. "And since you mentioned West Congo when you called last night, I'm guessing whatever you've got in mind involves discreet, untraceable transfers of large sums of cash? How much?"

"I'm thinking $75 million for openers. Think you can handle it?"

Before responding, I did the X's and O's on my mental blackboard. Twenty years ago, at the Agency, $75 million would have been considered real money, but today, it's chickenfeed—a drop in a global torrent, especially now that China's in the equation, and that's good. Thanks to connections at Langley and elsewhere, I fancy I'm pretty state-of-the-art when it comes to the tradecraft of laundering money. The transfer points are pretty much the same today as twenty years ago: Andorra, the Caymans, American Samoa, Vanuatu, Malta. As regards conduits, transfer points.

When I was at Langley, we liked to use closely held offshore corporations that own a lot of McDonald's and other cash businesses; $1,000/day added to the day's receipts between the cash register and the bank and who's to know? Enough of these and you're talking real money. We had special software that mashed up tax registers, phone books, voting records, and so on to create the illusion that what was actually five people at keyboards in a Washington suburb was an entire demographic of smallholders. There are also certain foundations where—for a slight commission—the administrator will be helpful in setting up a cutout. In its heyday, if you added up the assets of the not-for-profits the CIA used in this fashion, you'd've been looking at one of the largest charities in the world. The gap between then and now is mainly one of scale and digital technology.

The trick is to break the money up into bites sufficiently small and scattered to fly under the electoral regulators' radar, and digital technology has made this a no-brainer.

"You think $75 million will get the job done?" I asked. U.S. politics has become the most expensive game ever thought up. You need enough money to set up a multistate campaign infrastructure, involving thousands of people ringing doorbells and hitting the phones and computer keyboards. Enough money to buy game-changing media exposure. Enough money to finance all kinds of events and functions. Enough money to pay for hundreds of hours aloft in hired jets.

"It'll be a start," Mankoff said.

"Let me ask you this, then. Am I right? Do I recall reading somewhere that the guy's pledged to limit his campaign spending to public money?"

He assured me I shouldn't worry.

"OK," I said. "Next question. You've told me where the money's going, but I also need to know where it's coming from. In general terms, that is. I can't handle—I won't handle—anything dirty. Mexican drug money, money from countries under sanction, Russian oligarchs: none of that shit. You know what I'm talking about?"

He chuckled. "Well, I guess that lets out HSBC." Then he turned serious. "I assure you the money's clean."

"That's good enough for me."

So there's the proposition. Mankoff wants me to negotiate and execute an arrangement by which $75 million will be made available to the senator's campaign.

"And what exactly do you think you're going to buy with this?" I asked. "You're sure as hell not going to get any promises in writing."

He smiled. "The money will go into the campaign in return for certain policy and personnel understandings."

"Such as what?"

He reached into his pocket, took out a standard three-by-five index card, and handed it to me. Three names were written on it: *Harley Winters. Thomas Holloway. Eliza Brewer.*

The first name was instantly recognizable: Harley Winters, former deputy treasury secretary (international affairs) and adviser to presidents, MIT star economist, former provost of a major university, former *Time* and *Forbes* cover boy. He's a "public intellectual" who gets $100,000 a speech, a guy universally known as "the smartest guy in the room, just ask him." He's also what influence peddlers value most, he's what they call "flexible": finger in the wind 24/7, changes his stance more often than he changes his shirt.

If Winters is a high-profile type, Holloway's not one at all. He's the officer at the New York Fed who oversees the big Wall Street finance houses, including STST. From what I've been told, Holloway's policies are so aligned with Wall Street's desires that if he left the Fed tomorrow he'd have his pick of $5 million/year employment offers.

"The deal will be this," Mankoff explained. "Assuming the

senator makes it to the White House with our help, he'll appoint Winters and Holloway to head up his economics team. Winters in the White House, and Holloway high up at Treasury."

This was a no-brainer. Winters and Holloway have a 99.9 percent Wall Street approval rating. They've drunk the Kool-Aid. To them America is all about freedom of capital to do whatever the hell it wants without Uncle Sam laying on a finger. Anyone with a reform or prosecutorial agenda is going to have to go around them or through them and they can be counted upon to oppose it or stall it to death.

"And Eliza Brewer?" The third name had me completely stumped. Not a clue.

"A very smart securities lawyer. We need to get her a key slot at Justice where she can play backup just in case anything gets past Winters and Holloway."

"Like what? Inconvenient criminal prosecutions?"

"That's the idea."

"I think I dig," I said, and handed the index card back to him. He tore it into little pieces.

At this point, Gentle Reader, I know what you're thinking. If I agree to do this job—and it's odds-on that I will (I'll get to that)—and if I pull it off, it'll be one of the biggest political scams in American history, probably the biggest ever. Corruption at a level never before scaled: Boss Tweed or Teapot Dome with six zeros. I can't say I ever considered myself hall of fame material in the political corruption department, even though some of our CIA gambits were pretty virtuosic, but then again, there's always a first time.

"OK," I said. "Suppose I sign up. Where do I start?"

"The guy who's calling the shots is named Homer Orteig. Old friend of the candidate, from the University of Chicago. You'll need to get with him. Ideally, the deal you'll cut will be strictly between you and Orteig. The senator doesn't even need to know. In fact, it's probably better if he doesn't."

"And how do I do that?"

"We'll figure it out. We have time. Right now it's early days. You know how it is: people get overexcited. The usual early adopters—Soros and that lot—write checks in order to get on the inside track, just in case. The first quarter money-raising numbers for both Clinton and the senator should be pretty spectacular. The second quarter will most likely show a huge drop-off, and that's when we should make our move."

Mankoff was making a good point. Political enthusiasms are like overnight fevers. The camps of both Clinton and OG are in the throes of that first, fine, careless rapture when everything seems possible and money drops from trees, from $10,000 Hermès handbags and from the pockets of $5,000 Kiton suits. This top-table ecstasy will probably last another month or so. Then people will start to get real, will sit down and calculate the odds—and the money flood will slow down. That'll be the time to float a tasty $75-million fly under the trout's nose.

"OK," I said, "assume we figure out how to get to the campaign. We've been talking about $75 million. Is that my limit?"

"Consider yourself to have discretion up to $75 million. Beyond that, we'll need to talk. So there we are. You up for this?"

I told him I'd let him know within twenty-four hours. There was still stuff I needed to think about. Stuff I didn't want to talk about with him—ethics-type stuff I thought he'd understand only in theory.

He slid out of the booth, leaving his usual lousy tip, to which I added $5. He paid the cashier for our breakfast and I followed him out onto Madison Avenue, where his car was waiting.

"Back to Bach?" I asked. He nodded with all the enthusiasm

of a man being led off to the gallows. He has a sprawling old-fashioned house in Woodbridge, Connecticut, on the outskirts of New Haven, where he and his wife Grace go on weekends. She's a former music librarian he met in Washington during our CIA tour. She can turn the pages for him while he's learning a new piece, and in return he indulges her passion for decorating. They have two grown sons who live out west—indeed, they're about to close on a place in Santa Fe near their elder son and his family.

In Connecticut, Grace gardens and reads decorating magazines, and Mankoff practices the harpsichord. He has three: an original Kirkman from 1787 on which Haydn is said to have played, the others modern-built—on which he takes weekend lessons from a member of the Yale Music School faculty who once taught William F. Buckley. By his own estimation, Mankoff's not bad. Not great—but not bad.

"Bach is proving too much for me," Mankoff lamented as his driver ran around to open the door. "His *Three-Part Inventions*. I just can't get certain fingerings."

"My sympathies," I said.

As he started to climb into the car, he turned back and said quietly, "If we get Orteig on board, and swing this business, and even if we don't and there's a crisis, this may be just one of several . . . let's call them "diplomatic" missions I'll be asking you to carry out. You're someone I can trust, Chauncey, and you know your stuff. There aren't many of those."

"I appreciate that," I said, adding quickly, "but it's something I want to think about. I think you understand why. I'll let you know by Monday."

"That'll be fine," he said. "Take whatever time you need." He sounded confident that I'd get on board—and why not? He thinks of us as attached at the hip. He had mentored me at the CIA, made important introductions and godfathered a business that lets me pursue work I like and a lifestyle I enjoy; I owe him. Besides, we were both Skull & Bones, and greater love hath no man, etc. etc.

I watched his car turn east on 76th Street. And that's when I had the idea for this diary.

So there we are. This puts you up to speed as to why Mankoff summoned me to Three Guys two days ago.

Now all I have to decide is do I do or do I don't. The decision isn't as cut-and-dried as I may have made it sound.

I called Mankoff a couple of hours ago and told him to count me in.

Gentle Reader, I know what you're thinking. What about those civic and communitarian virtues in which I was "marinated" by upbringing and education? If I do this, will I ever again be able to look in the eye those portraits and monuments on chapel walls I used to study during dull moments in prayer services? Am I not betraying where I come from them by accepting Mankoff's assignment?

The way things are today, 90-plus percent of the electorate don't think they have a friend in Washington. They're convinced that the fix is in, that the government is run strictly to promote the interests of the rich and powerful—and they have a point. Provided his message gets out, OG will look and sound to them to be the man to turn the tide: a great leader by, of, and for the people. The man to restore the American Dream. Someone who isn't all about the money, as one suspects the Clintons are.

Let's suppose a crisis comes just as Mankoff predicts, with Wall Street as the eye of the storm. The voters will expect that whoever they elect as president next year will go after "the malefactors of great wealth," just as FDR did in 1933, and they will be entitled to that expectation. They will want justice and justice is what I will have contrived and connived to deny them. Do I want to do that?

That's the question I've debated over the past couple of days. I've felt like Larry, the character in *Animal House* played by Tom Hulce, when he is presented with the opportunity to have his way with a young girl he's gotten drunk at a Delta House toga party. *Animal House* was my old man's and my favorite movie; we must have watched it together a dozen times, and I still watch it every year on Pop's birthday. *"Animal House,"* he used to say, "provides all the tools a man needs to chop his way through the thicket of modern life."

Anyway, if you're the cultivated soul I consider myself to be writing for, you'll remember the scene and the moment when two tiny figures pop up on Larry's shoulders: on one, a devil who exhorts him to fuck the girl, and on the other, an angel who admonishes him, "Don't you dare!"

That's how I felt as I deliberated Mankoff's deal. On one shoulder was an imp peddling the thrill of the chase, the sly pleasures of reliving Agency days, plus what I feel I owe Mankoff. On the other is an angel arguing for my upbringing and education, the values that my schools claimed to stand for. Underline that word "claimed," because at Groton, we fifth- and sixth-formers were expected to help out on alumni weekends, and many's the time I overheard FDR—surely the school's greatest alumnus—being cursed as a traitor to his class, sometimes by people born after his death, who'd obviously been indoctrinated by the sort of purse-worshipping, Upper East Side Republican parents and grandparents to whom tax rates were the lodestar of existence. Such people constituted my Yale Daily Themes professor's definition of the "upper crust" as "a bunch of crumbs held together by dough."

My father, Groton '51, wasn't like that at all. He didn't seem to care all that much about money, despite the fact that he spent his working hours trying to add to—or at least protect—the wealth of his clients. Like certain of my teachers and housemasters, men my father's age and younger, he preached that noblesse oblige, looking out for others, was the brightest thread in the Groton fabric, the woof to the warp of "Do unto others . . ." and that the New Deal was essentially the application of these ideals to the conduct and policies of government.

It was a kind of civic catechism that we were taught, a lesson in moral citizenship, but today its ruling principles appear to have been relegated to the metaphorical dusty vitrines to which the folks who push the buttons and pull the levers that consign to the wastebasket ideas inconvenient to their self-enriching plans for the nation. I'm talking about ideals like "city on a hill," "I have a dream," "Ask not . . ." and—as I've pointed out—almost anything FDR argued for. Pop also saw decent behavior as a practical matter of self-preservation: "Flaunt your advantages long enough, and loudly enough," he once told me, "and it will occur to someone to come and take them away from you." The bottom line is that there's enough residue of this kind of idealistic thinking left in me to cause second thoughts about Mankoff's proposition.

People are saying that communitarian democracy is withering away into a kind of oligarchic feudalism in which a tiny fraction of the populace ends up with the power and the goodies. Do I want to further that process? That's the big question facing me. If I do this job for Mankoff, I'll have perpetrated a fraud on the people who vote for OG, assuming he gets the nomination—no sure thing—and then wins the White House. Whose urging should I heed: the imp's or the angel's?

Well, I've decided to accept his proposition.

Why? Lots of reasons.

Number one is that I really don't fancy the idea of Hillary Clinton as my president. It's not so much her as the thought of her husband trading on his White House connections—and trade you can be sure he will; look at his record since he left the White House, for everything from cash to women. This country really doesn't need a First Lecher doing shady deals in the Rose Garden.

Number two is the opportunity to see whether I've still got game. Once you've tasted the heady intoxicants of undercover intelligence work, you don't forget how great it is to be a guardian of big secrets, to know what others don't, to deploy skills and resources that can alter the fates of people, institutions, even nations. I like my day job, but it's not exactly blood-stirring. Helping to arrange the funding for a Jane Austen workshop at Oberlin, a named professorship at Berkeley, or an Edward Hopper exhibition in Berlin doesn't carry the same thrills, chills, and technical satisfaction as blowing up the offshore accounts of some especially vile and genocidal sub-Saharan dictator.

Number three plays itself. You can't really call my mission a bribe. It's really a wager. In a proper bribe, there are few or no contingencies between cup and lip. What I'll be doing for Mankoff will be like the bets I placed for my old man when he twisted his ankle playing tennis and couldn't make it to the $20 window in 1975 when we went out to Belmont to watch Seattle Slew complete his Triple Crown. This is no sure thing. The senator has to knock off Hillary in the primaries to get the nomination, and then he has to win the election eighteen months from now. Suppose Mankoff's got it wrong; suppose a financial crisis doesn't occur and the anti–Wall Street issue is a nonstarter. The odds on OG getting it done definitely lengthen, whether we're talking about winning the nomination or beating whoever the GOP puts up in the presidential election. Maybe the Republicans have their own OG lurking in the wings. Or he can get hit by a bus, or turn out to be a closet pedophile, or there'll be another 9/11.

So there you have it. If I do Mankoff's bidding I will be adding a mite of my own to the pandemic of corruption that has afflicted nearly every atom of American public life. If I pass on his offer, I'll miss out on a chance to remake history. If I don't pass, I'll have an exclusive on what will potentially be one of the big game-changing moments in American history, what the chinstrokers in the pundit class will call "an inflection point." If you have a chance to leave your footprints on the sands of time, my housemaster at Groton used to say, jump with both feet and land hard.

And finally there's this: if I don't take the job, Mankoff will surely find someone else who will. I know this is a lousy reason to pursue a given course of action, but I'm human, aren't I?

My plan is to limit myself to a personal account of what I do for Mankoff; who I see, who I deal with, what's said. No personal stuff unless absolutely essential. Nothing about my friends, my love life such as it may be, my lifestyle, my personal metaphysics, or, except when absolutely necessary, my innermost existential yearnings. Apart from weekends or as the result of exigent circumstances, at the end of every day I'll set down events while they're hot and fresh. No backdating, redacting, lily-gilding, *pensées d'escalier*. Just plain vanilla accounts of planning and negotiations in which I'm involved, meetings at which I'll have been present as they happened, recorded as accurately as my memory and as soon as is practical.

All of this is protected by encryption software I've installed on this laptop, which itself has no phone, Internet, or Wi-Fi connection. That way it'll be eyes-only for me—and, of course, depending on what I eventually decide to do with this account, for you, Gentle Reader.

So off we go, friends. Fasten your seatbelts.

As the Lone Ranger used to shout, "Hi-yo, Silver: away!"

That's "silver."

As in thirty pieces of.

# FEBRUARY 20, 2007

Future readers of this account may need a bit of background on STST.

The firm was founded in 1903 by Lembert Struthers and Herman Strauss, ambitious young clerks chafing under the yoke of their senior partners at Harriman & Co. and Kuhn Loeb & Co.

They had a very clear idea of what kind of business they would do, and how they would do it, which they laid down in a series of fourteen precepts. The first and uppermost of these statements of principle was this: "We comply fully with the letter and the spirit of the laws, rules, and ethical principles that govern us . . . and our clients come first" is the exact wording.

I have it on good authority that the passage is displayed wherever one turns in STST's far-flung empire: when the firm's traders, whether in Prague or Johannesburg, turn on their Bloomberg screens at the beginning of the day, there it is—the first thing they see in the crawl; it's posted in every conference and waiting room from London to Hong Kong, in every restroom and vault between Las Vegas and São Paulo; you can't agree to a deal or take a leak without the noble motto hitting you in the eye.

Let it be said that there are many on the Street who are disinclined to take STST's pious exhortation of client primacy at face value. Finance capitalism, as it's called, likes to drape itself in a thick, warming blanket of self-congratulatory tributes to its concern for the customer, but when I listen to some of my clients and read the financial news closely, the more convinced I am that in transaction after transaction after transaction, the STST client who *really* comes first is STST itself. The firm itself rationalized such outcomes during the height of the '20s boom, when (as would later come out) it was unloading pretty egregious junk on its customers. Here's how Struthers put it in his 1927 Christmas letter to the staff: "Our first loyalty is to the client rather than the transaction. Now and then these coalesce, and we can in all honest good faith serve two masters."

This is apparently STST's justification for a string of deals they've put together with the hedge-funder James Polton that one of my clients has told me about, transactions that strike my untutored sensibility as treading an ethical borderline—which is why I wouldn't dare bring them up with Mankoff. There is one person at STST with whom I feel safe discussing them: Lucia van der Poole, STST's head of communications.

Lucia's become about my closest STST friend, mainly because we're kindred spirits with somewhat similar backgrounds and because the nature of her work leaves her desperate for someone to whom she can unburden herself. Her remit as senior vice president for communications covers everything that has to do with the firm's image: media relations and PR. In addition, two years ago, STST added Washington to her portfolio, so she also supervises its extensive lobbying effort, as well as its Capitol Hill and executive branch relationships.

A friend who knows Wall Street calls Lucia "STST's house agnotologist," a ten-dollar word I had to look up. Agnotology turns out to be the art (some might say science) of creating and disseminating ignorance. Ignorance, misconception, misperception, disinformation. Confusion and complexity. The essence and core of Wall Street public relations, of most "corporate communications." Both Wall Street and Washington are heavily into agnotology, and by all accounts, no one's better at it than Lucia.

Since corporate philanthropy falls under image-building and -control, it was inevitable that Lucia's and my paths would converge. They did about four years ago, when she and I were both involved in a big dinner at the Metropolitan Museum sponsored by

STST, and we've since grown close in the way of friends who see each other intermittently but stay in close touch. We exchange a lot of phone calls. We feel we can trust each other with the latest and hottest gossip.

She's a bit older than me, turned fifty on her last birthday (she says; I'd add a couple of years), a cultivated Englishwoman of flawless pedigree. Would be totally at home at Brideshead, would know exactly how to conduct herself with the sort of dowager grandee played by Maggie Smith. Her family is prominent and long-descended. One ancestor gave offense to Henry VIII and was beheaded; another was a fleet captain under Nelson; a third went to the Galápagos with Darwin. An uncle just retired as deputy chairman of Royal Dutch Shell, and a cousin is high up at Coutts. She has that special effect on your run-of-the-mill U.S. senator or billionaire—like a witch's spell, really—peculiar to polished English persons of her type: an aura that suggests fancy country weekends staged around titles, adultery, and hunt suppers. She's highly educated, read history at Cambridge, where she got what they call "a starred First," equivalent to our summa cum laude, and speaks several languages. She can talk about anything. Einstein remarked that genius is an infinite capacity for taking pains, which certainly describes Lucia, but she's not exactly chopped liver in the intuition department.

Physically, I find her appealing. She's narrow-featured, dark eyes and a Virginia Woolf nose, and model-slim, but with good breasts. An elegant figure set off in all weathers by clothes that explain why her expense budget is a matter of considerable admiration and envy around STST, along with speculation, in which she rejoices, as to who she had to sleep with to accomplish what she does.

She arrived at STST in late 1999, when Rich Rosenweis met her at some "City" function in London and hired her—she'd been a confidential adviser to the chancellor of the exchequer—to oversee the public-relations/media aspects of the grand opening of STST's big new London office in Canary Wharf. By all accounts, she did an amazing job—which will come as no surprise to anyone who's spent time with her. Mankoff was impressed, and lured her across the Atlantic to weave her magic spell over STST's initial public offering. His timing was perfect. Lucia was ready to leave England. She and her aristocratic husband had grown apart, and he had a mistress stashed at Le Touquet, but divorce was out of the question because it would screw up his entail. Here was a way out. She liked Mankoff's offer, and liked him, and so to New York she came at the turn of the millennium.

Once in New York, her ascent was meteoric. Today, she's universally regarded as the public face of STST, almost as well known in terms of "brand identification" as Mankoff or Rosenweis. Certainly she has built up as good a Wall Street/Washington web of information and influence as either of them.

Lucia and I get together a couple of times a month for lunch or a drink. She tells me who's up and who's down; passes along the latest hot rumors that the SEC or the Feds are taking a close look at this or that firm or individual; which big respectable bank is said to be doing "no-no" business like money laundering; what's what on Capitol Hill. Since part of her job is to keep the firm from shitting its own nest, she monitors STST's e-mail traffic and isn't above showing me choice bits now and then, in the way that friends who really trust one another exchange secrets too good to keep to oneself. I reciprocate with gossip much less titillating, but it's the best I can do: things like who's being considered for a Carnegie Hall or Penn trusteeship; which university, on what terms, is pursuing which private-equity mogul to endow what; which museum director is sleeping with his deputy.

"Ever heard of someone called Eliza Brewer?" I asked her. "A Washington lawyer."

"Lizzie Brewer? Everyone's favorite insiders' insider? Little Bo Peep in chain-mail armor. Why do you ask, darling?"

"Someone mentioned her name in a way that sounded like I should recognize it. I didn't. And you know how I hate to appear less than au courant in the who's who department."

"I do indeed. Ah, sweet Lizzie. She'll cut your throat for tuppence ha'penny. She's the tiny iron fist in the velvet glove of C & B."

C & B: a name I did recognize. Stands for Coppercoat & Barley, one of the capital's hardest-charging law firms. Four hundred lawyers and growing. As well known for its lobbying prowess as its jurisprudential skills, and no wonder. Its pride of lawyers already includes four former members of Congress, two ex-Cabinet secretaries, the niece of a recent vice president and God knows how many former Congressional staffers and clerks to Supreme Court justices. It's a place where the so-called revolving door spins at Mach 5.

The more Lucia told me about Brewer, the more clearly I could see why Mankoff included her in his triumvirate. Winters and Holloway can be counted on to divert or hold up policy initiatives unfavorable or threatening to Wall Street, but if matters get out of hand, and an investigation or prosecution needs to be shut down or an indictment blocked, Brewer's the girl for the job. She'll know which doors to bang shut, what to cram down whose throat to shut them up, how to stifle regulatory actions that would affect a banking house's public image and possibly even its access to credit, or—worst case—land its higher-ups in the pokey.

We moved on to the transactions that Lucia calls "our firm's peculiar arrangements with James Polton," and how these can be made to appear to jibe with "the client comes first." STST is presently in the process of buttoning up what is supposed to be the final Polton deal, a structured ziggurat of mortgage debt and derivatives called 2007 Protractor.

Lucia doesn't like the Polton deals. She thinks STST is pushing the ethical envelope with these transactions, and that they may in the end come back to bite. She would never say so out loud within the firm, because Polton's hedge funds are huge revenue generators. He's one of the top hedge-fund operators in the country, whether your benchmark is Assets Under Management (AUM)—$170 billion—or Internal Rates of Return (IRR)—average of 27 percent over the last five years.

In the summer of 2006, he came to the conclusion that the securitized credit markets, those great discrete pools of mortgages and consumer debt and the derivatives that can be attached to them, had moved into bubble mode, and sooner or later were going to burst. At that point, he began to short everything in that sector that he could. By the last quarter of 2006, however, others had seen the same opportunity as Polton, and there was little available in the market to sell short on the scale he likes—it was like a trout stream being depleted through overfishing—so he came to STST and Deutsche Bank and a couple of other big players in the mortgage-backed securities market and proposed that they look into creating credit pools specifically for him to bet against. He and his attorneys had figured out how to do this within the letter of the law if not its spirit.

Polton was willing to pay handsomely. The sugarplum visions he set dancing in the minds of structured-finance people at STST and elsewhere got them all in a tizzy of greed, and so, apparently without bothering about ethical niceties such as "should we sell our clients stuff we've designed to go bust?," the firm's math nerds went to work on the algorithmic equivalent of IEDs.

This is how I understand it to work: Polton gives STST a list of sure-to-default mortgage-related debt securities. STST packages them into a multi-tier investment pool. These work on the theory that although if you stack garbage high enough, by the time the lower layers are consumed, the topmost layers will hang in there and somehow get paid off. This qualifies these layers, however, for a top rating from S&P and the other rating agencies, which means they can be bought by and sold to certain limited-risk clients—German regional banks, for instance—willing to rely on the ratings rather than their own credit judgment in return for a smidgen of additional yield. They're taking long positions on stuff that Polton, STST, and coconspirators are simultaneously selling short in the parallel derivatives market. This is why such clients are called "mullets," a word for the fish whose sole purpose of existence is to make a meal for larger predators.

This isn't one of those instances where STST has taken a short position in order to help a valued client complete a trade or round out a position. Pure proprietary profit is the goal here; it's the trading equivalent of swearing an oath with your fingers crossed behind your back. To dress this murky business up, a third-party front with a reassuring name like Derivatives Analysis Inc. is hired to put its stamp of approval on the garbage selected by Polton et al., and to take the fall when the top layers go kaput according to plan. That's also when the client figures out what's been done to him and calls his lawyer.

Lucia claims the Polton deals are models of probity compared to some of the other shit going down elsewhere, and for all I know, that's right. There's gossip that another big firm has pasted together a deal called Amethyst that they just keep refilling and refilling with garbage pulled from other, busted deals that they then can short over and over again. They've done $500 million so far—and still they find buyers. Even better is a huge scam at Citi, where the traders' sleight of hand is shoving unsold, unsalable pieces of older deals—stuff too fragrant for even the most obtuse German provincial bank to swallow—onto their own bank's balance sheet. They book those transfers as regular-way sales and immediately "pass Go" and collect their individual bonuses, notwithstanding that when these trades blow up, it's their own bank and its shareholders that will take the hit.

The arrangement with Polton isn't the first time that Struthers Strauss has engaged in financial origami and created elaborate and deceptive paper structures that are eventually so complex that scarcely anyone is able to figure out how it all fits together. "Complication is the first refuge of the scoundrel," says my elderly chum Scaramouche, about whom I'll tell you more shortly.

STST showed its mastery of fraudulent complication back in the 1920s, another time when the markets were in the grip of what the economist John Kenneth Galbraith has called "a gargantuan insanity." The firm pyramided interlocked "investment companies" with down-on-the-farm names like Appalachian and Clinch Mountain and, at the very summit, the Struthers Strauss Trading Company. These were sold to clients at nice prices with very nice built-in commissions and management fees. I suppose it was these deals that Struthers had in mind in 1927 when he issued the dictum about serving two masters.

In 1932, Herman Strauss, who was technically in charge of the firm's underwritings, was hauled before the Senate Banking Committee. The questions thrown at Strauss were pretty softball—Washington was trying to cover up for Wall Street—but nevertheless he had to admit that in 1928 and 1929, the firm that he and Lembert Struthers had built with such pride and scruple had unloaded barge loads of garbage on the investing public for $50 a share, financial waste matter that three years later was selling for pennies. As it turned out, Strauss got off lightly. A year later, with FDR having replaced Hoover in the White House, the committee was reconvened with Ferdinand Pecora as chief counsel and the banks were eviscerated.

By now, Gentle Reader, you're asking how a firm like STST can look itself in the eye. The answer is it doesn't. If the lawyers will sign off on it, go for it! "Legal" and "illegal" are as close as the Street comes to "right" or "wrong." No matter what you and I may think, these Protractor-type deals are perfectly legal, approved by $1,000/hour lawyers.

There are people who argue that Wall Street is the natural habitat of the psychopathic personality. There's a ten-point list called "the Hare checklist," after the psychologist who formulated it, and I have to say I've seen striking examples of these attributes and tendencies in many if not most Street types I've encountered.

(1) glib and superficial charm
(2) grandiose self-perception
(3) a constant need for stimulation
(4) pathological lying
(5) organic lack of conscience and empathy for others
(6) talent for manipulation
(7) no feelings of guilt
(8) shallow emotional responsiveness
(9) refusal to accept personal responsibility
(10) difficulty maintaining long-term personal relationships

One more thing. What STST expects of its own people, it expects from those with whom it does business, and that includes outside consultants like me. Absolute discretion. Omertà that makes the Corleones look garrulous. Talk to anyone, especially the media, about your dealings with STST, and should someone there hear about it, you're toast. If they knew about this diary, they'd be putting out a contract on me.

It's the despair of my chum Lucia and her staff that Mankoff won't do media—no talk shows, no *Fox Business News*, no sit-downs with most-favored journalists like Charlie Gasparino,

Maria Bartiromo, or Michael Lewis. Although Lucia would like to put him on *60 Minutes* or *Charlie Rose*, she has to admit that Mankoff's "mystery man of Wall Street" shtick probably works in the firm's favor.

Of course, the firm's top analysts take public and publicized stances on stocks and sectors on which they develop opinions and make buy-hold-sell recommendations, and now and then, if it suits a particular transaction or strategy, Lucia will orchestrate a leak.

There's definitely a Big Brother aspect to life at STST. Lucia says the phones are swept every day for bugs, and hard drives are subjected to random checks. And as I said, e-mails especially are carefully monitored. I don't know what it is, but there seems to be something about e-mail that brings out the indiscreet in people. Traders in particular are blowhards by nature; with them, digital boasting can be reflexive, even though employees are regularly reminded of a favorite saying of Arnold Braum, the Wagnerian gnome who is the managing partner of Corbett & Charles, STST's principal outside law firm: "the 'e' in 'e-mail' stands for 'evidence.'"

STST recruits the best and the brightest and most ambitious products of the famous universities; year in, year out, the firm ranks first in recruitment at Stanford, MIT Sloan, Amos Tuck, and other top-rated business schools. The pace of the place is brutal: eighty-hour weeks are standard even in summer, and the firm's on the brain 24/7. I think of it as a kind of hyperbaric chamber spun from gold. As you rise closer to the organizational summit, you have less and less time or energy left for the wife and kids, who are expected to compensate for the parental/spousal gap by buying stuff with your seven-figure take-home pay and black AmEx card or sleeping with the personal trainer.

You give yourself body and soul to STST. There's no time for romance or the upward rounding of the mind and feelings or for moral or social or cultural reflection and improvement, and no space in the spirit for any emotion other than ambition and greed. One mistake and you're gone. If you can survive there for twenty years, till you're forty-five, you'll be rich enough to quit and learn to play Chopin or do good works in the barrios of South America or stalk the snow leopard or smell the roses.

No firm is defter at dealing with accusations of conflict of interest. That's probably why the Polton trades have gone down so easily. So far. Here's how they're treated in *The Firm: The History of a Great Institution*, the first authorized history of Struthers Strauss, which will be published early next year. Lucia slipped me a copy of the manuscript, and I have to say it's really very good: stylishly written, admirably researched. Here's the book's take on the Polton trades: "*. . . the firm and its own investors enjoyed the substantial profits . . . produced by taking an astute and almost unique short position in the subprime mortgage market. While some would question whether the firm did not have an overarching fiduciary responsibility to all clients and customers to share its expertise . . . senior management was and is clear: Each business unit is responsible and accountable for doing its best to complete the mission of that particular business—period. No business is its brother's keeper. Each tub on its own bottom.*"

"Each tub on its own bottom." You can't get more sweetly evasive than that.

I suppose all firms at some point have to deal with situations where some clients are more equal than others. Triaging clients is part of the business; why shouldn't a firm go the extra mile, ethically as well as financially speaking, for the client who writes $100 million a year of business as opposed to one who throws in an order now and then? Polton is surely more profitable to STST day in, day out, than the German banks who've been the lead mullets in the Protractor-type offerings. But God knows how STST responds if faced with Lucia's blackest nightmare: an insider whistleblower with the facts and documents who can walk the SEC or Uncle Sam through the scheme, layer by layer.

So that's STST, creed and culture. Further comment from me would be superfluous, other than perhaps this: every now and then, away from my business, I run into STSTers past and present. Only the ones who no longer work there seem remotely happy—at least as I define the word.

# FEBRUARY 26, 2007

One final bit of background. I feel I should tell you a bit about San Calisto, nicknamed by me for the Roman palazzo where the Vatican stashes its superannuated cardinals. On days when I'm still in the office in the late afternoon, or when I have nothing on my plate for lunch, I'll wander across the elevator lobby for a drink or a sandwich.

San Calisto currently houses four engaging relics (down from a half dozen when I moved in next door) from the era when STST was an old-fashioned partnership. They still pine for those bygone days, although they understand why the firm went public in 2000. Trading activity had grown in volume, risk, and technical complexity to a point that the then-partners' personal wealth might have been imperiled. Incorporation and a listed quotation protected against that dire contingency.

Still, they all agree that something changed in their beloved firm's vibe. New faces were coming up fast; room needed to be cleared at the top; relationships with certain corporate clients were changing as those clients' own executive composition changed. The generation that had steered STST to postwar glory had outlived its day.

San Calisto was Mankoff's graceful way of shoving these elders gently aside. He was cool with the idea that STST's history be recognized in a living way, but equally insistent that a respect for tradition not be allowed to interfere with present-day operations and attitudes. STST values its senior citizens' experience and knowledge up to a point, but it doesn't want them wandering around the firm spreading dangerous old ideas or talking up antiquated concepts like "conflict of interest." Mankoff prefers history to be inside books and museums and glass cases, not shuffling around the byways of his realm, sticking its head into offices, inquiring about things it can't really comprehend, spreading possible confusion with talk about "what we used to do . . ." or "what we used to think . . ."

Frankly, I think the Street's mistaken to ring-fence its elders. One thing that really bothers me about Wall Street nowadays is that everyone's so *young*. Where's the experience? They'll tell you it's built into the algorithms that they depend on, but I don't buy that. For these young people, it's all about now, never about then. Of course, if you have no past—didn't grow up with pictures of ancestors on the dining-room wall, or worship in chapels with war memorial tablets—why should you give a damn about *then*?

The San Calisto gang talk about the past but aren't stuck in it; for a group whose age must average seventy-five, they're pretty up to date. That doesn't mean, though, that they're crazy about today's Wall Street. If there's one philosophical point they're agreed on, it's that back in their day, the work was about *building*: raising money for new companies, new factories and stores, new processes. Today it's mainly about *extracting*—whether what's under the microscope is a company being hollowed out financially in a leveraged buyout, or practically everything in the magic slice-and-dice world of securitization.

Visitors to San Calisto are buzzed in to a small reception area where a handsome, middle-aged receptionist plays Cerberus. The rest is a warren of small offices, conference rooms, a dining room catered by a chophouse down the block, and a closet-sized, dreary "business center" that looks like it was plucked from your local Marriott. San Calisto has its own separate Bloomberg account and LAN computer network. The overall décor is Ralph Lauren traditional—cut-glass decanters on imitation Chippendale sideboards, mediocre English watercolors of landscapes and racing scenes, a scattering of old nineteenth-century "Spy" caricatures, and etchings of Old New York

The old boys' offices are heavy on STST memorabilia: old photographs of the original Broad Street partners' room; Lucite blocks with miniature prospectuses embedded in them; model airliners dating back to the heyday of the Lockheed Constellation and Douglas DC-6 and Boeing 707, bearing the insignia of airlines that are mostly no longer in business; models of ocean liners long since consigned to the scrapyard; miniature oil-drilling rigs; photographs of prime-of-life San Calistans shaking hands with company CEOs on shipyard launchways and airport tarmacs, in factories, beside oil derricks, and with politicians and statesmen; framed fountain and ballpoint pens from notable closings: underwritings, private placements, mergers. And, of course, in every room, suitably framed, *"Our clients come first."*

By now, death and dementia have reduced the San Calisto population to four noble remnants. I call these old guys "the Wrecking Crew," after characters in my beloved P. G. Wodehouse golf stories. I'm not a golfer, but when I was around seventeen, my father tried to seduce me into taking up the game and gave me a volume of the Wodehouse tales. I hated the game—it takes forever—but I love those stories, several of which feature a foursome of elderly Wodehouse players nicknamed according to their playing styles: "The First Grave Digger," "The Man with the Hoe," "Old Father Time," and "Consul, the Almost Human" (after a half-man, half-ape sideshow attraction popular in Wodehouse's youth). My own personal Wrecking Crew consists of the Nitmeister, who never met a factoid or data byte he couldn't discourse on at length; the Ancient Mariner, a walking anthology of Wall Street and STST anecdotes, who'll buttonhole you in a trice and relate something dreadful that Kidder Peabody did back in 1979; the Warrior, a much-decorated fighter pilot in Korea, who wears his ancient valor like a halo; and, finally, my favorite: Scaramouche.

The latter is a bright-eyed old guy, ruddy-faced with an astonishing shock of white hair. His name is Clement d'Arcy Spear. He was born in 1934, the same year as my father, attended Boston Latin, Harvard, and Harvard Business School, did the then-mandatory two years in the peacetime military ("too young for Korea, too old for Vietnam"), volunteered on JFK's successful 1960 campaign, and joined STST right after that election. He was head of Industrial Finance in the late seventies and eighties, retiring in 1992 as a limited partner.

I nicknamed him after the title character in a 1920s potboiler by Rafael Sabatini. The opening line fits him: "He was born with the gift of laughter, and a sense that the world was mad." Not that I've ever read the book—I did see the movie once on TV—but when the Yale library was built back in the 1930s, some wag had this sentence carved into the façade, alongside quotations from Dante, Shakespeare, and other immortals.

Scaramouche has a highly developed feel for the ludicrousness and folly of so much of modern life. He has a champagne personality—he himself boasts that he's "a revel-rouser," but there's a strain of hard-eyed realism running through it all. He's got a wicked mouth on him and fancies himself a coiner of aphorisms, and I have to say, the more I see how the world really works, the more accurate his quips seem. It was of Rosenweis that Scaramouche first uttered his immortal aphorism that "90 percent of the world's problems can be traced to three causes: sex, money, and short men." I asked him once about how STST justifies being on every side of every deal, and he observed: "Chaunce, old boy, if God hadn't wanted it this way, He wouldn't have given us two sides to a mouth." Another of my favorites is: "They say character is destiny, a sentiment with which I agree. The problem is, it's usually some other man's character and my destiny."

It's from Scaramouche that I picked up a useful epistemological tool called "Hanlon's Razor" (nobody seems to know exactly who Hanlon was), which posits, "Never attribute to malice that which can be adequately explained by stupidity." He holds that this accounts for most conspiracy theories. Of today's Wall Street, he says, "Nowadays computers have made it possible to profitably trade obscenely, almost embarrassingly small fractions of money. But to make those add up to a decent profit in absolute terms, you have to add cogs and capacity to the machine—A makes B turn, which makes C turn, which makes D turn and so on—and there's a danger there. Let a tiny grain of sand get in one of the gears, and the whole damn thing will blow up." That might be Mankoff talking, although Scaramouche is no admirer of STST's CEO; he thinks Mankoff lacks style. Another good one is: "I've made more money from what I've read upside down on other men's desks than what I've read right-side up on my own."

And it was Scaramouche who explained the financialization of the U.S. economy in terms that I'll be able to pass on to my grandchildren, if I ever have any. "Once upon a time," he told me not long after we met, "GM sold cars with loans attached; today they sell loans with a car attached. Apples and oranges, if you ask me." And Scaramouche who summarizes a great deal of what goes on in Wall Street today with "complexity is the first refuge of a scoundrel."

Some say that Scaramouche could have ended up running STST if he'd gone for it, but he didn't. I asked him about that once. "The problem was," he told me, "that to do that, I would have had to become one of these people, and I would rather have bamboo slivers under my fingernails than end up inhabiting the persona of someone like Rich Rosenweis." He likes to tell himself what he swears is a true story about how one day quite recently, he was walking along Rector Street and ran into a man, a few years younger than himself, whom he'd known fleetingly in the old days. This fellow looked Scaramouche up and down and then asked, dead seriously, "Are you who I think you used to be?"

The way my friend tells it, for once in his life, he was at a loss. Finally, he mumbled, "God, I hope not," and they went their separate ways.

The old boy basically doesn't give a damn. He says what he thinks and doesn't care whom it rubs the wrong way. He frankly admits that he grew to hate Wall Street even as it made him rich. In the 1980s, when everyone was flirting with Michael Milken and his magical money machine, he announced that if STST did junk bond business with Drexel Burnham he'd quit and take his corporate clients and best people to Morgan Stanley. STST rejected Milken's overtures and thereby dodged a regulatory and financial disaster.

Scaramouche was Merlin Gerrett's lead investment banker back in the day, helping Gerrett build Arrow Northumberland into the country's most-admired investor (and second-richest man after Bill Gates). Scaramouche himself didn't do badly out of the relationship; rumor has it that he still owns $80-odd million of Arrow Northumberland stock, bought for peanuts when he first began to handle Gerrett's investment-banking business. It's said that Gerrett still privately seeks the old boy's advice, notwithstanding that Mankoff is now the firm's designated Gerrett connection.

There are times everyone needs a good, bracing jolt of companionship, and so, today, after accepting my assignment from Mankoff, still harboring lingering doubts about whether I'm doing the right thing, when cocktail hour rolled around, and my long day's work was done and evening drew nigh, I walked across the elevator lobby to San Calisto.

This evening the crowd was down to just two: Scaramouche and the Ancient Mariner. I poured myself a whiskey from the sideboard and joined them just in time to hear Scaramouche say, "Now tell me that isn't the damnedest funniest thing ever to happen on Wall Street! If it isn't, I don't know what the hell is!"

I asked to be included in the joke.

"Have you heard about the transactions the firm's doing with this fellow Polton?" Scaramouche asked me. "The hedge-funder?"

"A bit."

"Well, what I hear is that when Polton and his minions started to canvass the Street for willing coconspirators, this firm and Morgan Stanley and Banque de Seine and others were quick to sign up. But Bear Stearns, of all people, turned him down. Did you hear me? Bear Stearns! Can you believe it! Turned him down on what they said were ethical grounds, quote unquote. That is probably the only time in the Street's history that the words 'ethical' and 'Bear Stearns' have appeared in the same sentence!"

He let us savor that remark, then turned to another matter. "Chauncey, you talk all the time to Lucia van der Poole. Has she ever mentioned something called Samarra/Hatton?"

"Samarra? You mean like in the John O'Hara novel?" I responded. *Appointment in* was one of my father's favorites.

Scaramouche shook his head. "The one I'm talking about is a redneck mortgage servicer way down south in Dixie. One of those fly-by-night outfits that uses door-to-door representatives and strip-mall offices to peddle mortgages to poor people who they know won't be able to keep up the payments. I gather Rosenweis has made a deal to acquire their business. Mankoff must be nuts to let him. That a firm like ours would involve itself in such a contemptible business beggars belief! It's worse than penny stocks!"

I Googled Samarra/Hatton afterwards. I could tell quickly that this would be a lily that Lucia—who had never mentioned the name to me—would despise having to gild. I could understand Scaramouche's disbelief. This is a low-rent, Shylockian business on a level with payroll lending. Samarra/Hatton gives mortgages to people with "less than pristine credit histories." In other words, people whose prospects of paying back a mortgage are between zero and none. It then sells these on to Wall Street, which repackages them into structured deals, like the ones STST is doing with Polton. Scaramouche is right: it's a contemptible business.

Scaramouche wasn't finished. "A firm of our size and dignity has no business peddling this penny-ante stuff! It's like the Morgan bank going into payday loans! Disgraceful!"

The Ancient Mariner and I raised our glasses and drank to that.

Scaramouche went on: "The real risk in buying a low-grade business is the low-grade people who come with it. Not that the Wall Street people I see nowadays at the Stuyvie (short for Stuyvesant Club, the old-line midtown club where I'm also a member) fit anyone's definition of high-grade. They make you yearn for the good old days when the Street emptied out by six, and everyone would be home in the bosom of their family or mistress, or having a martini at their club. I must say, the more I hear about what takes place inside those cloistered walls downtown, the harder it is to imagine that there was a time at the firm, at least while Herman Strauss was still alive, when we were told in no uncertain terms 'only to go after first-class business, and only in a first-class way.' Anyway, I shan't be surprised if the whole bloody mess comes to a hideous and inglorious ending. To say nothing of expensive."

Walking home later, I started thinking about the nuts and bolts of the job I've agreed to do for Mankoff. This fellow Homer Orteig, OG's right-hand man and campaign strategist, seems a good place to start. The question is: how and where do I get to him?

## MARCH 6, 2007

Inevitably, I find myself wondering about OG. Not that it makes any difference to what I'm up to for Mankoff, but I suppose it's normal for me to want to have a better sense of the kind of person he is. His followers seem to think he's Abraham Lincoln, Jack Kennedy, and Martin Luther King rolled into one. When he delivers a speech, you get a feeling of what the atmosphere on the Mount must have been like when Jesus got going on the Beatitudes.

But how good a president will he make? I can't seem to help asking myself that, even though it has nothing to do with my assignment. He's a great campaigner, tremendous with crowds, but how is he at the one-to-one make-the-other-guy-blink stuff where policy gets thrashed out and workable legislation negotiated? Mario Cuomo famously observed that we campaign in poetry and govern in prose, and look at how little poetry counts for in modern life.

His career path has been impressive and variegated, and his credentials look amazing. The guy's been a lot of places, done a lot of things. He's been his own John the Baptist, preparing the way with two books, an autobiography a while back and a book last year about the power of hope, about how if we dream hard enough, America can be a better place. Self-help books that pitch a wishing-will-make-it-so philosophy sell in the millions, so in that sense OG is preaching to the converted. I don't read self-help books, and I doubt I'll read either of OG's.

Everywhere he's been, everything he's done has garnered success and acclaim—although there are a few critics who point to unkept promises, discarded relationships, grand plans not implemented. The usual broken eggs that go into making a tasty-looking career omelet. But great résumés—or great minds—don't necessarily make for great or significant president. Look at the first George Bush.

I'm no expert, but if OG is elected, I'm guessing he may run aground on Capitol Hill. There are people in Congress today who make it look like the doors to the loony bin have been thrown open. The country is polarized to a degree I've never seen, and it's reflected in the Congress. The middle ground, where socially and fiscally essential policies and programs were once worked out, is a barren wasteland. Nothing grows there. I look for Congress to be a problem, what with the static generated by the 24/7 news cycle and the deceptions of the spin doctors and "news" dispensers like Fox.

These days, the more intellectual a politician is, the more suspicion he's likely to arouse. What is it the prophet says? "Come—let us reason together." But that's not how the system works, maybe never has. Politics is about cutting deals: you give me this, and I'll give you that. I'll slip you $75 million, you deliver Winters, Holloway, and Brewer. Certified intellectuals like OG have difficulty buying into that process. They can't grasp why their acute, analytical, three-diploma, mother-knows-best perception of the right policy solution isn't always immediately conceded by all concerned. Why their skillful rhetoric and polished reasoning don't inevitably carry the day. They never seem to understand, or simply disregard the notion of the instinctive mistrust ordinary people feel for those who flaunt their high IQs. That in politics, principal with an "al," as in wealth, counts more than principle with an "le," as in truth, beauty, and the American way. In other words: show me the money.

Well, OG is certainly smart—a member in best standing of what the pundit class calls "the technocratic elite": the people who oscillate between the public sector and the world of universities, think tanks, corporate boards, white-shoe law firms, and investment banks; who turn up postpaid at Davos and Aspen; who get the highest speaking fees. These are people who talk and talk and talk without much benefit to the ordinary voter. More important, few of them seem to have earned a living, once you eliminate schoolchild stuff like mowing lawns or selling Girl Scout cookies. They organize and appear on panels; they accrue consultancies and fellowships; garner talk-show/op-ed exposure.

OG strikes me as a prize example of the species—and that turns me off. I read him as a narcissist of a pretty high order. My battered Webster's *Ninth New Collegiate Dictionary* refers the reader to "egoism" and "egocentrism," which makes the point without needing to turn the page. If there's anything in the known universe the guy appears truly to get off on, it isn't "We, the people," it's himself.

But whether I dig him or not is of no practical concern to my immediate task. There's no doubt in my mind that with enough early funding, a candidate as charismatic and exhortatory as OG can definitely put away Hillary, who exudes zero messianic glamour and whom nobody—whether they lean right or left—really seems to trust. Getting past her is the key. Outspending her is likely to be the tactic that will work best. After that, the White House should be a lock, especially if there's a GOP-killing financial crisis. And you have to say that, given the evidence, this is also starting to look like a sure thing.

I had lunch with Lucia today. It was obvious when she sat down that she was in a sour frame of mind. When I asked her what was wrong, she complained that she'd had to devote a good part of an already overscheduled morning—on Rosenweis's direct orders—to trying to spin the *Post*'s "Page Six" gossip column about a ridiculous fracas in the Hamptons that involves an STST higher-up, a woman who was paid a $20 million bonus to come over from Deutsche Bank to be cohead of the firm's Global Equities division. It seems that this woman, whom Lucia describes as a great business getter but a "godawful" person, and her husband, a bigtime Manhattan dermatologist, have gone to war with a neighbor, a hedge-fund stud with a new Russian wife and $12 billion Assets Under Management. At issue is some dune grass the latter party is alleged to have cleared out to make way for a path to the beach that runs along on the property line of the STST woman's Amagansett McMansion.

I let her blow off on this subject, then asked what else was new on the Rialto.

"Well—this, for starters, also courtesy of Richard," and from her cell phone Lucia read me the following e-mail:

From: Richard Rosenweis to Desk Chiefs: re: Axes: "Our current largest needs are to execute and sell our new issues—CDOs and RMBS—and to sell our other cash positions . . . I can't overstate the importance to the business of selling these positions and new issues.

"Axes?" I asked. "What are 'Axes'?"

"A term of art, dear boy. 'Axes' are what we call the stocks or other products that we are trying to get rid of because they are not seen as having sufficient potential profit and may even produce losses."

"In other words, dumping your losers on your clients?"

"Preferably not, but if all the world's your clients, that's a problem. Then there's this, passed along by one of my trading-desk spies."

This one was from Sam Monday, cohead of International Trading, to an associate. The message was direct: *"Boy, that wolferine deal was really shitty."*

"What's 'wolferine'?" I asked.

"'Wolverine,' you idiot! You know perfectly well that most of our MBAs can barely spell their own names. It's code for some swaps deal our Singapore office has unloaded on some poor little hedge-fund lambs in Auckland. Wolverine only closed last month, but already it's in its death throes and looks as if it's going to take the dear, sweet, naïve, trusting Kiwis down with it."

She showed me another e-mail, this marked "Confidential" and signed by the firm's ace market strageist:

We . . . remain as negative as ever on the fundamentals in subprime, but the market was trading VERY SHORT, and was susceptible to a squeeze. We began to encourage this squeeze, with plans of getting very short again after the short-squeeze causes capitulation of these shorts. The strategy seemed doable and brilliant, but once the negative fundamental news kept coming in at tremendous rates, we stopped waiting for the shorts to capitulate, and instead just initiated shorts ourselves immediately.

The object is to cause maximum pain for existing holders of credit insurance. We should start killing the . . . shorts in the street; this will have people totally demoralized.

"Pretty stupid to put that on e-mail," I said. "How confidential is 'Confidential'?"

"Perhaps three or four hundred people—not counting hackers."

"What about the Braum doctrine that 'e' stands for 'evidence'?"

"If we're lucky, we can bury it before the SEC gets a whiff."

Strolling back to the office after lunch, I once again thanked whatever gods may be that I don't have her job.

# APRIL 8, 2007

Mankoff is starting to look prescient. A week ago, New Century, the biggest subprime mortgage mill in the country, filed for bankruptcy.

He and I talked about this a bit on the way to a meeting at the Morgan Library about a trove of eighteenth-century French musical manuscripts that the museum has its eye on. Time is of the essence. Another big Wall Street hitter is rumored to be looking at the same collection for Juilliard.

According to Mankoff, the Federal Open Market Committee, the star-chamber group that sets Federal Reserve monetary policy, refuses to buy the notion that anything's rotten in the state of Subprime. Either that or they simply can't face the fact that they've allowed the situation to get out of control. Apparently Bernanke and his colleagues, with one or two exceptions (most notably the guy from the Dallas Fed, whom Bernanke can't stand, and vice versa), sit around fiddling with their algorithmic models like kids playing Legos, while the rockets' red glare lights up the financial landscape outside the window. This intelligence—obviously from a mole inside the Fed—has encouraged Mankoff to step up the tempo of STST's beat to quarters.

# MAY 18, 2007

Last night the phone rang just as I was getting ready to watch Jon Stewart. It was Mankoff.

As usual, he got right to the point.

"You know what the Bohemian Grove is, right?" he asked.

"*Natürlich*," I replied. The Bohemian Grove is the summer encampment staged by the Bohemian Club, San Francisco's equivalent of the New York's Century Association or the Garrick Club in London: originally started by artists and writers and other creative types but now pretty much taken over by investment bankers, academic politicians, and corporate lawyers.

The "Grove," as it's called by people who've actually been there and those who pretend they have, is held for two weeks every summer in a redwood forest the club owns on the Russian River, a hundred-some miles north of San Francisco. It's one of those meet, greet, and pontificate confabulations that act as junction boxes through which pass the world's currents of influence and interest: the Global Economic Forum at Davos is probably the best known, and then there's the Council on Foreign Relations and the Clinton Initiative and the Aspen Institute, and Bilderberg, and Allen & Co.'s media jamboree in Sun Valley. "OK," I said, "why this curiosity about the Grove?"

"Think you can get yourself invited?"

"I can try. Yeah, probably—there's a guy I know out there who's asked me before. Mind telling me why?"

"Orteig's going to be there—from July 19th to the 21st. This may be our best shot."

He explained that Orteig had been the feature attraction at a dinner that one of our hedge-fund clients had held to drum up support for OG. Ordinarily Mankoff wouldn't have gone—he hates those things as much as I do—but the host is a good client, and Mankoff reckoned he might pick up some OG intelligence that could be useful for our grand design. Which he did: in the course of cocktail-hour small talk, Mankoff learned that OG's #1 is planning to attend Bohemian Grove in July.

The situation plays itself. If I can wangle an invitation for those dates, and then execute a neat bit of "managed serendipity" and accidentally on purpose happen to run into Orgeig . . . well, do I have to draw you a picture?

I told Mankoff I was pretty certain I could get myself invited. There's a San Francisco lawyer who's on the board of the de Young Museum, for which I helped work out a major loan of medieval and Renaissance tapestries from a Mexican media potentate. He has several times spoken to me about coming out as his guest to "the Grove," which he speaks of with the same reverence with which an imam might speak of Mecca, but our schedules have never quite fit.

So when I got to the office this morning, I waited out the time-zone difference, then called my friend in San Francisco, and weaseled out of him the information that he's planning to be up at Healdsburg for the entire Grove fortnight. I then fibbed that I would be on the west coast between July 19 and 21, so maybe this could be our year, for at least a couple of days. He was delighted at my news and suggested at once that I join him at the encampment. I blushed prettily, thanked him effusively, and called Mankoff's office and had them lay on a jet for July 19, open return but no later than July 21. Game on!

It's a little after 10:00 a.m., EDT, and I'm in a chartered Citation X at 30,000 feet climbing to 45,000, headed for California to see a man about an election.

The plane is on charter from Air Magus, which is owned by Merlin Gerrett; because of the longstanding relationship, STST charters exclusively with them. Please don't get the idea that I routinely travel in this grand fashion. To have a private jet on standby is an integral part of Mankoff's and my Orteig scheme. It did occur to me as I boarded at White Plains that when Morgan dispatched his "man" to Washington to talk with Teddy Roosevelt's "man," he may well have sent him by private railroad car. In those days, it would have taken as long to get from New York to Washington as for me to fly today from White Plains to Santa Rosa, the airport nearest the Bohemian Grove. Our flying time is estimated at four hours and thirty-two minutes, which allowing for the time difference will put me on the ground around noon PDT. From the airport to the Grove is a little under an hour. If all goes according to plan, by dinnertime I should have "bumped into" the object of my potential affection.

Things continue to deteriorate in the world of Big Money. A woman I went to Yale with, who now writes for *The Wall Street Journal*, says that the mood on Wall Street reminds her of the early days of AIDS, before HIV had been identified and people were confused about the causes of the disease and how to fight it.

The root cause seems to be that everyone's got so much going on with everyone else, in all shapes and sizes, in all degrees of transparency, liability, and opacity, that when one gets sick, others must, too. We could be looking at a credit pandemic. Three days ago Bear Stearns shut down its hedge funds on short notice, which has led to rumors of a possible credit boycott of Bear. If Bear has a hard time rolling over their overnight borrowings, others will get dragged down. Trust will disappear, and lenders will insist on more and better collateral, but there probably isn't enough paper available to satisfy these demands. As always happens, gimmicks are starting to replace credit judgment and good security. Take Citi, which is desperately trying to pare down its balance sheet, and has started to sell CDOs subject to what they're calling a "liquidity put," which allows buyers to sell the crap back to Citi if they can't move it in the market.

Mankoff has been certain all along that Washington must sooner or later get involved: worst case, as a lender of last resort. Yesterday he got word that certain key aides are pressing his friend the Secretary of the Treasury to rein in the subprime market, which has gone completely Wild West. The problem is that an enforced slowdown—even a moratorium—on subprime origination and securitization would probably lead to a chain reaction that would require an outlay from either the Treasury or the Federal Reserve.

Washington's trying to avoid that, and is seeking ways to prod the system into fixing itself, which Mankoff says is like pushing on a string. If there has to be a bailout, he told me the other day, he wants STST positioned to take profitable advantage of it—and he hinted that there may be a role for yours truly in that process. But for now, Orteig has our full attention.

Do you remember that old movie *Zulu*? It's set in the 1880s and starts with a bunch of British soldiers at an outpost in South Africa going about their routine daily tasks when they suddenly become aware of a sound like thunder in the distance. This turns out to be a thousand Zulu warriors stamping the ground as they work themselves into a battle frenzy. That's how Wall Street feels right now. There's thunder in the distance, but is it big trouble or just weather? In the Battle of Rorke's Drift, as the ensuing battle in *Zulu* was called, the most Victoria Crosses ever handed out for a single engagement were awarded. When the shit hits the fan on Wall Street, I doubt there'll be many medals pinned on pinstriped lapels.

I like the deal I'll be proposing to Orteig. The $75 million, leveraged in the way political dollars can be (Mankoff estimates 5–1, meaning our $75 million could generate $375 million in cash-and-kind campaign contributions), will put OG head to head with Hillary. As for our side of the trade, the brilliance of Mankoff's concept is that it doesn't involve secret understandings with Winters et al. He's betting solely on past form, ego, ambition, and character to make sure that what Mankoff wants, Mankoff gets: Winters to make sure the White House sticks to a policy that puts Wall Street's welfare above all others; Holloway to protect the banks; Brewer to neuter any eager beavers at Justice who have grand ideas of criminally prosecuting Wall Street executives; and a fourth name, Patrick Vollmer, to supply the halo. Vollmer is the man who dragged America out of the Carter stagflation of the 1980s. He wasn't on the index card at Three Guys, but Mankoff has decided to secure the fortifications with an old CIA trick. At the Agency, we always tried to mask our shadier gambits by bringing in a front man of impeccable reputation and soaring self-regard. If there's anyone who can still provoke admiration from more than one side of the aisle, it's Vollmer. And word is that he's dying to get back to Washington to try to undo the mess that Greenspan and Bernanke have made of monetary policy.

Sounds like a long shot, doesn't it, to make a bet like this? Just remember Scaramouche's remark about character and destiny. I'm confident of success. Orteig has to be a practical yet imaginative sort to have brought his man this far this fast. He'll bite.

The captain just came on the speaker to tell me that we're an hour away from starting our final descent into Santa Rosa. Gentle Reader, are you ready to rumble?

# JULY 21, 2007

"Mission accomplished."

That was the message I left on Mankoff's voicemail an hour ago, as soon as we were wheels-up out of Chicago's Midway Airport after dropping off Orteig.

I'm not going to bore you with the details of my forty-eight hours among the Bohemian Grove's redwoods. What's it like? Well, if you're the sort who thinks it a mark of status to be able to watch a European prime minister take a piss on a sequoia, or to be able to tell the folks back home what Henry Kissinger "dressed down" looks like (a pretty gruesome sight), you'll love the place. It's funny. The official motto of the Bohemian Club is a line from *A Midsummer Night's Dream*: "Weaving spiders, come not here." But if you just sat back and watched the goings-on among the giant redwoods—the sucking-up, the deal-seeking, the obvious social calculation—you'd conclude there's nothing but arachnids on the make (including yours truly) all baked into a gigantic pastry of self-congratulation. Think Davos with trees and you've got the picture.

I went right to work, and it took just a bit over an hour for carefully planned happy coincidence to cause me to be introduced to Homer Orteig at an afternoon function.

He's a guy of middling height and weight, whose sleepy, heavy-lidded eyes and old-fashioned brush mustache are the distinctive features in an otherwise uninteresting face. Not someone you'd notice even in a small crowd, but take a second, closer look, and you'll see that here's a guy to watch out for at the weekly Friday poker table at the Lions Club. I knew him to be a couple of years older than me, a longtime Chicago lawyer, sometimes professor of law at the University's downtown campus, and an established

Cook County political insider, notwithstanding that the word on him is that he's a total straight shooter; I sized him up at once as someone I could do business with.

I contrived to run into him again at cocktails at Mandalay, the fanciest of the camps. By the second Ramos Gin Fizz, we were fast becoming new friends. I'd done my homework and played the right Chicago cards: sympathy concerning the Cubs and Bears, hatred of the White Sox, enthusiasm for the Second City, Steppenwolf and the Lyric Opera and Mies van der Rohe's Lakeside towers. My research had established that his favorite hangout was a North Side deli called Sonny's, so I told him that I'd heard it compared favorably in the smoked meat department to Katz's down on Houston Street. Then I threw in my love of the novels of Patrick O'Brian and Gilbert and Sullivan. By the time I finished, we agreed that we seemed to be kindred spirits, and wasn't it good luck that we'd met?

We walked together to the lakeside theater (the Grove offers two theatrical presentations, "the High Jinks" and "the Low Jinks"), and after the show, over more drinks, I learned that he was planning to fly back to Chicago in two days, on Saturday the 21st. Commercial, of course, which meant driving through weekend traffic to Oakland to catch JetBlue.

This was the opening I'd counted on. I was betting on the assumption that at this stage, OG's campaign has to watch its pennies, and chartered jets aren't an option for anyone except the candidate himself.

"Look," I told Orteig, "I have a consulting client who's flying out here tomorrow night for some big wine hootenanny in Napa. I was just talking to him on the phone, and he told me the plane has to go back to New York on Saturday to pick up his wife. I need to get back, so I asked him if maybe I could snatch a free ride and he said fine. Let me check with him and see if it'll be OK to drop you off in Chicago on the way to New York. I know he's a fan of the candidate, which ought to cinch the deal. I'll check with him just to make sure."

Show me an American male or female who'd turn down a freebie on a private jet and I'll show you a freak of nature. I went off to a Wi-Fi zone, pretended to call, then returned and gave Orteig the thumbs-up. His smile let up the glade. Still, I had to figure that behind the beaming, grateful face, the political animal would be wondering if there'd be a quid pro quo, and if so, what it might be. In Orteig's world, there's no such thing as a favor without a price tag.

First thing Saturday morning, a taxi ferried us over to Santa Rosa, where a spick-and-span Falcon awaited us on the runway. By eleven o'clock we were en route to White Plains by way of Chicago-Midway.

The opportunity to start my pitch came about an hour into the flight, just after we tucked into the gourmet sandwiches provided by the French Laundry, the three-star Napa restaurant that I'd arranged to cater the flight home.

Orteig looked across the table at me and said, "This is great chow." Then he asked me: "You told me you do some consulting for various Wall Street firms?"

I couldn't have scripted it better. I'd figured he might take the initiative, if only to get a sense of what I might be looking for as a return favor—as well as to see whether I might have other uses. After all, I'd made him well aware by now that I routinely worked with some pretty rich people.

"That's right," I replied. "A few. Hedge-fund people mostly. A couple of firms. My big investment banking client is Leon Mankoff at STST. You probably know who he is." That "probably" was, I thought, a bit of an artful touch.

Orteig nodded. "Who doesn't?" He took a couple of thoughtful bites, then asked: "How do people like Mankoff see things shaping up politically for next year?"

"At the moment, if you're a betting man, you have to send it all in on Hillary. She's hit the ground running, and she's raised a ton of money. Still, people have reservations about her. Even people who say they support her. People just don't trust the Clintons. If there's a financial crisis, which Mankoff and others think is likely, given what Washington's let the Street get away with—not to mention what the Street's let itself get away with—there's likely to be a lynch mob calling for the Street's blood. And Hillary will be leading it. It doesn't matter what she or her people have said or promised so far—if they see real political opportunity to do an ideological one-eighty, that's the way they'll go.

"You say Mankoff thinks a financial crisis is likely? Any timing on that?"

I shrugged. "Who can say? There's going to be a point at which a lot of the bad stuff can no longer be swept under the carpet. Subprime credit, for example. And nobody really has a handle on what's going on with derivatives. If any of this blows up at scale, you might be looking at a major convulsion. Still, these things always take longer than people expect. One of my clients is always quoting Keynes to the effect that the market can remain irrational much longer than you can remain solvent. Wall Street can fight the inevitable off for a while: borrow more money, uncover a fresh bunch of greater fools, pray for divine intervention. It's all a function, really, of how much money how many people can invest in keeping the balloon afloat. Once they run out of money, or inclination, or blind courage, or trust, or stupidity—although there's no way this country can ever run out of *that*—it's finished. Once they've got no more skin left to put in the game: game over!"

"And you think this will happen when?"

I gave it the old "who knows" with the hands, then said, "The storm might hit tomorrow, but it equally might hold off until next year, which is how Mankoff's betting. It's really a function of how much bad money people are willing to throw after good."

I watched Orteig digest that, then added: "One sure thing—if there's a crisis, the GOP is dead meat. The Democratic candidate will be a lock. Hillary won't even have to campaign. She can just sit on her ass in Chappaqua and watch her husband fuck the help."

I gave him a minute or so to think about that while I munched on my sandwich, then added, "Too bad your guy got started so late. He's an attractive candidate. Born to run. Great stage presence, impressive CV. Obviously very smart. People I know who've met him have been impressed. He has that 'it" factor that Hillary lacks. But he's got an awful lot of ground to make up. Speaking honestly, how do you think he's doing? Really doing."

"We're gaining momentum," he said, trying to sound positive and only half-succeeding.

"How much have you raised so far?"

I knew it was a question he wouldn't care to answer, and he didn't. "We're OK. Just starting to get traction."

That was bullshit, and yet it wasn't. My Internet research suggests that OG is doing better than Hillary in terms of current fund-raising, probably something around $40 million since the beginning of the year, but that's not translating into good poll numbers. But those would shift overnight if Orteig had $75 million to put to work next week.

"Who knows?" I said. "You still may have a shot."

I paused. Time to drag the fly under the trout's nose.

"From what I'm hearing," I said, "there's a lot of firepower out there that hasn't committed. That's still on the sidelines."

I watched him think carefully about his next move. Then he leaned forward until his face was practically up against mine and asked, in a low voice, almost if he feared the plane might be bugged:

"You work with a lot of big-money people, Chauncey. If you were in our shoes, how would you reach out to them?"

Bingo!

I didn't want to move things along too fast. "Well, I'm no political pro. But right now, I'd have to say, you need to hook up with one or two really big hitters. Dribs and drabs won't get it done; I'm talking tens of millions. Just to take an example, how much do you figure that party at the Museum of Modern Art raised for your guy? That was a pretty fancy crowd. Still, you probably cleared what? A couple of million?" I knew the answer, but I was highballing him to set him up.

"Half a million," he replied. He looked disconsolate. Then he brightened and added, "But probably more to come. And we've been doing a lot better." He didn't sound confident.

"When's the convention?"

"August 25 next year—in Denver. But before that, there are the primaries and caucuses, starting with Iowa in January."

"Not a lot of time. Your guy's made a strong start. The books, the Lincoln connection, and the throwdown at Springfield: all good shit. Apparently the money's coming in OK, but just. To get off the schneid, you're going to need a quantum jump: money for the Internet, state volunteer organizations, advertising—a ton of very expensive infrastructure. They don't give that stuff away."

I let that sink in, then set the hook: "Let me ask you this, Homer. Say you had an incremental $75 million—I'm just picking a number out of the air—that you knew you could count on right now. Money you could start laying out next week. How big a difference would that make?"

"You're speaking theoretically, of course?" he asked.

"Of course."

There was no need for me to wink. Orteig's a pro. He got it. I watched his expression change, his features sharpen, eyes wake up.

The smell of actual money does that to people. Greed, opportunism, the anticipation of real spending power, even a hint of potential victory: all were visible as I watched Orteig mentally translate $75 million into a powerful political database and its corollaries: websites, server costs, office space, thousands of volunteers and their care and feeding and deployment, call centers, TV time, chartered jets, Nielsen ratings points, audience share.

And rising poll numbers.

Finally, he said: "Chauncey, I'll level with you. If we got an injection of $75 million right now—even half of that—we could win this darn thing! We've got the right candidate, we've got the right message: all we need to be able to do is get it out, to secure funding sufficient to build out the brand and the campaign organization. If you know where I can get that kind of money, the candidate will kiss your ass in a Macy's window at high noon."

"That won't be necessary," I said, then decided it was time to bring out the net. "Homer," I said, using a voice full of fellow feeling, "I have to come clean with you. Our bumping into each other at the Grove wasn't entirely a matter of chance."

He grinned. "You know, I'm just starting to pick up on that. For someone who professes to disdain politics, you're a pretty sharp operator."

"Flattery will get you everywhere," I responded. "Now listen: there are people—wealthy people, influential people—who feel very strongly that if there's a crisis, Mrs. Clinton's not the person they want dealing with it. They've deputized me to come and talk to you."

"I don't suppose you're willing to disclose who these people might be?"

My turn to grin. "You don't suppose correctly," I replied.

"Why don't you tell me exactly what you have in mind?" We were on the same wavelength.

"Happily," I said. "I've already described to you the crisis my people see coming. Some of them think it might even compare to 1929. You know those World War II documentaries on PBS that show people picking through the rubble of Berlin in 1945? Or London after the Blitz? That's what they think this economy's going to look like."

"Jesus."

"I agree. OK, let's take as a given that the shit hits the fan sometime next year. If it happens before November '08, the likeliest scenario, that'll be on Bush's watch, and this administration's immediate problem. Coming on top of Iraq and Katrina, what this'll do to Bush's historical rating won't bear thinking about. Buchanan'll look like Lincoln next to Forty-Three. You with me?"

He nodded. "Go on."

"Now: here's the thing. You can bet they'll act quickly, because the people who'll be running the show from the Treasury are Wall Street types. You know: invest and then investigate. Which means they'll try to resolve over a couple of weekends a disaster that's been decades in the making. They don't know how to think long-term, or in terms of the wider community, what you and I think of as Main Street. The first thing on their minds will be to save Wall Street from the consequences of its greed and folly—and Washington's—so they'll try to fix the mess by throwing the taxpayers' money at it. They won't do what they should do, which is to keep essential overnight credit flowing, and throw the rest of the subprime and other garbage into a kind of global cesspool and let the rats fight it out. They should close down or nationalize the busted banks after segregating insured deposits, fire their boards, and put the bums who brought us this mess in handcuffs, along with the CEOs who let them get away with it. Let the banks' stockholders take the hit. But this isn't what'll happen, which is why the next president will have a problem."

I thought I got that little rehearsed speech out very glibly. You would have even thought I'd written it myself, although the words were Mankoff's. Orteig seemed impressed. "I think you'd better explain," he said.

"It's very simple. People on the Street will tell you that it takes roughly twice as long to get out of a crisis than to get into one. This means whoever gets elected a year from now is still going to have to deal with the problem. Whatever the GOP puts in place will be hard to get out of. But what will still be possible is for whoever enters the White House in 2009 to take it out of Wall Street's hide the way FDR did back in '33. That's when we got Glass-Steagall and all the other protective regulation that Phil Gramm and his patrons got rid of under Clinton."

"I see."

"And that brings me to your candidate. Let's start with your guy's declaration that he's the candidate of change. Change Washington, change the way the country functions, and so on. And change equals reform, agreed?"

Orteig nodded.

"The question, then, is: what kind of reform? Or, to put it another way, reform of what?"

"Wall Street, I should think."

"That's our guess. But reform needs to be implemented coolly and thoughtfully, not against a background chorus of 'off with their heads!' with lynch mobs gathering on Capitol Hill and tumbrels rolling down Wall Street—but when the next president is inaugurated, he or she will be under pressure to set policy simply to satisfy the mob's or the media's call for necks for the guillotine. But lynch mobs, guillotines, and heads on pikestaffs are hardly what the economy's going to need at that point."

"I take your point, but if there's a crisis, you can hardly expect a candidate not to exploit it politically."

"Of course. The people I'm speaking for don't much care what the candidates think and say about Wall Street up to the election. You tell the girl what she wants to hear in order to get her into bed, but that's not the same as a marriage proposal. What musn't happen is that we end up with a president-elect and a bunch of advisers who try to put an anti–Wall Street, anti-business campaign rhetoric into actual practice. That would be a disaster for the country. For a new administration to take office with a policy based on retribution and punishment would be a terrible mistake. Bad for Wall Sure, to be sure, but worse for the country. It'd be a case of starving the patient just when he needs to be fattened back to health. The people won't see it that way, of course, but off the evidence of the past twenty years they haven't exactly shown themselves to be capable stewards of their own best interests."

"The public won't stand to see Wall Street bailed out."

I grinned. "What if they have no say in the matter? Besides, hanging Wall Street out to dry shouldn't be at the top of any serious president's policy want-list. There's health care. There's Iraq and Afghanistan. The Main Street economy will require a bit of lip service, and maybe even some real money. There's China, Latin America, the drug war, other big stuff. More pressing and painful issues than putting a few people in Armani into minimum-security prisons. Your man is an inspirational type. If he captures the electorate's fancy and gets elected, they'll cut him some slack, no matter what he may have promised during the campaign. And what you and I are really here to discuss is how to make sure there *is* a campaign in which he can make promises."

"What about the media?"

"The media? Come on! The last time the media made a real difference in the way things get done in Washington was Watergate, and that was what—almost forty years ago?"

He pondered that. I decided to switch to sympathy mode.

"Look, Homer. I'm no fan of a lot of the stuff I see going down on Wall Street. But I do appreciate that if there's a crisis it's important that the markets see the prospect of stability for as long as the big banks need to get their houses back in order. If a new administration comes in having made all sorts of wild reform promises about throwing the passengers in the Bush lifeboat to the sharks—and then keeps those promises—the result could be chaos."

Orteig smiled and shook his head as if laughing at some inner joke. "I see," he said. "God help me if I ever find myself pitted against you in an election."

"You flatter me," I said. "Here's the thinking of the people who sent me to talk with you. If they could be privately—and I emphasize 'privately'—assured by you that in the eventuality your man is elected, his economic team will consist of men and women who understand the importance of functioning capital markets and banking institutions to the overall welfare of the nation, they're prepared to commit up to $75 million to the campaign."

He whistled softly, then nodded to himself. Then he fixed his gaze on mine and asked, "And what if he doesn't get the nomination?"

"If he doesn't get the nomination, obviously the money's down the drain. Nothing ventured, nothing gained."

"I see. As far as an economic team, I trust you have certain people in mind?"

"I do." No more playing around, I thought. I reached into my jacket pocket and took out an index card similar to the one Mankoff had shown me at Three Guys, on which I'd printed four names.

Orteig reached for it, but I held it back, and said, "Before I show it to you, one thing must be understood. The people whose names are on this card have zero knowledge of what I'm proposing to you, and it has to stay that way. We're making a Pavlovian bet here.

Ring the right ideological bell, and these animals can be counted to salivate, if you get my meaning. A sort of conspiracy by reflex."

Then I handed him the card.

He studied it, then looked up. "These names aren't going to go down very well with our base," he said. "Especially Harley Winters. He's a living symbol of crony capitalism."

"Base?" I asked. "C'mon, Homer: without money you don't have a base. Chances are your campaign's already starting to run on the vapors. And as far as Winters symbolizing anything, he stands for whichever way the wind is blowing—which hasn't prevented him from failing upward higher and faster than any man alive."

He thought about that for a moment. "I guess my boss might be OK with Winters," he said. "What would you have in mind? Chairman of the Council of Economic Advisors? Secretary of the Treasury? He's been there, done that."

I had a ready answer. "You offer him the job he'll see as just one rung below what he really wants."

"Which is?"

"Chairman of the Federal Reserve."

"We can't get rid of Bernanke. He only got the job last year."

"Bernanke's tenure is up in 2014. So you tell Winters that if he joins the team and plays ball he'll get the Fed job then. You might drop a hint that if he turns you down, Stiglitz and Krugman are next on the short list. He hates those guys, because they've got Nobel prizes and he doesn't."

"OK," he said. "Let's say Winters takes the bait. What about Holloway? I don't know much about him."

"Holloway is the New York Fed's point person with the banks. They love him because he's all theirs. If the present administration stitches together a bailout, he'll be a key player."

"I see. And where do you see him fitting in?"

"High up at Treasury would be a good spot. Maybe the top job. He's got the skill sets and experience. Someone once described him as a Hall-of-Fame technocrat."

Orteig nodded. "And Brewer?"

"Maybe the head of the criminal division at Justice," I suggested. "More behind the scenes than out front. She's a top securities lawyer with a ton of regulatory experience, and a good sense of the appropriate parameters of reform and prosecution. She'll make certain nothing gets out of hand, in terms of punishing individual bankers."

I've concluded that Brewer is perhaps the key player on Mankoff's little list. Winters and Holloway can divert and distract and throw sand in the policy gears, but if things get "down to the lick log," as one of my oil-patch clients, a huge Oklahoma collector of Plains Indian art, likes to describe a tight business corner, you need an ace stonewaller, someone who knows how to kill a prosecution before it gets off the ground and stifle the jangle of handcuffs. Think of Brewer as an All-Pro deep safety in a prevent defense.

"I see you have Patrick Vollmer on your list," Orteig observed.

"Strictly window dressing. The man's a giant in the earth where the media are concerned, and having someone like Vollmer at least notionally on board alongside the likes of Winters and Holloway will help keep the press in line."

Orteig reflected for a moment, then: "Take a step back. What if I can't sell this arrangement to my team? You realize that if there's a crisis, fingers will be pointed to deregulation as the major culprit. Winters and Holloway were key players in pushing that through."

"If there's a crisis, Homer, fingers are going to be pointing every which way. The only question you and your people need to face up to is how bad do *you* want your guy want to be president?"

Orteig fell silent. I said nothing, just watched him debate with himself for a minute.

Finally, he looked up. "So that's it? We agree to slot these four people as suggested and you'll find me $75 million?"

I nodded. Then added—of my own volition, just to cinch the deal: "Let's say $75 million minimum. The people I'm working with seem to know what they're doing, and that's their number, but there could be more. It all depends on how things go."

"So how would it work?"

"You mean how will the money get to the campaign?"

He nodded. "You know there are strict rules about political contributions," he said. "How exactly would you set it up?"

Now we were in my area of expertise. I laid out roughly, on a no-names basis, the plumbing of an operation like this, a network of cutouts, blind screens, and slice-and-dice shops that will feed the green stuff into Orteig's designated operating accounts. Was it Mao Zedong who said that revolutionaries must swim like fish in the sea of the population? So it will be with the increments of Mankoff's money—minnows as it were—that I will toss into the great turbulent streams of money circling the globe.

"The key to moving large sums is to break it down," I told Orteig. "I'll break the money into pieces that average $200 to $500 per, which works out to 150,000 names at the max. You've already set up political action committees and volunteer organizations in all fifty states, so we're looking at $1.5 million per state, on average. That's not a lot of money, although it's more in Alaska than in Illinois, say, so we'll vary the inputs to reflect population, voter demographics, and so on. People have learned from Abramoff's mistakes."

My reference was to a Washington fixer who went to jail last year for a scheme of political bribery so crude that you'd think a six-year-old would have spotted it. A six-year-old, that is, who hadn't been paid to look the other way. "Anyway," I finished up, "$1.5 million per state divided by a $150 average contribution works out to only 10,000 contributors, which leaves me plenty of room to maneuver. I'll make it look like thousands of little people out there are dropping their grimy tens and twenties in the offering plate."

He shrugged in a half-convinced way. "I see." Then a thought seized him and for an instant he seemed to turn pale.

"You're not talking about laundered money?" he interrupted. "God, that would be the kiss of . . ."

"Not to worry. I assure you, it will all be perfectly legal, and the money will be absolutely clean. You have my word on that."

I paused to let him arrive at a conclusion as to the creditworthiness of my pledge. I had the advantage of my upbringing, the way I look and sound. No one thinks that, coming from someone like me, my word won't be money-good, that I'm one of those fools who still believes in stuff like honor. He thought the matter over for perhaps fifteen seconds, then nodded. "Go on."

"What we're talking about has been going on for years. Think about 1960, when Daley fixed Cook County for JFK." I thought that sounded pretty authoritative—especially since I was one year old when the dead of Chicago rose from their graves and elected Joseph Kennedy's son to the presidency.

I could see Orteig was doing his own thinking. He wasn't going to come out and say "yes" out loud, but that's what he was saying with his expression, with his body language. Still, for form's sake, he had to dot all the "i's" and search out all the chinks.

"You're aware that the candidate has pledged to use public financing if he's nominated?" he asked me.

"A girl can always change her mind," I said cheerfully. "He won't have to make that call until next summer. Let's see what happens."

I figured it this way. By summer 2008, we'll know whether OG will be the Democratic candidate. If he is, and he decides to opt out of public financing, his adherents won't care. Why should they? By then they'll be beside themselves with hope and enthusiasm.

"One other thing," I added. "I know I've said it once already,

96

but perhaps it's best we keep this just between you and me. Who knows how your guy might react? Plus there's his wife; they say she calls a lot of the shots, and we're not casting *Macbeth*."

Orteig looked uneasy. I could sympathize with his situation, the position I was asking him to put himself in. What I was stipulating would be a kind of betrayal, a secret kept from someone with whom everything up to now had been on the table. Still, Orteig struck me as the sort of operator for whom ends always justify means, and so it proved.

Finally he smiled. "Don't worry," he said, "I'll deal with it."

I stuck out my hand. "So do we have a deal? I'm assuming you're one of the three people left in the world to whom a handshake means something?"

He studied my face carefully, then took my hand.

"Deal," he said.

The fix was in.

In the forty minutes or so before we began our final approach into Chicago-Midway, we established a few simple ground rules and protocols. Orteig will give me names and accounts to which to direct the money. If we need to talk, we'll do so either face-to-face or on secure landlines or drugstore cell phones that can't be traced. Above all, no e-mails. As Lucia and I have discussed, the form turns normally closemouthed operatives into indiscreet blabbermouths and exhibitionists.

Orteig had one last question as we dropped through a high scrim of clouds over Lake Michigan.

"Suppose, God help us, we don't get the nomination?"

I shrugged. "Didn't I make myself clear? If your guy doesn't make it to post time, so be it. Rub of the green. But if my people thought that between the brand you're promoting and the financing you're now going to have behind you, there was any significant chance of that, we wouldn't be sitting here."

An hour later, when I'd dropped Orteig off and was back in the air, headed for home, I called Mankoff on a disposable cell phone I'd brought along for the purpose and left my "Mission Accomplished" message.

He called back twenty minutes later. I gave him a report, choosing my words carefully. It was a million-to-one against anyone eavesdropping, but if someone was, I might have been talking about a lecture series we were setting up at some college. He sounded pleased. Well, as pleased as he ever sounds.

"Thanks, boss. We aim to provide good service," I told him just before we rang off.

As my plane rushed eastward through the slowly darkening sky toward White Plains, I reviewed my conversation with Orteig. All the bases had been covered; of that I was sure. I ran through the questions he hadn't asked. Possible dog that didn't bark in the night stuff. I couldn't think of any. This arrangement was loaded with imponderables. A situation where we liked the odds but didn't really have control. Acts of God had to be considered: suppose OG gets hit by a bus, develops congestive heart failure? Suppose Winters or Holloway are offered the jobs we have them slotted for, but turn them down? I regarded that as an extreme long shot— Winters still has a number of items left on his Rule-the-World bucket list, not to mention a "Get Even With" roster the size of the Manhattan phone book—and as a sniper's nest, it's hard to beat 1600 Pennsylvania Avenue.

As for Holloway, the guy's been #2 again and again and again. There's no more narcotic urge in the human spirit than the thirst for stardom of one's own, especially if one has dwelt in stardom's proximity, or shadow, for any appreciable time. When the time comes, if it comes, Winters and Holloway will take the bait, count on it.

I have to admit I felt exultant. I supposed this is what a trader's high feels like, or a gambler when he bancos the top table at Monte Carlo. I had pulled off one of the all-time political fixes.

Our final approach took us over the Hudson. It was a spectacular evening. From the west, the setting sun set the metal-and-glass face of lower Manhattan ablaze. I could pick out the skeleton of STST's new headquarters, just north of where the Twin Towers had stood. It's perhaps the greatest monument anywhere to what's called "crony capitalism": private profit using the people's money. The bronze and glass sheathing is already well advanced and gleams brilliantly, almost golden. Something about the building reminds of the slab at the beginning of *2001: A Space Odyssey*. No one seeing it like this could miss its message, could miss what it stood for.

I wallowed, briefly, in pride at being even a tiny part of such a huge piece of business, a facilitator for such power. Twenty minutes later we were on the ground. I shook hands with the captain, thanked the flight attendant, and went to find my car service.

And that, Gentle Reader, is how I fixed the 2008 presidential election.

## AUGUST 9, 2007

A tipping point may have been reached. Certainly Mankoff thinks it's a big deal. I happened to be in his office discussing a grant application to his and his wife's private foundation from the alma mater of a major STST client when Rosenweis burst in without knocking, bearing the news that Paribas, the big French bank, has frozen its subprime bond funds because it can't figure out a way to value them.

"That's the party line," Rosenweis told Mankoff (as is normal with Rosenweis, he acted as if I wasn't there). "You ask me: it's a bluff. The Frogs have been hit with a ton of redemptions and don't want to cough up. Typical!"

It seems that Paribas is afraid of a landslide: it might get 80 for the first lot of bonds it sells to meet redemptions, but once the word gets out, the second batch might bring 70, and so on down the line to where the garbage can't be given away for nothing. For the time being, anyone with money in a Paribas subprime deal is locked in—as in jail—and since Paribas is a major junction box in these markets, if they're in trouble, the likelihood is that everyone else will be. This is a major step toward Mankoff's worst fear: a market freeze-up in which no one will lend to anyone else.

Rosenweis left with strict instructions to sell off what he can without making STST look panicky. I asked Mankoff if the Paribas action represents the first splashes of a Noah-style downpour. All he could say is that he hopes not, and that he'll accelerate plans for STST to build itself an ark.

It's no skin off my ass, really. I sold my STST back in February at $210 when Mankoff told me to; the stock's now selling at $175 and change. In a week I'm off to Nova Scotia for a brief holiday, and nothing but nothing is going to interfere with that. I do get the feeling that events are moving faster than Mankoff has foreseen, certainly faster than he would like. I feel for the guy, I suppose, although Wall Street doesn't exactly elicit sympathy in its best of times. Whether virtue is its own reward or not, greed is surely its own damnation.

# AUGUST 31, 2007

Unlike most people, I like to get summer over with before Labor Day. There's something invigorating about getting back to the office while everyone else lingers on at the seashore or in the mountains. I can clear my desk and set my agenda for fall without the phone ringing every two minutes.

I got back yesterday from a blissful fortnight in Canada. A *New Yorker* writer persuaded me and some others to go in on a month's rental of a nice cottage on the Nova Scotia coast about two hours south of Halifax. There were six of us: my friend and her significant other, her cousin, a cardiologist from Buffalo, a married couple from Wilmington who work at the Winterthur Museum, and myself. The place was definitely low-key. We had iffy but manageable cell reception if you stood on a dune facing southwest, and the nearby village had a coffee place with decent pastries and Wi-Fi. We spent the first two days reassuring each other how great it was to be out of the digital maelstrom.

Lucia just got back from the south of France a few days ago, and we had lunch together. She was waiting for me at San Pietro, sipping a stiff G&T and not looking happy. The first thing out of her mouth was how unspeakable the South of France has become. Never again, she swears.

Then, after ordering a second G&T, she shoved a sheet of paper at me, saying, "Take a look at this. You'll want to shoot yourself. I know I do."

It proved to be a list of all the good Wall Street news that has piled up since we last saw each other: *7/30/07: The Big German Bank IKB Cuts Profit Forecast Amid Rout in U.S. Mortgages; 7/31/07: American Home Can't Fund Mortgages, Shares Plummet; 8/02/07: Accredited May Face Bankruptcy, Merger in Doubt; 8/06/07:*

102

*American Home Files for Bankruptcy; 8/08/07: Fund of German Westlandischesbank Stops Payouts, Cites Mortgage Market Unease; 8/09/07: BNP Paribas Freezes Funds as Loan Losses Roil Markets; 8/15/07: Countrywide Financial "Risks Bankruptcy"; 8/17/07: Fed Cuts Discount Rate 50 Basis Points to 5.75 Percent; 8/21/07: Sachsen Landesbank has EU3 Billion in Subprime, Source Says; 8/22/07: H&R Block Taps Credit Line, Cites "Unstable" Markets; 8/22/07: Lehman, Accredited, HSBC Shut Offices, Crisis Spreads; 8/23/07: Fed Lends $2 Billion to Banks to Ease Credit Woes; 8/26/07: New Zealand Mortgage Fund Basic Return Files Bankruptcy over "Wolverine" Subprime Defaults.*

The last item especially interested me. It had taken Wolverine, that rotting CDO Rosenweis's minions had laughingly unloaded on a New Zealand hedge fund, less than six months to tank. I started to ask Lucia if that might be a new world record, but decided to hold my tongue. Without my asking, she volunteered that the Kiwis aren't taking it lying down but are having a tough time finding a jurisdiction in which to sue.

According to Lucia, this list ain't the half of it. The gossip *du jour* is that certain big banks—the name one hears most is Barclays—have been collusively manipulating the daily LIBOR fixings. LIBOR stands for "London Interbank Offered Rate" and is the benchmark for practically every interest rate in the world of finance: from what STST pays for $10 billion in overnight money, to what Joe Sixpack pays on his monthly $250 credit card balance. If Lucia's scuttlebutt is correct, God knows what fresh hell this will bring down on Wall Street's head!

At STST, Lucia reports, the banking and trading floors resound with lamentation and keening and the rending of bespoke garments. STST stock is now down to around $160 and change. I happen to know that Lucia's stock options clear at $180, so she's well underwater. I feel for her.

Still, Lucia believes there's light at the bottom of the toilet. "Did you see this?" she asked and handed me a clipping from a financial wire service: a transcript of the speech Fed Chairman Bernanke would be giving later to the Kansas City Fed's annual powwow at Jackson Hole: *"It is not the responsibility of the Federal Reserve—nor would it be appropriate—to protect lenders and investors from the consequences of their financial decisions. But developments in financial markets can have broad economic effects felt by many outside the markets, and the Federal Reserve must take those effects into account when determining policy."*

I pride myself that I can tell bullshit when I hear it, and if this isn't a prize example, I don't know what is.

Still, it's not as if I'm in a position to crow. Ominous as the financial news may seem, I can't say that things on the OG front look much better. So far I've fed almost $20 million into the campaign, but Clinton remains well in front, John Edwards retains his nuisance value, and the cause wasn't helped when, just before I left for Nova Scotia, OG gave a speech in which he said he wouldn't hesitate to go after Bin Laden inside Pakistan if he had to. So now he's a warmonger, and we already have one of those in the White House. He's tried to backtrack since, but it hasn't had much effect.

His reviews have been mixed. Here's a typical one: *"He slips into this tendency, which he probably learned as president of the* Harvard Law Review, *to overstate his premises before he states his position. In politics, you do the opposite of what you do in the* Law Review: *you state your position, then say your premises—if you ever get to them."* This strikes me as basically a paraphrase of Adlai Stevenson's great one-liner: *"Here is the conclusion on which I base my facts."*

That said, however, there are a couple of significant factors in play, according to Orteig, whom I spoke with last night. First, OG is "doing tremendous business" on the Internet—small contributions are really starting to come in, thanks to the expanded web presence our money has paid for; second, there's a good chance that Oprah will endorse him—which could be huge: her millions of viewers can translate into millions of votes for OG. Orteig's also high on what everyone calls "social media": Internet sites like Facebook and MySpace and especially something called Twitter, which has been in business a little over a year and apparently has already got 75 million users venting their opinions in 140 characters or fewer. I'm not sure I understand the vote-generating potential of these, but Orteig's convinced that the sheer weight of numbers and inter-connections generated on these sites will over time make a huge difference. He's confident that if his man can just hang in there and show well in the debates (there's an important one at the end of October in Philadelphia), and that if Clinton stubs her toe, which the record suggests she will, he can carry this thing off. Edwards, according to Orteig, is no threat. He's a pussy-hound—OG's team is lined up to leak names, dates, and dirty pictures—and when that stuff comes out, he'll be toast.

Bottom line: Orteig's convinced that the infrastructure he's building with our money will shortly start to pay off. The machine's beginning to hum. The mission now is to use the remaining commitment to put boots on the ground, as it were. Pollers, canvassers, voter-facilitation teams. There's plenty of time to do this before the Iowa primaries: four months is an eternity, given the shape-shifting speed at which modern life moves.

# OCTOBER 16, 2007

Lunch with Lucia again today. A new problem: it seems that one Allen Sloan, a very sharp writer at *Fortune* and *The Washington Post*, has figured out Protractor and its two-faced ilk. Here's an excerpt: "*Struthers Strauss said it made money in the third quarter by shorting an index of mortgage-backed securities. That prompted* Fortune *to ask the firm to explain to us how it had managed to come out ahead while so many of its mortgage-backed customers were getting stomped . . . The firm's profits came from hedging the mortgage securities it keeps in inventory in order to make trading markets. It said in a recent SEC filing, 'Although we recognized significant losses on our non-prime mortgage loans and securities, those losses were more than offset by gains on short mortgage positions.'*"

When she first read Sloan's piece, Lucia told me, she knew there would be trouble. And there was. Rosenweis got wind of it and naturally blamed Lucia as if she'd written it herself. She finally calmed him down with assurances that Sloan's article wouldn't cause a ripple—no one outside of business reads *Fortune*—and so far it hasn't.

From what I'm picking up on the Rialto, Mankoff isn't the only big hitter with misgivings about what's gone down in the credit markets and what will likely happen. The difference is that Mankoff is doing something about it at STST, while his opposite numbers elsewhere are praying that the cancer will just go into remission all by itself, the way cancers sometimes will. I'm no financial oncologist, but instinct and experience tell me this one isn't going to.

Here's what I mean: Lucia tells me that according to her most reliable Citibank mole, a guy quite high up in the mortgage department over there sent a memo to the bank's top executives, from ex–Treasury Secretary Rubin on down, warning about all sorts of shit going down in his bailiwick and even threatening to run to the Feds unless it stops. The Citibank policy in such matters is modeled on STST: "If you won't go down with the ship, we'll throw you overboard," and the guy has walked the plank: isolation ward, removal of supervisory authority, and, most dire of all, elimination of bonus. The key PR move will be to discredit the guy, and Lucia's willing to wager that Rubin's called his cronies in D.C. to make sure he doesn't get a hearing even if he turns up with reams of incriminating stuff. These days it's hard to tell where the Street ends and Washington begins.

## NOVEMBER 16, 2007

The media are wetting their pants over OG's trip yesterday to Silicon Valley, where he gave a campaign speech at Google—"Man of the future surfs wave of the future": that sort of BS. He avowed himself a "techie," which if I was your ordinary voter would make me wary: speaking solely as a voter, I'd prefer a president who goes with his gut, rather than the data sets provided by the squadrons of technocrats whom Orteig has deployed (using Mankoff's money; we're up to $35 million) to build into as efficient a campaign machine as this country has ever seen. It's not just data, however; there's no doubt that OG has touched a nerve. You can sense this just talking to people. They're worried; people they know are in foreclosure, getting laid off; no one feels safe. Fear is out there.

Personally, I find it paradoxical (and a bit guilt-making) to observe the electorate's emotions being reduced to unfeeling data points by cold-blooded cadres of geeks and nerds, but that's the way it is today. I recently went to the Bay Area in connection with an Oakland arts program for poor local kids, and took a day off to stop in Silicon Valley to pitch a bunch of prospective high-tech multimillionaire donors, and I regret to report that when it comes to the common rub of humanity and the general good of mankind, these people are every bit as indifferent and conscienceless as anyone I've run into on Wall Street.

# NOVEMBER 22, 2007

Thanksgiving Day: and on the political front at least, much to be thankful for. At long last, OG's presidential candidacy finally seems to be taking off.

If he gets the nomination, the turning point will probably have been the debate three weeks ago at Drexel University in Philadelphia. OG did well, was his usual fluid, fluent self, but the key was Hillary's bad showing, the kind of scratchy, ill-tempered performance that reminds many centrist voters why they never liked or trusted the Clintons to begin with, and certainly makes one think twice about giving her one's unconditional love.

I'm one of those disillusioned centrists. Bill Clinton broke my political heart. I thought he had what it took to be among the greatest presidents ever, but he turned out to be just another peckerwood led around by his dick—and that opened the door for Bush and Cheney and all that they've brought with them, from Iraq to the mortgage mess. No Monica, no Bush, is the way I see it.

Anyway, on October 30 at Drexel, OG broke clear of the pack. Clinton has led in Iowa from day one; now, overnight, that lead is no more.

Mankoff's breathing easier, although there's still a ways to go to the finish line. Then, yesterday, it was deus ex machina time: Orteig's fondest prayers were answered when Oprah endorsed our candidate!

This is huge!

How huge, you ask? Well, Orteig called a couple of hours ago to report a twenty-point straw-poll swing OG's way in the early-primary states (Iowa, New Hampshire, South Carolina) and to ask for a quick $20 million to seize the day. The money's on its way as I write, via a dummy fast-food chain in Dubai, a yacht charter service in Miami, and the phone listings of seven U.S. cities.

And it gets better: Oprah will be personally campaigning for OG.

I don't want to get in front of myself, but I can't help thinking "game over!" When one candidate garners the endorsement and in-person support of perhaps the most admired person in American public life, a bet on anyone else is foolish.

As predicted, the Oprah-OG combo is just killing them. Huge turnouts in Iowa and the other two states. Tens of thousands showing up to see their heroine in the flesh. This is one occasion where OG doesn't mind being second banana.

Many think Oprah should be running for president herself. One pundit described her as "more cogent, more effective, more convincing" than any of the declared candidates. Hell, if Oprah were a candidate, I'd probably vote for her. There's something about her that harmonizes with what this country's supposed to be about. Unlike Wall Street, where you have to wonder whether people deserve the kind of money they make for the kind of work they do, Oprah has earned the vast wealth she's accumulated.

Not that people on the Street are paying that much attention to politics. Most are focused on Citi, about which ever more dire rumors swirl. The general view is that Citi is already in full zombie mode but is trying to hide the fact in hopes that divine providence will come to their rescue. Back in mid-October, their CFO did a conference call during which he asserted that Citi's exposure to subprime was $13 billion. What he left out, one of Lucia's agents-in-place reported right afterward, is that the bank is actually on the hook for another $40 billion of those "liquidity puts." Whatever—or whoever—induced their accountants to let them get away with that without putting adequate loss reserves on their balance sheet is a matter for conjecture—or the U.S. Attorney.

Someone at Accenture passed along a choice bit of gossip currently circulating in high-level accounting circles: namely, that if Citi were to undo its current bookkeeping evasions, and restored to its balance sheet the stuff for which it has real liability in the form of contingent guarantees and "put backs," its leverage ratio would shoot up from around 25 to 1 to closer to 50 to 1! At that level, writing off a roll of paper towels would render Citi technically insolvent. One big hitter went on TV the other day to proclaim that he shorted Citi stock at $55 a year ago and expected to cover the short at $5. He's already looking good.

Can it get worse? You bet it can.

# DECEMBER 18, 2007

Last night Rich Rosenweis gave a big Christmas dinner at the Weir, the upscale uptown men's club he bought his way into a few years ago. I have no idea why I was invited. Lucia says he's envious of my "special relationship" with Mankoff. It's the Skull & Bones connection that particularly galls him, apparently, although why that would bother someone who didn't even go to Yale makes no sense to me.

In the interest of keeping the peace, my Rosenweis policy has been to make nice. I've gotten him choice opera tickets, wangled him onto the Met Museum's business committee, arranged for his wife to be featured in a couple of benefit group photographs in the *Times* Styles section and on a blog, widely read on Park Avenue, called *New York Social Diary*. If something happens to Mankoff and Rosenweis takes over at STST, I'd probably kiss his butt to keep the account because I like my lease deal and I'd hate to be parted from my chums across the hall at San Calisto. But the main reason I accepted his invitation is because the Weir is famous for its cooking and its wine cellar.

Lucia was going, too, so I picked her up en route. Our plan was to have a drink at the Saint Regis, exchange Christmas gifts (she's off to England to see her family in Shropshire or Hampshire or wherever and won't be back until after New Year's), then walk over to the Weir.

"This could very well be an evening right out of Juvenal," I muttered to her as we got out of the taxi.

"Indeed," she said. Lucia knows who Juvenal was—she did go to Oxford—but it was odds-on that we would be the only two people at Rich's dinner who would.

"Incidentally," she added, "I heard something interesting today from a chum in the Justice Department. Apparently the FBI's looking into possible fraud in the mortgage market."

"That's serious. On the sell or the buy side?"

"Both, I gather."

"Any names in particular?"

"The usual." She didn't need to spell out that any list would include the Wall Street crème de la crème, including STST. These days, no one's skirts are clean.

We split a pint of Pol Roger and exchanged gifts: a very fine bottle of 1956 Armagnac for me, a silver-gilt Edwardian pin for her that I'd spotted in the crowded window of a vintage jewelry store up on Lexington Ave. She seemed pleased.

The party venue was the top floor of the Weir. It's a club I've visited since I was at Yale and my godfather used to take me for lunch. The place certainly isn't as I first remembered: standard-issue WASP beaten-up leather and furniture. A well-worn look to everything, including the members. It's clear that new money has taken over—a bulletin board inside the front door lists Rosenweis as a member of the house committee—and converted it into today's idea of swank and posh and what is considered "exclusive." The place looks like a Ralph Lauren showroom.

Still, it could be worse. The Weir's museum-grade, eighteenth-century English silver—ewers, chargers, candelabra and such—is still there to be admired (it's been catalogued by a curator at the Victoria and Albert), and the British portraits and racing scenes are of ducal quality and provenance. As the hymn says: every prospect pleases, and only man is vile.

Rosenweis pulled out all the stops at dinner: private-stock Bollinger to go with the clams and oysters; limited-edition vodka for caviar smuggled out of Iran; a great *Beerenauslese* Moselle to mate with the foie gras, which the menu noted had been purveyed by Daguin, the famous restaurant in the heart of Armagnac country. Then there was rib-eye steak—Rich made sure his guests understood that "I had Peter Luger's guy choose it personally"—accompanied by a '61 La Tache, and so on and so on, ending with a cheese board also "personally" selected by Eric Ripert at Le Bernardin that was paired with a flight of '82 Bordeaux—Château Pétrus, Château Cheval Blanc, Château Haut-Bailly—and to end the parade, an espresso soufflé, served with a Château d'Yquem, followed by Cognacs and Armagnacs that may have passed under the nose of Dumas *père*.

Apart from the menu there was a minimum of ostentation—the Weir does that to lesser mortals—and I must say the mood during cocktails was pretty jolly. And why not? It wasn't all that long ago that people at STST were hitting the panic button because the stock had dropped below $170. Well, STST closed a bit over $210 yesterday, which means it's up about 5 percent for the year 2007 even as great swathes of the Street are tanking. According to Lucia, the gospel on the Street is that Mankoff and Rosenweis have navigated the gathering storm better than anyone else: what balance-sheet markdowns they haven't taken are pretty much offset by short positions and money-good swaps.

When we sat down, at the Weir's famous "long table," with the club's famous silver ranged down the middle, end to end, I found myself seated next to the wife of Arnold Braum, STST's senior outside counsel. I know her from some work I do with NYU's Institute of Fine Arts, where she's going for a late-in-life PhD, and we had a nice chat about Caravaggio until, with the arrival of a second course, she turned to her other side and I swiveled my attention to the diner on my left, a ruddy-faced older man whose white hair was flattened into a pretty drastic comb-over. He sported a Weir club tie. His place card identified him as Walter Hardcastle.

We'd never actually met until then, but I knew who he was.

A big deal in the social and institutional circles I work with: high up if not at the very peak of the alumni and financial councils of Princeton, trustee of the New York Public Library and the Museum of Modern Art, importantly connected to museums in Houston and Portland. He's also on the board of STST, and one of the firm's largest outside stockholders.

Hardcastle interrogated me swiftly and sharply as to who I was and what I did, trumping my responses with dropped names, along with allusions to his own splendid lifestyle: residences in Santa Barbara, Houston, and Tulsa, a suite at the Pierre Hotel, and a "cottage" at Windward Harbor, Maine, one of the best-known last redoubts of this country's Old Money. He also let drop that he's heading to Florida tomorrow "to try out a new Gulfstream."

He did most of the talking, and quickly shifted the conversation to the outlook for oil prices and then on to politics, which I am never at ease talking about, especially with someone this aggressive on all subjects.

"What do you think about the presidential race?" he asked me. "This fellow from Illinois? You think the country's ready for a nigger in the White House? I sure as hell don't!"

I replied with something noncommittal. I wondered fleetingly how he'd react to the news, conveyed by Orteig a couple of days ago, that every portent indicates that OG is going to kick Hillary's ass in Iowa. Not well, was my guess.

I tried to steer the conversation away from race. OG may not be entirely to my taste, but race is no part of the equation and people like Hardcastle disgust me. I can't say I was entirely successful—I doubt I've ever heard the "n-word" used so often in polite conversation—and I was immensely relieved when a waiter broke in with the next course and Hardcastle turned away.

Dinner was a long process, and I was glad when dessert was finished and Rosenweis tinkled his glass, then got to his feet and proposed a toast to the season and the continued prosperity of those present. We all stood and murmured our approval.

Outside, while we waited for Lucia's driver—she was dead-heading on a client's jet scheduled to depart White Plains for London at midnight—I asked her about Hardcastle. "The guy strikes me as epitomizing everything that's wrong with so-called 'crony capitalism,'" I said.

Lucia didn't disagree. She filled me in. It turns out the guy's Old Money—or the next thing to it, although he sells himself as a modern Horatio Alger. He was born and brought up in Wilmington, where his lawyer father took care of a branch of the DuPont family. He went to Saint Andrews prep and Princeton, and then, thanks to a fellow member of Ivy, the "eating club" to which he belonged, got a job in Tulsa after graduation and went west to enlarge his fortune. Along the way he made a socially strategic marriage to a daughter of an old Boston-Maine banking family named Longstreth. The name sounded vaguely familiar.

"I shouldn't be surprised," Lucia said. "They're people like you, Chauncey: born to be painted by Sargent. I gather his in-laws loathe him."

She added that for all his loathsome qualities, Hardcastle's a big deal, a member of many boards and councils in addition to STST, where he's the fourth- or fifth-largest stockholder. Lucia says he's Rosenweis's guardian angel.

That pretty much told me all I cared to know. Lucia's car pulled up, and we embraced and went our separate ways.

I couldn't help feeling depressed. Christmas is maybe the one time of the year in this cruel, usurious country that we're supposed to think of others, people less fortunate or advantaged, which if you're in the upper echelons of Wall Street means maybe 99.9 percent of the world's population. To glorify wealth at a time when it's clear that a lot of people are in trouble seems vulgar and coldhearted. I found myself wondering if the Street ever shows what we used to call noblesse oblige. Is it such a luxury, a moral pearl beyond price? Is it a sign of weakness? And don't even start asking whether what they do to make all that money is socially useful in any meaningful way.

Then I told myself that this is the way we live now—so deal with it. The Rosenweises and Hardcastles are what they are, Wall Street is what it is—so just shut up and take the money. And the foie gras.

I rolled out of bed early, shuffled into my bathrobe, made a light breakfast, read the papers, got dressed, and decided to walk uptown to 60th Street, where I'm meeting Scaramouche at the Veau d'Or for our annual Christmas lunch. It's my favorite Manhattan restaurant. I'm very fond of M. Treboux, who owns the place—and if I should ever think of getting married, his charming daughter Catherine, who runs it for him, will be near the top of my list. Scaramouche's been going there forever. So long that he boasts that he's on his third set of owners.

When I got there he was already halfway through a bottle of champagne. He looked ruddy, content, and prosperous; there's a kind of sparkle to the man that makes one instantly glad to see him.

A fresh glass was poured for me and we clinked toasts to the season and each other.

"So what's new?" I asked.

"All I can say, Chauncey my boy, is beware of old age. It has little to recommend it."

I promised to age cautiously. We ordered—tripe for him, kidneys for me: a common passion for offal is another cord that binds us—and chatted about cabbages and kings right through lunch, but I couldn't help thinking he had something larger on his mind. He waited until we were served the *Île flottante*, the restaurant's signature, then turned serious. "Not to put a pall on this splendid occasion, but I don't suppose you've heard of something called 'the Santorini Shuffle'?"

I shook my head.

"I must say, every time I think the Street can't pull a faster one, it does. This Santorini gambit is very hush-hush, and no wonder, because if you ask me, it stinks to high heaven."

"Do tell."

"The sordid tale begins around 2001. Greece wanted into the eurozone, to open up certain markets, and the eurozone—the Germans especially—wanted to admit Greece, in order to stimulate trade the other way round. Trouble was, Athens's balance sheet didn't meet the standards for admission. Too much going out, too little coming in: the usual problem.

"So, roll the drums, maestro, if you please. Wall Street was summoned to the rescue! A top-secret confab of major Wall Street houses, the Greek government, and some ex officio EU types from Brussels was held on the volcanic island of Santorini, far from prying eyes and ears, and they came up with a scheme that used options and overnight repurchase agreements and all sorts of other now-you-see-it-now-you-don't to cover up the shortfall long enough to satisfy the EU's standards for admission. It was a simple affair of cooking the books. The firms, ours among them, earned a handsome fee and have continued to profit ever since."

"Isn't that the Wall Street way?"

He smiled. "Well, of course it is. The trouble is that it never seems to have occurred to the parties concerned that the essence of a nation's sovereignty is control of its currency, and you give that up, and with it the power to adjust exchange rates, when you join something like the eurozone. Now, predictably, Greece's economy is imploding and it looks like they won't be able to meet their obligations."

"Wow. I thought nations didn't go broke. Wasn't that Walter Wriston's great claim?"

Scaramouche twinkled. "It was, and it's absolute twaddle. But it gets better. One reason Greece is falling apart financially is that the Street baked all sorts of self-serving options into the cake, and when those kicked in, Greece suddenly found itself in the hole for tens of billions of euros with no way out. And it's only gotten worse, thanks to the idiotic notion that you can borrow your way out of debt. Does the name Harley Winters mean anything to you?"

"Sure," I said, trying to keep my voice level.

"It's the same kind of mess he got my alma mater into when he was head of the endowment committee. It looks as if it's going to cost the university the better part of a half-billion dollars to extricate itself from the tangle."

"So what's going to happen to the Wall Street firms that cooked this deal up?"

"If history is any guide: nothing. They'll just whine that they were only serving the needs of a valued client, just doing what they were asked to do. That's the way the Street works nowadays; hell, it's the way the world does. It's always the other person's fault. Up to him to realize that what he was being sold is junk. Up to him to recognize that the merger he's being pitched is pointless. Where were his lawyers when our lawyers were writing up the terms? If you look at the record, nothing ever happens to the Street in such affairs. This wouldn't be the first time Wall Street's involved itself in a massive swindle that literally involves the fate of nations, and they've always come out untouched. Why should this time be different?"

He shook his head at the thought, refilled his glass, and raised it. "Well, my boy, here's to finance capitalism. Long may it prosper. What a world!"

A few minutes later, we shook hands on the sidewalk and wished each other the best of the season. He's off to visit his daughter and her family in Oregon; I'll be here through Christmas Day, which I'll spend making the rounds, as Manhattan bachelors have always done.

# DECEMBER 24, 2007

Well, here we are: Christmas Eve. Quite a year, a terrible year actually—but 2008 promises to be even more scary, what with the election added to Wall Street's troubles and the world's uncertainties. OG's looking strong; Orteig sounds as jubilant as Orteig can. Iowa is only days away.

I'm keeping my usual footloose, casual Christmas. In my loft, the décor is modest: a small tree, a couple of wreaths, and a sprig of mistletoe just in case. In a couple of hours I'll head for Riverside Drive to spend Christmas Eve with a couple who extend the hospitality of their grand Tweed-era apartment to me and assorted other "orphans" every year. On Christmas Day, I'll stop by friends for eggnong, then others for brunch, and around 5:00 p.m. I'll meet some chums for our annual Christmas movie at Film Forum or the Angelika, and afterward, a burger or plate of red-sauce spaghetti somewhere easy.

On Wednesday the 26th, Boxing Day, in what has evolved into an annual custom as regular as the sunrise, I'll pick up a rental car and drive up to the Berkshires, where I'll stay until New Year's Day with Rex and Millie Hastings. It'll be a good time for long snowy rambles with their three Labrador retrievers, while I ponder my misspent middle age and reflect on the eternal question posed by Wordsworth: whether, getting and spending, I've laid waste my powers, whatever they might be. I can't escape a growing suspicion that I may have. And what's true for me may also be true for the entire country.

Enough of this. It's Christmas Eve, goddamn it! God bless us, every one. And to all, a good night! See you next year.

# JANUARY 1, 2008

I left the Hastings' after breakfast, dropped one of the other house-guests off on West End Avenue around noon, returned the rental car to a garage near my apartment, and was home in time for a late lunch and a cheering glass of bubbly and some special smoked salmon from a fish caught and cured at a client's "camp" on a river in New Brunswick.

The routine in the Berkshires had been the same as always: home-and-away dinner parties; visits exchanged; rambles in the woods and fields with the dogs; time for myself alone in a fat armchair in a fire-warmed corner with a book; a trip into William-stown to see an interesting exhibition at the Clark Institute and have a coffee with the chief curator to discuss his plans; a matinee at the Playhouse; the New Year's Eve feast: same food and drink, same people as the year before and the year before that and the year before that.

There's something wonderfully comforting and consoling about this kind of year in, year out continuity. My hosts and the circle they move in are decent, old-fashioned people. Intelligent, overeducated, bookish, commonsensical, a bit naïve really, not sure that they understand the way we live now, somewhat worried about money (but who isn't), which is one reason they've ended up several hours distant from the blazing lights and frantic, chat-tering, costly pace of Manhattan and Boston.

My passenger on the ride back to New York was a former professor at Pace, now head of economics research at a big pri-vate foundation. He's part of a study group—journalists and academics—who are pursuing conclusive evidence that what Hil-lary Clinton has called "the vast right-wing conspiracy" actually exists. Their thesis is that starting at various points between 1968 and 1980, the United States has been the target of a concerted and coordinated effort by Wall Street and Corporate America to undermine our particular form of social democracy and convert our political economy to a closed system controlled and owned by a web of financial interests and their political courtiers.

According to the professor, this theoretical conspiracy had its roots in 1973–75 when, to quote him, "the three legs of the perch from which we ruled the world were kicked out from under us." Our economic hegemony was overthrown by the OPEC price increases and the stagflation; military hegemony came to an end in Vietnam and Carter's disaster in the Iran desert; our moral hegemony was killed off by Watergate and Nixon's resignation. This left the national mood susceptible to Reagan's soporific mix of palliatives and platitudes, which provided cover for a conservative coup far more extreme than anything Goldwater had stood for in 1964.

"You'd have to say this," he told me as we whizzed by the sign for the Tappan Zee Bridge, "the project has succeeded beyond anyone's wildest expectations. It's a Gilded Age all over again. Money rules absolutely. Corporatism and finance have totally taken over American politics. There isn't a pore of the body politic that doesn't stink of corruption and rot and bribery! This is what living in France must have felt like on the eve of the revolution. Or Germany just before Hitler."

His words hit home, pricking concerns I've managed to keep at a distance. Fenced off mentally where conscience can't get at them. Just for a second, I found myself wondering if there might be more at stake in this mission for Mankoff than simply keeping Wall Street out of jail. Am I just a tiny cog in a giant conspiracy intent on turning America into a fascist oligarchy? If my Groton history teacher, the one who worshipped FDR and the New Deal, were still alive and knew what I've been up to, he'd kick my ass and cross me off the list of his favorite ex-pupils. As it is, maybe he'll come back to haunt my slumbers, the way Marley's ghost did to Scrooge. I find the notion very troubling to think about, but the die is cast, the money's been moved. Only $8 million left to play with. I must say that in terms of political bang for the buck, there's never been anything like the Internet.

As for the other stuff: like Scarlett O'Hara, I'll think about it tomorrow.

# JANUARY 3, 2008

Did someone say "Game on!"?

Well, you better believe it, because OG has swept the Iowa caucuses. The competition's putting on a brave face, but based on what Orteig told me last night, this is the beginning of the end. Obviously this kills Hillary's hopes for a political blitzkrieg. She won't go easy, of course; there's no quit in her. Orteig expects her to redouble her efforts, and that she'll probably do well on Primary Day, when a bunch of states go to the polls, but that'll be her last hurrah. In other words, the lady is toast.

Naturally, OG's Iowa victory speech, which I just finished listening to, was a combination cock-of-the-walk and cock-a-hoop. Awfully confident, considering where we are, with a long way to go between now and the convention in Denver in August. There's no quit in Hillary, and she can be expected to drop the gloves and let it all hang out. Still, I like OG's chances, especially if the Wall Street apocalypse lighting up Mankoff's crystal ball comes to pass.

Ooops! The phone's ringing. It's Mankoff. This late, he can only be calling about Iowa, and he's got to be pleased. Gotta take this call. More anon. On to New Hampshire!

# JANUARY 8, 2008

The final tally in New Hampshire primary is in. There was a huge turnout. OG came second: 38 percent to Hillary's 39 percent.

Orteig's not surprised—or all that disappointed. He tells me it was to be expected that Clinton would win a round or two before OG finally puts her down for the count. Orteig left no doubt that it's our contribution that's made the difference, and I must say, to judge by the results, he's leveraged the money I've injected into OG's campaign—$71 million so far—with an efficiency you have to admire. When Mankoff and I spoke after the final New Hampshire numbers were in, he told me that the investment in OG may ultimately reap returns as great as any in STST's storied history. From the way he said that, I couldn't escape the feeling, no more than a glimmer, really, that there's more at stake here than simply the Winters-Holloway "insurance policy." He also said that when this is over, he may ask Orteig to come on board to run STST's wealth-management business.

Enough of politics. According to Lucia, what's on the mind of everyone on Wall Street right now is, first, the rumor that Bank of America (BofA) is going to acquire Countrywide and, second, that Bear Stearns may finally go bust.

"The unspeakable acquiring the uneatable." Scaramouche paraphrased Oscar Wilde's sarcastic definition of foxhunting when I asked him about the rumored BofA-Countrywide deal at lunch today. The San Calisto consensus is that this is the stupidest deal ever. Apart from the fact that its CEO looks and sounds like an extra on *The Sopranos*, Countrywide is apparently a mess of bad assets, crummy governance, hard-sell sales techniques that verge on the criminal, and very suspicious Washington interfaces (especially at Fannie Mae, whose management is well into a second generation of bonus-seeking corruption): all in all, a recipe for huge financial and regulatory headaches down the road.

As regards Bear Stearns, the consensus seems to be that by Easter Bear will be extinct, either in a bankruptcy chapter, taken over by one of the big banks, or absorbed and dismembered by the dripping jaws of vultures and hyenas: a joint here, a chop or a limb there. Regarding this, one of my clients claims that the New York Fed's been sounding out the Street to see who might participate in a you-get-this-and-I-get-that breakup of Bear.

The problem is that no one will want to take on the garbage on Bear's balance sheet with a make-whole from Uncle Sam, and that's not in the cards. Not yet, at least. People are calling in loans, asking for better collateral, and generally making life miserable for whoever it is—Jimmy Cayne's apparently indicated—who's running the show in Bear's new trophy building at 383 Madison Avenue. So far the consensus favors a "good bank, bad bank" solution. The good stuff stays in "old Bear" and the crap goes into "new Bear," which then files for bankruptcy, where it can be profitably looted by attorneys, accountants and workout specialists. I hate to sound sacrilegious, but I can't help being reminded of the Roman soldiers dicing for Christ's garments at the foot of the cross.

And so it goes. Was it John Donne who said, "The new religion casts all in doubt"? Something like that.

# JANUARY 9, 2008

"A lot of people wouldn't mind seeing Bear out of business," Mankoff mused this afternoon when I was in his office reviewing a list of proposals. "They've been tough competitors, although not so much with Cayne running things as when Ace Greenberg was in charge. Jimmy's taken his eye off the ball every now and then; Ace never did. There's a lot of fast-and-loose going on over there that Ace would never have tolerated."

What worries him is that if Bear Stearns tanks, the contagion will spread—and rapidly. The signs are already there. "We've reached the point where people are taking a much harder look at each other's balance sheets and collateral, although so far no one's pulled the plug. But if one does, the rest of us may."

# FEBRUARY 25, 2008

Citi has replaced Bear as the epicenter of malicious Street gossip, at least for the time being. Here's my latest tidbit, gleaned from a MoMA trustee.

It seems that last Friday the big bank announced its preliminary 2007 results. Earnings from operations were lousy, but Citi still contrived to post a modest profit, thanks mainly to a fat tax credit. All blessed with the usual blah blah blah from the bank's "independent" accountants about how management believes that the bank's financial controls are effective and the auditors find no cause to differ.

The accountants' sign-off letter was apparently time-stamped last Friday, February 22. But a week earlier, on February 14 to be precise, Citi had received a harsh letter from the SEC criticizing its accounting, financial modeling, risk management, and valuation procedures and demanding that the bank fix them pronto. But get this: *Citi has elected not to disclose the SEC letter to the public, including its stockholders.*

The question is: did they show the SEC letter to their auditors? What happens if this gets out? If challenged on the SEC letter, will Citi lean on Shearman & Sterling, its main law firm, which probably generates hundreds of millions in annual billings from this particular client, to come up with a Wall Street version of "the dog ate my homework"? The guess up and down Wall Street is: for sure.

Citi and Bear Stearns are today's bad news, but from what one hears, Lehman is closing fast. The latter is apparently getting by thanks to a really dubious overnight funding scam called Repo 105. It's getting to be hard not to conclude that Wall Street has been as crooked as it has been reckless in its drive for bonus-generating profit.

130

# MARCH 1, 2008

The Campaign Finance Institute has released its estimates. To date, OG has raised $184 million, Hillary $129 million. Such is the power of leverage. A year ago, OG was barely a blink on the financial radar. They're saying that over 40 percent of contributions to the campaign are $200 or less, from small donors. Hilary's comparable number is under 30 percent. Not bad, eh? A glowing testimonial to my money-moving prowess.

Now I can sit back and gloat, because exactly as anticipated, the big money's started to flow to OG. Wall Street's all in on the candidate, falling all over its collective wallet to get on board the bandwagon before it's too late.

## MARCH 10, 2008

Happy days are here again!

Just kidding.

Yesterday, the European central banks played "Little Dutch Boy at the Dike" and pumped $200 billion into their credit markets with zero effect. This morning, there's an estimate floating around that as many as a million and a half U.S. subprime mortgages will go into foreclosure. A lawyer I see at Municipal Art Society meetings tells me that he hopes the banks have got their paperwork in order, because otherwise there'll be an ungodly mess; the scuttlebutt here is that STST outside counsel Corbett & Charles have been ordered to review Samarra/Hatton, the recently acquired redneck mortgage mill that got my San Calisto buddies so exercised. Fingers crossed.

From what I'm hearing, the banks have collectively let more than 40,000 people go. A leading financial newspaper is predicting that global layoffs may exceed 70,000. This estimate includes a large percentage of the 14,000 employees of Bear Stearns, which is said to be on life support. I know from Lucia that STST's headcount is being cut back, mainly at lower levels—equivalent, say, to furloughing a couple of dishwashers at the Four Seasons, but these waves tend to oscillate upward and people below the rank of vice president are definitely nervous. Another small sign of the times: a couple of my invoices to Wall Street clients are thirty days late.

One last cheerful fact. MSNBC reports that one bank—I forget which—has put out a forecast that subprime losses may exceed $200 billion. *$200 billion*, can you believe that! And since reporting disaster has become a form of media poker, S&P saw that number and raised it, with a forecast that total subprime losses may reach close to *$300 billion*. Either figure is frightening enough, but what I find ironic is that people are saying that a goodly portion of those losses will be on debt that S&P and its fellow credit-rating whores have rated AAA. Did someone say "fraud"?

Scaramouche advises that anyone looking at Wall Street today will do well to follow the immortal wisdom of Chico Marx: "Who you gonna believe? Me or your own eyes?"

# MARCH 13, 2008

These days Wall Street seizes on any figment of good news to jump for joy, and today the Street was positively hopping.

The reason? One of their principal adversaries has bit the dust. Eliot Spitzer is toast!

That's right! Eliot Spitzer, governor of New York since January 2007, the self-styled "Scourge of Wall Street"—and easily the person most hated by the financial community—will be resigning the governor's office effective next Monday. It seems that the about-to-be-former governor suffers from Bill Clinton syndrome: can't keep it in his pants. In Spitzer's case it isn't White House interns in irresistible blue dresses—it's hot and cold running hookers. Dickheads and their dicks: it never changes.

As regards the larger political canvas, OG had a bad patch back at the beginning of the month when it turned out that the pastor of the Chicago church he attends is some kind of a cut-rate Farrakhan who talks a lot of anti–white trash. You can see the problem this presented: no way do Orteig and his colleagues want OG to seem more than coincidentally black. They don't dare even breathe the word "race."

The Hillary people tried to make this a big deal—asked the voters to imagine "gangsta rap" in the Oval Office, etc., etc.—but one thing OG is really peerless at is smothering problems with blah blah blah, and he did. So after a few uneasy moments, the campaign's back on track. He did well last month on Super Tuesday (won 13 out of 22 states); he won in Mississippi two days ago, and continues to pick up delegates while Clinton's base is hanging on for dear life. Perhaps he should start working on his acceptance speech for the Democratic Convention in Denver in late August. Mankoff's looking like a genius.

# MARCH 14, 2008

Another long day. Mankoff called me at 7:00 a.m. to tell me he had a new mission for me and was coming by. This must be a big deal; apart from my Good Friday cocktail party, he's hardly ever visited me at home.

He was here a bit after eight. He apologized for bothering at home, but he's wary of people seeing us together too often at his office. I told him it was no problem, made him tea, settled him on the sofa and did the "all ears" bit.

"We need to move quickly," he told me. "The situation may be worse than even I pictured. To start with, Bear Stearns is in the shit so deep that Uncle Sam is going to have to bail them out with a steam shovel. I hear they're close to a deal with JP Morgan Chase to provide Bear with interim financing backstopped by Washington."

"Well, you've been predicting this," I said. "What's new? If you listen to the gossip on the Street, there isn't a firm that isn't on the brink. What kind of shape are you guys in?"

"We're OK; not great, but definitely nowhere near the trouble others are. JP Morgan Chase: same. So is Wells Fargo and Bank of New York and a few others. But here's the thing. What Washington ought to do is let the strong survive and the weak perish. But when the weak include systemically connected outfits the size of Citi or Lehman or even Bear, you can't walk away from them, because you may trigger a domino effect."

"So what do you do?"

"My guess is that Uncle Sam's going to have to come up with a 'one size fits all-let's pretend' plan that treats both the weak and the strong the same way. A plan that'll make it look like they have to bail out the system, and not just a few firms that screwed up. That'll give us leverage, because Treasury and the Fed will need us and JPMC and Wells to play along. Otherwise, any plan they come up will be dead on arrival, especially if we and the others turn our lobbyists loose on Capitol Hill to kill it. In other words, I want us to be in position to leverage our situation when the time comes."

As Mankoff sees it, Treasury wants to set up a bailout template now—and he wants to be sure that this template serves STST's interests and also wants me to negotiate it. He ran thorough his plan, satisfied himself that I got it, and gave me the number of the relevant woman at the New York Fed.

She was expecting my call. We made a date to meet in Battery Park at 11:30 a.m.

Over my second cup of coffee, I tuned in to MSNBC, just in time to hear the network report that JP Morgan Chase, "in conjunction with the Federal Reserve Bank of New York," has agreed to provide a credit line to Bear Stearns for twenty-eight days, the financing to be guaranteed by the Federal Reserve. When I left my apartment, Bear shares had opened at around $60; by the time I reached Battery Park an hour or so later, my BlackBerry told me they were under $30.

I found my contact waiting for me over near the walkway along the Hudson. Nice-looking, late thirties or early forties, nothing sensational. Typical high-up government girl: in four or five years she'll be back in the private sector, reaching for the brass ring in some big bank's compliance department or as a partner in a major law firm.

At this time of year, the marina outside the World Financial Center was empty, and the little park was virtually deserted. We strolled along the water, her stiletto heels clacking on the cement, until we found a suitably isolated bench. When we sat down, she looked at me curiously. "Can I ask you something? They tell me you're an arts consultant. Why am I talking to you?"

"Because I have the confidence of my client. He and I did some work of this kind a long time ago in another galaxy. Let's leave it at that. Now: let's get down to business. The word on the Street is that you have a deal with JPMC to take over Bear Sterns. Is that correct?"

She shook her head vigorously. "We don't have any kind of a merger arrangement on Bear. With Dimon or anyone."

I figured she was bluffing, in hopes of finding how much our side knew.

So I responded, "You know, we can waste our time pretending—or we can get real. Our information is that you've agreed to provide Dimon with backstop financing, you and Treasury that is, because he's not about to take the crap on Bear's balance sheet on to his own, even if it's guaranteed by you people, without some kind of kicker. My client feels the same about his role."

"There's some kind of mix-up here," she said. "Your client's not involved."

Time to play my trump card. "In this mess," I said, "everyone is involved. Here's the way my client reads the situation. JPMC merges with Bear Stearns, by contamination if not by law it becomes an investment bank, which throws into question whether it can continue to draw on your discount window or any other source of low-cost or no-cost taxpayer capital normally available to banks of deposit."

"That's ridiculous!"

"What can I say? It may be, but there's enough substance there to inspire some strike suit lawyer to file for an injunction, and that'll put whatever discussions you've been having with JPMC on the public record."

She stared out at the harbor and the boats and the Jersey shoreline and said nothing.

I went on. "It gets better. It's the view of my client, and my client's counsel, that the Fed can hardly extend a loan to JPMC secured by the very same assets it wouldn't let Bear Stearns borrow against three days ago! All this leads my client and his counsel to conclude that there are excellent grounds to enjoin any merger of Bear into JPMC that involves a taxpayer or Federal Reserve back-stop or indemnity."

"There's no indemnity in the Bear Stearns package," she said, sounding indignant.

"Maybe yes, maybe no. It's common knowledge that JPMC is chomping at the bit to become a broker-dealer without losing its bank status and the funding privileges that go with it. So here's where my client and his attorneys come out: if you use the term-lending facility or the discount window or any other Federal back-stop to help Mr. Dimon buy Bear, fairness demands that you open said term-lending facility etc. to all the rest of the Street. Without conditions and using collateral similar to what you'll be financing against in the Bear Sterns deal. One size fits all. Isn't that what you people are after?"

"Why should we do that? JPMC is stepping up to the plate on Bear. You're not!"

"Oh, really? How exactly is JPMC stepping up? Bear has 14,000 people working there. Is JPMC guaranteeing the job count? They get the building, and the good stuff, *and* the equivalent of a $30 billion loan of the taxpayers' money that they can use any way they like, because the word is that once the deal is done, you'll be taking the crap onto Uncle Sam's balance sheet. You could have done that directly for Bear when they came begging."

"We rejected a direct loan to Bear Stearns because they aren't creditworthy."

"As we see it, you might with equal justice make the case that Bear wasn't creditworthy because you rejected them. If you did for Bear on its own what you're doing for JPMC, they'd be alive and dealing. Speaking of which, what sort of deal do you have with Dimon regarding Bear's stockholders? Do they get wiped out completely, or will they get a few crumbs?"

"We have no arrangements regarding Bear's stockholders."

"I see. I wonder what the market's saying about that." I checked my BlackBerry. "Aha! Bear's stock is under $20. Here, you want to see?" I made to shove the BlackBerry at her, but she looked away.

"Bottom line," I said, "the smart money is saying there's no there there. Without you guys, Bear goes poof! My client simply wants the funding advantages that JPMC's getting. My client has his lawyers standing by with a motion ready to be laid on shortest notice before a certain judge whose name you can guess, a judge who is seldom if ever well disposed to Wall Street and who can be relied upon to enjoin any deal involving JPMC taking over Bear. We don't want to go to court, but we will if we have to. I doubt Bear can stand the delay—or that JPMC won't back out of the deal."

"This is blackmail!"

"You can call it whatever you want," I said pleasantly. "All we're trying to do is balance out a simple asymmetry of interest."

She thought that over for a minute, then stood up. "Look, the best I can do is pass your message along. You understand that I can't give you the least assurance . . ."

"We know that," I replied. "All any of us can do is try. Just make sure it gets through loud and clear."

We shook hands and left it at that.

Will the Fed cave? In Mankoff's mind, after I related my brief meeting, without a doubt. What choice do they have? If you follow Mankoff's reasoning, they aren't ready to let a big firm go completely down the toilet. Washington's preference is always to try to buy time, presumably in the expectation that some deus ex machina will descend from Mammon's halls and make matters sort themselves out, or some kind of "rescue" can be stitched together. But Bear, unpopular and unrespected as it is by the loftier exponents of high finance, is simply too interconnected for Washington to walk away from. The result could be a punch to a nerve center that paralyzes the entire system. Something has to be done *now*.

And so, Gentle Reader, when next year or the year after that or whenever, you ask yourself how come the Fed did a one-eighty with respect to letting the investment banks belly up to the discount window, thereby hammering home the final nail in the coffin of Glass-Steagall, you'll know the answer.

# MARCH 17, 2008

As Mankoff expected, Uncle Sam has caved and Bear has vanished down Jamie Dimon's maw. As initially announced, Bear's stockholders were to be virtually wiped out, receiving only $2 for shares that were selling at fifteen times that when the lady from the New York Fed and I chatted in Battery Park. This was subsequently deemed to be cruel and unusual punishment and was revised upward to $10. The official excuse was a drafting error on the part of JPMC's lawyers, although Mankoff thinks that Jimmy Cayne threatened to oppose the deal. Ever the gambler, he would have been willing to take his chances rather than accept a lousy two bucks for his stock, and at that point the deal was still too fragile to absorb even a flicker of contention.

So Bear is *finito*. Thousands of blameless people will lose their jobs, longstanding client relationships will be ground to dust, an old and prominent Wall Street name will be effaced—but the system will be saved to blow itself up another day. The official announcement reminded me of that famous statement by a U.S. officer in Vietnam: "The only way to save the village was to destroy it."

The bet that Mankoff delegated me to place has paid off. The Fed has announced that it is opening the discount window to broker-dealers for the first time since the 1930s. The Bear people, who asked for exactly this concession a week ago, and whose firm has now been swept out from under them, are beside themselves and crying foul. Anyone whose schoolboy heart was tenderized with notions of fair play, as mine once was, might argue that they have a point.

One down, how many to go? Who's next? Lehman is now the odds-on favorite. I can hardly sit down with a Wall Street client without being told a new Lehman horror story.

Some are saying that the real problem at Lehman is its real-estate portfolio. It seems that Richard Fuld has been mesmerized by his current favorite at court, a kid named Mark Walsh, into betting the firm on commercial real estate, and the consensus is that if Lehman buys the farm, it'll have been real estate that delivered the coup de grâce. And remember those Repo 105 swap-outs that I mentioned last month? Conditional sales that allow the notional "buyer" to return the merchandise if he feels like it? Lehman's accountants are allowing these to be booked as bona fide dispositions of assets that would otherwise be subject to killer write-downs. When those chickens come home to roost, one client told me—during discussions about a Bonnard show in Philadelphia—they're going to be the size of 747s. Even the SEC has finally wised up to the situation at Lehman and has seconded teams of observers to keep an eye on things, but chances are Uncle Sam's people won't understand what they're looking at, or looking for.

What also isn't helping Lehman's cause is that apart from Fuld's immediate family and court retinue, you're going to be hard-pressed to find anyone who has a good word for the guy. People who know him swear that if the waves start breaking over the bow, he'll toss his closest and longest-serving colleagues overboard before himself. This does not encourage the kind of loyalty one needs from the crew when the ship begins to founder. I'm also told that Washington hates the guy, from the Treasury Secretary on down. Not the man you want to be worrying about when you show up with your tin cup.

It's all a bit much to get one's head around. So as I've often done in the past when I've felt the need for a refreshing perspective, I strolled across the lobby to San Calisto. As I expected, the place was pretty much deserted; at this time of year, old bones start to need warm weather, so most San Calistans are off to the Caribbean or Palm Springs or Scottsdale, and there were only two at the table, the Ancient Mariner and the Warrior. Each had a cocktail in front of him, and each wore an expression that pretty eloquently said he was sick of the other's company and conversation—so both of them were happy to see me.

The talk naturally turned to Bear.

"Never a first-rate firm," said the Ancient Mariner. "I was always surprised that anyone would lend them money even in flush times. We treated them better than they deserved. Herman Strauss for some inexplicable reason liked Cy Lewis."

"Who was Cy Lewis?" I asked.

"Back in the sixties, he *was* Bear Stearns," the Warrior explained. "If you needed some sharp dealing to be done, Cy was the man to front it for you. Sort of fellow, you saw him in the locker room, you took your wallet into the shower with you. I'll say this for him though. He could spot talent. He found Ace Greenberg and Ace was very, very sharp. Poor Ace, to see the firm he built disintegrate this way."

"That's the trouble with this business," the Ancient Mariner interjected. "You build a great firm, employ thousands of people good at their jobs—and a single son of a bitch can spin out of control playing with the firm's credit and destroy a century's good work! Look at what happened at Barings."

"You might say the same about the Federal Reserve," the Warrior responded. "It's all Greenspan's fault. Met the fellow a few times. Never liked him. Pompous ass, bloated with self-regard and a bunch of lunatic Ayn Rand theories about the way the world ought to work. And so very anxious to please. Here's a bit of interesting history for you, Chauncey. At the very end of the 1960s, we were making these crazy conglomerate loans, financing take-over bids, none of it adding a penny to the economy, but at least we weren't risking the firm and taking these loans onto our own balance sheet. Still, it got the Fed's dander up, and Bill Martin, who was then the Fed chairman, or maybe it was Art Burns, his successor, came down to Wall Street and told us to cut it out."

"And did you?" I asked.

"Of course. We had no choice. Back in those days, the Federal Reserve jawbone, properly wielded, was a fearsome disciplinary tool. Of course, Martin probably kicked off a bear market, but I'm not certain, looking back, that it wasn't a good thing. The Street was out of control, financing terrible takeover deals with bank loans and dubious bonds. Abuse of credit is the rogue gene in capitalism's DNA. It's always the same. We got through that, and then in the eighties along came Milken and his junk bonds, and the savings-and-loans—and now this mess. Mankind's curse is easy money badly lent and badly borrowed."

They were very eloquent in their disgust, and I was quite impressed, yet when I finally left I found myself wondering whether, to such people, the present is ever qualitatively equal to the past. Practically everywhere I've ever been, past hates present, and present has little but contempt for past. Few can manage the transition from then to now. Most Street veterans remind me of certain older faculty at Groton who doubled as coaches of club hockey; they used to pine for the days before the school got artificial ice.

I've pointed out that I'm a bit of a worshipper of olden times and noble traditions. Remember General MacArthur's speech at West Point? "The corps, and the corps, and the corps." I didn't go to West Point; I never served in the military; but I never hear or read that speech without tearing up. This is a key aspect of the allure that San Calisto holds for me. While I'm over there, I can pretend that there was once a world governed more or less by the principles I was raised and educated to hold dear and essential. Principles not found in the "eat what you kill" gangsta rap that Wall Street now dances to.

I'm probably fooling myself, I know. In their day, I'm sure these old guys prided themselves on the scalps on their belts. Cut every corner they could and double- and triple-dealt and engaged in every chicanery and manipulation they could—just like their successors do today. It's human nature.

## MAY 10, 2008

I'm surprised at how totally the media have bought into OG's act. I mean, I'm no pundit or political expert, but I can't believe that no one in the so-called "mainstream" media has called attention to qualities that were evident to me the first time I took a hard look at him. Most of the stuff is positively fawning. Not that I put much practical store by op-ed blathering. I have a friend who argues that pundits should be licensed like drivers. They should be made to take a test to get a pontification license, and then be subject to a point-penalty system for the punditical equivalent of traffic offenses: getting facts wrong, making grossly inaccurate predictions, laying down the law about subjects of which they have no practical grasp, relying on Iraq-quality unnamed sources, displaying pomposity and moral self-love, and so on. Pile up X number of points and your pundit's license is suspended or revoked— meaning no Sunday morning talk shows, rejection slips from the op-ed editors at the *Times* and *The Washington Post*, no Charlie Rose or Jon Stewart, no *Vanity Fair* profile, no $25K lecture fees and fat advances for mailed-in books with nothing new to say.

If only!

Late last night Mankoff telephoned to tell me to expect an envelope to be delivered by messenger early this morning. He sounded hyper-secretive.

"What am I, your private intelligence agency?" I thought as I gracefully assented. The fact is, I have a lot on my own plate just now. When Mankoff first mentioned that he might have other jobs for me, like the meeting in Battery Park, I assumed these would be brief, few, and far between. Now I wonder. Where will it stop? Should I ask for a commission?

"Bring it with you to the meeting this afternoon," he told me. "In the meantime, read it. I want you to have an accurate sense of what's *really* going on."

At 8:03 a.m. my doorbell rang. It was Pedro, the guy who's at the desk in the lobby on weekends, with a plain brown envelope.

Inside was a printout of a letter on Lehman letterhead written by a Lehman senior VP to the firm's top people. I'll just quote a couple of the juicier passages.

To begin with, here's how the writer sets the stage:

> I have become aware of certain conduct and practices, however, that I feel compelled to bring to your attention, as required by the Firm's Code of Ethics, as amended February 17, 2004 (the "Code"), and which requires me, as a Firm employee, to bring to the attention of management conduct and actions on the part of the Firm that I consider to possibly constitute unethical or unlawful conduct. I therefore bring the following to your attention, as required by the Code, "to help maintain a culture of honesty and accountability."

Then he gets down to cases. Hard cases:

> The Firm has tens of billions of dollars of inventory that it probably cannot buy or sell in any recognized market, at the currently recorded current market values, particularly when dealing in assets of this nature in the volume and size of the positions the Firm holds. I do not believe the manner in which the Firm values that inventory is fully realistic or reasonable, and it ignores the concentration in these assets and their volume size given the current state of the market's overall liquidity.

Handwritten addenda on the back of the memo state that Lehman is currently running more than 100,000 derivatives positions, 10,000 of which they can't account for. That's a 10 percent slippage in a system where 3 percent is considered catastrophic! Moreover, it seems that many of these positions are in trading portfolios whose computer systems don't communicate. That is a shitload of shit! And if you take a large percentage of those trades and link them to other people's balance sheets—including STST's—and then link those balance sheets to still others, you can see how terrifying what one San Calistan calls the Mrs. O'Leary Effect really is: a cow kicks over a lantern and before the ensuing conflagration peters out, most of Chicago is in ashes.

When I gave Mankoff the envelope, he read through it quickly. Then he stared at the ceiling, obviously weighing how to act on this new intelligence, probably trying to decide whether to pile on and short Lehman, as I know Rosenweis is urging him to do, or to let Fuld find his own way to his doom. Evidently having made up his mind, he turned his back to me, punched a number into his phone console, and murmured a few instructions that I couldn't quite catch. Then he hit me with a nice bit of news: "Merlin Gerrett's going to endorse the candidate. He'll make the announcement next week." This could be helpful. Really helpful when it comes to raising big money on the Street. Which is good, because I'm down to $2 million and pennies, and Orteig keeps hinting he could use more. Politicians are as bad as my friends' ex-wives: there's never enough.

After the meeting, on the way out, I stuck my head in Lucia's office just to say hello and how goes it.

"Can't talk now," she told me. "We've just gone into full panic mode. The auditors have been called in and everyone has been told they'll be working nights and weekends to make certain that our financial controls and valuations are as tight as they reasonably can be and that our books are up to the minute. Where we hold illiquid positions, they're to be marked down another seventy-five basis points. Oh yes: Lehman's just been declared a no-fly zone. We're not trading Lehman for our own account, long or short, nor are we accepting orders in Lehman stock and options that aggregate more than 10,000 shares, and then only for Class A clients and counterparties and only on the long side. Now: off with you!"

It isn't even Memorial Day, but already this is starting to feel like it will be a very testing summer. What fresh hell awaits?

# JUNE 8, 2008

Terrible hangover today: the only presences at last night's celebration were me and my TV—and the latter doesn't drink, so I
polished off most of a fifth of Lagavulin all by my lonesome.

Celebration of what, you ask?

Because Hillary has conceded! OG will be the nominee!
Which means that yours truly has played a decisive role in placing
a winning bet on the longest-priced dark horse in the whole history
of presidential elections, at least since Truman in 1948. Does that
make me the bigtimiest fixer in American history? I sure as hell
think I'm in the running.

And that means, the way things are now on the economic
and financial front, that he will surely be elected president.
Which in turn means that barring an act of extreme bad faith
on Orteig's part, come next January Winters and Holloway will
be whispering in the new chief executive's ear to lay off Wall
Street. Do you know the famous Titian painting of Pope Paul
III and two of his so-called "nephews," a pair of prize schem-
ers by the look of them? It's a fantastic painting; I saw it in
Naples a few years ago, and it has stayed with me ever since. If
I thought Mankoff would appreciate the joke, I'd get a postcard
of it and paste OG's face on the pope, and Winters's and Holloway's on the nephews—and give it to him the next time we see
each other.

The horizon looks bright. When Orteig called with news of
Hillary's concession, he told me they've passed $500 million.

The news from the Street also favors OG. The smart money's
saying that Bernanke et al. are committed to fighting the wrong
opponent—inflation—while in fact a deflationary collapse in ev-

erything from house prices to junk bonds is underway, spelling an outbreak of defaults and foreclosures. If things continue to deteriorate at their current rate, the electorate should be in a proper anti-GOP frenzy come Election Day.

On to Washington!

# JUNE 21, 2008

Lunch with Lucia today at Le Veau d'Or on my nickel.

First item on the agenda: OG's announcement two days ago that he's opting out of the public financing system, and that his campaign will rely on private contributions. Let me add, quickly, that Lucia brought it up, several times employing the word "hypocrite." She reports that people are saying it's a flat-out renege on an earlier promise for which, according to her, OG is famous. She made it clear that she doesn't trust him as far as she can throw him. Too slick, too ready with answers. I had no comment. I simply smiled and called for another *kir*.

When she finished ranting, we moved on to other gossip, some of it cheering, some not. As we parted, she put her arm on mine and asked, "Chauncey, do you by any chance own any GIG?"

That's Global Insurance Group, probably the biggest, widest-reaching, and most powerful financial company in the world.

"You know, I think I do. My old man got them when they bought a Dutch insurance company he'd put money into and he left them to me. It's been a great stock—until recently. Now it's probably too late to sell. Better to hang on and see what happens. Why?"

"You should sell."

"Really? Why?"

"Because something is better than nothing. Those shares could be worth zero."

"Why do you say that?"

"Some fairly reliable people on the inside are telling me that the Treasury Department and the Federal Reserve are drawing up lists of which firms are to be saved and which left to die if things get much worse. GIG's near the top of the list of those to be taken off life support."

"Ahead of Lehman?"

"People down there won't speak the word 'Lehman.' Just take my word for it on GIG."

I said I'd look into it.

Which I may. Frankly, until after the election, I don't plan to trade anything, long or short. I don't want to stumble into someone else's disaster and get tagged as an insider.

# JULY 31, 2008

*Was für eine Katastrophe!* as they say in Zurich. Back in February the big Swiss bank UBS estimated that write-offs connected to U.S. mortgage-backed securities and securitizations might reach $260 billion. Six weeks later, the IMF bumped that figure to $950 billion. A month ago, James Polton went public with his estimate, probably self-serving in view of the huge short position he's got, some of it in league with STST, via Protractor, that the right figure's probably around $1.3 *trillion*, but of course he's probably talking his book. Still, one of my clients, a very plugged-in and steady-minded bond manager, says that she hears the correct number might approach $2 trillion.

How the hell is the Street going to fill a $2 trillion hole? There's only one answer.

Uncle Sam. Aka We the Taxpayers.

It's evident that 90 percent of the electorate is completely in the dark about the size of the bill they're going to be handed to cover Wall Street's mischief. Oddly, OG hasn't brought it up in his campaign speeches. I put this down to Orteig's political shrewdness. The worse OG makes Wall Street look, the greater will be the pressure on him to roll out the guillotines, and the harder it will be to put over my Winters-Holloway ticket on campaign insiders who aren't party to the scam. Besides, OG has plenty of ammunition as it is.

The big picture indicates that anyone who thinks "the people's money" belongs to the people is about to find out otherwise. So far, talk about "subprime" and "counterparties" and "moral hazard" and the like is just so much Sanskrit to the man on Main Street.

But this can change.

We're going from bad to worse, from portentous to downright

ominous. Early this month, the FDIC moved in and seized a financial conglomerate called Indy Mac, which started life as a spinoff from Countrywide. Last night, I had drinks at the Regency with a professor at MIT who's head of the acquisitions committee at a regional museum that I'm trying to help out. He told me that, based on his statistical workup, Indy Mac alone may end up costing taxpayers and investors more than the entire savings-and-loan mess back in the '80s.

On top of that, Lucia reports that the Street consensus seems to be that the next big shoes to drop have to be Fannie Mae and Freddie Mac, the housing market's Fasolt and Fafner. The latter are the twin giants who built Wotan's Valhalla, another splendid Masters-of-the-Universe edifice that gets burned up in the end thanks to the arrogance of its inhabitants.

Fannie and Freddie were created to supply liquidity to housing finance by buying mortgages originated in the private sector. They're half-beast, half-man. Their debt is backed by Uncle Sam but their shares are owned privately. They're supposed to apply certain credit-quality standards to the mortgage paper they take off the Street's hands (and balance sheets), but the rating agencies have allowed that threshold to become meaningless with their cheap AAAs. A reliable source tell me that these "AAAs," which bear about as much relationship to genuine credit-worthiness as an Orchard Street "Rolex" does to the real thing. They're based on the assumption that bad paper issued or endorsed by great and famous institutions will be made whole by Uncle Sam in the event of trouble. It's like getting a rich cosigner on one's gambling debts.

Not everyone's fooled. Fannie's shares alone have lost two-thirds of their value in the past month, while the technocrats try to figure out if there's some way to resolve the mess short of outright nationalization, which is the Street's worst nightmare. You can see why: if Fannie and Freddie can be taken over, why not GIG, why not Citi?

Apparently Polton has accumulated a massive short position in Fannie and Freddie stock using STST as his prime broker. According to Lucia, Mankoff took a look at the account and called Rosenweis in just the other day, cut him a new one and ordered him to tell Polton to move his short position to another firm. I gather Rosenweis was really unhappy, but at STST it's Mankoff's unhappiness that calls the tune.

Two weeks ago, *The Washington Post* ran a story reporting that OG's campaign had solicited ex-Fannie CEO Franklin Raines for "his advice on mortgage and housing policy matters." Mankoff saw it and commented that a lot of people think that Raines is a jerk-off with slimy ethics, and isn't someone OG should be seen in public with and definitely not someone for the press to perceive as a member of OG's inner circle. I passed this on to Orteig, and he promised to take care of it.

The pain is metastasizing. As far as which firms people are betting on to fail, Fannie and Freddie sit atop the Las Vegas tote boards, with Merrill Lynch, Lehman, and Citi close behind, and BofA next up, thanks to its stupid acquisition of Countrywide. Layoffs on the Street are said to have finally reached the magic number of 100,000. Some of this is in the junk end of the mortgage market, jobs that probably should never have been created in the first place, but most of the hit is being taken by order clerks, cafeteria servers, contract cleaners. Scaramouche contends that this is standard Wall Street procedure: the money gushes up, the trouble trickles down. Always the little people, never the big shots whose lack of executive judgment allowed the mess in the first place. STST's not letting people go, not yet; Mankoff hates to fire people, and he's allowing normal attrition, opportunism, and nervous stomachs to reduce his headcount.

He hasn't canceled shore leave, but executives with primary desk or departmental authority have been told to stay within three hours' travel distance of the office just in case. People are hoping for a quiet August, for a respite during which to mentally regroup and screw their courage to the sticking place. But no one's under any illusions. This isn't August as usual. Party time in the Hamptons and Monte Carlo.

The name that people at STST can hardly bear to speak without crossing themselves and praying is GIG. A year ago, the insurance and finance colossus was thought to be totally impervious to harm, but no firm is insulated from internal idiocy, and that's what's nailed GIG. The word is that the man in charge of their "Special Finance" unit in London went apeshit in the derivatives market and has stuck GIG with positions that might cause it to implode. Among those positions is $20 billion due STST that Mankoff's going nuts trying to figure out how to get out of. Right now, Lucia tells me, it's a standoff: STST puts the arm on GIG for more collateral; GIG argues the number, then grudgingly agrees to post additional collateral, to which STST applies a discount (generically called a "haircut") that GIG disputes, and the Sisyphean process starts start all over again with STST stuck with $20 billion in bad paper.

Then there's Lehman. No one can figure out how bad it really is over there. On top of a $3 billion loss last quarter, they're admitting that $130 billion of their assets are impaired. God knows what other balance-sheet bombshells are about to drop. There's a stage when "*l'état, c'est moi*" types like Dick Fuld transition from denial to delusion as their empires collapse about them. Lucia hears that Fuld sees only a diminishing circle of colleagues he trusts when he isn't wandering the world in his jet like Diogenes in search of someone, anyone, who'll put up enough money to get Lehman through the end of the year. Today, Dubai; tomorrow, Seoul; day after that, wherever. The gossip is that Fuld tried to make a deal with Merlin Gerrett, and that Gerrett actually made a conditional offer, but that Fuld thought Gerrett's terms were too tough and walked away.

Politically, all the news is good. Orteig has offered me a floor pass for the Democratic Convention next month in Denver, but I've declined. I can't imagine anything worse than a week in the Rockies surrounded by shrieking yahoos in funny hats.

And now, if you'll excuse me, I'm going to take off for a long weekend on the Vineyard with a Yale classmate and his family, followed by a fortnight in Nova Scotia.

Talk to you after Labor Day.

# SEPTEMBER 5, 2008

Do you want to know what a political death wish made flesh looks and sounds like? Start with a reasonably pretty face concealing a brain evidently empty of all useful knowledge and any fond regard for truth. Add a nasal voice, the kind that Wodehouse says can open an oyster at twenty paces, in which is delivered gaffe after gaffe, often employing some very unusual grammatical constructions, along with a kind of "mean girl" knowingness, and what have you got?

Sarah Palin.

She's the ex-governor of Alaska who's just been nominated to be John McCain's running mate on the GOP ticket. A walking, talking recipe for political suicide. Better than hemlock.

Don't put any stock in the jubilant immediate reaction from the usual suspects: a great victory for women's rights, a magnet that will draw millions of white women to the GOP, etc. The McCain campaign is boasting that $7 million poured in after Palin's nomination was confirmed at the GOP convention.

Bullshit. Or should I say: "So what?"

Don't take it from me. That's Orteig's opinion, and he's normally a cautious guy who considers going an inch out on a limb the very definition of imprudence. Orteig thinks that Charles Krauthammer, a right-wing pundit that OG's team heartily detests, got it right when he wrote the following last week in his *Washington Post* column: "The Palin selection completely undercuts the argument about (the Democratic candidate's) inexperience and readiness to lead . . . To gratuitously undercut the remarkably successful 'Is he ready to lead' line of attack seems near suicidal."

Orteig thinks Palin's selection may be the single dumbest maneuver he's seen in all his years in politics.

Having watched the lady on the tube, I can't disagree.

# SEPTEMBER 8, 2008

New York is going through what Parisians call *la rentrée*, the time when everyone returns to the capital after a summer at the beach or in the mountains and goes back to work after the long August vacation. Magazines run forecasts of all the cool stuff that's on the agenda and the elite's shopping list; Wall Street cranks up, as do publishers' lists, shows on Broadway and the Museum Mile. The culture vultures flap their giant wings and take to the sky. The aspirational obbligato of so-called "socialites" approaches concert pitch.

But not this year of our Lord 2008.

Over this past weekend Uncle Sam finally ran out of excuses and evasions concerning his beleaguered stepchildren and pulled the plug: both Fannie Mae and Freddie Mac were taken into "conservatorship" by Washington. I suppose that's a polite way of saying "nationalized." Uncle Sam had no choice, given the other horror shows now turning the financial horizon an angry red, with Bear Stearns interred inside JPMC, Lehman dismasted and half underwater, and Merrill's mainsail flapping uselessly, while the crew runs out the lifeboats.

Great and bloody has been the carnage. Fannie shares closed last Friday at $13 and change, opened this morning a tad under $4, sank as low as $2.50 during the day, and closed at $3. The price action reflects the bill Washington is charging for picking up the pieces: new stock representing a 79.9 percent equity interest that translates into a loss of tens of billions to existing stockholders. The latter are moaning, and here and there you'll encounter the occasional murmur of sympathy, but let us not forget that these were *huge* institutional stocks, owned in million-share blocks by endowments, mutual funds, sovereign wealth funds (including China), and wealth managers, and these institutions and their advisers, from what I hear, simply sat on their hands and watched as Fannie and Freddie charged headlong into subprime to juice their stock prices and fatten their executives' bonuses. It's also said that they had a good one-third of Congress "on the pad," lest anyone in Washington get any ideas about throttling back.

From Mankoff's general disposition, I gather STST is OK, although it's turning out to be a closer-run thing than anyone would have thought six months ago. The firm still has some $20 billion of credit quality and maturity mismatches that they haven't been able to lay off, and that's on top of the GIG swaps, but STST has avoided the worst "by the hair on our chinny chin chin," which is how Lucia puts it. Even so, STST is thought to be in manifestly less worse pro forma shape than everyone except JPMC and possibly Wells Fargo, and a definite competitor in a game in which the last man standing will get first dibs on whatever's left.

## SEPTEMBER 9, 2008

Mankoff summoned me to his office late this afternoon, ostensibly to talk about a big Rubens show at the Royal Museum in Brussels, where the firm has opened a branch to be close—"within convenient bribing range" as Scaramouche puts it—to the EU parliament. He slid a slip of paper across the desk to me.

Here we go again, I thought. I suppose I could have said "enough's enough" and slid the paper back—but of course I didn't. The truth is, I can't stand not to know what's coming next.

On it was written "Ian Spass" and a 917 cell phone number. The name meant nothing to me. "Who's this guy?" I asked.

"He's the guy you'll be working with in Washington from now on. There's going to be some serious negotiating to be done with both the group that's in power now and whoever succeeds them after the election. Treasury and I have agreed not to speak directly; these days, you never know who's listening in. I need someone I can trust absolutely who doesn't have this firm's name on their business card, and Washington feels the same way about their end. I'm going to want you to be on call for at least the next six months. Same thing for Spass."

He filled me in on my new counterpart. Ian Spass was about my age. Harvard undergraduate, Harvard MBA. He'd been a mergers-and-acquisitions star at a big bank, had done a stint in the Bush Treasury Department, and now works as a freelance consultant.

I said I understood. I didn't say that the name of my new opposite number amused me: *Spass* is German for "joke."

This could get exciting. And I have to say I'm flattered that Mankoff reposes such a high degree of confidence in me.

# SEPTEMBER 12, 2008

Spass and I spoke for the first time today. I could tell from his tone and choice of words that he's a member in best standing of Big Swinging Dickdom, Washington version, where it's not about the money but about who'll take your call. I made sure to sound impressed.

Ours was a short chat, its main purpose to get a dialogue going between us. According to Spass, this coming weekend will tell all: either the fever breaks, or the patients start dying one by one. Lehman will be out of cash by Sunday night, apparently, with Merrill right behind them in the headlong rush to insolvency. Wachovia has suddenly turned out to be a major problem, but at least they are a true bank, with a big insured deposit base that might appear fetching to a buyer like Wells Fargo or JPMC. Same for Washington Mutual, which is poised to do an Olympic-quality plunge into the toilet. Funny: two years ago, these were among the hottest names on the Street.

He wanted to know about our end, and all I said was that they're reviewing their options like everyone else. I do know from Lucia that Arnold Braum has been pushing Mankoff to become a bank in order to access the funding privileges that a depositary institution enjoys. It seems the means are at hand, because it turns out that STST actually owns a real bank way up in northern Michigan, which was part of a regional investment firm STST bought in 2005. It has a deposit base of only $123 million and a scattering of ATMs at local stores and service stations. Chicken-feed by today's standards, but suddenly, given the direction events seem to be heading in, potentially priceless, because it may be a way around Sheila Blair, the hard-nosed, no-bullshit woman who runs the FDIC and is no friend of Wall Street. She wants Washington to deal with the Lehmans and their beleaguered ilk the way she dealt with Indy Mac: shut the fuckers down, pay off the legitimate depositors, let the counterparties fight it out among themselves, and screw the stockholders. Even banks like Citi, she argues, are liquid enough to make their depositors whole; if their trading books drag their stockholders and lenders under, that's just too damn bad!

# SEPTEMBER 13, 2008

I called Spass at the end of the day and relayed Mankoff's strongly held view that Washington should think twice about bailing out Lehman: "Lehman's a special case," I told him. "Their balance sheet is pure fiction. Nobody will touch their collateral. With them, it's all about real estate. You rescue Lehman, and you're going to have Harry Macklowe and those clowns that did the Stuyvesant Town buyout and every other real estate mega-deadbeat on your doorstep, looking for handouts."

I expected a brief lecture about the need for financial patriotism in this hour of national crisis, and Spass delivered one, but I held firm. Yesterday, Treasury contacted Mankoff and some other big hitters to ask them to come to Lehman's aid and was turned down flat. Partly on the terrible credit fundamentals, but also because those who are solvent, even if just barely, are convinced that when Lehman goes under, the golden doors of Washington's various vaults will be thrown open with free money for anyone who needs it or says they do.

After hanging up with Spass, I reflected that this isn't the way his side has expected things to play out. His mission is to tell Mankoff via me how Washington has decided things are going to be, and that will be that. But my mission is just the opposite: to deliver the Mankoff/Wall Street decision as to how things are going to be. No one other than Leon Mankoff tells Leon Mankoff what's what. He's carefully discarded his way to a strong hand, and now he intends to play it for all it's worth.

# SEPTEMBER 14, 2008

Long years ago, when I was still at Yale, my roommates and I took off for a ski weekend in Vermont. By the time we got to within twenty miles of our destination, early winter darkness had descended along with a snowstorm; the road was icy, visibility poor. We hit a skid and the back end fishtailed. The driver did what he was supposed to and steered into the skid, but this didn't seem to work, so he jerked the wheel the other way, with the rest of us shouting helpful contradictory advice, but this didn't seem to work either, and so finally he just said the hell with it, took his hands off the wheel, and let the car find its own way—a long, slow, sliding arc of maybe fifty yards that carried us gently into a snow bank. When we recovered our collective breath, we got out, managed to push the undamaged car out of the drift and back onto the road and resumed our journey.

While watching Washington handle the Lehman situation this past weekend, I was reminded of that experience. Like our driver long ago, Uncle Sam's minions finally froze at the wheel and allowed Lehman to drift freestyle off the road.

But this skid has not ended gently. This is a full-speed-ahead, brakes-failed crash into a brick wall, killing all aboard and probably a few roadside pedestrians. Washington's inaction has left the 150-year-old firm no alternative but to file for bankruptcy. Harvey Miller and his crack Chapter Eleven team at Weil, Gotshal & Manges have been given hours to prepare a filing that should properly have been done in an orderly manner over weeks, if not months. At the beginning of the year, Lehman stock sold for $62. (I just looked it up.) It closed Friday at $3.65. It will probably bring pennies when the markets open tomorrow.

At one point, it looked like Washington had cut a Lehman deal with Barclays along the lines of its Bear-JPMC "rescue." But no deal got done, because the UK version of our SEC invoked some legal technicalities—stockholder rights, due diligence, that sort of inconvenient stuff—that caused Barclays to back off. Worse still, the financial media are now reporting that under UK bankruptcy law, Lehman's London operations, and by extension its EU and other London customer balances and trade settlements, will be frozen. This could be huge, since it was in the London legal jurisdiction—presumably for tax reasons—that Lehman booked and cleared its global trades, held collateral and clients' securities, and so on. Bottom line: according to the experts, we are about to see total constipation in the credit markets. And if no one will lend to anyone else . . . sayonara, baby!

Despite all this, Mankoff seems remarkably cool. He's certain that Washington has now painted itself into a corner and will be forced to bend over backwards to avoid a repeat at, say, Citi—which could be a catastrophe several orders of magnitude more dire than Lehman. This could prove a windfall for firms like JPMC and STST.

So here's the way things stand on Sunday evening, September 14, 2008. Despite the widespread conviction that the entire Street's on the brink of insolvency, a small number of big firms are in OK to semi-OK shape: STST, JPMC, Wells Fargo, Bank of New York Mellon, and a few others. But only if overnight credit keeps flowing. On the brink, no matter how you cut it, are Wachovia and Washington Mutual, both said to be in almost as bad shape as Lehman was, and then there's Citi, of course, and Morgan Stanley. And the 10,000-pound elephant in the room, whose name no one dares breathe: Bank of America, which has just done a deal to merge with Merrill Lynch. Why Kenneth Lewis, BofA's CEO, wants to stack Merrill's mortgage difficulties on top of the fraud-suffused pile of crap he bought with Countrywide is anyone's guess. The inside skinny making the rounds is that Washington forced his feet to the fire.

Finally, there's GIG. The word on the latter is that unless they're bailed out within forty-eight hours, they're down the tubes, and now you're talking real money. Amazing! GIG was the great spider squatting at the center of the giant web of global finance and now it's roadkill.

So we're at precisely the point Mankoff foresaw when he summoned me to Three Guys. Widespread collapse in the financial sector, Washington flailing, rumors swirling about with cyclonic velocity. What must follow is some form of general bailout in which the measures used to save the weakest will be gravy for the strongest. It remains to be seen how rich a harvest it will yield for STST. More tomorrow, when markets open, and we can get a feel for how bad it's going to be. People are saying: Wall Street in 2008 is going to resemble Hiroshima in 1945. Stay tuned.

## SEPTEMBER 15, 2008

The immediate result of Lehman's death is exactly what Mankoff feared. Credit markets worldwide are simply shutting down. STST stock is off 20 percent since Labor Day, when Lehman rumors turned deadly serious, although the broader market's done a bit better; month-to-date, it's about flat. As for Lehman, it closed today at $0.21.

I have a friend over there—just a friend, not the sort of person who traffics in insider gossip—who has a million Lehman shares vested in his benefit plan. At Christmas just a year ago, he went to his bank, took down $15 million from a credit line secured by those shares, and went shopping: he bought his wife a knockout Seaman Schepps bracelet and a Dennis Basso fur jacket, pledged a donation to a Hamptons charity sufficient to secure his wife a committee slot at its big charity bash, gave $1 million to his prep school, and got his name on the girls' locker room. He also paid $5 million for a co-op in a building that doesn't allow "financing" against the property, which means that he paid for it with another loan secured by his Lehman shares. And he hired Hal Norden, NYC's decorator du jour, to do over the new digs. He told me this over lunch at Nobu, where the sushi goes for the price of a Southampton rental, and wanted me to come along with him after lunch to the Ferrari dealership. That was a year ago. He called yesterday to ask where he could buy some hemlock cheap—and he sounded like he was only half-kidding.

What we're dealing with here is a form of PTSD that has led to a complete and systemic loss of trust. The world hasn't run out of money; there's a ton of it out there, but it's frozen like a deer in the headlights. No one on any side of a transaction now believes the other party or parties will be good for the money come settlement.

This is the real damage Lehman has wrought. Good faith even among fraudsters is what greases the wheels of finance. Lose that, and the whole bloody engine races out of control and then blows up. Trust on Wall Street has long since abandoned honesty or character as measures of reliability; fuck the handshake, it's all about the balance sheet, and what someone thinks your paper is *really* worth versus what you say it is. Right now, Wall Street has essentially ceased to function, and it'll remain that way until someone comes along with the antifreeze. And that means Uncle Sam. Who else is left?

Worse still, I'm hearing the "r-word"—as in "recession"—more and more often. The Street's already laid off close to 150,000, and you can add one or maybe two zeros to that figure to estimate what the collapse of finance will amount to in the larger economy. Construction has imploded, and retail is close behind, they say. And those are two categories that have recently employed a lot of people. In addition, thoughtful observers are scared by the amount of consumer debt, what Mankoff calls "retail." Ours is an economy largely dependent on aspiration, and when people can't earn enough to close the gap with the Joneses, they borrow— on credit cards, in home equity and second mortgages and so on.

These are interesting times. We are told we should consider ourselves lucky to live in them. Whichever Chinese philosopher said that can go fuck himself.

# SEPTEMBER 21, 2008

The bad news has come so thick and fast since my last entry that I decided to hold off until I could catch my breath and do a sort of omnium-gatherum of what's happened since Lehman went under.

After a week when it seemed the world might be coming to an end, seem to have quieted down, but no one thinks we've seen the worst. So Wall Street is staying close to its Bloombergs. Lucia and I had lunch at Balthazar the other day, and it was practically empty.

It's understandable. At times like these, one doesn't feel social; you never know how this crisis may have affected friends, since the kind of friends I prefer don't make a big deal of how much or how little money they have. I decided to stay in this weekend, so on Friday night, I stopped at Szechuan Gourmet on 39th Street and picked up enough stuff to get me through to Sunday. At home, I had a few drinks and watched a bunch of first-season *Law & Order* episodes on DVD. Saturday, I devoted the morning to dry cleaning and getting a pair of shoes resoled. Back home, I thought about calling my tailor and canceling an order for a couple of new suits, but then decided not to: why punish him for the mess stirred up by a bunch of mindless Wall Street greedheads? Obviously if this continues, my own circumstances may compel me to join the chain reaction, but thankfully, not so far. The people who handle my mite are by nature cautious, and I'm in OK shape financially. But it would be foolish not to expect some contraction of my consulting business, in which case I may have to cut staff. God, I hope not. For me, there's nothing worse than having to fire someone, even for cause.

Now it's Sunday and a good time to review the bidding. Let's begin with the big news of the moment, fresh from Lucia: STST and Morgan Stanley will shortly announce that they're becoming regulated bank holding companies, just like JPMC and Citi.

This will give them unlimited access to the few taxpayers' pockets they don't already have a hand in, presumably including basket privileges at the Fed's printing presses. Better still, it will qualify them to participate in any bailout, backstop, make-whole, or other form of government handout that Uncle Sam offers banks like Citi. Such as the "extraordinary" exemptions that allow them to transfer "assets" such as STST's residuum of billions of unsalable derivatives and other junk into their insured bank subsidiaries, from whence they can be stuffed onto the Fed's balance sheet in return for free cash. This is what is meant by "privatizing the profits and socializing the risks." Democracy in action—with We the People participating in the great events of the moment.

Now let's turn to the Lehman chain reaction. Since Lehman filed for bankruptcy last Monday, overnight credit has dried up. By Friday, it was like Aunt Augusta's cucumbers in *The Importance of Being Earnest*: none to be had anywhere, not even for ready money, and not even for "safe" houses like JPMC and STST. Indeed, Lucia's fighting off Street gossip that if Morgan Stanley implodes, STST must surely follow. Everyone's arguing about collateral values, and nobody's yielding an inch.

Tuesday the news got worse. The culprit this time was the Reserve Fund, the giant money-market fund where corporations and other big players stash their free cash balances, money needed for bills and settlements coming due, the make-whole side of swaps transactions, calls for collateral, even payrolls. As a consequence of writing down its $785 million position in Lehman paper to zero, Reserve's shares, redeemable at $1 since the beginning of time, have "broken the buck." This means that for each dollar you'd put on deposit you'd get back ninety-nine cents or less. Nothing like this has been seen since the bank runs of 1907. Washington has granted Reserve permission to suspend redemptions, equivalent to a major bank closing its doors. Interesting factoid: Reserve's assets, which stood at $60 billion two weeks ago, had shrunk to $23 billion by last Friday. Don't tell me someone didn't know something.

In financial circles, the innermost ripples are starting to look like whirlpools. The word on the Street is that close to $300 billion in hedge-fund and sovereign money has been taken away from institutions rumored to be shaky and redeployed to *theoretically safe havens* like JPMC and the big Swiss and German banks. The Street's seeing squeeze upon squeeze. Even STST isn't immune; Lucia whispers that the firm's "liquidity pool" has been cut by roughly a third. Bottom line: the overnight funding market is a $3-trillion-plus operation. If it seizes up, the entireworld economy will suffer a coronary.

Finally, tjere's our old friend GIG. Uncle Sam marched into their downtown headquarters last Tuesday and effectively took them over, extending an $85 billion emergency loan and extracting an 80 percent equity interest. Negotiation by confiscation, you might say. People are whining about "nationalization," but what alternative is there—especially since the word is that Washington loathes the GIG management with almost the same passion it hates Fuld. Still, it's amazing: three years ago, GIG was one of the biggest and most admired financial institutions in the world. Now it's bust, a ward of Uncle Sam, brought low by derivatives bets made in London that apparently no one at GIG headquarters in midtown Manhattan understood. People are saying that this is a major root cause of the crisis: firms have been destroyed by bonus-seeking termites, traders booking transactions that generate immediate bonuses for the individual, but clobber the firm and its stakeholders when these trades crater down the road.

What's weird is that the numbers argue that GIG was in even worse shape than Lehman, and yet it got rescued (so to speak) on exactly the same terms Fuld and his people were begging Washington for. Same as Morgan and Bear Stearns back in March. These "rescues" seem scripted by Orwell: some animals are more equal than others. Let's see how STST fares if the going gets really hairy. Any way you cut it, a financial pandemic is what we're looking at, the twenty-first-century version of the Black Death that killed half of Europe seven centuries earlier. Money-market plague. No one gets spared.

It may be that my ears are fooling me, but for the first time I'm hearing traces of concern in Mankoff's voice. I know about the bad GIG swaps—that's a $20 billion potential write-off that doesn't qualify for a bailout (even Uncle Sam has to draw the line *somewhere*)—but God knows what other crap there may be that Rosenweis wasn't able to offload and that Mankoff doesn't know about. Even STST may be in one of those situations where it's what you don't know that'll kill you.

The media are doing their bit, of course. The TV networks keep showing clips of Lehman people exiting their Seventh Avenue building with cartons of personal effects, picking their way among sneering people carrying placards condemning "greedy, reckless bankers" which is the cliché du jour. The Street's response has been to send those few of its high-visibility CEOs who still retain a shred of credibility onto MSNBC and Fox to convince the world that the subprime collapse is someone else's fault—mainly Washington's—but this doesn't seem to be having much effect.

In this alternative reality, Uncle Sam and the borrowers were the real fraudsters. The mortgage promoters, lenders, and packagers were just poor saps, mere putty in the hands of indigents and incompetent, crypto-socialist bureaucrats.

I must say that I'm not surprised the public's not buying

this pitch. To accept that a vast conspiracy of bureaucrats and barely literate, basically innumerate working people at the bottom of the wage pyramid has somehow duped a self-professed elite of hugely well-paid people with degrees from the finest universities, working off financial models designed by Nobel laureates, into lending them the better part of a trillion dollars takes a level of imagination I don't have. I can't help thinking that knowingly putting people in houses from which it's odds-on that they'll be evicted only months later is an act of cruelty and cynicism unworthy of a nation that boasts of its generosity and great communitarian heart with a fervor worthy of Emma Lazarus. When John Winthrop spoke of America as "a city on a hill," I doubt he foresaw his vision financed with thirty-year ARMs with teaser rates.

Well, we'll just have to see what tomorrow brings.

# SEPTEMBER 23, 2008

I feel like I've been present at the Creation. Allowed to watch the Almighty at work.

It started last night with another call from Mankoff.

"I need to use your apartment," he said without preamble. "See you at four o'clock."

"You want the place to yourself?" I asked. "I can make myself scarce."

"Don't be ridiculous," Mankoff said. "I want you there. I may need a witness."

He showed up on the dot. He checked out the place, lingered briefly and approvingly over my bookshelves, asked for a glass of water. "The person I'm expecting," he told me, "he's on his way in from Teterboro now. Should be here in another half hour."

"Mind telling me who our mystery guest is?"

"All in good time." He smiled. Although hardly the playful sort, now and then he likes to tweak my curiosity.

At around 4:45 the house phone rang to advise me that my guest was on the way up. A couple of minutes later, I opened the door and there, to my shock and amazement, stood the so-called Sage of Shawnee himself, Merlin Gerrett, ranked by *Forbes* as the country's second-richest man, with a net worth of $69.8 billion in holdings in financial services, transportation, retail, energy, fast food, and God knows what else.

His nickname derives from his hometown of Shawnee, Kansas, where he still lives and where Arrow Northumberland, his holding company, is headquartered. He's the town's economic patron saint; over time he's bought up half the businesses in Shawnee, many of which he's put back on their feet with sensible advice and hard cash. Arrow Northumberland has been an incredible ride for investors; if you'd bought a hundred shares back in the late '60s, you'd have paid $2,500. Those shares would now be worth just under a million dollars.

The man's considered about the best argument for capitalism going. He's built his enormous fortune by buying decent businesses at advantageous prices, hiring good people, and giving them free rein. He plays for the long term, doesn't go for quick profits by manpower attrition or cutting lines of business, or drowning his companies in leverage with which to pay quick dividends the way the fast-money private-equity types do. Most of his cash flow derives from his wholly owned insurance businesses, cash cows that provide nourishment for the rest of Arrow Northumberland.

Not everyone buys his act. Gerrett's detractors complain that when Gerrett dishes out the down-home, deep-dish, "aw shucks" wisdom he dispenses on television, in the op-ed pages, and, most notably, in the letter to shareholders that accompanies Arrow Northumberland's annual report, he's no different from any hedge-fund hustler "talking his book," saying stuff that'll redound to the benefit of his investments. His worshippers say this kind of criticism is mostly sour grapes.

Maybe yes, maybe no. For instance, there's his big position in Morton's, the credit- and bond-rating house, which one commentator has called "perhaps America's largest *financial disservices* company." When Gerrett bought into Morton's, its ratings were blue-chip and gold standard. Today they're more problematical, what with the triple-A ratings the house bestows on the topmost layers of pyramids of junk-debt and derivatives. You'd think someone who called derivatives financial thermonuclear bombs would steer clear of the stuff, but the Arrow Northumberland statements show swaps exposure running to the tens of billions. Usually, when one of Gerrett's portfolio companies has faltered either ethically or financially, Gerrett hasn't hesitated to step in, chop off heads, and set matters to rights. But he's allowed Morton's to go on its merry way, rubber-stamping as AAA debt deals that ought to have the same kind of "bad for your health" warnings that cigarettes carry. Ah, well, who was it that said that a little hypocrisy is the price we pay for civil society?

But back to business. After Mankoff introduced me and I made Gerrett a cup of tea, we settled ourselves on the sofa and chairs surrounding a low coffee table, and the two men got down to cases. Namely, the terms of a $10 billion investment in STST by Arrow Northumberland.

Gerrett opened the bidding. He took some papers from his briefcase and placed them on the table, then said, "Leon, I've looked over these spreadsheets you e-mailed me. Did a little sharp-pencil work of my own. It looks to me like you people are in a lot better shape than I would have expected. Much better than most of the competition, and I can tell you I've seen a whole bunch of *their* statements in the past ten days, because everybody's out in the streets looking to raise equity.

"By my reckoning, you don't really need me, although you *could* use new equity, but more as a cushion than as a matter of survival. By my calculations, your present balance sheet can take a hit of, say, $40 billion and still keep afloat, if only barely. Does that sound right to you?"

Mankoff nodded. "Pretty much."

Gerrett went on: "You now have access to really cheap money, thanks to your turning yourself into a bank. As a taxpayer I find this disagreeable, although as a stockholder I applaud the strategy. Anyway, you look OK to me. Am I missing something?"

Mankoff smiled. "Technically, Merlin, you're right. We could get by without raising outside equity. But I'm thinking longer-term.

Down the road, there are going to be opportunities, big ones. We could be looking at half the competition we faced as recently as the first of the year. Bear's gone, Lehman's gone, Merrill's gone, Morgan Stanley's on the ropes, and BofA and Citi are halfway down the crapper. Everything's terrible right now, but nothing goes on forever, and when things start to turn, even if it isn't for a year or two, I want to be ready.

"Then there's this. We don't want bureaucrats and politicians telling us how to run our business and how much we can pay our people. I want to put us in a position to negotiate from strength with Washington. And if I had you as a partner . . ."

He let the thought die.

"So what do you have in mind?" Gerrett asked.

"Ten billion. Five billion from you, plus another five we'll raise from the market."

"With you on board, yes."

For the next half hour, it was like watching two world-class poker players. Bluff, check, raise, call, check. Mankoff cold-eyed, polite, understated. Gerrett exuding a kind of dumb-as-a-fox country innocence. Norman Rockwell would have loved the guy.

Finally Gerrett said, "OK. Here's my final offer. We'll buy $5 billion of preferred stock, with a 10 percent annual dividend, reasonable call protection, and warrants or a similar conversion feature to buy $5 billion of your common stock at a favorable price, say 10 percent below where the market is right now."

Mankoff did some quick figuring, then made his counteroffer. "Our stock's at $123 and change, which means you're looking for $110."

"Around there."

"That's pretty rich. I'm not sure I can get my board to go along at that level."

"I recognize that, but I have my own stockholders to think of."

"How about $115?" Mankoff asked. "That'll make it easier for me to sell."

Gerrett reflected briefly, then nodded. "I can live with that," he said. He extended his hand, and Mankoff took it.

Mankoff turned to me. "Chauncey, you must have a legal pad around here somewhere." Of course I did. I got out a pad and wrote down the terms of the deal. Mankoff and Gerrett reviewed these, made a couple of tiny emendations, and initialed the sheet. I signed as witness. Then I went to my printer and made two copies

The two agreed to get their lawyers on it pronto so that Mankoff could lay the transaction before the STST board via a 7:00 p.m. conference call. Press releases and regulatory filings would be put in the works. Neither foresaw any problems. Gerrett shook hands and departed. Thus do great men settle the affairs of nations.

## SEPTEMBER 25, 2008

Yesterday STST successfully completed the second half of the Ger-rett deal, a $5 million equity offering. So Mankoff has now got $10 billion in new equity to play with, and he's hit the ground running, already contriving to take over $5 billion in busted Lehman deriva-tives positions on the Chicago Mercantile Exchange for essentially zero cost, positions STST can probably liquidate for a couple of billion, or pledge back to the Fed at par as collateral for more free money—on top of which STST is being paid a fee of $445 million in cash just to take the paper off the Chicago Merc's hands. Which adds up to 2,445,000,000 reasons that a crisis is too valuable to waste. And I can't help but feel that this is just the beginning.

Eighteen months ago, Mankoff summoned me to Three Guys and laid out a long-term strategy that involved pretty tricky financial and political maneuvering. So far, everything's fallen into place. Depending on how things play out, STST may be on the cusp of the biggest windfall in its entire glorious one-hundred-year history.

Even Scaramouche is impressed. "Nobody but Leon could have pulled this off," he said over a twilight-hour martini at San Calisto. "Of course, poor old Bagehot must be spinning in his grave, seeing what the Fed's up to."

He explained. Walter Bagehot was an influential nineteenth-century English journalist and editor of *The Economist*. In a crisis, he wrote, the central bank should lend freely, but on good collat-eral and at a penalty rate of interest. The Fed is lending freely all right, but against dubious collateral and at a giveaway rate.

# OCTOBER 3, 2008

Congress finally approved TARP. Bush signed it into law, and Wall Street's breathing easier.

The gratification wasn't instant, though. Congress sent back Treasury's initial proposal, telling the public that the bill didn't do enough for Main Street.

Of course, that's bullshit. The party the draft bill didn't do enough for is the 1 percent, so it was back to the honey pot. It's Wall Street that instructed Capitol Hill to complain and use Joe Sixpack as the straw man. Like Oliver Twist, the rich and powerful always want more, and they have both the Speaker of the House and his notional right-hand man, the House Whip, in the pockets of K Street. The redrafted bill includes all sorts of special-interest add-ons, such as a tax break for manufacturers of toy wooden arrows, for fat cats whose beachfront cottages have suffered storm damage, for Hollywood producers, stock-car racetrack owners, Virgin Islands distillers . . . you name it.

You'd think there'd be some public outcry to the effect that if the people's money is to be given away, some of it might be given to the people. Indeed, what about "of the people, by the people and for the people?" Ask Wall Street that question, and you'll likely as not be told, "Where's the money in that?"

# OCTOBER 9, 2008

This has been a long but really productive day. It's 10:00 p.m. and I'm on the Acela, returning from the nation's capital to New York. I judge my Washington mission to have been a success. Not only have I come away with what I was dispatched by Mankoff to negotiate, but also with a $20-billion-dollar "bonus" add-on thanks to a brilliant bit of last-minute improvisation by yours truly. Maybe I have a future in investment banking after all. I can't help reflecting that if I worked at STST or any of the big firms, the deal I concluded today would be worth a bonus of $100 million, minimum. However, I'm working *pro bono oligarchia*, so my only reward will be the satisfaction of a job well done and the approval of a man whose respect I crave. It has occurred to me that if I'm going to work these long hours for him, maybe I should get paid at my normal rates. Then I reflected that I really do owe the guy, and the thrill of the chase and the insiderness—the chance to really see how power and money operate in these United States—is recompense enough. Besides, I have a feeling that if payment were added to the equation, I couldn't do it. So I'm going to hold on to my amateur status.

OK, let's take it from the top. Mankoff summoned me to his office yesterday at twilight. Things are heating up. He's had a call telling him to keep next Monday, October 13, clear for an important meeting in Washington at the Treasury Department, at which Uncle Sam's plan for TARP will be put on the table. The same summons has been issued to Dimon and other Wall Street CEOs.

Mankoff wants me to meet with Ian Spass to make certain that whatever Treasury's planning to put on the table will benefit STST. Based on what he's been able to learn from sources in Washington and elsewhere, he's convinced that Uncle Sam has no choice but to dictate a "one size fits all" solution that will lump the biggest firms together, the ones in pretty solid shape, like STST, alongside those in deep doo-doo, like Citi. If Treasury and the Fed try to negotiate bank-by-bank, with one set of terms for strong institutions like JPMC, Wells Fargo, or STST and another for the likes of Citi and Morgan Stanley, it could take forever, and Wall Street will be out of business by Thanksgiving, with breadlines running up and down Pennsylvania Avenue and Main Street screaming for blood.

Mankoff likes his negotiating situation. STST has bank-holding-company status and therefore access to free money, come what may; it can leverage the $10 billion in equity it raised back in September from Merlin Gerrett; hedge-fund clients and other important sources of liquidity are returning to the fold. All in all, he's in a strong enough position not to have to take any government offer he doesn't buy 110 percent. This is the message I was dispatched to Washington to deliver.

This was going to be the first time I'd dealt with Spass face-to-face. In all negotiations, venue is a key element. I took the initiative and booked a junior suite at the Embassy Suites on 22nd Street NW. I was gratified to hear him sniff audibly when I told him my choice. He's obviously a Ritz-Carlton/Four Seasons–type guy.

My train was more or less on time; I got to the hotel a little before one and had room service send up some coffee and bottled water. Spass turned up at 1:30, right on time—which I considered a good sign. When Washington people think they have all the cards, they tend to be late, just to show the other side who's who. He was a bit less lean and hungry than I expected—clearly a man who tends to his vittles. Standard big shot turnout: dark suit, Hermes tie, asshole shirt (white collar, striped body, the sort of thing Rosenweis considers chic), Ferragamo loafers, flag pin on his lapel. We wasted no time getting down to cases.

"I'm authorized to give you a general preview of our TARP program for you to convey to your client," he said for openers; "in total confidentiality, of course, on deepest background. If we know he's on board before we sit down on the 13th, it will be very helpful to the Secretary."

I said I understood.

"Fine. I know from our prior conversations that you know what's what, Chauncey, and so do I, so let's skip the bullshit. We'll play cram-down if we have to, but frankly, if your client and a few others sign up early, it'll be easier to sell to the rest of the Street."

He gave that a moment to sink in, then started to continue, but I judged this a good place to interrupt. "Look, Ian," I said, "You have a plan, we have a plan. I think we can save ourselves both time and aggravation if I go first, since we're the ones you have to persuade to go along. Us and JPMC and Wells. Citi and the others have no choice."

I could see he didn't like this, but he's too smart to debate the merits this early in the conversation and lose the thread, so he let me continue. "The word on the Street is that you're dumping the idea of buying bad assets and moving to a capital-injection model, despite what the Secretary has told Congress. We have no objection to that in principle. Provided, of course, the price is right."

He *really* didn't like this. "We're here to discuss ways and means," he responded, "nothing else. As regards terms, I'm not empowered to negotiate on that issue and I expect you aren't either. That's a decision that will rest with the Secretary. He expects the banks to go along."

"In which case," I parried, shooting him my best ace-in-the-hole poker face, "we have nothing to worry about, since I assume the Secretary will cut his friends on the Street as sweet a deal as he made for himself when he took the job."

We both knew what I meant. The Treasury Secretary had

cashed in $500 million of his former bank's stock tax-free, thanks to special congressional dispensation.

"Let me see if I can help us sort out what's what," I said in my most helpful voice. Using Spass's own words was pretty artful, I thought, as I told him, "The way my people see it, any plan your people come up with is going to have to acceptable from the get-go. After Lehman and GIG you can't risk another big failure, and a couple of the biggies are said to be right on the brink."

No reply. Just a shrug.

"The way we see it is," I went on, "unless *all* the big banks go along, you could be looking at a really treacherous situation, because the markets will perceive that the banks that stay out of the bailout are strong, while those that go along are weak. That'll set the latter up for further deposit withdrawals and incremental credit cancelations, and that'll only require additional infusions of the taxpayers' money. To put it rather crassly, you have to have us— and to get us, you have to accept our terms."

Spass frowned. He's no dummy. He had to guess what was coming, but he said nothing.

"OK," I continued, "let me outline what my client thinks the options are and what he proposes. To repeat myself, not everyone you have to include in the bailout, to make it work at all properly, is in the same financial position. Many on the Street will need Washington's help to survive, but the people I represent and a few others don't. I'm talking about JPMC, Wells Fargo—hell, we both know the names. They're the banks you need to make your program fly on Capitol Hill. If they spurn Washington, saying they don't need the taxpayers' money, it's going to be tough—maybe impossible—to sell a rescue of the likes of Citi and BofA and Morgan Stanley without doing what you did to GIG: namely wiping out the stockholders and unsecured creditors. You with me?"

I paused for effect, then played what I thought was a killer hole card: "And one other thing. How do you think the taxpayers and their elected representatives will react when they learn that the Fed has put out a ton of green stuff to prop up a bunch of dipshit European banks that went berserk chasing yield by loading up on subprime garbage?"

I was taking a chance here, as it might have occurred to Spass that when it came to flogging subprime paper to guileless Europeans, no one had done better than STST. But he let this pass.

"So the real question is," I continued quickly, not wanting to yield the floor, "what will it take to get the healthy parties like my people to go into TARP and whatever other schemes Treasury has up its sleeve? To act as if they need Washington's money when the odds are that they can get along without further investment? That's the trillion-dollar question. Of course, you do have a couple of due bills out: JPMC may have no choice but to go along with Washington after the sweet deal you cut them on Bear and Washington Mutual. Same with Wells Fargo: you curtseyed very prettily and let them buy Wachovia out from under a deal with Citi, a deal that you guys had brokered. Why you let that happen will probably never be known."

Spass still said nothing; he now looked as if he'd eaten a bad clam. I went on.

"Now let's look at my client's situation. If you know anything about these people, it's that they don't do something just because someone else has. They went out and raised $10 billion in fresh equity capital while everyone else was sitting around waiting to see which way Washington would jump, or whether they could do a number on the Koreans or Singapore. We hear the deal Seoul offered Fuld was on better terms than STST got from Gerrett. Hell, if you people had been willing to take Bear and Lehman under your wing on the same terms you gave GIG, or if you'd given GIG the same kind of deal you're giving Citi, you and I wouldn't be talking. But you didn't, so now it's my side that gets to make the rules. To put it another way, Ian, they've have made themselves impervious to the stick; what they want to see is the carrot."

"This is ridiculous!" Spass sneered. "Ancient history."

"You're right about that. Unfortunately, ancient is as ancient does," I replied. "So here's the bottom line. My client is convinced that unless he get a deal he likes, he's under no compulsion to go along with whatever bailout program you've concocted. And if he refuses to participate, do you think Dimon will? And then what? Will you nationalize the banks in trouble? Just think what a run on Citi might look like."

I'll say this for Spass. He's a realist. He wasted not a second palavering about blackmail or patriotism. "Tell me what you have in mind."

"We understand you're looking at a preferred-cum-warrants capital injection similar to what my client did with Merlin Gerrett. Which is fine with us, but don't for a minute think we'll pay Washington what we had to pay Gerrett in terms of dividend rate and conversion ratio. Taking that into consideration, we think an interest or dividend rate of 5 percent is fair, although they'll agree to a bump on the back end for cosmetic purposes. An increase in the rate after, say, ten years to, say, 8 percent."

He objected immediately. "Your client is paying Gerrett a 10 percent yield. Twice what you're proposing to offer the Treasury. That's unacceptable."

I smiled sweetly. "The way my client—and the market—look at things, Uncle Sam doesn't command the same respect as Gerrett and therefore isn't entitled to the same rich terms. Washington's name on our paper isn't as strong a backstop as Gerrett's. Now, moving on: we think that a fair equity kicker would be 5 percent of pro forma outstanding shares at a 10 percent premium over whatever the market price is when the deal—*if* the deal—gets signed."

I paused, like a matador preparing to dispatch a bull, then added, "Oh, yes, and we'd want the right to redeem the preferred after a year without a call premium. And the shares will, of course, be nonvoting."

He looked at me with disbelief. "What you're proposing is a stickup! You can't expect us to cut a deal on behalf of the taxpayer that's nowhere near what you're paying Gerrett for the use of his money! You're suggesting that the Treasury accept an option on STST stock at 10 percent *over* market, while Gerrett's warrants were priced at 10 percent *under* market."

I nodded but said nothing. I suspected it was time for his prepared remarks, and—sure enough—here they came: "If STST thinks they can blackmail the United States of America, they have another think coming. We are not going to tolerate this sort of crap! Especially when the national interest is at stake!"

I gave my chin a few thoughtful strokes in best punditical fashion, then replied, "I think we can cut the national interest crap, my friend. Just do the numbers. What we're proposing is peanuts compared to what JPMC and Wells have walked away with already, and peanuts compared to what you're going to end up throwing at Citi and BofA/Merrill just to keep them from going under.

I let him think that over, then continued: "There are a couple of other aspects of all this that need to be on hte table. When—*if*—this deal gets done, Treasury will grandstand about how it will stimulate the general economy, but you and I know that's rubbish. If it makes sense to lend to Main Street, my client will consider it, but if it doesn't, he won't. He intends to employ whatever money comes his way from Washington as he sees fit, not as Treasury does, or Bernanke, or *The New York Times*, or MSNBC, or anyone else. He'll pay all the lip service you want, but the reality is, he's going to run his business for the stakeholders he cares about, not like some kind of glorified Community Chest. If the market wants to infer that without TARP we'd be in the soup, he'll play along; he'll neither confirm nor deny. So that's the deal."

As Spass weighed those points, I thought it useful to add, "Let's say my people don't go along and instead march to their own drummer, not yours. What are you going to say when six months from now, they start to show profits that have people gasping—profits that they will have earned without the bailout because of all the business they swept up from their weak sisters? There'll be a lot of explaining to do. About why the weak and reckless were bailed out, while the strong and prudent could go their own way."

"That's ridiculous! Our program is specifically designed to unblock the nation's credit arteries! Are you suggesting that the Treasury is lying?"

"Oh, bullshit," I said. "You know and I know and Treasury knows that adding capital to the banks won't thaw the credit freeze. Besides, who wants to borrow? Buisness is scared shit-less, and the consumer's out of gas."

As I watched him chew on that, I had a sudden bit of inspiration, and almost as if some mysterious power was working me like a ventriloquist's dummy, I heard myself saying: "Oh yes, one more thing. My client has close to $20 billion in underwater swaps and hedges with GIG that are now under your control and therefore in your gift, shall we say. We need to get those made whole. A hundred cents on the dollar, no matter what the market thinks they're worth. We don't care how it's done, and we don't care how long it takes—as long as it's by the end of the year. And nobody need be told about it until it's a done deal."

I still don't have the slightest idea where the thought came from. Perhaps my suppressed investment-banking id.

Spass seemed genuinely shocked. "This really is blackmail," he exclaimed.

"You can call it what you want. No GIG, no bailout." The

190

moment I said them, I wanted those words back. If Mankoff had heard me, he would've had me snuffed. And yet something told me this wouldn't be a deal-breaker.

"You know we can't do that!" Spass insisted. "GIG was never on the table."

"Ian, my client's councel thinks that Treasury can do this. A bunch of overseas banks are locked up in GIG swaps the same way we are; they're screaming to get paid and the State Department's all over Treasury to do it. There's a wrinkle in French law that will give you an out, and we can piggyback on that. Get your own lawyers to check this out."

"What I'd said was true—something I'd heard Arnold Braum tell Mankoff when I happened to arrive at the latter's office just as Braum was leaving.

"I don't know," Spass muttered. But he was on the hook. This was a guy who had to make a deal. Had to. The GIG swaps were just icing, someone else's problem. I could see him thinking the same thing. What's another $20 billion? Especially when it's not your money.

In my excitement about GIG, I'd completely forgotten a concession Mankoff was insisting on. I hated to stick it to Spass on top of the GIG ploy, but I had no choice. "One final point: there's talk this plan of yours may include limits on banker bonuses. That's a deal-breaker. No limit on bonuses or other compensation. Understood?"

"You can't be serious! The Congress—the people, the voters—won't stand for that! These are the very people who brought this crisis down on the country and you're insisting they continue to be paid as obscenely as they have been?"

I understood his reaction. To go on paying tens of millions in annual compensation to people who might have wrecked not only the capital markets but the world economy, as well, would strike most people as a gross miscarriage of justice. Justice is not Wall Street's objective, however. Money is.

"The Congress is well paid both above and under the table to keep its mouth shut and vote the way they've been told to vote," I replied. "It'll be years before the voters and taxpayers figure out what's been done to them. Besides, Congress has given you people carte blanche on TARP. So what do you say? Deal?"

He didn't reply. "Don't look so gloomy," I added consolingly. "People are clutching at straws. Down the line, those straws may turn into machetes, and Washington will looklike Hotel Rwanda. You pull this off now, you'll be heroes."

I've fished in enough troubled waters to have a good sense of when the monster fish I'm after is on the hook. When Spass finally departed, I was certain we had a deal. I hit my cell phone and gave Mankoff a coded thumbs-up. I said nothing to him about my GIG swaps garnish. Better to wait and see if Spass's people go for it. Fingers crossed.

When I left the Embassy Suites, I called a curator at the National Gallery to see a if she was free for a cup of coffee. Might as well turn a few cents of Mankoff's dime to my own account. On the way over, my cell phone buzzed. It was Mankoff. Bloomberg was reporting that some asshole at Treasury or the Fed leaked the rumor that Wall Street was going to get hammered by Washington and made to pay heavily for its sins. Net result: the market in finance stocks had cratered. STST shares, which stood at $113 this morning, were down to $101 by the close.

I assured Mankoff that all is well in hand and that my best judgment is that he shouldn't worry. Just in case crossed fingers don't get the job done, let us pray.

What a day!

As you by now may have guessed, Gentle Reader, every so often I feel twinges of revulsion at the big-swinging-dick braggadocio exhibited by a lot of the people I have to be involved with professionally. This evening, however, I felt some of that myself. Real "King of the World" shit. I doubt that I'll experience this big a kick even if OG wins the election three weeks from now, as the smart money is saying he will, and big.

It seems that everything has gone pretty much exactly the way I put it to Spass—including the GIG lagniappe. The payoff has been immediate. STST, which finished last week at $88 after trading as low as $74, closed today at $111, up 25 percent. But that's not the principal reason for my exhiliration.

As you know, Mankoff had been told to hold himself free for a meeting this afternoon at Treasury. He did so, and was en route back to New York by early evening. He called me from Reagan National (he had the brains to fly commercial to Washington, unlike certain assholes who've become media jokes) and told me to meet him at the Bemelmans Bar at the Carlyle for a drink and a heads-up. From Three Guys to the Carlyle, I reflected; the news must be good.

When I got there, the place was a lot busier and jollier than it had been a couple of weeks ago when a friend and I stopped by for an early nightcap. The atmosphere positively dripped testosterone. A good day on Wall Street will do that for New York watering holes. The rats come out of the woodwork, feel their biceps, and start baying for Cristal and fifty-year-old single malt as if it were 2006 all over again.

When Mankoff arrived, I could see he was a happy camper, and his handshake told me that he was definitely pleased with yours truly.

Here's how the meeting went.

The Treasury Secretary, who handles most negotiations as if he's rushing the passer, started off by talking tough, making it clear to the assembled big shots, the heads of the nine biggest banks in the country, that what he was about to propose was set in stone.

"We were being told it was take-it without the leave-it, and the inference was that anyone who even hesitated to go along would suffer the wrath of God," Mankoff told me.

When the Secretary spelled out the specifics of the plan, Mankoff says the bankers around the table practically wet themselves with joy and relief. Contrary to being taken to the woodshed, they were being offered the biggest giveaway in U.S. financial history, tricked out to look like a get-tough Federal initiative.

Bottom line: Wall Street got everything it wanted. Everything I had demanded of Spass, practically word for word, item by item, basis point by basis point, virtually the entire scheme. I can't help but wonder if future historians will refer to this as the Spass-Suydam Plan, the way they talk about the Treaty of Brest-Litovsk.

Here's the deal. Treasury proposes to invest $135 billion in nine firms: $25 billion in each of the three big depositary banks (JPM, Wells, and Citi), $25 billion to BofA in two slices ($15 billion to the bank plus $10 billion to Merrill Lynch), $10 billion each in STST and Morgan Stanley, $3 billion to Bank of New York Mellon, and $2 billion to State Street. This is on top of all the other guarantees, collateral buyouts, and additional relief the Street's already gotten from Washington, as well as the windfall from Uncle Sam picking up Fannie's and Freddie's markers.

Best of all—and this I can't believe; even when I proposed it, I really didn't think that Treasury would go this far—the firms can do whatever they want with this money and no one is obliged to report to the government concerning how the funds are being used. As Mankoff summarizes the program: federal funding intended for survival will now be available for speculation.

What about a CNN report earlier in the day that a key point of the program was to flow money through Wall Street to help out distressed homeowners and get credit recirculating?

"Pure bullshit," Mankoff told me. "Strictly to shut Congress up."

It was agreed by all in the room that Treasury wouldn't have to make public the specifics of this arrangement until later this month. The more time that's allowed to pass without full disclosure, the worse economic conditions will get; layoffs will spread, small businesses will shut down, projects will be canceled, infrastructure will be pared. The deeper and more widespread will be gloom and despair. Focusing on their own misery will blind voters and taxpayers to the fact that hundreds of billions of their money has been given to the very people who bear a significant responsibility for the mess the country is in—on terms none of them would ever be offered in a dozen lifetimes.

I left Mankoff around seven, feeling very upbeat. As I stood on 76th Street, trying to decide whether to go home or walk over to this place on Lexington and commemorate the day with the best pastrami in New York, my cell phone buzzed.

It was Spass.

"Just want to tell you, that swaps matter we discussed?" he said. "GIG?"

"Yes?"

"Consider it a done deal. A hundred cents on the dollar. We can't do anything until November, however. We need to let things settle down, get everyone safely on board."

"I'm sure that'll be fine." We hung up.

It took a few seconds for the news to sink in. I'd pulled it off, by God! I had fucking pulled it off! Who else at STST has recently hauled a $20-billion deal from out of the toilet into the profit column?

Then I thought: how am I going to explain this to Mankoff? I decided to tell him the truth—sort of. I said it was strictly improvisation: just came up and I'd gone with it on the off-chance Washington might bite. He sounded very pleased. Very satisfied. Thanked me for a job well done. Even for Mankoff, $20 billion is a meaningful number.

And there you have it, the way we live now. In one of Fitzgerald's Jazz Age short stories, he writes, "If you wanted it to snow, you just paid some money." That about sums it up.

Is this good? Is it evil? Right or wrong? You tell me. It's just how it is.

# OCTOBER 24, 2008

The nation has been treated to the unmistakable sound of a rat scrabbling down the anchor chain of a sinking ship. Alan Greenspan, appearing before a hearing held by the House Committee on Oversight and Government Reform, recanted his previous statements that Wall Street could always be counted on to do the right and proper thing with all the cheap, easy money he'd thrown its way. He didn't use the popular new catchword "banksters" (as in fraudsters) but he might as well have.

Here's the great man's written testimony:

> Those of us who have looked to the self-interest of lending institutions to protect shareholder's equity, myself especially, are in a state of shocked disbelief. Such counterparty surveillance is a central pillar of our financial markets' state of balance. If it fails, as occurred this year, market stability is undermined.

At this point, committee chairman Henry Waxman, one of those high-IQ homunculi who over a long career make their way to the heights of Capitol Hill, where they spend ever so many enjoyable hours sticking pins in the big boys, asked: "You had the authority to prevent irresponsible lending practices that led to the subprime mortgage crisis. You were advised to do so by many others. Do you feel that your ideology pushed you to make decisions that you wish you had not made?"

To which the maestro replied: "Yes, I've found a flaw. I don't know how significant or permanent it is. But I've been very distressed by that fact."

Of course, one has to ask, what's a mea culpa worth in an

age without shame? Not much, is my guess. My money says that Greenspan, in the wake of possibly the greatest and most damaging financial misjudgment since the South Sea Bubble, will most likely end up getting paid several million bucks a year consulting to hedge funds and banks that are sucking at Washington's teat.

One thing is certain: STST is sure to be picked on as a whipping boy, and Mankoff will be called to testify before Congress, along with his peers on the Street. I know Lucia's already working on a return-fire rhetorical strategy. You can expect *mucho* anti-government rhetoric about how Uncle Sam made the Street do it.

I hadn't checked in at San Calisto recently, so I dropped by for a drink on my way home, and asked the old boys what they thought about the bailout.

"A financial trap from which there's no escape, and morally a disaster." That was the consensus.

"But what was the alternative?" I asked. Surely Washington had saved the financial system just in the nick of time, and with it the world economy.

"You mark my words," said the Warrior. "The leopard doesn't change his spots. Ninety-nine cents on the dollar of this bargain-basement finance Washington is handing the banks will go for speculation. I would expect the stock market to double over the next two years. There's likely to be a sell-off first, while the smart money figures things out, but after that, the sky's the limit. And meanwhile, the general economy will simply stumble along."

"I agree," Scaramouche added. "At the very least, the Street should be compelled to use this free money to help individuals and small businesses reduce debt. The amount of usury in this country is disgusting. Look at home equity, credit card rates, student loans, adjustable mortgages, payday loans, and other marginal financing. At the interest rates people are being charged, they'll never get out of debt. Never in my life did I think anyone would hear me say this, but I think we ought to declare an interest rate holiday. Make people keep up payments, but apply them to principal."

That seemed to make sense—but what do I know?

Orteig called at the end of the day. The election is in less than two weeks. He doesn't want to sound overconfident, but he told me that Mrs. OG is looking at carpet swatches. In a word, OG looks like a lock.

# NOVEMBER 5, 2008

VICTORY! OG has won! And won big—just as Orteig has been predicting. Killed the opposition. I'm writing this late—1:12 a.m. by the clock—and a bit woozy. I watched the election at some liberal friends' big, sprawling Riverside Drive townhouse. If it wasn't firmly moored to earth by plaster and tie-rods and the weight of its owners' trust funds, the building would have floated up to the moon, so ebullient, so triumphant and vindicated, did everyone feel.

Toasts were drunk to the end of the long national nightmare of Bush-Cheney. To TARP being rewritten to ensure Wall Street gets what's coming to it. To doing something about the income inequality that's poisoning the lives of the vast majority of the population. I was cool with those, although I did feel a bit of a hypocrite raising my glass to the prospects of Wall Street being given a sound flogging.

I've warmed a bit to OG. He ran such a great campaign that it's difficult to imagine his presidency not living up to it. At least in great part. When the president-elect came out and made his victory speech in Grant Park, just for a second there, my eyes moistened up. Of course, you'd've had to have the emotional metabolism of a snake not to feel the hopefulness of that moment, the thrill of seeing a young, modern, articulate leader strut his stuff.

Right now, OG has what football players call the Big Mo. As in momentum. A nation at his feet, with the young people and the smart people and the decent people behind him, ready to join him in straightening out the country, and cleaning up Washington and making the Wall Street profiteers and usurers pay for their greed and recklessness. Even if the latter outcome's not in the cards, thanks to Mankoff's money and yours truly's negotiating skills, a lot can get done. Down the line, when it becomes clear that the banksters have gotten away with it, and that nobody's going to jail, some of OG's more rabid constituencies will feel betrayed, but their laments will be stifled by the positive energy unleashed by everything else that'll be going on.

For the moment, however, no regrets. We'll just have to see what the dawn brings.

## NOVEMBER 20, 2008

Six weeks ago Mankoff and the other bank CEOs trooped down to Washington and were given access to hundreds of billions of TARP and other bailout funding. The Street's expectation was that this would calm the markets and send the averages soaring.

Well, someone didn't get the memo, because this simply hasn't happened. Quite the contrary. The last six weeks have turned out to be sheer market hell. The Dow closed yesterday off 427 points and followed that up today with another 445-point drop, leaving the average at 7,552. When I began this chronicle back in February 2007, the Dow was at 12,700 and change. That's a 40 percent drop in eighteen months.

Bank credit is tighter than ever while the larger economy worsens. It's a perfect storm of financial self-contradiction. Businesses and households are in deepening trouble, which reduces their creditworthiness, which intensifies the banks' reluctance to lend. That's the official excuse. From what I hear, though, Wall Street has other uses in mind for its bailout money, and they don't include alleviating Joe Sixpack's misery. One could make the point that if TARP had been fed into the larger economy to save jobs, keep plants and stores open, and forestall foreclosures, the stock market might not have tanked so badly. But who am I to opine? I'm not an economist or a trader.

Yesterday, STST traded at $52, a quarter of what it was selling for when I met Mankoff at Three Guys. Less than half of where it was when Mankoff and Gerrett cut their deal. Ouch! The only bright spot in the slump in the price of stocks is that it has somewhat stilled the chorus of complaint that the taxpayer got a lousy deal in TARP, since Wall Street hasn't been spared. The financial stocks have taken a real beating, not only because business is terrible, but because the market figures the Street will be taken to the woodshed next year.

Mankoff views the carnage serenely. Neither he nor (he tells me) Gerrett is sweating STST's current price. By next spring, he's certain, once the new administration's in power and pump-priming with all its might (and the taxpayers' full faith and credit) and the market sees the kind of money STST is making, the shares will be back well over $100 and probably closer to $150. Let us note that everything he's predicted so far has come to pass.

# NOVEMBER 21, 2008

This has been a hell of a day. Break out the champagne. Orteig has kept his end of our bargain. The president-elect's transition team has put the word out that the incoming administration's economic team will be headed by Harley Winters in the White House and Thomas Holloway at Treasury.

When I heard the good news late this morning, I was a few blocks west of my office conferring with an important new client who'd been sent my way by a friend at Julliard, a hedge-fund guy named Leonard King, who looks like a complete thug, with a shaved skull and a mug that belongs on post-office walls, but who turns out to be an opera fanatic. He gets more of a thrill from what's in the bars and staves of a Mozart score than in the cells and columns of an Excel spreadsheet. You remember my idea for a series of operas based on Shakespeare? Well, my new client has bought into it, and we're in the early discussion stages for a series of new productions to be performed around the world: *Macbeth*, *Otello*, and *Falstaff*, by Verdi; *Roméo et Juliette*, by Gounod; and *The Tempest*, by contemporary composer Thomas Adès. This is a huge, costly undertaking that I've been thinking through for some time (it'll cost around $200 million), but its prospective underwriter is a man who earned $1.3 billion last year and whose net worth *Forbes* put at $11 billion. He has what Wall Street types call "three-comma money."

We were humming along, matching lists of singers' and conductors' availabilities and fees, when all of a sudden he got a call that he said he had to take and rushed out of the office. When he returned, he was lit up like a Christmas tree with positive energy, and when he told me the good news about the appointments, I felt like I was having an out-of-body experience.

"You know what this means, don't you?" he told me. "Half the Street's been thinking this new guy's going to do a Pecora rerun and put a bunch of people in the slammer, but with Winters and Holloway calling the shots, that's not going to happen. Both of them are on record as opposing criminal prosecutions. So it's hallelujah time! The Dow and the S&P are already through the roof, because you don't have to be a genius to know what this means. We could have a thousand-point spike in the Dow over the next few days." Then he sent me on my way, declaring that he and his troops had "to hit the mattresses."

On the way back to the office, I stopped off at a hamburger joint on Lexington Avenue I like, and while I was eating, finished reading this morning's *Times*. Today's op-ed section has a long piece by Marina Hochster, the take-no-prisoners financial reporter who's a major thorn in Lucia's side. There are few journalists that Lucia can't bring around to seeing things the STST way—but this Hochster woman is one of them.

To my surprise, the piece was very hopeful and conciliatory, almost prayerful, not at all in the saber-tongued, slash-and-burn, antagonistic style Hochster's famous for, which makes her a favored talk-show guest. She's publicly stated that she models her journalism on the famous muckrakers of Teddy Roosevelt's time—Ida Tarbell, Lincoln Steffens, and Frank Norris—and ours: Woodward and Bernstein, Matt Taibbi, and Seymour Hersh. I read somewhere that Hochster hopes in her career to do to the pin-striped crooks on Wall Street what Hersh did to the perpetrators of My Lai.

Well, I thought as I read that, lots of luck, dear lady. Muck-raking's not what it used to be. Back in TR's day, the journalists had the support of TR and his bully pulpit. And right up through Watergate, public indignation could be ignited and rallied. But nowadays, not so much—if at all. People are inured to scandal in high places—you can thank the Clintons for that—and have the Internet on which to vent their indignation individually. Who needs to join a rally when you have Twitter? Even Hersh gave up trying to rake the corporate muck a long time ago. He once said in an interview that while journalists may relish the thought of going after Big Money, editors and publishers don't.

Reading Hochster's piece made me feel kind of sorry for her. The column was all about how OG's election a couple of weeks ago will usher in a bright new era, in which justice and brotherhood will prevail and the bad guys will be made to pay for their malefactions. I'd give anything to see her face when she hears the Winters-Holloway news. You don't have to be a cynic, or to know what I do, to grasp that this just isn't going to happen, not the way the nation is run today.

You have to admire Orteig's timing; he's sprung the trap at just the right moment, with the nation still drunk on expectation and giddy with idealism, and in no frame of mind to sit back, look hard, and ask, "What the hell is *this* about?" The way I think I would, were I not in on the game.

The effect on the markets was just what my client said it would be. By lunchtime, a giant, shimmering spiky shudder of speculative relief had swept Wall Street. The Street works by the theory that disaster deferred is disaster eliminated. Gone were all fears of retribution from a Democratic administration. By the time the last weary trader shut down his Bloomberg terminals, the Dow was up nearly 500 points, and the smart money is looking for another 500 come Monday.

The financial stocks lagged the rally, STST among them. It opened at $47 and change, closed at $53. Still a one-day bump of over 10 percent isn't to be sneezed at. I reckon it will take time for investors and traders to process the true potential for Wall Street of the appointment of two committed laissez-faire, pro-finance, anti-regulation types to manage a so-called "liberal" administration's economic and financial policy. Under OG, the Great Bush Giveaway, as Scaramouche calls the TARP bailout, will continue to roll on like the mighty ocean, splendid and implacable and teeming with sharks.

Anyhow, it's fair to say that my day passed in a kind of egotistical euphoria, tempered by mild disappointment that there's nobody out there whom I can tell about the coup I've masterminded. Just as I was getting ready to leave the office, Lucia called and we talked briefly about Winters-Holloway and what it meant. Her Washington connections report that some of OG's inner circle—including, curiously, his wife—are unhappy because they were never really given a chance to participate in the decision.

It was at the end of the day as I made my way downtown to meet a friend for a drink, brimming with pride and self-congratulation, that I recalled the famous passage from *The Great Gatsby* in which a shady type is pointed out to the narrator as "the man who fixed the World's Series back in 1919." I wonder if someday people will point me out as "the man who fixed the 2008 presidential election."

Will I be pleased? Only time will tell.

## NOVEMBER 27, 2008

OG's transition team has now formally confirmed the leak that drove the market up 1,000-plus points in five days. Harley Winters and Thomas Holloway will head the new administration's economics team, Winters as chief economic counselor to the White House, Holloway as Secretary of the Treasury. No mention of Brewer and scant mention of Vollmer. I imagine that Winters has already seen to it that the former Fed chief is marginalized.

When I spoke to Orteig this afternoon to wish him a happy Thanksgiving, he told me that the president-elect already seems to be developing a man-crush on Holloway. That doesn't surprise me. They're both technocrats with exceptional skills in career advancement. As for Winters, OG totally buys into the He Who Knows Everything image. He's one himself.

From what I hear, the Street's celebrating Thanksgiving with caviar and noble vintages. As well it should. Regulatory Armageddon has been postponed, if perhaps canceled. Hedge fund managers can shred their Cayman Islands visa applications.

Last Monday, following Friday's 500-point spike, the market opened up big and stayed up big, with the Dow gaining another 400 points. STST closed at $67. By the time I landed Wednesday at Montego Bay (I'm staying with friends in a villa with a beautiful, unobstructed view of Ralph Lauren), STST had broken back up through $70, a recovery of over 40 percent in just three sessions; it closed at around $76.

Of course, a decent interval will be required—a new president inaugurated, the Winters-Holloway nominations confirmed by Congress—before the Street can get back to business as usual. I had coffee with Mankoff the day before I left for Jamaica and he's very bullish. It couldn't have worked out better for STST: greatly reduced competition, risible cost of capital, zero transparency, and the prospect of an extra $20 billion to play with, thanks to my GIG prestidigitation. Mankoff thinks the second half of 2009 may be STST's best and biggest ever.

One amusing note. Just before I turned in, I caught an MSNBC rerun of an interview with Marina Hochster. She's a nice-looking, strong-featured woman, with a marked New England accent. The type people call "handsome." She wouldn't look out of place on a Nantucket widow's walk, scanning the far horizon for her menfolk's whaler. She was asked about the Winters-Holloway appointments, and responded, "It's like appointing a couple of Ku Klux Klansmen to run the NAACP." I thought that was pretty good?

Ah, well, so go the politics of this great corrupted republic. Bring on the turkey and the ackee and jerk sausage stuffing. In other words: Happy Thanksgiving and God bless us, every one!

# NOVEMBER 29, 2008

It's generally agreed that Mankoff runs one of the tightest ships plowing the mighty seas of global finance. Its balance sheet reflects plausible valuations; the firm takes generous haircuts on illiquid or unmarketable securities and recognizes losses promptly. Relatively speaking, they're as clean and honest as you'll find on the Street. They're in no regulatory difficulties as far as anyone knows: no inside trading, exposure to the Foreign Corrupt Practices Act or RICO, money-laundering, sanctions-busting. In other words, STST isn't HSBC.

Nevertheless, the financial crisis is so all-enveloping that not even the most risk-averse firms can avoid taking a few hits. Beginning last March with the fall of Bear Stearns, STST began to take write-downs and reserves against its trading book. These have been worsened by a severe falloff in business since Lehman. According to Lucia, Mankoff advised his board that the firm could show a loss for 2008 of almost $1 billion.

Now it appears that won't happen. The numbers sorcerers have ridden to the rescue.

You remember *Groundhog Day*? Where Bill Murray wakes up every morning to find that it's always yesterday? This is sort of the scheme STST's smartest numbers jugglers and its most ethically flexible senior accountants have concocted. It's a scheme that to my untutored and ethically naïve eye makes Enron's accounting look like IBM's, but apparently I'm being naïve again, because it's perfectly legal. On Wall Street, never forget, legality is the sole animating principle of morality.

Here's how it's going to work. For as long as anyone can recall, STST has been on a "November fiscal year." Each November 30 they close the books on the twelve months past and the next morning,

December 1, they open a fresh set of ledgers for the upcoming twelve months. For fiscal 2009, however, STST is switching to a "December year," one that will begin on January 1, 2009. The switch will take place after the books are closed on the (present) November 30, 2008, fiscal year. Which leaves the entire month of December 2008 in limbo or, if you prefer, purgatory.

So what will become of the missing month?

It seems that December will just vanish. That's right. It will be effaced from the face of time with a few clicks of an auditor's mouse. Those souls who calibrate their working lives to STST's calendar will go to bed this Sunday and won't wake up, from an accounting perspective, for thirty-one days, until January 1, 2009. Talk about Rip van Winkle!

The missing thirty-one days will have their earthly uses, be sure of that. They'll constitute a sort of arithmetical septic tank, into which will be dumped what's left in the way of loss-making junk on STST's balance sheet. Write-offs and markdowns that have been postponed will now be taken. December's shaping up as a lousy month for business, anyway, so this way they'll kill two birds with one pass at the abacus. And here's the best part: December 2008 will only have to be shown in next year's annual report as a footnote. Isn't it amazing what an accounting firm can do with only a pencil and a set of spreadsheets?

You'll also be pleased to learn that STST just got a very nice check for $19 billion from the Federal Reserve that closes out the GIG swaps problem. Some of this windfall will be paid out to make certain most favored counterparties whole, but Lucia says about $4 billion will stick to STST's ribs. According to her, the Bush Treasury insists that no disclosure be made by Washington until next year after the inauguration, when it'll be the new team's problem. Seems fair to me.

# DECEMBER 17, 2008

Last night Lucia attended Rosenweis's annual Christmas party. I had an important client to entertain and couldn't go, so she called this morning to report.

Among the big shots assembled around the table, the consensus was that Bernanke's going to take the discount rate straight to zero, a course of policy that, "in terms of benefit to Wall Street," will be like "waking up to find Jennifer Lopez sucking your dick," as Rosenweis colorfully put it.

At the end of the evening, Rosenweis asked Lucia to stay for a nightcap. No way he'll get into her pants, or even come close, and they both know it, so this postprandial chat was all business. Apparently, Rosenweis thinks Wall Street is getting a bum rap. Here's Lucia's recollection of what he said: "You need to do a better job next year. We all do. I know people are angry. But hey, we just did what Uncle Sam told us to do. No one told us to stop: not in 2004 or in 2006 and 2007, and even in 2008 until the bottom fell out. We're not the people who are supposed to be looking out for the taxpayer. That's the government's job. We need to get that message out."

I will refrain from editorial comment.

In times like these, that try men's souls, small rays of sunshine give outsized warmth to the troubled spirit.

Orteig called me at home tonight to give me a heads-up to pass along. It seems that Barney Frank, the Massachusetts congressman whose potential to be a pain in the butt is exceeded only by his talent for hypocrisy, has teamed up with Senator Chris Dodd, a man who (according to Lucia) has never seen a payoff he didn't like, to write some law—now universally known as "Dodd-Frank"—that will require a certain percentage of future TARP disbursements to be used for mortgage forgiveness.

Normally Dodd-Frank wouldn't be something Winters and Holloway would be in a position to head off. Technically they're powerless with respect to legislation until after the inauguration next month, but Orteig reports that Winters has persuaded OG that the mortgage crisis is a policy matter that now belongs to the new administration and must therefore not be allowed to move ahead legislatively without the president-elect's agreement. OG has bought that argument, and word has been conveyed to Rep. Frank that if he expects as much as a single jeep to be budgeted for military installations in his district, he better table any legislative initiative until after the inauguration. Dodd is less of a problem; with him it's just a question of how big the check needs to be.

Every day, it seems, there's new news that paints the mortgage industry as a hotbed not only of reckless lending but also of outright fraud. Apparently Citi has an operation in deepest Missouri in which thousands of worker bees at computers spend their day "kosherizing" bad or defective mortgages. Loans in which the come-on was fraudulent, the terms misrepresented along with the borrowers' financial position, the paperwork incomplete and therefore not legally binding. These weren't loans created to put America's little people in homes of their own, mind you. These were loans created to generate fees and spreads for Wall Street. Less than 15 percent of subprime mortgages written during the past few years were for first homes; the rest went for flips, second homes, and home equity.

It makes one wonder how many lanterns Diogenes would have gone through searching the dimly lit corridors and corners of Washington for an honest man—but I keep telling myself to stop thinking like this. Become more tough-minded, more the practical man of affairs for whom the bottom line is all. After all, Mankoff says there's work still to be done, which will doubtless call for yours truly to affect a clear eye and a hard heart.

# DECEMBER 23, 2008

Nobody can wait for the midnight clear, that's for sure. Wall Street still resembles Humpty Dumpty: patched up along the fault lines but the cracks still very evident. Here's hoping Uncle Sam's fiscal Super Glue holds. Apparently Citi has had to have major additional transfusions of the taxpayers' money to bail out its "Structured Investment Vehicles," or SIVs. These are the "let's pretend" off-balance sheet entities Citi and its lawyers created to stick the big bank's worst garbage in. I'm told there was a highest-brass meeting with their accountants and lawyers during which they were told either to fix the SIV problem and bail out certain internal hedge funds—including the fund they bought for $900 million from the slick Indian gent who's now running the bank—or risk a big fat qualification on their audit. Word is that this may result in Citi having to bring as much as $100 billion of toxicity back onto their balance sheet.

BofA remains iffy, especially with Merrill included (that merger finally closed last month). Other year-end tidbits gleaned here and there include a Fed program that goes by the code name "ST OMO," which stands for "single-tranche, open-market operations," whatever the hell that's supposed to mean. Apparently the fun and games now in place could cost as much as a trillion dollars. Money is money, but what I find somewhat troubling is that, according to one of Lucia's sources, Uncle Sam—both past and present administrations—intends to keep this $1 trillion giveaway a secret from the taxpayers.

People are totally puzzled by what the Fed's up to. One suspicious hedge-funder I spoke with wonders if the Fed might not be engineering "a reverse dump": lending Wall Street the money to buy back some of the garbage collateral Bernanke and Co. vacuumed up earlier, thereby making the Fed's own year-end balance sheet look better. This sounds like "double secret greed" to me.

Another bit of news about our central bankers is that, in uncontrollable save-the-world mode, they've thrown $30 billion of the taxpayers' money at a shadowy Luxembourg outfit called Dexia, which is a major insurer of U.S. municipal debt. In this time of crisis, when hundreds of thousands if not millions of American households are squeezed, losing their jobs, being put out on the street, tens of billions of your full faith and credit and mine are being shipped overseas to foreign banks. Does that make any sense?

Frankly, I'm beat, I'm tired, I'm ground down. The office will stay closed through the long weekend, and on Saturday I'll head north for my annual New Year's sojourn in the Berkshires—and that'll take me into 2009. And STST will be back in sync with the calendar.

One final note. Apparently a couple of weeks ago the president-elect was confronted by an influential senator who begged him to rescind the pending appointments of Winters and Holloway. This is a legislator who thinks Wall Street—especially Citi—is being let off too easy and whose opinion of Holloway, in particular, is not repeatable in polite society. He's said to have made no bones to OG about his belief that these are the wrong people at the wrong time.

OG told the senator to stuff it—presumably after consulting with Orteig. I can't help wondering if or how much OG knows about my deal with Orteig, but for some reason I can't make myself ask. Don't I remember a novel called *Shall We Tell the President?*

So here we are on the brink of 2009. How'll it turn out? It has to be better than the year we're leaving, all eleven months of it. Gentle Reader, a very Merry Christmas to you. See you in 2009.

# JANUARY 1, 2009

New Year's Day in the Berkshires.

I had a tough night sleeping. It was late—maybe 1:30 a.m. when the last guests left, and my hosts and I cleaned up and dragged ourselves upstairs to bed. By then, my mood was already dark, although I managed a bright face and a frisky line of chatter right up to the moment I closed my bedroom door behind me and flopped down on the bed.

So, you ask, whence this gloom? I might call it a crisis of conscience.

Ever since I got here, I've felt like an alien life-form among people with whom I used to feel real intellectual and moral kinship. I look at them, and listen to them, and then I think they're no longer (although they don't know it) "my" people, "my" sort. Or I'm not theirs. Not any longer.

The very first night, my hostess, Millie Hastings, turned to me at dinner and said, "How can you stand to work with those Wall Street people, Chauncey? It's going to be a pleasure to see those people pay for what they've done to us!"

This is a woman for whom, two or three years ago, I went to bat with some of "those people" and secured $1 million in grant funding for a lecture series at her alma mater. It helped, I suppose, that the people I approached had children applying to that college.

I responded with what's become my stock answer: "The way I see it, Millie, is that I help what some consider bad money find its way to good ends. Besides, 90 percent of the finance types I work with have nothing to do with the kind of stuff that's caused this crisis." Already I'd had to spend a certain amount of time establishing that my friend and patron, Leon Mankoff, isn't the same as one Bernard Madoff, despite the similarity in the spelling of their surnames. It was disclosed about a month ago that the latter has been running a $60 billion Ponzi scheme, and since then Mankoff has been driven crazy by people confusing him with the swindler and whispering and pointing him out in places like Carnegie Hall.

I can understand how my Berkshires bunch feels. They're basically all of a type: well spoken, candid, cultivated, liberal, humane, old-school; mostly acquaintances of long standing, along with a couple of new additions. They're people who accept the rules and play by them—and expect the same of others. The problem is they live by premises no longer in force—you simply cannot disdain money in a culture that worships it. And the current crisis has left them in shock. They could pride themselves as being the flower of society, guardians of the minds of our youth and of the great cultural traditions, but what use are those attainments when overnight their 401(k)s have evaporated; the value of their houses has dropped by half; their friends and colleagues suddenly find themselves unemployed; their departmental budgets are slashed; their exhibitions, fellowships, lectureships canceled.

And the worst part, the complaint I've heard most often in the five days I've been up here? Their children are mainly interested in making money. I know how they feel; I recently read that over 50 percent of this year's graduating class at Yale signed up to interview on Wall Street, and all I could think was that something has gone terribly wrong somewhere.

So where does that put me? Do the missions I've successfully carried out for Mankoff make me a traitor to my class, as FDR was accused of being? You tell me.

I'm glad I won't be around when my friends up here see the kind of profits STST expects to report. They've had to give up vacations, pet projects, and other life enhancers, and there's more to come, while the people that caused these sacrifices are emerging from the crisis richer than ever. I know Lucia's concerned about how to respond if STST shows juicy earnings barely six months after being handed billions in taxpayer money, but that's just an image nuisance. Mankoff himself is concerned that if STST's profits get back up to where they were in 2007, his top people are going to want their compensation levels back up to where *they* were in 2007. I can hardly expect that fat Wall Street bonuses are going to sit well with Main Street, where "For Rent" and "Going Out of Business" signs are already sprouting like winter daffodils, but with the crazy way we live today, you never know.

I hear people stirring in the house. I'll go down to breakfast and make cheerful New Year's Day noises, then say my goodbyes and head back to the city. Happy New Year.

# JANUARY 7, 2009

Orteig called today with two bits of interesting news. Like all good fund-raisers, he likes to keep his patsies warm and toasty for the next time around. Politics is the gift that keeps on wanting, and I can tell he's already thinking about 2012, even before OG is inaugurated.

It seems there's this economist close to the president-elect, a woman named Romer, who's pushing OG to up his stimulus package from $800 billion to $1.9 trillion. She has Main Street in mind as the beneficiary, through massive new federal investment in infrastructure and possibly even direct cash contributions, but Winters has persuaded OG that the most beneficent restorative for the economy will be via the financial/banking system, which will pipe the money to the nation's farms, small businesses, and distressed homeowners. Romer is understandably very unhappy. Personally, I think she has a point about infrastructure: New York City's streets look as if they're maintained by Rwanda's Department of Transportation.

Orteig also reports that OG summoned Holloway to the White House, along with the woman who heads up the SEC, and the three of them had a session about implementing serious oversight of the financial system, but that Holloway managed to get that can kicked down the road, pleading that the Street needs to concentrate all its energy on the present.

# JANUARY 8, 2009

I strolled across the elevator lobby at the end of the day, and found the Nitmeister and Scaramouche engaged in a discussion of a scam in Detroit, a city that was once a bastion of this country's industrial might but which in recent years has deteriorated into a slough of poverty and criminality, with a good third of its decrepit housing stock either abandoned or in foreclosure. It seems that the city's credit rating has been downgraded to junk levels, which will trigger $200 to $300 million in penalty payments to the banks that sold Detroit a complicated swaps issue back in 2005. The transaction was designed to protect the city in the event interest rates rose; when they instead declined, thanks to a crisis brought on in large part by the very people who sold the city on swaps "protection," Detroit was on the hook for huge make-whole payments to Wall Street. The city doesn't have the money, and has asked for forbearance, but Wall Street is playing hardball, even threatening to seek a lien on the priceless collections of the Detroit Institute of the Arts, one of the great museums of the country. It appears the Street is within its legal rights to do so; as is not the case with other major museums, DIA and its holdings are city property and therefore legally vulnerable.

"It isn't just towns and cities and water districts that fell for this garbage," Scaramouche was saying when I sat down. "What about places like Harvard? I hear it's going to cost them close to half a billion to get out of a deal they let themselves be talked into."

"No doubt we missed a splendid opportunity," the Nitmeister commented, his canny old features scrunched up with remembered greed. "Once these swaps deals with municipalities became common currency, you and I should have shorted a bunch of XYZ municipal bonds, then bribed someone at S&P to drop the ratings and held the issuers' feet to the fire. As I have no doubt someone may have. We'd've done very nicely."

Scaramouche smiled. "You're right, Ira. It does bear thinking about, whether someone at one of the rating agencies hasn't gotten a kickback. Of course, we'll never know, not with the way things work today."

A cheering thought with which to kick off a new year.

# JANUARY 18, 2009

Mankoff knows how to pick 'em! If Harley Winters never does another thing, as an investment, he's already a winner, and inaguration's still two days away. It's been widely reported that Winters has been working Capitol Hill and has managed to quell residual anger over where most of TARP has gone. Congress only just woke up to the reality that money intended to help Main Street has instead been handed out to Wall Street, and several congresspersons were urging cancellation of the last big bundle of TARP handouts.

Winters promptly dispatched two letters to Congress that eloquently paint TARP as a genuine and far-reaching populist initiative that will be channeled via Wall Street purely in the interests of economic efficiency.

Lucia showed me copies over drinks. I can't recall when I've read such skillful examples of technocratic twaddle. I asked her if she'd had a hand in writing them. She shook her head vigorously. "All Winters," she said. "The man *is* a genius."

I don't believe her. Nowadays, I don't know if I believe anyone about anything.

# JANUARY 20, 2009

OG's inaugural address was a big nothing. No economic call to arms, no rallying cry, no anti–Wall Street rhetoric. If I was a raving supporter, I'd be upset, possibly suspicious. The public was expecting an FDR or Honest Abe; instead it got a corporate-style pitch, PowerPoint without the slides. Management in place of government, as I recall Christopher Hitchens writing somewhere.

# JANUARY 22, 2009

Lucia bought me breakfast at the Regency this morning. The place is as reliable a barometer of the plutocratic mood as any venue in the city. This a.m.'s buzz was definitely upbeat—and so was Lucia. She's just returned from D.C., where she did the whole inauguration deal: balls, buffets, tribute breakfasts, check-writing fiestas, embassy receptions, chic Georgetown lunches—all sandwiched around strategic huddles with her K Street janissaries.

She brought back one bit of news that I found very interesting. Apparently, the president had barely left the Capitol steps following his grade Z inaugural address when the GOP called a meeting of its congressional delegations at which they pledged their life, liberty, and sacred honor that from this day forward they will oppose every single initiative, policy, reform, or what-have-you that OG or his administration puts on the table. Clearly, they feel his wishy-washy inaugural address signals a shift from the supercharged populism that carried the election, and that they have only the president to go up against, not the will of the people. Whatever the White House asks for, the GOP will oppose it. If the president says he wants to go the john, they'll move to have the lock on the men's room changed.

"If I was calling the PR shots for the president," Lucia said, "I'd play it the way Roosevelt did. Tell the people that he's well aware that Wall Street hates him, and that he welcomes their hatred. Get Main Street into a proper Us against Them frame of mind. Apparently his wife feels the same way. But this is a man who seems to think that life is a gigantic moot court, in which reason and the rule of law will prevail, with himself playing the Great Conciliator."

Fat chance, I reflected. With the GOP laying down artillery fire from the front, and the fifth column established by my compact with Orteig subverting behind the lines, "Hope and Change" isn't going anywhere.

# FEBRUARY 2, 2009

Had lunch with Lucia today at the Veau d'Or, my check. We seem to be going steady, but life's like that. You'll see a certain friend every day for a month and then they vanish from your existence. When I asked her what she'd been up to recently, her reply was concise: "Sowing confusion as always."

"Anything in particular?"

"The bailout. People are starting to ask, did we *really* need Uncle Sam's money or didn't we?"

It seems that the Fed is covering its TARP ass by passing the word that twelve of the thirteen biggest banks were on the brink of insolvency last fall. I think a good one-third of the banks represented at the Treasury meeting last October could have gotten by without TARP. But of course, everyone's new favorite guessing game is *Which was the exception?* The smart money likes JPMC and Wells Fargo, but there are a few influential holdouts for STST.

One thing's for certain: Citi couldn't have survived without TARP. Which is an irony, because Citi's the prime poster child for the lunacy of deregulation. The amending and subsequent repeal of Glass-Steagall, which many believe lie at the heart of the present crisis, were concocted precisely so that the banking and investment banking components of Citi could be combined into the present unmanageable mess. Of course, if Citi had gone under, there would have been a huge popular demand for the reinstatement of Glass-Steagall or something like it.

We also discussed our new president's press conference last week during which he used the tough language on the subject of Wall Street that many had expected to hear in his inaugural address. I doubt that one tenth of one percent of the people who watched the inauguration watched this press conference, which is probably the point. Here's how the *Times* reported it: "'There will be time for them to make profits, and there will be time for them to get bonuses,' the president said during an appearance in the Oval Office with Treasury Secretary Thomas Holloway. 'Now's not that time. And that's a message that I intend to send directly to them.'"

Naturally the Street's in an uproar. How *dare* he? From the outset, Orteig has assured me to "watch what we do, not what we say," so I brushed it off. But not Rosenweis, who obviously hasn't been clued in about Winters-Holloway. He's urging that STST and the rest of the Street team up with the GOP in a concerted, tough-talking propaganda pushback and has given Lucia orders to initiate a boycott of the forum of an event next month at which Holloway is scheduled to announce the administration's grand plan for reform. Lucia doesn't think that's a good idea, but she's unwilling to take on Rosenweis, who's already making her life hell about Davos. For the past eight years, ever since he and Mankoff took over at STST, Rosenweis has attended Davos and peacocked among other "world leaders." This year, however, with Wall Street taking desultory fire for lining its pockets while the rest of America is turning theirs inside-out, Mankoff thinks STST ought to skip Davos and has instructed Rosenweis to cancel

Lucia called with an interesting bit of news.

"Remember you once asked me about a lawyer named Eliza Brewer?"

"Vaguely." I'm really getting good at this.

"Well, she's just signed on at Justice. Deputy Attorney General for the Criminal Division. The sigh of relief up and down K Street practically crashed a couple of buildings. The lady apparently doesn't believe in criminal prosecutions for anything short of outright felony. You'd have to be Bernie Madoff to get her attention."

Winters, Holloway, and Brewer, I thought: the trifecta is complete.

The markets are tanking, but STST stock has been heading straight up. The shares sold below $50 at its 2008 low, so to be back at almost $90 is a hell of a bounce. Lucia's concern is that the firm's success, including the nice recovery in its stock, may be exploited by the envious and beleaguered to make STST the prime target for the anti–Wall Street faction. We shall see.

Yesterday, with much fanfare, Holloway unveiled the new administration's plan to deal with the financial crisis—and laid a total egg. Which is surprising, considering that he threw the Street a total softball. Here's how the *Times* summarized the occasion.

> In the end, Mr. Holloway largely prevailed in opposing tougher conditions on financial institutions that were sought by presidential aides, according to administration and Congressional officials.
>
> Mr. Holloway . . . successfully fought against more severe limits on executive pay for companies receiving government aid.
>
> He resisted those who wanted to dictate how banks would spend their rescue money. And he prevailed over top administration aides who wanted to replace bank executives and wipe out shareholders at institutions receiving aid.

Still, it's too early for Wall Street to sound the all clear. Lucia tells me that a Bloomberg reporter named Pittman is raising a ruckus with a lot of questions about loan guarantees to GIG, BofA, and the like. This is not information Treasury or the Fed has the slightest intention of letting non-insiders get hold of, I'm told, and they're turning their chanceries inside out searching for whistleblowers while they repel Pittman's information-seeking sorties with salvos of doublespeak and denial. Sooner or later, of course, Bloomberg's going to file a Freedom of Information Act request and then the fat cats may truly be in the fire, although it's likely to be a year before Uncle Sam's obliged to cough up any really embarrassing disclosures. In the meantime, Wall Street's lobbyists are painting critics and truth-seekers as "unrealistic, misinformed, advancing ulterior motives, and damaging to U.S. competitiveness."

Lucia's Washington sources also report that Winters and Holloway are scrapping noisily about how Citi should be broken up. Not about *whether* it should be, but about *how* it should be—and which one of them should handle it, since it promises to be a maximum-visibility assignment. This is good, since it lengthens the odds against anything concrete getting done. I wouldn't be surprised if squabbling between the two hadn't figured in Mankoff's calculations from the outset.

# FEBRUARY 15, 2009

For many on Wall Street, Valentine's Day wasn't happy. The *Wall Street Journal* reported yesterday that the Dodd-Frank bill is back on track. You'll recall this legislation was shelved for review late last year at the request of the incoming administration. The new draft legislation still includes a clause forbidding the payment of bonuses to executives of the big banks, as well as outfits like GIG and GM that have received bailout aid.

When this got out, great was the keening and rending of bespoke garments up and down the Street. "Where's the gratitude?" they whine, noting all the campaign moolah that Dodd has sopped up over the years. While a bonus clawback or holdback might seem perfectly reasonable to thee and me, Gentle Reader, indeed, some might say richly deserved, the Street of course doesn't see it that way because the crisis is all the government's fault. You've heard the spiel: if it hadn't been for Fannie and Freddie's urging, subprime would never have existed, and so on.

According to the *Journal* article, Dodd has already heard from—guess who?—Winters and Holloway urging that he withdraw the penalty clause.

Certainly no one at STST is sweating it—not according to Lucia, who I ran into at a function at the Metropolitan Museum. She's prepared to wager good money that by the time the Dodd-Frank bill approaches becoming law, sometime in the twenty-second century at the rate it's being fiddled with and bent out of shape by K Street, etc., the bonuses will have been cashed and spent.

## MARCH 15, 2009

Beware the Ides of March!

Whoever said that first certainly got it right.

Last Monday, both the Dow and the S&P touched lows not seen since the dot-com bust. This has not proved beneficial to Wall Street morale. STST suffered a mini-collapse to the mid-'70s, although the shares are still nicely up from last September.

On top of this, Washington chose yesterday to reveal at long last that it had made STST whole on its GIG swaps. Now the firm really is everyone's whipping boy of preference, a kind of two-word synecdoche for all that's rotten about Wall Street. The media have spiced their accounts of the GIG deal with words like "favoritism," "graft," "backdoor rescue," "Washington–Wall Street revolving door," and the like. Uncle Sam's secrecy on these matters is made out to be a capital markets version of Abu Ghraib. Even Fox News, which Lucia practically owns, is having a tough time lipsticking this pig.

The Fed's taking the position that this segment of the bailout was essential, and that as a matter of comity it was legally obligatory for them to include STST in a package that mainly benefited overseas banks.

Lucia utterly discounts the likelihood of Joe Sixpack reacting to this news and reaching for his pitchfork, because a great deal of thought and money has gone into making sure that Joe S. doesn't really understand what derivatives are. What he probably does understand is the pink slip and foreclosure notice laid out on his kitchen table. For these he'll blame Washington, not Wall Street.

It really is amazing how much Wall Street gets away with, considering how idioticallyh suicidal they can be. Take the following e-mail that a usually discreet white-shoe lawyer showed me. Dating from last year, it was addressed to GIG's top executive echelon by a high-level member of the company's legal staff. It read: "In order to make only the disclosure that the Fed wants us to make we need to have a reasonable basis for believing and arguing to the SEC that the information that we are seeking to protect is not already publicly available."

"Only the disclosure the Fed wants us to make"! Are these people stark, raving nuts?

Here's what's worrying Lucia now: because STST seems to have emerged from the crisis relatively unscathed while Citi and BofA and the rest of them are staggering around like lamppost drunks under the weight of hundreds of billions of bad paper, people are starting to say that STST must have been crooked. How else could they be in good shape while all the rest are damn near dead? people will ask. The answer's obvious: they had to have cheated.

## MARCH 18, 2009

While flipping channels after lunch, I happened on CNN, and there was Senator Dodd lamenting that "special interests" have neatly excised the restriction on executive bonuses from the financial reform bill that he and Rep. Barney Frank will be sponsoring, and have replaced this proscription with language practically demanding that these bonuses be paid, even to the GIG fraudsters. The White House has said nothing on this subject, which represents a complete 180-degree turnabout on the part of the administration, given that it was just a fortnight ago that the president himself attacked the bonuses. I thought about getting hold of Orteig to say thanks and congratulations but decided not to. As they say on the Street, discretion is the better part of value.

# MARCH 22, 2009

Three days ago, the House passed a bill that imposes a 90 percent surtax on bonuses paid to executives of bailed-out firms. Wiser, cooler heads are now prevailing, I hear, as Wall Street comforts itself with the realization that there is little Washington can do that the Street cannot either evade or castrate. TARP was largely symbolic, anyway, and the banks in good shape that signed up simply to show themselves to be financial patriots will soon start paying back those forced investments and departing the program. Not that this will matter. TARP may be gone, but there remains no shortage of troughs.

Tonight, on *60 Minutes*, OG turned in a sterling performance. "We can't govern out of anger," he told Steve Kroft, which is pretty cool, considering that it was the anger of millions that got him elected.

I had a 7:00 p.m. meeting with Mankoff in his apartment that I wasn't looking forward to. I'd be bearing bad tidings: a program that Mankoff is personally funding at a leading music school has run seriously over budget and needs $50K pronto. On top of that, he'd spent the day in Washington—working Capitol Hill, I assumed—and having to kowtow to those idiots would put Pollyanna in a black mood. Not that the horizon is totally dark. The Dow Jones has closed up almost 500 points for the week, up 1,000 points for the month and back within hailing distance of 8,000, and that surely is something.

I was in for a surprise. When Mankoff opened the door himself, I could see that he was in as jolly a frame of mind as I could remember. Bluebirds perched on each shoulder merrily chirping away, chipmunks chortling at his feet, that sort of thing. He showed me a nice little Matisse he's trying out, one of those 1912 paintings that gets the Mediterranean sky just right, made me a drink, and then, without my having to ask, explained the reason for his upbeat mood. It has nothing to do with the market.

It seems that the Washington trip had nothing to do with Congress, but with a top secret meeting at the White House, to which Mankoff, Dimon, and the rest of last October's original TARP group had been personally summoned by OG. To a man they reckoned that what they'd feared since last fall had at last come to pass: with the country in the terrible shape it's in, the president and his people had decided to make good on his campaign committment to "fix" Wall Street. Mankoff told me he hadn't been that nervous since Tap Day at Yale.

When they were all seated, OG's opening remarks hadn't

soothed the heaving bosom. "My administration is the only thing between you and the pitchforks," the president said. He hadn't smiled when he said it. Here it comes, Mankoff had thought: Christmas in reverse. Instead of visions of sugarplums dancing in his head, what he pictured were excess profits taxes, limits on executive compensation, tough new capital controls.

But that isn't what came next. OG's a bit of a ham, and he was having fun playing all these big shots. He'd looked around the table, pausing to study each of his guests' nervous faces, and then, with a big grin, said, "You guys have an acute public relations problem that's turning into a political problem. And I want to help . . . I'm not here to go after you. I'm protecting you. I'm going to shield you from congressional and public anger."

With that, the smiles broke out around the table, and Mankoff swears there were even one or two loud sighs of relief. Then everyone put their serious faces back on, and listened gravely as OG delivered a few platitudes about thinking long-term and everyone pulling his oar and the best interests of the country. Then it was time for cheese and crackers and for everyone to have their picture taken with the president before he had to leave for another meeting. Winters and Holloway came in, along with Orteig, and worked the room pretty effectively, and made everyone feel that their interests were being properly looked after.

After the president departed, Orteig had drawn Mankoff and a couple of the other bigger hitters aside and asked for a return favor that shows just how clever a politician he is. Essentially, what he's asking from the Street is to launch a chorus of complaint about being roughly treated by the White House.

"We don't want anyone to get the idea that we're in bed with Wall Street," he told them, "and some blowback from you people will help dispel that misconception."

That's Orteig, I thought when Mankoff told me this: don't listen to what we say, watch what we do.

Wall Street is an amazing place; it must be the only line of work whose practitioners have zero moral perspective.

# APRIL 15, 2009

STST just released its first quarter results, a day earlier than expected, in order to keep the markets a bit off balance. Here's the good news: the market was looking for 1Q profit of $1.60 a share; the firm actually earned $3.30, more than double the consensus expectation. Most of the profit came from fixed-income trading, a fact STST was reluctantly required to disclose, and it will take the media a while, if they ever can, to figure out that a good part of this profit came from the "carry trade," from leveraging Uncle Sam's zero-cost TARP money into Treasury securities that pay between 1 percent and 3 percent. A neat double-dip into the taxpayers' pocket.

Of course, the deal I made on TARP with Spass has left STST free to trade as it pleases, while the weaker competition has to use its bailout money to paper over balance sheet cracks and fissures. BofA, for instance, is still sorting out the crap that came with the Countrywide acquisition—a deal that, in retrospect, seems to have involved between one and three minutes of serious analysis on the big bank's part. In addition, the situation at Merrill Lynch—which, to be fair, BofA was pretty much bludgeoned into buying by the Bush Treasury when Washington was in one of its "got to get this done before Asia opens on Monday" panic attacks—is said to be enough to cause a risk manager's hair to fall out. Citi and Morgan Stanley remain in resolution mode, which means fewer hands to share out the goodies, and goodies there are aplenty.

This doesn't mean that STST is entirely free and clear. Based on what Lucia tells me, old stuff keeps crawling back to nip at STST's ankles. There are nasty rumors about other dodgy overseas financial sleights-of-hand that STST took part in. Greece and Lybia, in particular. Whether any of this will actually cost STST is open to question. It never seems to.

Then there's the Month That Never Was. It took a while for the media to catch up and catch on, but not long ago, the *Times* ran a piece about how STST made December '08 vanish just like that, and others have followed up. I rather liked this phrase from a recent *Wall Street Journal* article on the subject: "Struthers Strauss provided as much detail as it could."

*As it could!* Though to be fair to the *Journal*, its story then went on to ask the right questions: "Struthers booked an unexpected profit in the first quarter; would that have been true if it had to count December?"

Finally, probably the largest and potentially most dangerous of the giant chickens on final approach, there's Protractor and Jimmy Polton. The news that Polton *personally* cleared $5 billion last year—that's *personally*, and that's *billion*—*mainly* shorting subprime has hardly elicited great gusts of approving admiration among the chatterati. That a significant part of this obscene profit derived from deals designed in collusion with STST to go snap, crackle, and pop overnight has not escaped general notice. Lucia's had an ominous tip from her Washington minstrelsy that the SEC, which has been looking for a way to land a shiner on Mankoff and his colleagues, thinks it's found gold in Protractor and is considering issuing STST with what's called a Wells Notice, a formal notification that an investigation is under way with a view to possible prosecution. No word as to how the SEC will treat Polton, but I'm damned if I can see how Uncle Sam can go after STST without looking at Polton as an indictable coconspirator.

The good news is that none of this concerns 1600 Pennsylvania Avenue, where it's suddenly all health care, all the time. I'm told that anyone who thinks Wall Street is a pack of blood-sucking rent extractors is in for a shock when Big Pharma sinks its fangs into whatever health plan gets passed through Congress—if one does. A guy who was in Bones with me is an executive VP at one of the major drug companies, and what's he's told us in the sanc-tuary of the tomb about that industry's plans for universal health care—should it pass, no sure thing—would make your hair stand up straight.

Yesterday, a Frenchman with one of those ten-barrel *Almanach de Gotha* names killed himself out of shame at losing close to a billion dollars of his friends' and clients' money with Bernie Madoff. I'm as surprised as I am saddened. I thought shame and disgrace, fearsome forces in my upbringing, had long since ceased to count in the way we live and behave now. That honor has become a moral non-starter. Our national emotional policy doesn't grant them official recognition. I can understand this poor guy; the social culture he was born into left him no choice. There was no way he could wave a wand and make the money stolen by Madoff reappear, and his own resources weren't sufficient to make his investors whole. All he had left was honor, which demanded that he do the right thing. I grieve for him, I grieve for his family. I grieve for all of us. It's always puzzled me how the noblesse oblige can't ever seem to grasp how dishonorably and innocently other men act, often for money.

There are times like this when I just don't get it. I need a vacation.

# MAY 6, 2009

Lucia passes along an interesting bit of gossip from a K Street source. There's a newcomer to Washington who is making a lot of noise and has the potential to be a real pain in the ass to the inner circles who decide who gets what and how much. She's named Elizabeth Warren, a Harvard Law professor who's been appointed to one of those congressional oversight panels set up to keep an eye on Uncle Sam's various giveaway programs. Apparently Warren isn't buying the numbers that Treasury is putting out about what a great investment of the people's money TARP and other bailouts have turned out to be, and won't shut up about it. She's apparently a person of principe.

The White House isn't happy with Warren's complaints, and so OG deputized Harley Winters, no less, to sit the lady down and instruct her in the ways of Washington and consensual democracy. She, of course, naturally told the media about this conversation, in which Winters advised her that to have any influence you need to be an insider, and to become an insider, you do not start by not pissing on those who are.

Now I'm sure the lesson was effectively put. To have Harley Winters fill you in on the niceties of crony capitalism and insiderness is like having Albert Einstein as your freshman physics teacher. But Warren wasn't buying, and now she's made him look like a self-important jackass and gained herself an enemy for life, although maybe she figures that over the long term, that won't matter. On this she may be right: if the past is any guide, the winds will shift and Winters will tack off on another heading.

# MAY 10, 2009

Jon Stewart has a great shtick about people who say one thing and do the opposite. I'm a big Stewart fan although I wonder sometimes whether he does more bad than good by turning everything into a joke. Nowadays, everything, even matters of urgency and importance, is converted into entertainment of one sort or another and thereby loses its heft and bite.

I wonder if Stewart and his writers will pick up on Merlin Gerrett's newly released first-quarter report. Thanks to big write-offs in its position in derivatives, Arrow Northumberland not only showed a loss for the period, but was stripped of its triple-A credit rating by all three big services, including Morton's, where Gerrett is the biggest stockholder. I guess hypocrisy can be a two-way street.

Lucia tells me that in the wake of Gerrett's first-quarter horror show he's signing up Washington types left and right to lobby Congress and the regulators to exempt certain vintages of derivatives from regulation. If this isn't crony capitalism, which Gerrett has also excoriated, what is?

## MAY 20, 2009

Over drinks today at San Calisto, I happened to observe that the Murdoch empire, notably Fox News, the *New York Post* and *The Wall Street Journal*, seemed to be on OG's case big time. What is that all about? This is not a president you'd normally feel sorry for, but I wonder about the hard treatment he's getting from Murdoch's minions. In business, Murdoch adheres closely to the "You put up and I'll shut up" formula, so one has to wonder what he wants. The thing is, there's not much left in this country that Murdoch's wanted that he hasn't already gotten. So how come when you turn on Fox News, the first thing you hear nowadays, either from some blonde ditz, or from that prize asshole Sean Hannity (next to whom a cretin like Rush Limbaugh looks like a combination of Socrates, Gandhi, and Bismarck) is that the president is physically incapable of carrying out the duties of his office?

The guy has his shortcomings, and on the basis of what we've seen so far, his presidency isn't shaping up as one of the all-time greats, but there's stuff he's trying to do—health care, for example—that only Scrooge McDuck would begrudge. My job was to insulate Wall Street from prosecution and disgrace, and that seems to have worked, at least in the sense that the Bush administration's giveaway polices are being ably defended by the Winters-Holloway cohort. But there's a lot else wrong with this country and the world that could stand a bit of fixing—and not the kind of fixing I've been involved with for the last two years.

In the course of the Murdoch discussion, the Ancient Mariner informed the table that his son-in-law, a lawyer with an important Los Angeles firm, says that Murdoch was himself inclined to go easy on OG. After all, Murdoch was asshole buddies with the Clintons and Tony Blair; basically, he likes to be on the winning side, no matter where on the ideological spectrum that happens to be located at a given time. It turns out, however, that when Murdoch passed the "lay off" word along to Roger Ailes, the Falstaffian character who runs Fox News, Ailes's massive jowls quivered so violently with rage that the building shook, and he threatened to quit. Naturally the Dirty Digger (as the English satirical magazine Private Eye calls Murdoch) backed down, since the latest ratings indicate that one person in four gets their news from Fox, and Fox, period.

That's not surprising. We're living in an era that's made a religion out of self-expression, and the Internet has provided a platform for every nutjob out there—someone recently joked that "the Internet has given millions of people with nothing to say a place to say it." So Fox has had no trouble finding a huge audience for its weird ideology.

How ironic it would be, I thought, as I walked home later, if in some strange, counterintuitive way, OG should end up being the catalyst for a racism-tinged, crypto-fascist Big Money takeover of this country. When I agreed to do this job for Mankoff, this was not something I expected to be part of. Did I help the progressive element in this country vote for its own doom? Oy!

# JUNE 20, 2009

STST stock is back up to 143. "Oh joy, oh rapture!" resounds through the marble halls.

Granted, the firm is showing solid fundamentals, but it's not hurting matters that the Fed's printing presses are driving the equity markets upward.

Meanwhile, the great game continues. Last Wednesday, June 17, STST announced it was paying back the $10 billion of TARP money Treasury "forced" them to take just eight months ago. It was naturally implied by the MSNBC end of the media spectrum that STST's ability to repay was the result of sinister if not outright crooked doings, like using dirty money from the GIG swaps buyout. On Fox, it was reported as good guys doing the right and honorable thing—and looking out for the taxpayer.

And the sea rolls on, as Melville says.

# JULY 4, 2009

Lucia's ready to slit her wrists.

About the worst thing that can happen in PR is when someone comes up with a derisory nickname for a client company. Once it gains traction, it's like being squeezed to death by a boa constrictor or eaten slowly by a Great White. There's no escape.

Such a fate has now befallen STST. Marina Hochster, the muckraking journalist, has hung the tag "TARPworm" on them in a piece in a popular magazine. The article is entitled "A Monster Parasite." In less than a fortnight, it's already racked up ten million hits, and I'm told that the magazine has gone back for a million-copy second press run.

Here's how Hochster's article begins: *"America's vital financial organs have been invaded by a rapacious, bloodsucking parasite called the TARPworm, also known as Struthers Strauss."* On the facing page is a cartoon of a giant faceless creature, something like an elongated slug, but with stubby tentacles and gaping suckers. Its surface is covered with the symbol "$T$T.," and it's coiled around a clump of cartoonish buildings marked "Congress," "Federal Reserve," "Treasury," "GIG," "White House." The caption? "Meet the TARPworm."

The article accuses STST of being the main perpetrator and profiteer in every bubble and other untoward episode in the capital markets since its founding: the '29 Crash, the merger/conglomerate craze of the late '60s, the 2000 tech bubble, the Fannie-Freddie housing finance scams, the securitization game in subprime and elsewhere, you name it.

Following this bill of particulars, Hochster wonders why everything has seemed to break STST's way in the current crisis, including the GIG make-whole. In particular, she takes a hard look at

Protractor and the obviously collusive (quote unquote) Polton deals, (crediting Allen Sloan's 2007 *Fortune* article) and wonders why Uncle Sam has never lowered the boom there.

It's a savage piece of work. There's no doubt the lady's done her research, and knows what she's looking for and looking at; she knows which files to probe, what numbers to call, what a between-the-lines perusal of financial statements can reveal—such as that STST only paid $14 million in cash taxes on 2008 profits of over $12 billion. This is not the sort of factoid likely to inspire good feelings in a debt-drained, overtaxed electorate.

According to the piece, STST long ago developed a template by which it has engineered one lucrative boom-bust cycle after another. Here's how Hochster describes it:

> The formula is relatively simple: the TARPworm positions itself in the middle of a speculative bubble, selling investments it knows are crap. Then it hoovers up vast sums from the middle and lower floors of society with the aid of a crippled and corrupt state that allows it to rewrite the rules in exchange for the relative pennies the bank throws at political patronage. Finally, when it all goes bust, leaving millions of ordinary people broke and unemployed, the TARPworm devours hundreds of millions of other people's money to repair the damage it wrought. And then it begins the entire process over again.

Frankly, I think Hochster overstates her case. There's another side to the story, as I've come to realize. Opportunistic firms like STST, who get it right fairly regularly, do a hell of a lot less *lasting* damage to the economy and the taxpayer than the clowns who get it wrong—either accidentally or on purpose. It wasn't STST who put Bear Stearns down the tubes, or GIG or Lehman or Countrywide or Washington Mutual, or flew Merrill Lynch into a mountain, or messed up Fannie and Freddie; it was the idiots, incompetents, and fraudsters that ran those outfits. And while we're at it, how about GM and the auto companies, or GE, both of which have sucked up billions in bailout money?

Rational opportunism is STST's modus operandi. To paraphrase a nineteenth-century New York politiican, "They seen their opportunities—and they took 'em." They make their own good luck—as much as they can. But they also "mark to market" when no one else does, and they know what their risks are, and they understand that the only way to make very big money in this business is to cash in on the so-called inflection points, when anything can get sold, everything gets bought, and there's credit aplenty to grease the wheels. Read an article like Hochster's, and you'll come away thinking that STST was the only firm to profit from subprime securitization, the only firm to make money out of the bailout. That's just crap: off the top of my head, I can name a dozen players, starting with Jimmy Polton, who made more money shorting subprime than STST did, and are every bit as guilty of profiting off subprime as Mankoff, Rosenweis, and their minions.

Still, say "Struthers Strauss," and the knee-jerk response you get is "You mean the TARPworm?" The name drops from the ceiling like Groucho Marx's duck in that silly quiz show my old man liked to watch.

Around STST, of course, it's all Lucia's fault. She's the person in charge of image. How could she let this happen on her watch? She should have known about it—doesn't she have moles in all the important media?—and put a stop to it. She's done that before. I feel for her and wish there was something I could do to defend her, but I'm helpless.

Last Monday, Bernard Madoff was sentenced to 150 years in

the slammer. The consensus at San Calisto is that he should have been given a medal instead of a prison sentence for showing the world how easily fools and their money can be parted. As always, someone's going to profit. The fees and commissions some court appointee will be paid for cleaning up after Madoff should run into the tens of millions. Just think what Lehman must be worth to its liquidators. Billions, for sure.

## JULY 17, 2009

If Lucia's hitting the Tanqueray extra-hard these days, you can blame Marina Hochster. Wall Street stories now simply refer to the firm as the "TARPworm," as in "The TARPworm reported record Q3 earnings . . ." "The TARPworm's involvement in the scandals now roiling Europe . . ." "How much influence does the TARPworm have at the Fed . . ." "CFTC investigating TARPworm hijinks . . ." Et cetera, et cetera. I've even seen TARP redefined to stand for "TARPworm Armed Robbery Payoff" instead of its pompous official name.

# JULY 22, 2009

It just gets worse: STST has now been served with the Wells Notice people were afraid of. Now the firm is facing possible future prosecution by the SEC, not just a regulatory slap on the wrist. What's specifically under scrutiny is STST's role in Protractor.

There's a dispute with STST about how, when, and whether to disclose this. In Lucia's opinion, the Wells Notice is a big deal and should be promptly disclosed to the markets to show there's nothing to hide. Rosenweis is fighting the idea. He hates transparency and has gotten the firm's outside lawyers to affirm that merely receiving a Wells Notice about a puny few billion dollars isn't a material event, given the size of STST's balance sheet, and therefore it's up to STST to decide if and when it will tell the world. What I find difficult to understand is why *the SEC* doesn't tell the world, but apparently that's not the way things work nowadays. Mankoff will make the ultimate decision, of course, but I gather he's wavering.

This is odd. Mankoff is usually the most decisive person in the room, but Lucia reports that for the first time since she came to STST, he seems distracted. His edge dulled, his focus not keen. She worries that he might not be well. I've noticed the same thing. I don't think he's been as sharp as usual in our recent interchanges. He seems tired, impatient, overburdened. On the other hand, why shouldn't he? This has been a bitch of a stretch going all the way back to Bear Stearns, GIG, and Lehman, plus all the shuttling back and forth to Washington to answer the same sets of questions put to him by different congressional committees—and the shit just keeps raining down. Add it all up, and even a superman would start to feel the weight of the world.

There is one bright spot out there, although the size of a

pinhead compared to everything else that's going on. The House bill levying a 90 percent tax on bonuses paid to executives of bailed-out firms? Well, it has just plain vanished. Kidnapped in the course of the treacherous journey from House to Senate and hasn't been seen or heard from since. *Fortune* recently reported that once the media lost interest, so did the Hill, and that was that. Strange and discouraging are the workings of republican democracy.

# AUGUST 6, 2009

An interesting development, perhaps not unexpected. A source close to the White House tells Lucia that all is no longer hearts and flowers between Winters and Holloway. For whatever reason, Winters is now pushing for a stimulus that would put money in the hands of the people but Holloway remains the banks' guy, continuing to argue that every last nickel of bailout/stimulus money should go to Wall Street, and essentially without conditions.

You have to admire consistency. When he was involved in overseas banking and credit crises (Brazil, Argentina, Thailand, and so on), Holloway was "Mr. Tough Guy," arguing for all sorts of concessions by the debtor nations, but now that the crisis has gone domestic, with the palpable culprits being Holloway's chums at Citi and its ilk, it's free money for all, no questions asked.

Lucia's source tells her that Holloway is prevailing in most of these squabbles, thanks to OG's man-crush, and this is driving Winters batshit.

Talk about biting the hand that both feeds you and wields the whip.

And talk about being stupid.

OG came to Wall Street today to give a speech and no one turned up. At least none of the biggest hitters. Not Mankoff, not Dimon, and none of the CEOs of the other big banks, with the exception of Richard Parsons, whom Uncle Sam has installed as interim chairman of Citi. What OG got was a nondescript gaggle of hedge fund types, the usual government-in-exile panjandrums like Roger Altman and Pete Peterson, and a bunch of second-stringers who made it clear with their body language that even they had more important things on their plate and would rather have been somewhere else. When OG strode to the podium, he must have said to himself, "Here I am, the most powerful man in the world, and look at this sorry collection."

The president basically told his audience to clean up their own houses, or he'd do it for them. "You don't have to wait to put the bonuses of your senior executives up for a shareholder vote," he urged. "You don't have to wait for a law to overhaul your pay system so that folks are rewarded for long-term performance instead of short-term gains."

Same old, same old—and received as such.

According to Lucia, when he delivered that last bit, his audience cleared its collective throat and ostentatiously checked its collective BlackBerry. And when OG went on to say: "It is neither right nor responsible after what you've recovered with the help of your government to shirk your obligation to the goal of wider recovery, a more stable system, and a more broadly shared prosperity," the audience simply sat on its hands.

As Orteig said to me when he called later, they could at least have faked respect if not enthusiasm. As it is, OG left the building with what one can only imagine was a major case of the red ass. I'd have liked to be a fly on the wall when he got back to Washington and did the "how went the day" bit with his wife, whose favorite game is hardball and who's said to hate Wall Street.

Meanwhile, on the home front, STST has responded to the Wells Notice. The response document drafted and submitted by Arnold Braum's firm runs 49 pages and probably represents $5 million in hourly billings. The main thread of STST's defense is that the people who bought Protractor and similar deals were big boys totally capable of looking out for themselves and that STST was merely responding to the demands of the market and the perfectly legal requests of a good client—just as a responsible firm should.

Lucia and I had a good laugh over the phone when she read me the assertion by STST's lawyers that the SEC's theory of the firm's misconduct "relates exclusively to the role of Polton Partners, Inc.—now recognized as a heavy bettor against the subprime market but at the time a relatively unknown hedge-fund manager."

Bullshit.

Toward the end of the response comes something that Lucia says must have sent STST's founders spinning in their graves: the excuse that the firm was forced to do Protractor as a competitive necessity because others were doing it. Talk to the old boys at San Calisto and they'll tell you that Messrs. Strauss and Struthers were absolutely opposed to taking on a line of business simply because someone else was. Today, I guess you might say it's a case of every tub on someone else's bottom.

## SEPTEMBER 19, 2009

I spent a couple of incredibly boring hours last night plowing through a hard copy of STST's response to the SEC about Protractor. The boilerplate was beyond incomprehensible—but I understood enough to wonder about certain details. For instance, the response claims that in 2007 it wasn't generally known that Polton was shorting subprime and related securities and options. Well, I already knew about it back when I met Mankoff at Three Guys in February of that year, and if I did, real Street insiders must have known twice as much, twice as early.

None of the documentation I've read answers the question that's bugging me. Why isn't the SEC coming after Polton as a coconspirator? You'd think that if the regulators would have anyone in their sights, it would be Polton himself, given his centrality to every side of the deal—it's a trade that he thought up, and from which he made around $1 billion. Yet it appears he's being given a pass. How come?

I've asked Lucia about this, but she has no more knowledge than I do. She has other issues to cope with. For example, will the Protractor litigation have to be included in the STST annual report come next March? How much do stockholders need to know? Worst case, she tells me, they could end up paying $2 billion in penalties, an amount that is peanuts when you have a $900 billion balance sheet, and therefore, in the lawyers' opinion, probably isn't "material."

## OCTOBER 7, 2009

I went down to Washington last Saturday to see a fantastic exhibition of Venetian Renaissance sculpture, stuff that may not rank with Donatello and the Florentine big boys, but is wonderful nevertheless. It seemed to be a good occasion to catch up with Orteig, so we arranged to take a spy-novel stroll along the Mall.

He fed me some inside poop on how the administration is dealing with Citi. The big bank is no nearer being out of the woods than it was at the worst of last fall's crisis. The game that's being played is a high-finance, capital-markets version of "Let's Pretend." In this case, "Let's pretend that our balance sheet is stronger and cleaner than a year ago." This is probably why Citi stock is up some 50 percent off its lows, but then most finance stocks have had a tremendous rally. Hell, STST has nearly quadrupled off its bottom: it traded yesterday at $190.

If Citi's situation doesn't improve in the relatively near future, Orteig told me, the bank could be facing true nationalization along the auto industry model: the equity will be wiped out; the debt will be worked out, with the bank's creditors taking a massive haircut; and the really bad assets will go to the dumpster. Naturally, all parties want to avoid this, but it's going to take a great deal of imagination and a great deal of taxpayers' money.

Orteig says that the man in the Oval Office is all over his aides to come up with some kind of rhetorical ploy that will (a) make it look as though he's keenly determined to face up to the Citi problem, and thus deflect any charges of Wall Street favoritism; but (b) will simultaneously make clear that his hands are tied legally and so nothing can get done. I guess you'd call this having your cake and throwing it up, too.

If you ask me, reading between Orteig's lines, the only thing that'll be done about Citi will be to feed it more and more money. This hould qualify Holloway for a private-sector paycheck that should run into a neat eight digits per year when the time comes, plus book royalties. He may not equal the $100-plus million payoff from his Washington stint that former Treasury Secretary Robert Rubin has gotten, but he'll do just fine.

Meanwhile, people like Marina Hochster are loudly complaining that the White House is frittering away its political seed corn on its health-care legislation. The moral standards on which Big Pharma operates are every bit as negligible as Wall Street's, but are harder for journalists to run down. Keep this up and there may not be much of this great republic left to sell, but every little bit counts, right? That's how people get to be really rich: watch the pennies, and the billions will take care of themselves.

## OCTOBER 13, 2009

Today is a green-letter day in American history: it was exactly one year ago that Mankoff, along with Wall Street's other biggest shots, trooped down to Washington to have $135 billion of the taxpayers' money forced on them on giveaway terms. A decent portion of that largesse has since been largely repaid on a basis that Washington has persuaded the media to accept as having provided Uncle Sam with an annualized 25 percent return on his citizens' investment. According to a friend who understands accounting, the word "annualized" is a synonym for "bullshit." Still, why complain? STST stock is up over 40 percent this year.

Speaking of the TARPworm, I read recently that Marina Hochster is now engaged in background reporting on a long piece that will try to prove that Wall Street has staged nothing less than a coup d'état under the umbrella of the very administration that the voters in 2008 expected to clean up the mess and put the scoundrels in chains. What more proof does any thinking person need?

# NOVEMBER 4, 2009

I'm not exactly in the market for new friends, but yesterday in a bar I met a pretty interesting guy who may become one.

Here's the backstory. There's a Spanish movie I've had on my must-see list that's playing at the IFC Center, and as this was a rare free weekend, I arranged my Saturday to catch the midafternoon showing. As is my habit, I got to the box office two hours ahead of time to be sure of getting a ticket, figuring I could get a burger and a drink at the Greenwich Village Bistro around the corner.

I took a place at the bar and ordered a beer and a cheeseburger. As is also my habit, I checked out the guy on the next stool: a fellow about my age—I guessed—with an Asian cast to his features.

The book he was reading got my attention: John Le Carré's *The Honourable Schoolboy*. I'm a huge Le Carré fan, and this novel is one I particularly like, although it isn't as well known as *The Spy Who Came In from the Cold* or *Tinker Tailor*. It's even more complex and veiled than those novels are, which is probably why I like it.

"That's a great book," I said to him. "Too bad the BBC never adapted it."

Some people resent having their reading concentration broken into. This fellow didn't. He put the book to one side, took a contemplative sip of his dark beer, and smiled. "You have good taste," he said.

With that, we got to talking, the way men seated next to one another in bars do, and eventually introduced ourselves. His name is Arthur Han ("everyone calls me Artie"). He's a professor at John Jay College of Criminal Justice, where he teaches "Financial Forensics" and a seminar on fraud and other capital markets malefactions. He also consults on Wall Street, focusing on the

263

interaction of politics and markets; it turns out we have a few clients in common.

Somehow we got onto the subject of the corruption that seems to permeate every corner of American public and private life: everyone on the take, nothing that can't be bent or bought. Corruption in politics—the influence of bigger and bigger money—seems to be an obsession with Professor Han. A number of times, he brought up a lawsuit called *Citizens United* that the Supreme Court is deliberating, and then summarized the pros and cons as if I were a moot court. A decision is expected as early as the first quarter of next year. If the plaintiff is upheld, as Han tells it, corporations will be free to throw unlimited, unregulated amounts of money at political campaigns. And if that happens, he declared, you can write "finis" to representative democracy, which is running on vapors as it is.

"The Court's as corrupt as the rest of Washington," he declared. "People talk about 'regulatory capture' and 'legislative capture,' but they need to add 'judicial capture' to the list. It's the most dangerous of all in terms of what it can do to our democracy."

Artie doesn't think much of the present Court. He says that Roberts and Alito are like the Pacino and Duvall characters in *The Godfather*, capo and consigliere; Scalia is clearly certifiable; and the less said about Clarence Thomas, the better.

"What about Kennedy?" I asked. "Everyone says he's the swing vote, the make-or-break guy. What do you think of him?"

My new friend grinned. "You know what Kennedy is? He's every high school kid who figured out that the best way to get elected president of the student council is to kiss the ass of both the faculty and the captain of the football team. It's hard to imagine: that the fate of our system is entrusted to men like these. It's also interesting, and I think significant, that the troglodyte faction includes none of the women justices."

We shared a laugh at that. "Of course, nothing ever changes," he said next. "Corruption's as American as apple pie. Take a look at this. It dates from 1854."

He reached into his shoulder bag and pulled out a sheet of computer paper, which he let me keep:

Influences secretly urged under false and covert pretenses must necessarily operate deleteriously on legislative action, whether it be employed to obtain the passage of private or public acts. Bribes, in the shape of high contingent compensation, must necessarily lead to the use of improper means and the exercise of undue influence. Their necessary consequence is the demoralization of the agent who covenants for them; he is soon brought to believe that any means which will produce so beneficial a result to himself are "proper means," and that a share of these profits may have the same effect of quickening the perceptions and warming the zeal of influential or "careless" members in favor of his bill. The use of such means and such agents will have the effect to subject the state governments to the combined capital of wealthy corporations, and produce universal corruption, commencing with the representative and ending with the elector. Speculators in legislation, public and private, a compact corps of venal solicitors, vending their secret influences, will infest the capital of the Union and of every state, till corruption shall become the normal condition of the body politic, and it will be said of us as of Rome: *omne Romae venale.*
—Mr. Justice Grier, writing for the majority in the matter of *Marshall v. Baltimore & Ohio Railroad Company,* 57 U.S. (16 How.) 314 (1854)

Artie watched while I read it, then said, "what makes this especially fun is that a year or so later, Justice Grier was himself accused of accepting a bribe in a matter that came before the Court. Needless to say, he got off."

From that point on, until I had to hotfoot it out the door to make my movie, we engaged in a kind of serve-and-volley mutual deploration of the terrible state of affairs that America has become. Disgusting this, horrible that—and why have all these awful people ended up with all the money and most of the power? An obsession with making money must entail certain character flaws, we agreed.

But here's the problem. The more I found myself nodding in agreement—and I did agree, believe me—and the more vociferously I voiced my own disgust at how low the affairs of the nation had been brought, the more shamingly aware I became of that troubling inner disconnect I've spoken of already. There I was, with an absolutely straight face and all the sincerity of which I was capable, condemning corruption—the manipulation and distortion of government for monetary ends—while having been the perpetrator of perhaps the most massive and consequential fix in the whole stinking history of U.S. politics.

These were feelings I wasn't exactly keen to revisit, feelings I've generally managed to suppress. Now, talking to Artie Han, I found them returning more stingingly than ever. Up to now, I've sold myself on the proposition that the Wall Street patch I've caused to be protected is only a tiny, not very consequential piece of a vast reeking whole, and that I had nothing to do with the GOP in Congress pledging to obstruct *every single* measure that OG may proposed, or with holding health care hostage, or with threats to cut entitlements, or with the making of pointless war.

Anyway, I managed to put these thoughts to one side. When it came time for me to head for my movie, Han and I did the nice-to-have-met-you bit and agreed to meet again. We exchanged cards and coordinates. He lives in the West Village in a town-house he shares with a partner—my guess is he's gay, but who knows?—and a woman named Bianca Longstreth, a TV producer whose name I recognized from the credits at the end of a couple of Sunday night cable shows I regularly watch: spies, mysteries, and political hugger-mugger, interestingly cast, cleverly plotted, the writing sharp, literate, and relevant.

Han seemed to think she and I might hit it off and he said something about fixing us up, but people are always saying that to me. Still, you never know, do you, and he seemed like someone who's a good reader of people—just as I fancy I am—so I said I'd be delighted to meet her.

This will have to wait until next year, as Han's off to China this coming Wednesday to teach a course at a university in Shanghai. According to him, China is to corruption what Mecca is to Islam. He'll be back mid-January.

This morning I got an e-mail from him confirming our lunch date and also telling me to keep next March 21 free, because he and his housemates always give a party on the solstice to mark the end of winter. He adds that this would be the right kind of occasion to introduce me to Bianca Longstreth. I e-mailed back to say that I've put a hold on March 21, and that I looked forward to meeting Ms. Longstreth. *"Assuming I'm still alive,"* I added. The way life works nowadays, anything further than a week out seems to be tempting fate.

# NOVEMBER 17, 2009

After much press room fanfare, with the Attorney General behind him to one side, Winters and Holloway to the other—all three looking pious with hands clasped in front of them—OG announced the formation of the Financial Fraud Enforcement Task Force, which promises to deal forcefully with the Wall Street miscreants responsible for the crisis.

This brave new unit will operate within Justice, which means that any "enforcement" will have to be signed off on by Eliza Brewer, which in turn means there will be no meaningful enforcement. In other words, this "task force" is typical OG bullshit, claptrap to catch the groundlings (as was said in Shakespeare's time).

The in-the-know betting on the Street is that, come five years from now, the number of meaningful criminal prosecutions carried out by this lofty-sounding "task force" will be fewer than the fingers on one hand. We shall see. I look forward to hearing what my new friend Arthur Han thinks of this OG initiative. Not much, is my guess.

# NOVEMBER 18, 2009

The high spot of my morning was a long e-mail from Artie Han:

Chauncey: Greetings from Shanghai. Amazing city. Exhilarating and troubling at the same time. It was nice to meet you and have a chance to chat and I hope we can manage to keep in touch. I hope I didn't bore you with my focus on Wall Street psychopaths. I don't meet many laymen who are acquainted with Hare's famous checklist of the attributes of the psychopathic personality. A lot of fairly original research on the subject has been done by Professor Clive Boddy at the University of Nottingham in the UK, some of which I've tried to incorporate in my seminar on Capital Markets Control Fraud. Professor Boddy kindly sent me a draft of a paper on (tentative title) "The Corporate Psychopaths' Theory of the Global Financial Crisis" that he expects to publish early next year in the *Journal of Business Ethics.* Here's a sample—I hope you find it interesting:

... corporate collapses have gathered pace in recent years, especially in the western world, and have culminated in the Global Financial Crisis that we are now in. In watching these events unfold it often appears that the senior directors involved walk away with a clean conscience and huge amounts of money. Further, they seem to be unaffected by the corporate collapses they have created. They present themselves as glibly unbothered by the chaos around them, unconcerned about those who have lost their jobs, savings, and investments, and as lacking any regrets about what they have done.

They cheerfully lie about their involvement in events, are very persuasive in blaming others for what has happened and have no doubts about their own continued worth and value. They are happy to walk away from the economic disaster that they have managed to bring about, with huge payoffs and with new roles advising governments how to prevent such economic disasters.

Many of these people display several of the characteristics of psychopaths and some of them are undoubtedly true psychopaths. Psychopaths are the 1 percent of people who have no conscience or empathy and who do not care for anyone other than themselves.

Han ends his e-mail with the following: "Don't forget to keep March 21, 2010, open. I told Bianca a little about you, and I can fairly say she seemed vaguely interested, which isn't generally the case. She's run through most of the men in Hollywood and a goodly percentage of those elsewhere. Best wishes for all the holidays—AH."

A troubling day. Here's the story. A friend of mine, a curator at the Clark Museum in Williamstown, came down to lecture at the Met, and we had lunch in the museum's fancy restaurant. The food's not bad, even if you do pay for a *soufflé* approximately what the museum itself pays for a Rembrandt.

During lunch, Iona and I chattered merrily about cabbages and kings, until over coffee I mentioned that I haven't heard from the Hastingses, the couple I always stay with over New Year's. Usually, by now, I have that invitation all buttoned up. I expressed concern that either Rex or Millie Hastings might be ill.

Iona put down her cup. "My God," she said, "you haven't heard?"

"Heard what? Don't tell me . . ."

"Nothing like that. No one's sick. It's worse than that—at least as far as some of us are concerned."

Then she went on to tell me a sad story about how Rex had been talked into a no-risk sure thing by "his man" at Merrill Lynch. It's like stealing money, he'd been told. And so it had turned out— only in the wrong direction. Rex had literally bet the farm. Money had been borrowed to double down, stocks Millie had inherited from her father were sold, a second mortgage was taken out on the Hancock house. Then the margin calls started to come in, and finally the issue defaulted.

"And now the bank has foreclosed on the farm," she finished.

"Rex has a lot of friends up there," I said. "Surely he can work his way around that with the bank. Doesn't his wife have money?"

"We all thought that, but apparently not. As for the bank, they say they're out of the picture. They sold Rex's mortgage to some Wall Street firm that stuck it into one of those big pools and sold *that* to some bank in Tasmania. It's supposed to be serviced by some firm in Florida but nobody *there* seems to know anything."

"Are you telling me they're broke?"

"Stone-cold. Rex has his salary from Williams, of course," Iona continued. "And Millie does have a small trust from an aunt that couldn't be touched. But they have a daughter at medical school at Penn and a son at Michigan Law, and now all this debt . . . well, I don't have to tell you . . ."

She paused, presumably to contemplate the wreckage of our friends' lives, then continued: "They've put the house on the market—and, of course, it's probably worth half what it was two years ago—and are looking for something to rent. The children can refinance with student loans, I gather. It's so sad. Why is it always the good and decent and prudent who get torn to pieces by these things? Why aren't the crooks who came up with these investments, quote unquote, in jail? That was one reason we all voted for the president."

There was a lot I could have said to that. Prudent people don't buy CDOs and other stuff with asserted alchemical powers. Prudent people don't bend an ear to the blandishments of stockbrokers posing as "wealth managers." Prudent people take out only one mortgage, and in amounts not exceeding fifty percent of the value of the property. Prudence assumes the worst to be possible, if not likely.

But prudence and decency aren't synonymous. Some of the most prudent people I know are sharks, and some of the most decent people I know can be downright reckless; just look at Rex Hastings. Decent people reject the notion that others don't give a damn about them, are just using them to make money or gain social acceptance. I thought about the people I see every time I go down to STST, who would soon be collecting bonuses that would buy Rex and Millie a dozen houses, and for doing what?

For persuading German banks to buy the Polton deals? For soft-soaping the guileless New Zealanders who went bust thanks to Wolverine? These are buyers who are paid to be prudent. The trouble is, not enough people understand that prudence needs to incorporate a healthy measure of flat-out mistrust—especially when it comes to Wall Street.

So I said nothing. Iona, meanwhile, was just getting started, and I couldn't tell if she was simply venting, or because she had me in her sights.

"It isn't just Rex and Millie, of course. Half the people I know seem to have bought these securities—or worse. This man from Merrill cast a wide net. And the ripples have spread much, much further. Do you know a terrible man named Harley Winters?"

"Of course I've heard of him. Who hasn't? Sitteth on the right hand of the Almighty down in D.C., right?"

She nodded. "Well, he got the ear of one of the important trustees of a foundation I'm in touch with, and persuaded him to put a big piece of the operating endowment into something called a 'swap,' and it's lost them close to $100 million. They've had to cancel programs, cut fellowships and reduce benefits. You know that Palissy exhibition I've been working on with them for two years?"

"Of course."

"It's canceled. You should walk around our village. Businesses that have thrived in the town since World War II have had to close. That nice shoe store, for example. For the first time I can remember, people I know are using food stamps in the markets. It's horribly embarrassing for all concerned. You see what's going on, and you come to *hate* Wall Street. I'm surprised none of these bankers have been murdered."

This made me feel truly guilty—for perhaps the first time. These were people whom I knew—whose lives I knew—who had been hospitable and generous to me.

"It's really sad," Iona was saying. "Christmas is going to be awful. Everyone's depressed and angry and hardly in a festive mood. A whole way of life has collapsed around our heads, and people need to sort out their lives before they can begin to go on with them. I can tell you my own circumstances aren't what they were, but fortunately there's Mother—but even she's complaining that her bonds aren't doing as well as the bank told her they would."

Still, if you look at the situation with a clear eye, Rex Hastings has no one but himself and his "wealth manager" to blame for the financial mess he's in. But who has the luxury of clarity these days?

They say if you take the king's shilling, you're the king's man. So where does that leave me? I feel like a stiff drink might help. No wonder people become alcoholics.

## DECEMBER 13, 2009

The sleeping dragon has finally rolled over and opened one eye. Dodd-Frank has reached the Hill for markup.

It's a process that shouldn't take more than a decade. Wall Street will see to it that if and when Dodd-Frank passes, it will consist of several thousand impenetrable pages of bothersome but essentially toothless regulation. And that will only be a first step. Hundreds, more likely thousands, of administrative implementations (how the damn thing will actually function; who will have the power to do what to whom; and how; and when) will have to be written and incorporated into law, and that is when Wall Street will set its K Street wolves on the fold. The carnage should be terrifying.

# DECEMBER 23, 2009

Lucia reports that STST is a graveyard. Everyone's tired. No one above a certain pay grade is in the office; they're out spending their estimated bonuses (which are still paid before the actual trades pay off, so why shouldn't they spend them lest someone try to take them back?). This means good news for local Ferrari dealers, Hamptons real estate agents, people who sell $25,000 wristwatches and $100,000 earrings and $1,000/ounce caviar. Bonus time also activates the pheromones, and you can bet that in $500-an-afternoon hotel suites up and down Manhattan, comely young persons ranging from the crème de la crème of pole dancers to clients' "executive assistants" to junior analysts with degrees in English from Sarah Lawrence are celebrating the jolly season with their bosses.

The only sign of austerity at STST is Mankoff's ban—over Rosenweis's strong objections—on Christmas parties. Official STST Christmas parties, that is. Anyone is free to use his own dime to hire a private room at La Grenouille or Per Se or the skating rink at Rockefeller Center and haul in buckets of Veuve Cliquot and all the foie gras you can swallow. Just as long as it doesn't appear in Page Six or New York Social Diary. Caterers' people have eyes and ears, and have been known to sell what they've seen and heard to the media.

Publicity other than that disseminated by Lucia and her troops is now anathema at STST. No freelancing, no talking to journalists without prior permission. The less the public grasps how well the firm is doing while the rest of the economy is down in the dumps, the better for all.

By noon today, I had got through whatever was on my desk and brought my calendar and to-do list up to date, so I thought I'd risk the wild streets to finish my shopping. On the way out, I decided to peek in and see if anyone at San Calisto was around. Not that my expectations were high. Most of the old boys decamp for the Christmas holidays to sunnier places—Florida, the Caribbean, Arizona—returning to the city after New Year's for a brief spell of portfolio rebalancing before heading back to the sun or the slopes for the balance of the winter.

The Ancient Mariner was alone at the table where the old boys gather for drinks. He was engrossed in a thick book while he picked at a plate of cheese. I greeted him and asked what he was reading.

"It's this new history of the Morgan bank. Absolutely first-rate. Listen to this. It's from the summer of 1932. Roosevelt's running for president and he gets a letter from Russell Leffingwell, an important Morgan partner and a terrible busybody-about-Washington. Leffingwell starts out by pleading—and I quote—

"'You and I know that we cannot cure the present deflation and depression by punishing the villains, real or imaginary, of the first postwar decade, and that when it comes down to the day of reckoning nobody gets very far with all this prohibition and regulation stuff.'

"To which FDR replies:

"'I wish we could get from the bankers themselves an admission that in the 1927 to 1929 period there were grave abuses and that the bankers themselves now support wholeheartedly methods to prevent recurrence thereof. Can't bankers see their own advantage in such a course?'

"And then Leffingwell again: 'The bankers were not in fact responsible for 1927 to 1929 and the politicians were. Why then should the bankers make a false confession?'"

He put the book down and beamed at me triumphantly. "Who says history doesn't repeat itself?"

"Amazing," I said. We chatted briefly, and then I made my escape just before he launched into what I was certain would be a book-length discourse on the Penn Central collapse of the late '60s. As I waited for the elevator, my mind shifted to other matters, and my thoughts weren't happy ones. I was thinking about old times and past New Years in the Berkshires, perhaps never to come again. Other reflections on life's shouldn't-haves and might-have-beens crowded in.

There are days when life's no fun, no fun at all.

# DECEMBER 24, 2009

Usually I'm out and about on Christmas Eve, dropping in here and there on families who like to offer cheer to lost souls. This year I decided to stay in, have a few drinks and order in some Chinese, watch *A Christmas Carol* on DVD, and make an early night of it.

As I was going through a pile of mail, I happened across STST's 2009 Christmas keepsake, an elegantly printed, deckle-edged copy of the firm's fourteen commandments, which Lucia sent out to friends and clients. It's clearly intended to remind the world how virtuous an enterprise the TARPworm is, despite all the terrible things people say about it. I made myself a drink and read it through, all the way from "Our Clients Come First" to #14: "Integrity and Honesty Are at the Heart of Our Business."

It's hard to match up what I've observed firsthand at STST and the values propounded in its code of conduct. But what do I know? I'm among the unconverted, while STST's people believe themselves to be practicing a kind of religion. I wonder: before settling down to the day's affairs, do STSTers repeat the commandments to themselves, like nuns and holy men telling their rosary beads?

I wonder what kind of precepts Strauss would write today, now that his gentler, more gentlemanly Wall Street has given way to a tough, rough, callous, rent-seeking regime driven by computers that can do the numbers in milliseconds but conspicuously lack moral conviction or judgment. A Wall Street that has no place for gentlefolk or deals done on a handshake. If anyone's come up with an algorithm for fair play, I haven't heard of it.

And there I think I had better let the matter rest before I start thinking bad thoughts.

Merry Christmas!

STST opened 2009 at $84 and closed the year at $168. Wonderful performance, if you own the stock, handily besting the Dow Jones, which opened the year at around 9,000, sank to a low of around 6,500, and finished at 10,548.

I must say, this past week passed pretty quickly. I'd been dreading it; after all, it's been years since I passed New Year's in the city, but the Berkshires interlude is *fini*, so there you are.

I had planned to spend New Year's Eve alone, feeling sorry for myself, consoled with a special vodka and an even more special caviar a Moscow newspaper shipped over in the diplomatic pouch to Lucia, which she—generous soul!—passed on to me. But in the end the need for company prevailed, and I'm going to go along with some friends to a party that a Chelsea gallerist is throwing. He just sold a Jeff Koons "Diamond" (basically a Crackerjack favor blown up to industrial scale) for $20 million to a man who made a fortune marketing blow-dryers in Eastern Europe, so the champagne and nosh should be first-rate, and anyone who's anyone left in the city, which may or may not include anyone worth meeting, will be there. These days, one wants to be on the lookout for possible new clients more or less 24/7.

What have I done with my week? Well, for openers, I've caught up on some of the new and exciting stuff that Wall Street's getting up to now that they're once again confident that they can get away with anything.

The big news is so-called "HFT"—high-frequency trading. This is straight out of *Flash Gordon*, or a Kubrick movie. If you're one of those people who've been predicting that computers will take over the world, here's your proof. What we're talking about here are computers trading millions of shares per second or tiny fractions thereof—up, down, long, short, and sideways in search of infinitesimal splinters of profit. At these speeds, it's 100 percent algorithmic and electronic: all about beating the other guy's software and hardware.

I gather Mankoff is steering clear of high-frequency trading, even though the big concern is that HFT may not stay away from STST, in the sense of screwing up the execution prices of big orders.

Things certainly seem to have gone back to being too good too fast. I can't help thinking that one of these days, the computers are going to go apeshit in response to some trading asymmetry and produce a 1987-size up-or-down spike in a single session. This will represent a whole new set of opportunities for Washington to come down on Wall Street's head and write new "reform" legislation, which will only end up leaving "lay" investors worse off once K Street gets through modifying it.

In my view, getting rid of the human element in stock trading can only lead to the retreat of the human element from investing, and this will be a very bad thing. HFT has nothing to do with judgment, or value, or how a business is run, or what its prospects are, and the people who consider such factors important—the people who have been the backbone of this business for two hundred years—are going to shy away from markets dominated by Wall Street versions of R2-D2 and look elsewhere. And then?

So much for Chauncey's adventures in the magic world of high-finance high-tech. The New Year will bring new challenges. I expect to be more than unequal to them.

So: Happy New Year! And party on!

# JANUARY 1, 2010

It seems odd to look out the window on New Year's morning and not see snowy Berkshire fields backed by gentle forested slopes; not to be aware of the small warm sounds of a country household gradually coming to life, the smell of coffee, the dogs snuffling at my bedroom door, anxious to get going; the general quiet. For most of my life, I've been away from home on New Year's Day. Every year when I was growing up, Pop would take me south after Christmas to visit his old Groton roommates in places like Hobe Sound, Florida, and Aiken, South Carolina, both bastions of the WASP ancien régime.

Pop was everyone's dream houseguest: funny, up for whatever the "it" of the moment was, considerate, accepting of the house rules, good with the help, a generous tipper, always ready to make a partner at tennis or golf or the fox-trot, a fourth at bridge, an object of derision at charades. There were a lot of ways he mentored me, but none more effectively than in the business—perhaps it's an art—of houseguesting.

I had scant hope for the New Year's Eve party to which I got myself taken last night, and my expectation was right on the money. Same old, same old. Shrill, desperate, too much to eat, too much to drink, everyone talking a quarter note too fast and a semiquaver too high, most of the company worrying about their finances.

I was home by 1:00 a.m., where I had a good old-fashioned "Lonely Guy" welcome to 2010: a taste of almost-flat champagne and a few last spoonfuls of Lucia's caviar, and it was lights-out before 2:00 a.m. Too bad the evening was a bust, because right now, I'd like a little zip in my life. Frankly, I feel pretty lonely these days. I find myself rushing back to the apartment to get at this diary, which itself has become a force for solitude. I thought about getting a cat (unlike dogs, they don't have to be walked), but cats have unacceptable ideas about who's boss.

Funny: it used to be that I couldn't wait for tomorrow; now there are times when I turn the light out and hope the next day won't come. Not suicidally, you understand—just in the sense that maybe it would be kind of nice if everything just went . . . poof.

It's not that I don't have a lot of friends—I do—and not that my weekends aren't busy—if I want them to be, they are—or that I lack for social and sexual opportunities—I don't. But something's missing.

I need to address this hole in my life. My old man believed that every New Year should start with an unflinching personal review. A look back and a look ahead. No matter where we were, no matter how bibulous and late the evening before had been, he'd rise promptly at eight on New Year's morning, breakfast according to the dictates of his hosts, and then carry a yellow notepad and a third cup of coffee off to some secluded part of the house he was staying in and make a list of what to deal with in the coming year. There would be stuff left over from the year just ended that needed follow-up; more importantly there would be warning signs.

He was always after me to do a review of my own. It didn't take all that long, he'd urge, pointing out that he was invariably finished by the first Bloody Mary call and the first college bowl game on TV. But I'd resist, it just wasn't my style—when it comes to introspection and self-examination, I prefer to work in the moment.

But for whatever reason—my guess is that it has to do with being in New York, and not in some bucolic setting far from the madding crowd and the wails of the world—I awoke this morning determined to do such a review. And so, having risen at a reasonable hour, I sat down with a cup of coffee and reread what I've put in this diary going back to the very first entry, almost three years

283

ago, when Mankoff summoned me to breakfast at Three Guys to propose that I fix the 2008 presidential election.

More and more, as time has moved on, and we enter our fourth year together, Gentle Reader, I worry that I'm starting to set down too much about how I feel, what my reactions are. Editorializing mixed in with the news, if you will. Hard to tell where one ends and the other begins. I seem to talk an awful lot about my old man. The truth is that I miss him. There are times when I wish he was still around to tell me what to do, how to react. My San Calisto chums make up for some of that, but not enough. I'm very wary of turning them into surrogate fathers; they're just good, wise friends who happen to be old men. What's that line at the very end of *Lear*: "We that are young shall never see so much, nor live so long"?

I must say that I'm struck by my own moral inconsistency. One day I'm this, the next I'm that: like a little kid, I don't seem to know what I want. I worry that all the wheeling and dealing that surrounds me might be contagious. I fear I've turned out to be the sort of person that my father, that Groton, that Yale all tried to ensure that I would never become.

Is there such a thing as a moral vocation? If you went to Groton, you were certainly taught to think so. How much and for how long should we be bound by what we learned in the classroom or at chapel? Every day, I find it harder and harder to rationalize why I acceded so readily to Mankoff. Why I went for it so quickly, so thoughtlessly. Did I let myself get too much in the moment, as the saying goes? I realize that Mankoff casts a kind of spell on me. He was my senior at Bones; my commander in the CIA; my mentor and sponsor in the world I've tried to make for myself; in a way, he created the professional Chauncey. How could I have turned him down?

And yet . . . and yet . . .

I can't get my lunch last fall with my Williamstown friend

out of my mind. When Mankoff approached me, I never really appreciated the extent of the damage this crisis would cause among ordinary people. The lure of the game was too compelling—the old CIA stuff, all that. The sort of people I care about have had their lives wrecked, while the sort I tend to despise are better off than ever. There's something hideous and ugly about that state of affairs, and in a way I suppose I'm fractionally responsible.

So how guilty should I feel?

Not as much as many, more than some. I tell myself that most people on the Street or in Washington have euthanized the better angels of their nature, while I have merely anesthetized mine. So what happens when virtue awakes?

There's no knowing how all of this is going to end up. Maybe things will work out; maybe there'll be blood in the streets.

On which jolly note I'll close.

# JANUARY 4, 2010

Toward the end of the day, Lucia called to ask whether I'd be free for a New Year's drink. We met at P.J. Clarke's in the World Financial Center, a few blocks west of STST's new headquarters. She sounded pretty fraught.

I figured she had office drama on her mind, probably some new Rosenweis offense she needed to vent about. At least she's put her concerns about Mankoff aside, reporting that the boss seems in reasonably good fettle, with few reminders of the slack performance he displayed at times late last year.

This has been a tough two months for Lucia. The firm is taking fire from all quadrants and it's her responsibility to mount both defense and counterattack, working from here and from her Washington hotel. And that's just on the business end of her life. Who knows what's happening on the home front? I get the definite feeling that all's not hunky-dory on West 72nd Street.

It turned out that what's especially driving her nuts now is a flap about aluminum warehouses for storing the stuff, not built of it.

"Aluminum warehouses?" I asked. "For a bank?"

It turns out that STST is buying a bunch of aluminum warehouses in the Midwest. Because of the way the market for the vital metal works, STST will be able to control day-to-day prices by limiting the amount of physical metal released into the market at a given time. In other words, monopoly pricing power, worthy of a Thomas Nast cartoon. Naturally, it will fall to Lucia and her people to explain to this transaction to the public, no easy task when the firm's in an unfortunate position: anything STST does that looks like the slightest departure from "normal" lines of business is regarded as criminal.

# JANUARY 9, 2010

Bad, sad news. The Warrior is dead. He was up in Vermont staying with a daughter and her family and went out alone for some cross-country skiing yesterday; bad idea when you're coming up on 90 and it's starting to get dark. The San Calisto consensus is that the old boy got the sort of end he would have wanted. Or, in the view of the Ancient Mariner, deserved: "The old fool! Who goes cross-country skiing at his age?"

His family is planning a memorial service in ten days—the usual: Upper East Side church, followed by a reception at a private club a couple blocks away—but if it were my call, I'd stage a Viking funeral, a flaming pyre floating down the East River.

It's hard to escape the feeling that the Warrior's death marks the last hurrah of another era, a whole other set of values. He would never have blown his own horn, but when he wasn't around, the San Calisto regulars used to boast that the Warrior was the only STST partner ever known to have turned down a client who wanted to take over an Ohio steel company. It was the sort of deal that promised huge fees and a lot of publicity, but the Warrior was concerned about what it might do to the target company's community—plants shut down, jobs eliminated. And he refused to handle. Another firm took on the assignment, booked the fat fees, and in due course the plants shut down and the jobs were eliminated, and Wall Street had claimed the life of another community. Well, he's gone now, and in time the others in San Calisto will follow, and then who will be left to light the way back into the past?

# JANUARY 19, 2010

The Warrior's memorial service was held at St. James's, the Madison Avenue church where my old man sent me to Sunday school, although he himself only darkened its pews for weddings and funerals.

The Warrior's decorations were arranged on the American flag draped over the coffin. On the cover of the order of service was an old photograph of the man—he must have been in his early twenties then—standing by the nose of a vintage jet on an airstrip that I reckoned must have been somewhere in Korea. Under the photograph was printed, simply: "Roger Farnsworth Garson, 1928–2010."

For the hour the service took, it was as if I'd been fed into a time warp, as if I'd been transported back into the world I grew up in. The hymns and readings were familiar. There were two eulogies, both touching sentiments and standards no longer much honored. When I left the church, it was with brimming eyes. Fortunately, I'd thought to bring a handkerchief.

The second eulogy was given by the Warrior's eldest son, a man in his fifties, a chaplain at the Air Force Academy, wearing a dog collar with his dress blues, a light-colonel's oak leaves on his shoulders. He spoke movingly about his father, and what he'd meant to his family, his schools, his comrades in arms, the philanthropies to which he'd devoted time and money, and the business world in which he'd made such a success and enjoyed such a fine reputation. And then he said that he wanted to read a passage that he had for some years imagined would fit his father's end, whenever that came. It turned out be the famous passage from Bunyan's *Pilgrim's Progress* about the death of Mr. Valiant-for-Truth. I had a housemaster at boarding school who read this passage to us at least once a term. As a boy, I always found it moving, but this time, in St. James's, read in a fine, practiced voice from the pulpit, it nearly tore me in half.

> When he understood (he was about to die), he called for his friends . . . and said, I am going to my Father's; and though with great difficulty I have got hither, yet now I do not repent me of all the trouble I have been at to arrive where I am. My sword I give to him that shall succeed me in my pilgrimage, and my courage and skill to him that can get it. My marks and scars I carry with me, to be a witness for me that I have fought His battles who will now be my rewarder. When the day that he must go hence was come, many accompanied him to the river-side, into which as he went, he said, "Death, where is thy sting?" And as he went down deeper, he said, "Grave, where is thy victory?" So he passed over, and all the trumpets sounded for him on the other side.

After that, the service was a bit of a blur. For a recessional hymn, instead of "Onward, Christian Soldiers," the organ roared to life with the familiar strains of the Air Force hymn, and with lusty ill-tuned voices and hardly a dry eye, we sent our revered friend off into the wild blue yonder.

After passing through the receiving line, I decided to make tracks. Walking to the subway, I checked my BlackBerry, and learned that OG made yet another speech today indicating a harder-line stance toward Wall Street.

Some things never change, do they?

# JANUARY 22, 2010

Yesterday the Supreme Court rendered its decision on the *Citizens United* case, the one that has Arthur Han in such a swivet. Basically, the Court has ruled exactly what Artie feared: that money is speech, and that corporations have the same legal standing as people and the same First Amendment rights of free speech. They can therefore make political contributions virtually without limit.

One hates to think of the rich idiots this decision will empower. There are a couple of upmarket thugs from the Midwest named Donald and Douglas Dreck who have been pouring a ton of inherited right-wing money into politics. *Citizens United* should have those two licking their lips.

Corruption should be harder work than this.

# FEBRUARY 15, 2010

Artie Han has returned from the Mysterious East, and we got together for lunch at Le Veau d'Or.

The place wasn't crowded. Three tables of "Olde New Yorke" types, a young couple billing and cooing in the back corner, an elderly man alone with a formidable martini at a banquette under the famous painting of a sleeping calf (*Le veau dort*. Get it?). That's something else that I like about the Veau; it's one of the few places in the city where one can comfortably dine by oneself.

Artie looked like he'd lost his best friend, as well as his parents and his dog. "I'm sorry about *Citizens United*," I said, patting him on the shoulder.

"No worse than I expected from this Court."

It seems that he has a new jurisprudential bone to gnaw on: ACA, which stands for "Affordable Care Act," the complex universal health-care plan on which, in my opinion, OG has pissed away a fair piece—if not most—of the political capital with which he came into office. Compared to ACA, the offering documents on Wall Street deals are models of transparency. Artie's read the legislation, all nine million pages, and worries that, as drafted, it contains a real Achilles' heel: four little words that some clever lawyer for the bad guys may seize on as a basis for judicial nullification.

"And those four words are?" I asked.

"Established by the state, quote unquote," he replied. He went on to explain, between bites of celery remoulade, the damage this phrase, literally applied, might do. I won't bore you with that. Suffice it to say that Artie sees sinister forces at work.

"It'd be easy," he said, "the way Washington works nowadays, to pay off a couple of staffers with drafting responsibility to sneak the four little words into the final version and see that they stay there."

For the balance of lunch, our conversation centered on the seminar course in corruption in American politics that Artie is teaching in the spring semester, centering on the work of a young Fordham professor with the astonishing name of Zephyr Teachout. She published some of her research in the *Cornell Law Journal* last year, and Artie says it's original and terrific. He's been in touch with Teachout, given her his notes to use for the book into which she's expanding her Cornell article, and hopes to get her to speak to his seminar. Of course, if Artie wants someone who understands corruption from the inside to address his class, maybe he should sign me up as a guest lecturer.

"It's really unbelievable what's going on in this country," Artie went on. "Although not surprising if you look at the record. You realize, don't you, Chauncey, that what we're seeing in this country's politics right now is the endgame of a slow-motion coup that started in 1971. I trust you're aware of the so-called Powell Memorandum?"

I shook my head. "Never heard of it."

Artie explained. Lewis Powell was a big-time corporate lawyer, principally for Big Tobacco, who wrote a memorandum to the U.S. Chamber of Commerce in 1971, advocating a forceful pushback on many fronts against the leftist radicalism that he saw as threatening to overthrow the free enterprise system: unions, college faculties, a wide range of do-good organizations, and northeastern and west coast congressional Democrats.

Powell's ideas took hold, principal among them the one that Reagan made gospel: that government is the enemy of democracy. As Artie puts it, "Powell can be considered the grandfather of our present deplorable condition of government by plutocracy."

He shook his head at this. "Funny," he said. "I often think he would be as dismayed as you and I are at how his grand scheme has turned out. Not long after Powell wrote his memorandum, Nixon appointed him to the Supreme Court, where he turned out to be surprisingly moderate."

"So what would you do about it if you were king?" I asked.

"There's only one solution."

"Which is?"

"Fight fire with fire. Someone with the resources and the willingness to take on, say, the Dreck brothers. Financial civil war, if you will, with *good* big money pitted against *bad* big money. Find someone who recognizes what people like the Drecks are doing to this country and is rich enough to go toe-to-toe and head-to-head with them."

"That's a lot of money to go up against," I commented. The recent *Forbes* list, after all, puts the Dreck brothers' combined net worth at $30-odd billion. So who do you send into the ring against that level of political purchasing power? Bill Gates or Merlin Gerrett? Neither is known to be political. George Soros and the mayor of New York seem likelier candidates.

Artie and I played a few rounds of "Fantasy Billionaires," and then it was time to go. He'll be busy with his new seminar, and I have to go to Seattle and Honolulu on client business, so we probably won't see each other until his party next month. I'm looking forward to it. I've read up on Bianca Longstreth, and I'm intrigued.

# FEBRUARY 16, 2010

Had to go over to STST this morning to see Mankoff about his Yale project. Lucia's back to worrying about him, so I was alert for symptoms of mental slippage, but he seemed OK. He told me that the word has gotten out that STST's 2009 bonuses, due to be paid out in a few weeks, will be right up there at pre-crash levels, so everyone at the firm is alight with joy. They'll be smiling in Gerrett country, too: with STST stock roaring along at $169, the warrants he extracted from Mankoff are a couple of billion dollars in the money.

Oh, and there's been an entertaining development. Rosenweis has gone all English on us. He's taken a flat in the hyper-exclusive West End apartment house called simply "Albany" (never but never "the Albany," except by low-rent ignoramuses who also say things like "We're staying at the Claridge," meaning Claridges, the famous Brook Street hotel). Lucia says it's tarted up as if Lady Bracknell were expected for tea at any moment, accoutered at vast expense with furniture from Mallett, a Munnings racing painting over the mantel, portraits of other peoples' ancestors and estates scattered throughout, and a proper central casting English butler. Just like a Ralph Lauren store, in other words.

He's taken up shooting: paid £200K for a matched pair of 1947 Purdey 12-bore shotguns hand-tooled for a belted earl, signed up for lessons at the Holland & Holland shooting school, and this coming August has "taken" a week at Biddick Hall, the fabled estate near Durham, which the cognoscenti consider about the best grouse shooting in the UK.

He's pestering Lucia to use her family connections to get him into White's, the paragon of London men's clubs on which the Weir is patterned. The next thing you know, he'll be asking Lucia if she can arrange a royal warrant. I can just see it: "By appointment to Her Majesty the Queen, purveyor of junk bonds."

When I asked how this unfortunate development had come about, it seems that over Martin Luther King weekend in Palm Beach, the Rosenweises hooked up with the Duke of Sunderland (known to his friends as "Woody," as in Marquess of Woodbury, His Grace's second title), the sort of fellow who appears at royal occasions draped in scarlet velvet and ermine and carrying a mace, or a rod which he uses to dowse for rich Americans with opulent guest rooms in Palm Beach and Newport and consulting fees and company directorships to dish out. Lucia says he's right out of P. G. Wodehouse and would be at home at the Drones Club.

So powerful is the infatuation that His Grace has become STST's first "house peer." Lucia was summoned to Rosenweis's office last week to meet the duke, and was instructed, "Woody here's going to be consulting to our International Advisory Board, opening the right doors in London, that sort of thing, and I've assured him of our full support."

"Just out of curiosity," I asked Lucia, "what *are* the right doors in London nowadays?" I hear from my UK contacts that an entire cottage industry has grown up to service the lifestyle requirements of Russian, Middle Eastern, and Chinese billionaires, selling powder-room-quality Dufy paintings at Cézanne prices and arranging choice tables at restaurants like the Ivy. No one, after all, pants after money with the desperate enthusiasm of the English. They're more avid for cash than the Clintons.

I wished Lucia good luck with His Grace. What else was there to say?

# MARCH 7, 2010

I'm still a couple of weeks away from meeting Bianca Longstreth, but she's been on my mind more than I care to admit.

I Googled her right after Artie told me about her, and on the basis of her looks alone, I'm interested. "Aristocratic" was the first adjective that lit up in my mind. She has what I think of as Lampedusa looks: smoldering yet refined, aloof yet passionate. Dark eyes, a great Italian nose, a very direct gaze. She's forty-six, just three years younger than me, and divides her time between Manhattan and Los Angeles. She and her twin brother Claudio (someone in the family clearly felt strongly about Shakespeare) run a TV/film production company called Gemelli (Italian for "twins"!). Its biggest hit so far has been *Bad People*, which, in its five seasons on HBO, garnered enough Emmys and Golden Globes to sink an aircraft carrier and gave birth to a couple of moderately successful spinoffs. They also wrote the script for a new animated version of *Wind in the Willows*, which was nominated for a major Oscar and won a few minor ones. In the last couple of years they've worked on everything from Cirque du Soleil to theme parks, and there seems to be more to come.

Why wouldn't I be intrigued by a great-looking woman, obviously smart and articulate, probably makes a lot of money, and knows everyone and (yes, this matters at this point) is past the child-bearing age? I searched around, and she seemed to come up empty on the emotional entanglements front. All good.

The Lonsgtreth name itself also rang a bell, and, thanks to the miracle of Google, I found my way to Marjorie Longstreth, a formidable woman whom I recall meeting at a reception some years ago at the Fogg Art Museum in Cambridge. It turned out that she was the mother of Bianca and Claudio. Her husband is Thayer

Longstreth, H'60, H'06 Hon., retired CEO of a trust company that got sold to Merrill Lynch in 2003.

He's obviously the real thing, Cabots-speak-only-to-God Boston, members in best standing of the old, true patriciate, with all its courtesies and noblesse oblige. Marjorie's a trustee emerita at the Fogg and Wellesley; he's served as an Overseer at Harvard. They have homes in Brookline and Maine, belong to the Somerset Club and The Country Club, hold important Back Bay trustee-ships and corporate and charitable boards. One of their ancestors was surely in the first boat to row ashore from the *Mayflower*.

By now, you've surely divined that I'm more than a bit of a snob when it comes to this sort of thing. All in all, these sound like my kind of people. A vanishing breed. March 21 can't come to soon.

# MARCH 16, 2010

I've spent far too much time over the last few days thinking about Bianca Longstreth, a woman I've never even met. It's a problem I have, this romantic fantasizing, and I have to be careful. If I let it get out of control, daydreaming can get me into trouble. It has before.

Still, I can't help but find this woman utterly intriguing. Does she have a boyfriend? Is she a lesbian, a spinster, too busy for love? Does she hate commitment? Google doesn't supply the answers. I suppose I could ask Artie, but I don't want to appear too anxious too soon.

It doesn't help that I'm not particularly busy right now. The cultural front is quiet, although a trustee of the Metropolitan Museum is pushing me hard to find funding for an exhibition of some dress designer's work. I've made clear my strongly held opinion that the best route to Parnassus isn't Seventh Avenue, and that the sensible course of action is to work Anna Wintour and her friends for the funding of couture shows, and to come see me when Raphael or Etruscan art or something serious is on the table. It's the same everywhere: everyone—museum, university, performance venue—wants big box office numbers, as if art were a suburban multiplex.

STST is keeping a low profile, waiting to see whether there's another shoe to drop in the SEC's investigation of the Protractor deal. I'll bet everyone upstairs and down at the firm wishes they'd never heard of Jimmy Polton, but of course, at the moment, there's quite a lot that Wall Street wishes it had never heard of. If it were me behind Mankoff's desk, I'd settle with the SEC now: pay a fine and be done with it. In most regulatory tiffs, first out is usually cheapest; so sayeth Scaramouche. Apart from the SEC and the

Senate hearings where STST has been singled out (along with Deutsche Bank) as the bad guy in securitization, Washington has treated Wall Street with a gossamer touch, despite all the smoke and mirrors being deployed from the bully pulpit. But maybe that won't go on forever.

## MARCH 22, 2010

Well, not to keep you in suspense, Gentle Reader, I've met Bianca, and she's incredible.

Terrific, fantastic, sexy, smart, and beautifully spoken. Just unbelievable. Why she isn't married to someone like George Clooney, I can't imagine. She's everything my imagination hoped she'd be, and more. On the basis of a hour's acquaintanceship in a roomful of chatty people, I can't say that I've fallen in love: it's just too early, and I know I'm capable of acting impetuously. As I've gotten older I've gotten more cautious where big feelings are concerned. I prefer the gradual simmer to the fast boil.

Can this turn into a relationship? Conjectural. If I'm looking for anyone, it's probably a person I can come home to (though she'd have to have her own place) and put my feet up with, not a busy producer who's in Copenhagen on Tuesday and Rio the day after that and committed to two weeks a month in L.A. I definitely want to see Bianca again, and she didn't seem wholly indifferent to me, to put it politely. She told me to call her "B—everyone else does," so that's what I'll call her.

But let's start from the beginning. Yesterday was a mildish day for this time of year, temperature in the mid-fifties, the city pretty much dried out from the savage nor'easter that a week earlier had dumped almost six inches of rain on us. I decided to walk uptown, reckoning that my usual pace (allowing for window-perusing and assorted dawdling, perhaps a stop along the way for a shot of Dutch courage) would get me to West 9th Street around 1:45, which struck me as about right for an event beginning at 1:00 p.m.

As I turned into the block on which stood the brownstone shared by Artie and his housemates, my watch reading 1:44 p.m., I saw him talking on the sidewalk to a tall woman in trousers and a black turtleneck. A limousine idled at the curb. She looked vaguely familiar, although from that distance, all I could make out was that she was broad-shouldered, with closely cropped dark hair. Before I got close enough to meet and greet, she embraced Artie, climbed into the waiting car and was off.

"Who was that you were talking to?" I asked. "She reminds me of someone."

He smiled. "You don't know her? Gosh, I must introduce you. That's Marina Hochster. You know—the journalist. She's an old friend of Bianca's. She's on her way to JFK to catch a plane to Frankfurt."

No wonder I'd thought I recognized her; I'd seen Hochster just a couple of weeks earlier on Jon Stewart.

Artie went on with his explanation. "Bianca and Marina grew up together in Maine, at Leeward Harbor, where the Longstreths have had a place for generations. Marina's a townie, but in those places that makes no difference—or didn't used to. The Hochster family owned the local boatyard for about a century—until a bunch of private-equity vultures got hold of it four or five years ago and wrecked it. That's a major reason she's got it in for Wall Street."

I knew about Leeward Harbor. Anyone who knows his way around the WASP world does. If you grew up in a certain style in Manhattan, or Boston, or Philadelphia, or Baltimore, or even as far west as Lake Forest or Grosse Pointe, you'll have known about places like Leeward Harbor, Hobe Sound and Delray, Fishers Island. The last redoubts of old money, by which I mean *old* money: family fortunes that date back to the Industrial Revolution. No Russians, oil despots, or private-equity types. I'd visited the place once, many years ago, when I was still at Yale and crewing on a friend's boat.

Artie continued with the Hochster family saga as we mounted the steps leading to his front door. "There was a whiz-kid who'd made about a jillion dollars in private equity and had built a gigantic house in Porpoise Point, which is Leeward's fancier twin across the bay. This upstart had bought one of Hochster's famous harbor cruisers, and he looked around and decided there was money to be made building boats for people like himself. He got his firm to put up most of the money and brought in a few rich summer types, including Bianca's uncle Walter Hardcastle."

"Walter Hardcastle is your housemate Bianca's uncle?"

"Why—you know Hardcastle?"

"Met him once. He's a bombastic old shit."

"So I hear. He's married to B's mother's sister, who I gather is sort of a ditz. Nothing like Marjorie, I can tell you. Anyway, he and some other private-equity sharks whom he brought in for the kill talked Marina's father into selling out. Sweet-talked the old man with words like 'synergy' and 'grow the business' and promised to keep everything as it was, only bigger and better. Marina told her father not to listen to them, but he drank the Kool-Aid, especially when they promised that he could continue to run the business, but now with millions in fresh capital to draw on. So he turned a deaf ear to his daughter and went ahead and did the deal. Do you want to hear the rest? It's pretty depressing."

I thought I probably knew what was about to come. These private-equity horror stories are all the same. But it would have been discourteous not to let Artie finish.

"The new owners started by paying themselves a huge dividend with money borrowed against the boatyard assets. Business dropped off a cliff in 2008, and they defaulted and the creditors closed the yard the next year. It was like cutting the heart out of Leeward, a century's worth of skill and goodwill thrown away just like *that*. And as you can well imagine, Hochster's was the largest employer in that part of the island. The machinery got sold to some people in Taiwan; Hardcastle and his cronies bought the physical site out of bankruptcy and are planning to put up a bunch of luxury condominium townhouses, quote unquote. And that's not the worst part."

"Which is?"

"It's that people in Leeward have blamed Marina as much as her father and treated her so badly that she's sworn never to set foot in her hometown again. Which means that she and Bianca can only connect off-island. Pretty pigheaded of Marina, if you ask me, but you know how these Down East types can be. *Captains Courageous* and all that. Well, here we are. Follow me."

It's a tall house, five floors with a small elevator. Artie's partner Hal Norden is one of the city's top decorators, and his operation takes up most of the ground floor, as well as the parlor floor: drafting tables, metal shelves filled with swatch books and the like, pinboards on the walls devoted to projects-in-progress, a small office for the accountant. The third floor is almost equally divided between the large room where the party was gathering and, in the rear, a loftlike, open-plan dining area-cum-kitchen.

Arthur and Hal share the next floor up, and Bianca's quarters take up on the entire top floor. It's a deep building, so we're talking close to 2,000 square feet. Bianca's living space consists of a combined bedroom-sitting room, a bathroom that would satisfy Cleopatra (along with a formidable array of walk-in closets), and, at the rear, looking over a small, not especially well-kept garden, a home office that looks like it could give NASA a run in the technology department. I wanted to dilly-dally and give myself a chance to examine her photographs and books, but Arthur hustled me right along. "Duty calls," he said. "Let's go down and find Her Majesty."

There were about twenty people in the drawing room. It was magnificent. Old New York, right out of Edith Wharton and William Dean Howells. Dark wood, bookshelves to the ceilings, rich velvet, the furniture of a pleasing amplitude and comfort.

"Come say hello to Hal." Arthur took me by the arm and led me toward his partner. "Hal, you should meet Chauncey Suydam. I've told you about him. He also consults for your good client Mr. Rosenweis's firm."

Hal looked just like the photos I'd seen on his website. He has a smile that had me reaching for the Ray-Bans, and is in tremendous physical shape; it took my right hand a full ten seconds to recover from shaking his.

I moved away—Artie had hustled off to chat up a new arrival—and accepted a glass of something sparkling from a tray proffered by a pretty girl in a black bow tie, then stood off to one side, trying my best to case the joint before actually starting to work the room.

I saw a few faces I recognized—a couple of guests I knew I could latch on to, people I didn't know well, but at least I knew who they were. They, too, would know who I am, which gave a base from which to branch out.

I was deciding on my first move when I felt a tap on my shoulder. "You must be Chauncey Suydam."

I turned around, and there she was, looking just the way Google had promised. Gentle Reader, have you ever seen *South Pacific*? If you have, you'll recall one moment that has the entire theater clutch its heart. It's when the plantation owner Emil de Becque sees Nellie Forbush for the first time and literally *bursts* into song, "*Some enchanted evening, you may see a stranger; you may see a stranger across a crowded room.*" My old man had the original cast album, and he used to play that bit over and over.

Well, when I first saw Bianca, that's how I felt.

How shall I count the ways? Let's start with her looks. Her hair and eyes are deep umber, almost black; her features are finely, sharply cut, with an edge of perpetual amusement at the corners of the mouth; she's what I've always pictured the "Dark Lady" of Shakespeare's sonnets to look like. She's slim with a prominent high bosom. There's not an atom of "common" about her. She reminds me of an English actress named Emily Mortimer. She was turned out the way I was raised to think a woman should dress when receiving friends at home on a Sunday: a simple blouse under a cardigan, tailored trousers, very simple jewelry, rimless reading glasses on a silver chain.

"That's me," I said. "Happy at last now that I've finally met you."

She smiled at this. "Arthur thinks you and I might do well together. You must call me B, everyone does." She slid her spectacles onto her nose, placed her hands on my shoulders, and studied me. "Yes indeed," she said, "you may very well suit. Provided certain adjustments are made. I'm not sure about that necktie, for one. Come on—let's get some lunch."

We helped ourselves from the buffet and found a couple of seats. She continued to study me, which didn't bother me. Goes with the territory, I figured; casting is her business.

"You remind me of old photographs of my father," she told me. "When he was in his prime."

"I'm flattered. Our breed quivers on the cusp of extinction. I like to think that I carry it on."

"As do I," she replied, "as do I. Now, tell me everything."

I gave her the short-form version of my life story, with only one or two minor embellishments. She seemed interested. Out of the corner of my eye I saw Artie looking over at us. He gave me a discreet thumbs-up.

We talked for a good forty minutes. She's first-rate company, a good talker, a great listener. What she chooses to talk about, she knows about. Finally, she stood up.

"I don't want to run but life leaves me no choice. I have to catch a plane to L.A. Something's come up on a project we have going at Sony, and my brother and I have to meet with them first thing tomorrow."

"I understand. Will I see you again? I'd like to."

"Of course. I need someone in my life, and I think you're far and away the most appropriate candidate who's come along in a very long time. Provided I can get over your connection to the TARPworm, quote unquote. Arthur tells me you consult to them." Her grin was naughty.

"Only in a very limited way. Leon Mankoff, their CEO, is an old friend and mentor. He helped put me in business."

"I know that. You have to understand: I have rather strong feelings about that firm. Do you know a perfectly awful man named Walter Hardcastle?"

"Only in passing. He's on the board. And he is dreadful, based on very brief acquaintance. He's your uncle, I gather."

"By marriage. He's the husband of my mother's idiot sister Molly, although his one true love is money. If my brother and I ever do *A Christmas Carol* I intend to cast Uncle Wally in the lead. When shall we see each other again?"

"How about lunch? When you get back from the Coast?"

She thought about that, then shook her head. "I think dinner would be preferable. That way, if it really works out, we can go to your or my apartment afterward."

I smiled. "You'll get no argument from me."

"Fine. Pick a place and e-mail me some dates. I do hope you're not planning to take me to one of those trendy restaurants that make you wait an hour for indifferent food."

"I wouldn't dare."

"Fine—shall we make a date now?" She looked at her cell phone calendar. "How's April 21? That's a Wednesday."

"Exactly a month from today," I observed. "Very *An Affair to Remember.*"

She laughed. "We shall see, shan't we?"

"How about the Veau d'Or? 7:30. Do you know it?"

"I know *of* it. Mother and Daddy used go there went they came to New York. They said it was very Parisian. I can't believe it's still going."

"Stronger than ever."

She tapped the info into her phone, then got up.

"I'll be off now," she said, and without my making a move, she lowered her lips to mine and kissed me. "Mmmm," she murmured, "how pleasant."

"My sentiments exactly," I said, and raised my face for another go. She had already turned away and was on her way out of the room.

On my way home, I stopped at the Barnes & Noble on 8th Street and hunted up a DVD of *An Affair to Remember*.

Can April 21 come soon enough?

# APRIL 1, 2010

After work, I wandered over to San Calisto—just in time, as it turned out, for a celebration. The old boys were gathered around the dining-room table, watching Scaramouche wrestle the cork out of a magnum of vintage Pol Roger. A glass was brought for me, the wine was poured, and then Scaramouche raised his glass and declared solemnly, "Gentlemen, I give you the health of Mr. Benjamin Bernanke."

I guess I looked puzzled, because the Ancient Mariner hastened to set me straight. "What we're drinking to, Chauncey my lad, is the Federal Reserve's apparent desire to enrich those of us with capital and credit without regard to whosoever else it costs or where the money could be most helpful."

I still looked puzzled. "My dear, dear Chauncey," the Ancient Mariner said in a voice both soothing and condescending, "yesterday marked the end of the first quarter of what Mr. Bernanke in his wisdom has dubbed 'quantitative easing,' or 'QE,' whereby our central bank spends untold billions buying bonds from banks. While the final figures won't be in circulation for a week or two, I think when we see them, we who understand how things work in this country will see what others will not and we shall rejoice and take advantage."

"You'd better explain," I said. I'm actually up to speed on QE, but it seemed elementary courtesy to let my venerable friend tell it his own way.

He was happy to indulge. "As you may know, this QE nonsense involves massive purchases by the Fed of Treasury and other debt securities, in the expectation that the liquid reserves thus freed up on bank balance sheets will find their way into the general economy and stimulate a broad, demand-driven recovery up and down

Main Street. But of course that's not what will happen. Wall Street will see to it, and the Fed will say nothing. Main Street will gain little, if anything, but for the banks it's an absolute smasher. What happens is that the Fed's bond purchases will create liquidity in the finance sector that will gush into the stock and bond markets. Those of us who own securities will seldom have done better."

He looked about him and raised his glass: "Gentlemen, again, please—to the chairman of the Federal Reserve system and all who sail in him! Crony capitalism—long may you thrive!"

# APRIL 17, 2010

Yesterday was a bad day for Lucia. The Wells Notice shoe has finally dropped.

She called me to have a late drink and commiserate. She sounded so unhappy I couldn't refuse.

"Some mess, eh?" I commented after we got our drinks. "So how're Mankoff and Rosenweis going to play it?" I asked. "Stonewall? Try to cut a deal? How you going to get around those stupid e-mails?"

"I'm not sure. Leon's out of town, and no one can get hold of him."

"That's unlike him."

"It certainly is."

"Where the hell is he?"

"His wife won't say. He calls in twice day on his mobile, talks to his secretary and Richard, then turns it off."

This made no sense. Mankoff leaves New York on business perhaps a dozen times a year, only for certain special occasions and particular clients. The Milken Institute meetings in the spring; Merlin Gerrett's annual meeting circus in Shawnee a bit later; the Pasteur Institute in Paris; music at Salzburg, Leipzig, and La Scala; a few board meetings—that's it.

"So that means Rosenweis is handling the SEC? He wouldn't be my conciliator of choice."

"Exactly. Richard is good at creating pressure, not so good at dealing with it."

"So what about Polton? Sounds like he's being let off scot-free. Has he cut a deal with the SEC?"

"Polton and his people are denying any cooperation with the

SEC. They're saying that they didn't have anything to do with what specifically went into the CDOs that went bad."

"What's Arnold Braum have to say?"

"He's planning to put up the defense that Protractor wasn't ever material, given the size of our balance sheet."

"I could buy that," I said, "were it not for the inconvenient fact that when the SEC announced it was going after you, your stock dropped over 10 percent. That strikes me as, well, a pretty material instance of nonmateriality. What are your people thinking in terms of settlement?"

She shrugged. "Best guess: $50 million."

"Sounds low to me. If you get off at twice the price, it'll be cheap," I responded, signaling the waiter for another round. A lousy $50 million to settle an SEC rumpus? I've bought presidencies for less.

We moved on to other subjects, a couple of burgers, more drinks, and somehow ended up outside my place. When she suggested coming up, I didn't say no.

Riding back up in the elevator after chivalrously seeing Lucia into her limo at 3:00 a.m., I suddenly felt a terrible rush of dry-mouthed guilt, as if I had been horribly unfaithful to Bianca. Which makes no sense: B is a woman I've met once, whom I've talked with for an hour.

Oh well, we shall see. For now, to bed. Alone.

# APRIL 18, 2010

It seems to me that I've broken my original compact with you, Gentle Reader. I did say at the outset that this diary would be all business, and not personal. The secret life of Wall Street and Washington, but not of Chauncey Suydam.

It seems, however, to have swerved off into the personal—mainly, I guess, because that's what I now find interesting in my life. I'm bored with the tireless money-grubbing that now seems to drive this country. I'm bored with the corruption—it's too relentless and constant and everywhere—and that I'm technically part of it makes it worse. I've worn out my imaginary worry beads trying to figure out how the country gets out of the box it's put itself in.

I'm worried about Mankoff, but I figure that when he wants to get in touch, he will. I reckon that STST has extracted as much as it could reasonably have expected from the crisis and bailout; there's not much juice left in those oranges. From here on out, they'll mainly go with the flow, hang on to what they've got, and look for the next big thing—possibly even a new crisis offering new bailout goodies. Lucia reports that Rosenweis is calling more and more shots without checking with Mankoff, which has people edgy. Not that Rich isn't capable of running STST—he isn't Mankoff. No one is.

# APRIL 21, 2010

Just got home from my first date with Bianca. We had a very nice evening together: a good dinner, a kind of dowsing for possibilities, then goodbye.

I walked into the Veau d'Or at 7:10 p.m., twenty minutes early, as is my habit, since it gives me a chance to shoot the breeze with Catherine, the owner's daughter, before she gets busy with the other patrons. I told her whom I was meeting, and she seemed appropriately curious; apparently she's a fan of one of B's shows.

B turned up right on the dot. I introduced the two ladies, and could tell pretty quickly that they'd get along.

"I love this place!" B said when we were seated, and a couple of *kirs* and menus had been brought. "It's so real!"

In the course of dinner, we discussed this and that: measuring one another, feeling each other out. I asked her to tell me about her friend Marina Hochster. I find it fascinating, and oddly reassuring, that her obvious loathing of Wall Street has searing personal roots. "I'm sorry I missed meeting her. I've been reading her stuff for years. Artie gave me some background. Quite a story. Explains why she's so angry, why she hates Wall Street so intensely."

The girls had stayed close through their high school years; B was sent to Milton Academy, south of Boston, where her mother had gone, and Marina won a scholarship to Andover. They continued to see each other in the summers in Leeward, but when it came time to go to college, their paths diverged.

Marina had found a vocation in political science and the "idea" of America, the sort of calling that great secondary-school history teachers can convey to impressionable, excitable postadolescents such as yours truly once was. Marina went from Andover to Georgetown, until it began to change for her. She interned on

Capitol Hill and K Street, where what she saw in the way of corporate influence opened her eyes and wrecked her illusions about America. "She thought all bankers were like Daddy," was the way B put it.

A journalism course focused on the Tarbell/Norris era inspired Marina to become an investigative journalist. After graduation, she went back to Maine to work on a newspaper in Portland, where she stirred up a ruckus with a penetrating exposure of the financial hijinks underpinning a big construction project in Bangor. This led to Boston and the *Globe*, and from there she evolved into *the* Marina Hochster, Marina of "the TARPworm."

While Marina was making her way, B and her twin brother Claudio went to Harvard; that's what Longstreths do. What a Longstreth had never done was to quit Harvard for UCLA film school, which Claudio did after his sophomore year, following his election to Porcellian and Hasty Pudding. Off to Hollywood he went, never to return. B was progressing steadily toward business school, from which she graduated at about the same time I was thinking about setting up Maecenas. Her brother persuaded her to go west and work with him. After writing and producing for a decade, they started Gemelli. The rest is entertainment history.

Over coffee, she looked at me and said, "I was thinking that perhaps you'd like to come up to Leeward for Memorial Day. Before we start sleeping together, I want to see how you fit in with my family. They're very important to me."

What could I say to that?

"It's strictly family," she continued, "but Mother and Daddy always let us bring whoever's in our life. Claudio'll be bringing his partner Frederick, and Artie will be there, although Hal's going to be in the Far East, shepherding some ghastly Russian through the souks of Hong Kong and Shanghai."

"I don't think they have souks in Hong Kong," I said. "They have souks in places like Marrakech."

"Well, whatever. So would you like to come to Maine? I really do think you'll get on nicely with my parents, Mother especially. Separate bedrooms, of course."

"Of course. Memorial Day sounds terrific, although I'll have to move something around—I have sort of a commitment to go to Fire Island."

"Fire Island!"

"I have old friends who have a place on the very eastern tip called Point O' Woods."

"Good lord, Point O' Woods! Is that still going strong? I haven't been there since I was at Milton. My roommate's family had a place there. I never think of it as being on Fire Island, it's so buttoned-up."

"It still is." I find Point O' Woods very agreeable; it's so WASPy it makes Newport look like Bed-Stuy. I'm comfortable there.

We parted on what seemed to me to be very good—even promising—terms. I offered to drop B in the West Village, but she has a late-night shoot in Brooklyn and a car was waiting. She kissed me goodbye, with what seemed like more energy and feeling than she'd deployed the first time.

I stood on the curb and watched her car round the corner, just the way I had when all this began three years ago, with me standing on a Manhattan sidewalk watching Mankoff's town car pull away. Things connect up, and fate lays down the paving stones one by one on a road that has led from Three Guys to today.

# MAY 6, 2010

"Countries don't go broke."

Thus, some forty years ago (I gather), spake Walter Wriston, Jamie Dimon's spiritual avatar, the Citibank CEO who transformed banking into a growth business and in so doing destroyed it—if the consensus at San Calisto is to be believed.

Remember the Santorini Shuffle that Scaramouche told me about not long after I began this diary? That was the 2001 island meeting between Greek officialdom and a hit squad from Wall Street, where everyone happily figured out how to cook the books in a way that would qualify Greece for admission to the eurozone. Well, it seems that Greece is really going bust, can't pay its debts. And certain parties on Wall Street, having extracted hundreds of millions in fees and penalties from the mess, are scrambling to extricate themselves from the finger-pointing.

As it's being described in the financial press, what's going on with Greece sounds to me like a *Foreign Affairs* version of Repo 105, the sleight-of-balance-sheet stuff that helped sink Lehman. Apparently there have been nasty rumors for some time about the birthplace of democracy, but with the help of its Wall Street coconspirators it has financed itself by borrowing, since its GDP and balance of payments aren't up to the job. Add to that the fact that the richest Greeks keep their money and themselves mostly elsewhere, in tax havens like Switzerland. (Hence the joke that the second largest Greek city after Athens is Lausanne.)

So there's that. And now another fresh hell seems to have opened up. By late this morning, the Dow had dropped a thousand points.

*A thousand points!*

Why?

Some point to the incipient Greek crisis, but economic and credit fundamentals no longer matter to markets the way they used to. Instead, the smart money's calling it "a flash crash" and is blaming it on HFT—algorithmically generated orders: strictly computer-driven, untouched by human hand or mind—for millions of shares that crashed into each other the way that waves from opposite directions will sometimes collide at a breakwater. I don't really understand it—apparently most of the orders are phony, what they call "spoofs"—so I'm not going to try to analyze it. By the close the market had cut its losses by two-thirds, with STST closing at $148, so no real damage done. Still, the story has a clear moral: put not your faith in robots.

# MAY 7, 2010

Yesterday, thanks to Winters—or maybe it was Holloway—the Senate killed off something called the Brown-Kaufman Amendment. Named for the two senators who sponsored it, the amendment was intended to be incorporated into Dodd-Frank; basically it says that if you're too big to fail, you're too big to exist, and attacks the moral hazard that got the world into its present mess with a mechanism to break up the big banks.

Another piece of hot news that has the hedge-funders I work with jumping for joy is that Holloway is close to outright victory in a campaign he's been waging to have the Fed pick up the Street's absolute worst junk, using a program called Term Asset Lending Facility, or TALF. Meanwhile, Mankoff remains out of pocket. His assistant will only say he's still out of town. Something's obviously up, something serious. I'm starting to worry.

# MAY 13, 2010

I thought the world went topsy-turvy a week ago with the Greek business and the flash crash, but today was worse, for entirely different reasons. It was unsettling and upsetting.

Here's how it went. Around 7:30 this morning, my apartment phone rang. My regular landline, that is. No one calls me this early except maybe Mankoff, and I knew it wouldn't be him—I still haven't gotten through to the man.

To my astonishment, the voice on the other end was Ian Spass. I hadn't spoken to him for well over a year. Hadn't thought much about him, either. I guess I assumed that, like most of those who'd had a hand in the Washington side of TARP and other bailout giveaways, Spass had simply ridden off into the sunset and was now pulling down a nice seven figures at some bank or law firm or lobbying shop.

"Ian," I said, "long time no talk. What's got you up at this hour?"

"I wanted to make sure I got you. Will you be at home this evening?"

"If there's a God. Why?"

"I'm in New York. I need to speak with you about something."

"Sure. I'll be here after six. Drop on by."

He showed up a little after seven. I made us a couple of stiff drinks and settled him in my most comfortable chair. "The stage is yours," I said. "Is this an official or unofficial call? I thought you'd abandoned the marble halls for the dark side."

"Let's call it semi-official," he said. "The SEC wants to get a message to Mankoff. I told them you're the person to talk to."

"I'm flattered," I said. "Fire away."

"All right: here's the deal. Are you familiar with this Protractor business?"

"Familiar enough, I suppose."

"Washington—and not just the Commission—prefers not to go forward with a public prosecution. For obvious reasons, they'd rather it be settled out of the limelight on a basis that will sound reasonable to the public. There are bigger scandals brewing. The Brits have apparently stumbled on a possible manipulation having to do with LIBOR . . ."

"Everybody knew about LIBOR back in '08," I interrupted. "And nobody did fuck-all about it then."

"That may be," Spass replied. "We all had a lot on our plate, and at that particular moment, it simply didn't make sense to throw a huge price-fixing scandal into the mix."

"Especially when the commodity whose price was being fixed was money."

He shrugged. "What I'm here to work out with you is a suitable Protractor settlement."

"What do you have in mind? The usual? A large-sounding fine and a promise not to do it again. That is, a promise not to do again what you never did in the first place?" In most of their settlements with Uncle Sam, STST and other Wall Street houses are permitted not to admit to malfeasances they're totally guilty of. It's one of the best legal scams going.

"We're thinking of settling for $600 million," he said. "That's the word we wish you to pass along to Mankoff. It's his call. We're tired of Arnold Braum's theatrics."

I let out a low whistle. Still, in terms of the potential aggro, $600 million didn't sound all that bad. A large fraction, admittedly, but still a fraction of the money they've made on those Polton deals. And first out is usually cheapest, as the San Calisto wisdom has it.

"Plus the usual disclaimer?" I asked.

320

"Not exactly. In this case, we'd like to see some admission of wrongdoing."

"I'll pass it along," I said. "That's all I can do. On top of the mea culpas, $600 million's a lot of money. I'm not sure my former client will spring for that." There was no point to telling him that I didn't know where Mankoff could be reached.

"Not necessarily," Spass said. "Not if you look at it on a net basis."

"What do you mean 'net'?" I asked.

He grinned. "I don't suppose you've ever read the full SEC complaint on Protractor?" he asked me.

I shook my head. "All I've seen is STST's reply."

He reached into his briefcase, pulled out a document, a quarter inch's worth of stapled pages, and tossed it on the table. "I defy you to read through this as often as you want and find Polton's name in there," he said.

I said nothing. This was preaching to the converted.

"Have you got a computer here?" he asked. "You must."

I booted up the Mac Air I use for work (the other one, the one I write this diary on, was tucked away in a wall safe). From his pocket he produced a flash drive and slotted it in.

"I think you're going to enjoy this," he said. "And I know Mankoff will. It's a recording I made privately. The only people who know it exists are you and I."

The implication was clear. It seems that Spass had worn a wire on his own people. Talk about Washington being a nest of vipers!

He tapped a couple of keys and a recording began to play.

I could hear four voices: two asking questions, a third answering them, with occasional interruptions from a fourth. The only voice I recognized was the third: Polton.

It took me maybe another thirty seconds to figure out what

I was hearing: this was Polton being deposed by the SEC about Protractor.

Or, to put it more precisely, this was Polton ratting out Struthers Strauss about Protractor. Blowing the whistle on his principal co-conspirator in return for regulatory immunity, I guessed.

I could see why the SEC thinks its case is a lock. Polton has given them chapter and verse, down to the last penny. And Washington is willing to let Polton go if they can make an example of STST.

After it finished, I unplugged the flash drive and made to return it to Spass, but he waved me off.

"You may not think so, Chauncey, but I still have a vestigial sense of what's fair , even if it only amounts to honor among thieves. Mankoff and Rosenweis—especially Rosenweis—will be interested in this. It may inspire some thoughts on their part about how to finance the money settlement."

I took his point. We finished our drinks and he left—but not before leaving a final bonbon on my plate: "One last thing. There's a rumor that Polton shorted your stock after he made his deal with Washington. I doubt he's stupid enough to do that. Jimmy Polton may be many things, but stupid he isn't. Anyway, the Commission's looking into it."

This was something Mankoff had to know about—and pronto. I called him on his personal cell phone number, and his wife answered. That had never happened before.

"Is Leon there, Grace? I really need to speak to him."

"Oh, Chauncey, he went to bed early and I hate to disturb him. He's had an awful, long day. Can't it wait?" She sounded tired and sad, almost plaintive.

"Of course," I replied, "let him sleep. Will he be in the office tomorrow?"

"I expect so. You know Leon. Wild horses . . ."

"No problem. I'll call him then." As I got ready for bed, I found myself thinking about Spass. He must be like any human being with even a speck of decency in him. Sooner or later, there has to come a time when one can no longer stand another minute of this stuff—the lying, the double-dealing, the sheer rapaciousness. There was a hymn we used to sing several times a year at Groton that seems to capture what Spass must be feeling, and what I myself am starting to feel: *"Once to ev'ry man and nation / Comes the moment to decide / In the strife 'twixt truth and falsehood / For the good or evil side."*

I thought about that hymn all evening, although when I finally went to bed it was Mankoff I was concerned about. Something's terribly wrong. I'm sure of it.

# MAY 10, 2010

Marina Hochster has a good strong post on a financial blog today. Hard to disagree with.

She writes:

> It's time to put aside the idiotic notion that corporations should be run entirely in the interest of their stockholders, including executives with fat options deals. This disemployment-spawning theory, in aid of which Wall Street has prostituted itself, with Washington as its pimp, has not only grievously damaged the economy but has torn great holes in the nation's social fabric, as millions of households and tens of thousands of communities have been uprooted for the sake of a notion for which there is little basis in economics, and none at all in decency.

When I read that, I thought, I really would meet this outspoken lady, "TARPworm" or no. I called B in L.A. and asked her to arrange an introduction.

"Should this make me jealous?" she asked.

"Not at all. I just like people who speak their minds. My heart is pledged to thee." I spoke lightly, but put just enough feeling in my voice to arouse suspicion that I might be serious.

B promised to cook something up when she returns east.

# MAY 14, 2010

Mankoff's secretary called to tell me her boss is in the office and could see me at noon.

I thought he looked bad. Mankoff never radiates rude good health, but he looked especially pale, and he seemed to have shed a few pounds: his shirt looked baggy on him, its collar a half-size too large.

"You all right?" I asked.

He looked at me suspiciously. "Why? Has someone said something?"

I shook my head. "Just thought you looked a touch under the weather."

"Actually," he admitted, "I'm having some kind of intestinal blip the doctors are having difficulty getting a handle on. Nothing serious. So what's on your mind?"

"I had a surprise visitor the other night," I began. I told him about Spass coming to see me and suggested he get Rosenweis to join us. When Rich came in, I recapitulated my conversation with Spass. Then I played them the flash drive.

"So, bottom line, it looks to me like Polton's turned state's evidence," I said when it finished. "In any case, Spass tells me that Uncle Sam wants an up-or-down answer on Protractor by July 4: $600 million, *service compris*."

Mankoff nodded absently. "July 4," he murmured. It was as if he'd lost track of the conversation. Then, like a dog shaking off water, he seemed to refocus and told me: "You're right, what you just said. We should get more than $600 million . . ."

He broke off. For just a couple of beats, he looked confused, as if his train of thought had derailed. Rosenweis and I looked at each in wild surmise. This isn't Leon, we were thinking—this isn't the guy whose powers of concentration when attending to business are only equaled by Jack Nicklaus on the eighteenth hole of a major.

Then he recovered. "Let me mull it over."

"What I should tell Spass?" I asked.

"Tell Spass to tell his people that they'll have their answer on time. Leave Polton to us."

I got up and left. I was bothered. This was all been very unlike Mankoff. At least, the Mankoff I'd known all these years. The Mankoff I thought I knew. Of course, the kind of man he is, maybe I know nothing.

## MAY 15, 2010

It turns out I can't make it to Maine for the Memorial Day week-end with the Longstreths. An important Silicon Valley client is planning a private museum—a billion-dollar project—and he requires my presence for the long weekend, when he and I are to fly all over Europe to look at recently built museums and meet with their architects. Big names. Zaha Hadid, Jean Nouvel, Foster, Rogers.

B sounded unhappy when I told her, but promises to put me on the list for the Labor Day weekend. I'd be a liar if I didn't say I'm really disappointed, but what can you do?

The trip to Europe was worthwhile, but hardly pertinent to these notes. My client showed himself to be perspicacious and informed; at the moment I think he's leaning toward a young, hip firm based in Oslo, which would also be my choice.

Bianca's gave me a full report about Memorial Day at her family's place. As predicted, Hardcastle made a complete asshole of himself at lunch, and all were greatly relieved when he chugged off in his $200,000 Rolls.

"At one point, Uncle Wally referred to our president as 'a house nigger.' I thought Claudie was going to leap across the table and strangle him!"

"I hardly think of your brother as politically fiery," I said. "Not as you've described him to me."

"You'd be surprised. In Claudie the revolutionary fires burn deep and hot. You should have seen him at Harvard, especially when he and a bunch of Young Socialists picketed Daddy's bank."

"Otherwise, how'd it go?"

"Fair. Daddy was a bit down. He'd just come from his fiftieth reunion at Harvard, which seems to have been a bit of a bummer. Apparently the Class of '60's politics have taken a sharp turn to the right. All anyone wanted to talk about was money—even at Porcellian. Daddy feels that he and most of his classmates have spent their lives talking and thinking about money and business and that it's time now to smell the roses."

"I can understand that."

"They're very keen to meet you."

That pleased me. I could infer that I'd received a good report card. "And I to meet them," I said. "Anything else exciting?"

"I spoke to Marina on the phone. She's on her way to China. We'll get together when she returns."

Suddenly, there's much to look forward to.

## JULY 15, 2010

The SEC action on Protractor is a done deal. STST will pay $600 million in fines and penalties; there will be a mild acknowledgement of corporate error, but no individuals will be named.

The critics are pointing out—not unreasonably—that the fine is a pittance for a firm as rich as STST, and Lucia reports that the Street consensus is that STST has cut itself a fantastic deal, although nobody's saying as much, lest Uncle Sam get bigger ideas about future settlements with other firms. If Protractor was a $600 million malfeasance, the talk goes, what should BofA be looking at on Countrywide? $6 billion? Meanwhile the rumors about LIBOR are intensifying, with Barclays the name on the tip of everyone's tongue. The numbers being thrown around will surely run well into the billions.

As usual, ugliness is in the eye of the beholder. To 99 percent of the world, $600 million will sound like a lot of money, but Mr. Market clearly knows what's what, and the stock's at $150; a month ago, you ocula have bought it for $125 and change.

And so it goes.

# JULY 16, 2010

Mankoff called first thing this morning. He didn't sound like himself—half his sentences seemed to glitch in the middle—but he did manage to tell me that Rosenweis went to see Polton yesterday after the close, and the two men had a frank exchange of views centering on Polton's role in the SEC-Protractor outcome. It was made clear that either some accommodation must be reached, or Polton will never do another ten cents' worth of business with STST. That might not sound so ominous to us, but once the word gets out that Polton's on the STST shit list, a lot of other lucrative doors will close to him and he knows it. The upshot is that bygones are to be bygones, and Polton will personally pick up $350 million of STST's tab at the SEC. Who said virtue isn't its own reward?

# AUGUST 6, 2010

Like most people, I keep tucked away in my mind a list of my best and worst days. My best list starts with November 21, 2008, when the news of Winters and Holloway's appointments was released. There's also the day I was tapped for Bones; the day my old man and I won the father-son squash doubles at the Racquet Club. The destruction of the Bank of West Congo went under.

That's the good stuff. Yesterday, July 31, goes right to the top of the list of yours truly's All-Time Worst.

Most of the day had gone pretty well. A meeting with Maecenas's accountants concluded that we're in good shape. This was followed by lunch at the Morgan Library and a productive discussion of a future Lewis Carroll exhibition, followed by drinks at the Stuyvesant Club with a friend from Denver, who filled me in on the world of cultural investment and finance in the Rockies. I got home around seven.

B's crisscrossing the Midwest for the next ten days, scouting locations, so I'm on my own. Our relationship is progressing nicely: say, eight on a scale of ten. We see each other two to three times a week when she's in the city. We've developed an easy intimacy; sometimes she'll stay over, sometimes I will, most nights we return to our separate homes and separate beds.

So all seemed copacetic until about 9:30 p.m., when the house phone rang, and the guy at the lobby desk told me that a "Mrs. Lucia" was downstairs asking for me. Whatever this was, I thought, it was unlikely to be good news.

It wasn't. She looked terrible. "What's wrong?" I asked.

"First of all, I need a drink. Now."

I poured her a stiff single malt, no ice. She took a couple of unladylike swigs. When she spoke, her voice was a rasp.

"Leon's leaving," she told me.

"Leaving? My God." I sat down heavily, then got up and stiffened both our drinks. "Tell me."

"I've just come from the office. I was at the Four Seasons charming one of my lapdogs at the *Times* when I got a call telling me to get my fanny down to global headquarters posthaste. To Richard's conference room. The Executive Committee was there. Then Leon got on the speakerphone from Santa Fe.

"He told us that he has been diagnosed with early onset Alzheimer's. He's been everywhere: Mayo, Johns Hopkins, MD Anderson in Texas. At present, the symptoms come and go, but he feels the disease gaining on him. He's decided he can no longer responsibly perform his duties as CEO and has asked to be relieved, effective immediately. They've appointed a special committee to handle the matter of succession, but of course it'll be Richard."

She moved nervously around the room, fussing with her hair, stopping to examine a row of narrow shelves on which I'd ranged my old man's trophies.

"These are nice," she said, almost dreamily. "They remind me of the house I grew up in."

Then she returned to the sofa, sat down beside me, and patted my cheek. "Oh, Chauncey. What will become of you without Leon? How long have the two of you been together?"

"Thirty years this past June."

I poured another round. We talked about what life was going to be like at STST without Mankoff.

"I'll stay on board for a while," she said. "There's a lot about this firm that isn't easy to defend, but at least we're not a bunch of crooks. Not compared to some others I could name. And I fancy I haven't done a bad job. But I can't see working for Richard indefinitely. Eventually I'm going to move back to London. I'm thinking about joining with some friends in a social advisory service for rich foreigners. Everything from what school to apply to and which fork to use to travel, what decorator to hire, how to wangle an invitation to Ascot, how to get a good table at Harry's. It's the best way for people like us to use our taste and background to make really very good money teaching all these Chinese, Russians, and Arabs how to spend their jillions. God knows, Chauncey, I don't have to tell you about that."

"I'm not sure how to take that," I replied.

"Listen, being a whore is an honest business. These are riffraff who believe that unless something's expensive, it can't possibly be any good, which lets one mark up goods and services to three or four times their normal cost. I may ask you to help me now and then. Fix up a box at the opera, arrange for someone to sit close to Anna at the Costume Institute gala."

"I shall be delighted. If the price is right."

"You may assured it shall be."

I poured us another round. We talked for a long while, until suddenly Lucia exclaimed, "My God, look at the time!" It was getting on for 1:00 a.m., and she got up and rushed out the door, barely thanking me for the drinks and the sympathetic shoulder.

I stumbled to bed. My mind went back three years to that equally dull morning outside Three Guys, and all that had happened as a result. It was as if a life was ending, you'd have to say it was.

The issue now is, where the hell do we go from here?

## AUGUST 26, 2010

Just back from visiting the Mankoffs in Santa Fe. A tiring trip, whose emotional stress wasn't helped by a late flight, a missed connection in Dallas, and an overnight stay at a vile airport hotel in Nashville. It was 10:00 a.m. this morning when I finally dragged myself into the apartment.

So: Santa Fe. It started with a call a week ago from Grace Mankoff. Could I come down? Leon would like to see me.

To get to Santa Fe, you fly into Albuquerque and then take a shuttle bus a bit over an hour north, where you're dropped off downtown. On my trip out, I left at the crack of dawn, and by early afternoon, I disembarked in Santa Fe to find the Mankoffs waiting for me. Leon looked OK. Grace looked beat.

To my surprise, Mankoff was at the wheel, although I could see Grace keeping an eagle eye on him. The short trip proceeded without incident. Their house is about twenty minutes northwest of the city, in scrubland that's mostly undeveloped, but which is dotted here and there with large pueblo-style houses, low-lying in the pueblo style, and with vistas to die for. Their house is a very pleasant, homey place: big open rooms and porches decorated with Hopi and Navajo art, blankets, drawings, and pots. There's a music room with a harpsichord I recognized from the Connecticut house. Mankoff's other instruments, though—along with his musical manuscripts—have been given to Yale.

The visit went about a million times better than I expected. The atmosphere was upbeat; Mankoff wasn't the drooling, withdrawn, shambling being I'd anticipated. Now and then, he seemed confused by small things or simple tasks. There was one morning when we were going downtown when he seemed momentarily taken aback by the task of starting the car. Still, if you didn't know him as well as I did, you'd've said that the old engine was ticking over more or less normally. I did get Grace Mankoff off to one side one day to ask for a medical briefing; all she said was that her husband was like a refined orchestra that had been turned over to a tempestuous, quixotic, unpredictable conductor with a drinking problem. "All in all, it still plays reasonably well, but there are moments . . ."

I spent three full days in Santa Fe. On my last night, we ate outdoors at a pleasant cafe around the corner from the Plaza. When we got home, Grace retired with her book, and Mankoff suggested a nightcap. We went out onto the terrace and sat under the stars. You forget how big the sky is out west. Pretty amazing.

"Do we have any loose ends to tie up?" he asked after we clinked glasses.

"Not that I can think of, but your wish is my command."

"You do realize, Chauncey, that I'm losing my mind?"

"I understand the prognosis isn't good."

"It's like a slow tide washing over me. Who was that English king who ordered the time not to come in?"

"You mean Canute?"

"That's me: King Canute. In another six months to a year, the prognosis is that I'll be totally off in an impenetrable world of my own. Probably die not long after that. Grace will need you to help her sort out a few things. And Rich may ask you to stick around to help him with a few loose ends. I know you two don't like each other, but could you do that—as a favor to me?"

"I'll do whatever you want."

Now it was my turn. There's been a question I've had on my mind for a long time, but I've hesitated to ask it.

"The money you had me feed into the campaign three years ago."

"Yes?"

"One thing you never told me. And don't tell me now if you don't want to. Where'd the money come from?"

He thought the matter over. "I can't tell you. Does it matter?"

I supposed it didn't. You could probably go back from where we are now to where we were in 2007 and see who's made out best, and come up with some pretty plausible answers.

Suppose Three Guys had never happened. Without Mankoff's $75 million—without Saudi Arabia's or Citibank's or whoever's $75 million it was—would we be better off? OG has turned out to be a poor president in the way historians and pollsters judge things, but he's been just great for Wall Street, and wasn't that the point? The price of stocks is back up, and the rich are richer than ever before, so go figure. I sure as hell can't.

And I have to add one heartless note. When Mankoff disappears into that mental blackness, he'll take our secret with him. That'll leave only me—me and whoever reads this diary years from now.

Well, after several cancellations and delays, I've finally made it to Longboat, Bianca's family's place in Leeward Harbor, Maine.

Let me tell you a bit about Longboat, Gentle Reader. On a map, Pilgrim Island looks like a bunch of bananas dangling from the coast of central Maine. It's joined to the mainland by a short umbilical causeway. The island is split up the middle by a wide sound known as Satan's Sluice that thrusts inland from the Atlantic for a distance of nearly four miles.

Pilgrim Island is renowned for its natural beauty, which more than a century of strict conservation and generous environmental philanthropy has done a good job of protecting. Much of the island is now a national park embroidered with a capillary network of hiking trails that draw a million visitors annually. More than one writer has noted that it offers living affirmation of the famous hymn that for over a century has been sung in the island's churches. It truly is a place "where ev'ry prospect pleases / And only Man is vile."

Close your eyes and let your imagination take over, and it is not hard to imagine the island as it once was, the virgin evergreen forests, the Indian villages, not to mention the great flashing schools of cod and sun-darkening squadrons of canvasback duck that drew the attention of English seafarers in the late seventeenth century. Huge, dark green swathes punctuated with streaks of blue, and with the lighter colors of rocky uplands covered in meadow grass. The alternation of heights and water is dazzling. When Thomas Mann visited the island in the early 1950s, the writer remarked that the views compared favorably with his beloved Engadine in Switzerland. That the place has inspired the efforts of a veritable Parnassus of American landscape artists, including Winslow Homer and Thomas Cole, should come as no surprise.

To the south, where Satan's Sluice ends in a wide bay, the land is protected from the roughest bits of offshore weather by two uninhabited islands, Blueberry Major and Blueberry Minor. Inland from the islands is a wide bay. On its southwest shore sits Leeward Harbor; almost directly across to the northeast, settled on a tongue of richly forested land, is Windward Harbor, which includes the more social and moneyed enclave of Porpoise Point. Windward's topography is more dramatic than Leeward's, altogether flashier, its bluffs higher and steeper, its enclosing forests loftier and more enveloping, its colors richer.

Anyone remotely familiar with the landscapes of American privilege will recognize at once that this is Old Money Country. The key aesthetic principle in the local architecture seems to be circumspection. Even the largest Windward "cottages"—the local name for any dwelling larger than a fisherman's shack—are unpretentious by, say, Hamptons standards, notwithstanding that there are families hereabouts with resources sufficient to buy out every hedge-fund impresario between the Shinnecock Canal and Amagansett. But this is changing; the opportunity to be—or to claim to be—cheek-by-jowl with some of America's oldest money and bloodlines has proven to be catnip to a number of freshly minted money barons, and Windward prices have moved up steadily.

There are definite differences in social style between the two villages. People tend to characterize Leeward as "more Boston or Philadelphia" and Windward as "more New York," and there's some truth to that. The latter's more aspirational, less inhibited about wealth and its uses. It was mostly Windward money that paid for the runway at the nearby mainland airport to be lengthened to accommodate large private jets. It was mainly Leeward money that acquired and donated many of the larger tracts that make up Evangeline National Park.

A lack of pretension characterizes Leeward, what the sort of people who devour decorating magazines doubtless call "shabby elegance." Newer money is expected to tiptoe into town and tug its forelock as it waits its turn for coffee or the newspaper or a table at Cain's Lobster Pot, or for an invitation to play tennis or golf at the Viaduct Club, known to locals simply as "the club." As one wag has put it, "Over at Leeward, they must have spent all of $100 in the last ten years fixing up the yacht club. At Windward they spend $100 on a cleat."

Residents of both villages grumble about having to make concessions to an age when money has once again become the measure of all things, as it was back in the Gilded Age when wealthy folk first started to build their summer cottages hereabouts. Laying out a few million dollars for a fine property on either side of the bay is no assurance of immediate invitations to cocktails or dinner, or of membership in the Jug and Beaker, the exclusive local men's club, although $100,000 to the local hospital might help.

At the seaward end of the narrow crescent harbor, at the bottom of the bluff, occupying several hundred feet of waterfront along the easternmost arc of Leeward Harbor where the land hooks sharply back, is the site of Hochster's Boatyard. In the old days, the yard would be clanking, buzzing, busy, with one or two spanking new hulls ready to be masted and launched. Today, Hochster's is padlocked shut, with shreds of wind-tattered legal notices affixed to the gate.

Around Leeward Harbor, "Hochster" is a name no longer honored; it has become an epithet that stands for betrayal and venality and "Judas money," and on Saturday nights at the taverns where locals gather, an extra round often leads to declarations of violence and retribution against the family. No wonder Marina stays away.

If one turns left at the Hochster's site and heads uphill in a generally northeast direction parallel to the shoreline, one soon enters the residential parts of Leeward Harbor. These lie on wide bluffland with good long views of the bay and its outlet to the Atlantic. They're broken up by a web of narrow lanes signposted with the names of important residents—Longstreth, Anderson, Butler.

The longest of these pathways, stretching perhaps a quarter-mile from the main feeder road to the edge of the bluff, culminates in a white picket fence marking the turnoff into a short driveway. To the fence is affixed a wooden cutout of a nineteenth-century whaleboat that identifies the property as Longboat. This is the compound that for over a century has been the summer home of the Longstreth family. It comprises four buildings: a tall main house flanked helter-skelter by three smaller cottages. The oldest and grandest house, which gives its name to the compound and sits at the center of things like the manor on a feudal estate, was built in 1892 by Lucius Longstreth, great-grandfather of the present owner. The twin cottages named Moorings and Jibe Ho! were built in 1925, and the last and smallest, Gull's Roost, in 1948, when Pilgrim Island was regaining its pre-Depression, prewar social rhythm and summer at Longboat had once again become a continuous merry parade of Longstreth family and friends.

The main house is the heart of the place: assembly point, command post, war room, hangout, sanctuary, bolt-hole—especially during the frenetic stretch from July 4 through Labor Day, when life becomes a blur of tennis, barbecues, golf, sailing, and croquet, all punctuated by the clink of ice in tall glasses and the chugging of Hochster harbor cruisers returning from excursions to the outer islands.

Longboat is a fine old shingled edifice, with spacious porches overlooking the harbor, and a number of commodious function rooms, including a country-formal dining room dominated on onc long wall by a large, especially fine Fitz Henry Lane painting, dated 1857, of *Leeward Harbor Seen from the Bluffs*. I'm told that museums in Portland and Boston are drooling over this picture, and I can see why.

In the middle of the house, off to the right of the stairs, overlooking the water, is everyone's favorite room: a cozy, welcoming library that serves as a haven when autumn arrives earlier than wished or winter overstays its welcome.

There are two major family occasions on the Longboat calendar: the long Memorial Day weekend, when Longboat comes alive after its winter hibernation and the house is opened and made ready for the season, and, some twenty-odd weeks later, Labor Day weekend, when the compound is shut down for the winter. For an outsider to be included in one of these is a singular honor.

A few words about my host and hostess, B's parents, Thayer and Marjorie Longstreth. They're models—almost to the point of cliché—of a certain kind of New England distinction. Everything about them bespeaks long private and professional lives conducted with dedication, intelligence, and circumspection. True Yankee patricians: old names; old schools; old money, with family trees that boast bankers and merchants, parsons and schoolmasters. He can count Adamses, Cabots and Emersons on various branches of the family tree, as well as a mayor of Boston and a great-great-grandfather who died fighting at Gettysburg. He epitomizes a cultivated, tweedy, bow-tied, reticent style of getting and spending that's become increasingly rare, limited to a number of shrinking habitats mostly in New England within an hour or so of Boston, around Philadelphia, and—although these now hover on the very brink of extinction—on the Upper East Side of Manhattan. In the summer, this old breed can be found on Boston's North and South Shore, in one or two venues on Cape Cod, and in enclaves like Leeward Harbor or at Stockbridge and Lenox in the Berkshires.

Marjorie Longstreth, Thayer's wife of forty-seven years, is tall and spare; at seventy-three, a handsome long-nosed woman, straight of carriage, with shoulder-length gray hair going white. Refined, precise, elegant, with a good sense of humor and a profound feeling for her fellow beings. After a brilliant four decades at Harvard Law School that culminated in a deanship and a chair in in Intellectual Property Law in her name, Marjorie retired from active teaching two years ago. But she has kept busy in retirement: she serves as a trustee and chief counsel ex officio to the Fogg and Gardner museums and the Children's Hospital. Her résumé runs to thirty pages of positions held, honors received, committees and boards served on, not to mention innumerable articles, books, and distinguished visitor- and lectureships. Her 1987 book, *The Golden Brick Road: Gospels of Hope in American Politics*, was short-listed for the Pulitzer Prize, and her earlier book on *Roe v. Wade* remains the definitive text. During her time at Harvard, she got to know a young woman who is now the nation's First Lady, with whom she keeps in discreet touch (the Longstreths dined privately with the First Couple last winter, and were seated with the presidential party at Senator Kennedy's funeral in Boston).

It's apparent at a glance that money has been neither a problem nor an obsession in this household. It may be that the absence of the former leads to a lack of the latter. Thayer retired as CEO of Back Bay Fidelity Trust, the final stage in the evolution of the old family bank, six years ago: well before, as he puts it, "all hell broke loose on Wall Street." In 2002, wishing to assure himself and his family of greater liquidity, he sold the bank, which had been controlled by his family since the War of 1812, to Merrill Lynch for $800 million in shares. Of this sum, $260 million ended up in various Longstreth family accounts, with the balance going for taxes and to a family foundation that Thayer controls. That's something B and I have in common; both our fathers' banks—of

343

course her father *owned* his—were swallowed up by the Thundering Herd.

In 2003, barely a year after he sold the family bank to Merrill Lynch, a new man took over as Merrill's CEO, an individual whose blinding arrogance, Thayer reckoned, would carry to certain ruin a firm that he had always considered one of the most prudent and collegial on Wall Street. He promptly sold the family's Merrill Lynch stock, resigned his board seat, and urged various accounts over which he had influence to take their business elsewhere. We all know what happened to Merrill Lynch.

Since then, Thayer has busied himself with his trusts and clubs, with various civic, cultural, and charitable activities—and, above all, with Harvard, to which he has stayed deeply loyal, notwithstanding being outvoted on the Investment Committee in a bitter dispute with fellow committee member Harley Winters—yes, *that* Harley Winters—over a derivatives bait-and-switch that will end up costing Harvard nearly $1 billion to get out of.

Thayer is what he seems: a person of principle, common sense, and rockbound loyalty to family, schools, and country—the same qualities he displays in his supervision of the family office and its considerable assets, now lodged in the Boylston Street premises of a venerable Boston law firm. You'll recall that, according to B, he's been in a lousy mood all summer, although he seemed to be coming out of it this past weekend.

The Longstreth family's feelings about Longboat are intense. The ancestor who built the house, Thayer's great-grandfather, son of the Civil War hero, was in the Pierpont Morgan mold: a take-no-prisoners banker with an elaborated sense of noblesse oblige and a passion for music and art. He considered the material, environmental, and spiritual well-being of Leeward Harbor and its inhabitants to be his personal responsibility, and did his best to see that a similar sense of duty was inbred in his children and in theirs. Among the locals, the Longstreths are spoken of with deference and affection, lords of the manor who are mindful of the responsibilities that go with privilege.

Marjorie, too, has been coming to Leeward as long as she can remember. Her father and *his* father, successive heads of a famous New England boarding school with strong church affiliations, served as seasonal rectors of the village's nondenominational parish. With the exception of World War II, when gas rationing made the trip prohibitive and her family switched its base of summer operations to Boston's South Shore, Marjorie's long, happy girlhood summers were passed here, on the water and the tennis courts and at dances on the deck of the club, music provided by a borrowed Victrola, as she still calls a record player.

She made her debut here in 1958, at the Leeward Harbor Yacht Club, and was married at the club five years later. No less than her husband, Marjorie feels Leeward in her DNA, her marrow, her every fiber.

For me, being up there was bliss, like going back in time; it reminded me of the way, say, Bridgehampton used to be when I was a kid and my old man and I and another family shared a nice rented farmhouse for a couple of summers: simple, spacious, straightforward. No bullshit, no Ferraris, no clamor for restaurant tables.

It was interesting to talk to B's old man about changes in the area, especially what's happened to Hochster's. He hates Harborside, the new condo development rising on the old boatyard site—largely, I suspect, because a principal investor in the development is his despised brother-in-law Walter Hardcastle.

People like the Longstreths were in a position to block the project for the usual historical preservation reasons, but unlike the preservation terrorists of the Hamptons, whose money and genealogies usually date back no further than a month or so, they chose to take a long view, and ask themselves, "If not Harborside, what then? The boatyard isn't coming back. Where will this village find work?" At the end of the day, the only solution seems to be the one every so-situated American community has come up with: tourism and servicing the new rich in ways that range from building and staffing McMansions to catering and serving elaborate picnics and clambakes. According to Marjorie, ten years ago there were two long-established realtors serving the Harbors; today there are a dozen, including local offices for big New York outfits like Sotheby's.

For me, these are but zits on the face of perfection. I've come to think of Leeward Harbor and Longboat and the rest as B's dowry, although only metaphorically, since it seems pretty clear that she has no intention of marrying me or anyone else, and I certainly have no immediate plans to marry.

Anyway, it was a marvelous four days. The Longstreths are great and gracious hosts. B's mischievous twin Claudio and his companion Frederick were there, and I enjoyed them. B's right about her brother's politics: he's as outspoken a liberal as I've run across in years; his faith in OG remains undimmed; any shortcomings are completely the fault of the GOP and its captive Supreme Court.

Unfortunately, there was one night when we were condemned to dinner at the Hardcastles', a case of "having to fly the flag," as Marjorie put it. Claudio refused to go, but as a houseguest I had no option. It was all very grand—caviar, '82 first-growth claret ("96.3 in Parker," as Walter Hardcastle told us); monumental flower arrangements by the florists who take care of La Grenouille in New York; a chef recently recruited from a three-star Paris restaurant.

I reminded our host that we'd met several years earlier at Rosenweis's Christmas party at the Weir, but he drew a blank. He spent most of dinner telling the table about a book he's planning to write, about "the goddamn ongoing niggerization of America and how are we going to stop it." B says that if you want to see steam literally

346

blow out of someone's ears, just say the name of our current president to her uncle. We were back at Longboat by 10:00 p.m.

Otherwise, the weekend was perfect—and if things between B and myself keep on as they have, there'll be many more to look forward to. Great food and drink, great company, great weather. We picnicked, I was taken sailing, we hiked the national park trails, got in some downtime while the golfers golfed, and I loved every second. One day, Bianca and I took one of the little sailboats out and made for a small island that's only clearly visible when the fog lifts. We anchored, waded ashore, spread out a picnic, then ate and drank and lazed in the chilly sun until a good idea struck us both simultaneously and we went behind a big boulder and made love, at a pitch of excitement that I thought might burst the laces of my boat shoes.

"Well," she gasped after she got enough breath back to talk, "that's not the way we normally go about our lives here at Leeward Harbor, capital of old-fashioned circumspection."

"How do you know?" I gasped back. "What about your mother and father, back in the day? I'll bet they've got a few tales to tell."

"In their day, my buck, such tales weren't told!"

Point well taken, I thought. And another point for the Longboat Way.

Incidentally, I've tapped out this entry on a terrific new gadget, a present from B, one of those rare gifts where both the object itself and the feeling behind it are life-enhancing: an iPad. It has been on the market for maybe four months and has sold millions. Some people have all the brains.

# SEPTEMBER 16, 2010

End of week one of the Rosenweis Regime at STST. It's been two months since I last visited their offices, although my retainer payments have been direct-deposited right on schedule.

Lucia's still hanging on and plans to stay until the end of the year. Her role will be much reduced during this interim period. She tells me that Rosenweis kept his inner-circle shock troops in the office over the Labor Day weekend to rejigger the internal power grid, and when STST returned to work a week ago Tuesday and looked at the new organization charts, it was clear that the Mankoff regime is over.

San Calisto's worried; they fear their days are numbered—specifically that they will be evicted if or when the building is converted to make way for a London- or Monaco-style private bank for high-net-worth clients. I'll have to get out, too—so I've called a couple of brokers and set up appointments to look at office space. But nothing will replace those old boys across the way. No matter what alternative arrangements are made for them, an era is surely ending.

Which brings me to something else that's going to be shut down: this diary.

With Mankoff out of the picture, my career as a Wall Street secret agent is over. Mankoff is sick. Orteig is said to have made the First Lady's shit list and can no longer enter the Oval Office without knocking. Ian Spass is reported by the *Journal* to have signed on at a reported $5 million a year as senior Washington counsel to a gigantic Mexican telecom. So now it's time for yours truly to make my final bows and tiptoe from the stage.

At the end of the day, has anything really changed? Wall Street may not be back to all its exact same old tricks, but confidence is certainly running high among the traders and bankers that they can get away with whatever needs to be gotten away with to turn a fast buck. Winters has left the administration, and Holloway has announced that he'll be leaving soon, too, and no one on the Street has gone to jail.

The general economy remains stagnant. Can I say that the trillion or so that was diverted from Main Street would have made a difference? One would think so.

My Wall Street glory moment is finished, and with it, the point of this diary. I'm going to load it onto a couple of flash drives and tuck them away in my safety deposit box. I sometimes think of what could happen if I went public with it now, but I'm certainly not going to do that while Mankoff is alive. Or while I'm alive, for that matter.

Grace Mankoff reports that her husband is deteriorating. Almost as if separation from STST has cut into his will to live. She says that the tics in his speech patterns seem to be accelerating, the "lost" pauses seem more frequent. And yet the disease does have its peculiar compensations: Grace tells me is that his harpsichord playing has never been better; all of a sudden, "the fleetness and fluency Leon's been chasing for years is his," is the way she put it.

How odd life is.

# NOVEMBER 10, 2010

The Democrats and OG got killed in last week's midterm elections—as expected. The wonk set is declaring the Affordable Care Act a singular accomplishment, but it doesn't feel like it. I often wonder what the early days of the New Deal felt like. Bigger and better, I would guess.

The nation's politics are broken. The GOP has become a raving hive of lunatics, NRA-style gun fundamentalists, and wealth-worshippers. The rise of the Dreck brothers, who are willing to spend whatever it takes to turn the country hard right, is symbolic of the way things are going. The San Calisto crowd says the Drecks remind them of the German industrialists who backed Hitler; they better be careful of getting what they wish for.

And how do I feel about it all, given my own role in the events? As usual, I waver. The moral qualms haven't gone away, and I know I was too eager to dive in—too excited about a breathtaking mission. Still, I don't know that the alternative—any alternative—would have been much better.

# DECEMBER 18, 2010

And so, Gentle Reader, with this entry I bid you goodbye. It's been a long and winding road, hasn't it? Three and a half years: all the way from Three Guys, to a world without Mankoff.

A brave new world?

Where do I come out when my mirror and I engage in a little personal evaluation? I suppose I could say we are what we are, life is what it is, we end up where we end up—and leave it at that. But my mind doesn't work that way. I look at the past three-odd years and see three standout achievements. I cut a deal with Orteig that probably saved Wall Street from the gallows, in a manner of speaking. I blackmailed Washington into making STST whole on its busted GIG swaps. I developed a relationship with Ian Spass that led him to tell me about Polton turning state's evidence on Protractor, on the basis of which STST was able to reduce its out-of-pocket on settling with Washington by $350 million.

How's that going to look to St. Peter when he turns to my page at the day of reckoning? There was a Grantland Rice poem the Warrior liked to recite when he'd had a couple: *"When the one great scorer comes to write against your name, he marks not that you won or lost, but how you played the game."*

But what if the game itself stinks? Can the whole point simply be to make the rich richer? That seems to have happened, too—and do I want that on my conscience? The fact is, I really never thought through these outcomes when Mankoff asked me to be his man. If I were a true son of Wall Street, I wouldn't have given a shit then, and I still wouldn't today.

But I do.

February 17, 2007, to December 18, 2010. Three years, ten months, and a day, if I've counted correctly. A geologic era. A lot of water over the dam, a ton of money in play, and the further corruption of a political philosophy that was once upon a time the greatest melding of idealism and moral power on God's earth. Things have happened that maybe shouldn't have; things haven't happened that maybe should have. The earth regularly shifts beneath our feet. We'll let history be the judge.

That I should be thinking such thoughts now reflects a change in attitude that I attribute to my growing involvement with B's family, her parents especially, and what they represent: namely, the kind of American, "city on a hill" values I was brought up and educated to believe in. The more this country went on in the way it has since Reagan, the harder it has been to believe in that stuff. But in Marjorie's company, I do. Thayer's, too, although less so— he's a banker, after all.

I've made two copies of the diary, and I've erased the text from my computer. On Monday, these will go into my safety deposit box, and there they'll slumber until someone finds them after I'm dead.

So there we are. I thank you for being a great audience. One last word, if I may. I started this diary with a quote from Gibbon, so it seems only fitting that I finish with one. At the end of his *Autobiography*, the great historian describes the moment when he completed *The Decline and Fall*:

After laying down my pen I took several turns in a *berceau*, or covered walk of acacias, which commands a prospect of the country, the lake, and the mountains. The air was temperate, the sky was serene, the silver orb of the moon was reflected from the waters, and all nature was silent. I will not dissemble the first emotions of joy on recovery of my freedom, and, perhaps, the establishment of my fame. But my pride was soon humbled, and a sober melancholy was spread over my mind, by the idea that I had taken an everlasting leave of an old and agreeable companion, and that, whatsoever might be the future date of my history, the life of the historian must be short and precarious . . .

"Short and precarious." Let's hope not. Precarious is for Wall Street thrillers, and this isn't one. The thrill is gone, as the song says.

So there you have it, Gentle Reader. Over and out. Good night and good luck. See you in some other life.

PART TWO

# CHAUNCEY'S CHRISTMAS CAROL

December 25, 2014–January 1, 2015

# DECEMBER 20, 2014

Well, Gentle Reader, surprised to hear from me again? What has prompted me to pick up my figurative pen, you ask?

When I began the diary, I perceived it as a chronicle that would be useful to historians, a record of a slice of time, place, and activity that would have some value to scholars and readers of a later day. My thinking on that has changed. Changed completely. Bear with me.

Four years ago, I stepped away from the fray, ceased to be a participant, and became a mere onlooker with no skin in the game. For one thing, Leon Mankoff passed away two years ago, in September 2012. His death wasn't unexpected, but it was a huge blow, nonetheless.

Still, the last four years have been mostly positive. B and I go from strength to strength. Her family has become mine, as it were. Values and convictions I had carried away from my upbringing and education have been restored. I had been taught one kind of America, you might say, but somewhere along the way lost sight of it, just as the country lost sight of what it's supposed to be.

Now, with Mankoff no longer around and me completely detached from STST (when my consulting contract came up for renewal last year, I was advised that the firm "was now going in a different direction" in my area of competence, and that was that), I started to look at the state of the nation's affairs with a cold, hard eye. It's fair to say that I was—am—disgusted with what I saw. Increasingly so, day by day. Disgusted with the ignorance, the greed, the mediocrity, the total lack of proportion and rationality in every area essential to the moral and material well-being of the nation. And disgusted with myself for having played the role I did in the country's unconditional surrender to Mammon and his cohorts.

I'm not going to sermonize on the state of America in 2014 or about Wall Street, or about the stench of corruption and selling out that every pore of Washington exudes. There are just too many ills and evils to list, and any halfway sentient American knows what they are. The diagnosis isn't good, the prognosis is dire, and as we run up to the election two years from now, it will only get worse. Already the candidates who've announced for the GOP nomination would suit a circus clown car, and on the other side, of course, she's back. What I spent $75 million of Mankoff's money to prevent—Hillary Clinton in the White House—at this point looks like a done deal for 2016.

The only remedy for all that ails us, at least as I see it, is for this country to experience the kind of catharsis—a massive coast-to-coast convulsion—that will force open its eyes, eyes blinded for almost a generation by now by avarice and stupidity, and shove in its face an unignorable, true picture of what we have let ourselves become. The more I ponder the matter, the more I've concluded that there are only two ways out of the present swamp. One would be mobilize *good* Big Money against *bad* Big Money. I don't see that happening.

The other would be public outrage of a scale, intensity, and universality few Americans now alive will have seen firsthand. French-Revolution-quality outrage, pitchforks-and-tumbrels-quality outrage. I may be flattering myself, but I think my diary, properly and effectively presented to the electorate, could trigger such a reaction, and I intend to give it a shot.

What we need is a cathartic trigger I believe my diary could be the means by which to force such a catharsis. The twenty-first-century equivalent of Camille Desmoulins hopping up on a restaurant table in Paris and haranguing the crowd into a fury that led to the storming of the Bastille and all that followed. The kind of catharsis that the Civil War represented, that brought the end of slavery and for a time a genuine effort toward civil rights; that led to the New Deal; that brought to a nation awash in hopelessness the power that comes from thinking as a community in the way that World War II did. Hell, it was just such a catharsis, north to south, east to west, that created the United States.

If I make my diary public, I think, quite frankly, that it will have several times the seismic effect of Watergate. Just look at the differences in scale. It'll get people to ask, if this is the way the country can be jerked around by the money power, what else may have gone down that we don't know about?

The voters are mad or disillusioned. Racists hate OG, Tea Partiers hate him, his own party's disappointed at his feckless presidency—particularly his failure to take on Wall Street—and of course Wall Street hates him (even if they pretend they don't) out of fear that he may still have a regulatory wild card up his sleeve. Both sides of the "class warfare" aisle seem angry at him: either too much talk about inequality, or not enough. His tax policies favor the other guy, whoever the other guy is. People who can't find Iran on a map are furious with his negotiations with what Bush called the "axis of evil." Many of the noisiest voices in the room hate the Trans-Pacific trade agreement because there's nothing in it for them, which they just know means there must be something in there for someone they hate—and of course there is, most likely. To right-wingers, OG's a Socialist, to others he's a puppet for crypto-fascist corporatism. A lot of the threads are interwoven, which only turns up the heat.

So my solution is to declare "a plague on all your houses" and blow up the lot. I realize there are risks, but the way I see it, none that are crippling. The first word out of millions of mouths when they read what I've got will be "impeachment." I don't think that dog will hunt. I believe Orteig when he swears OG never knew what was being done on his behalf. He wasn't in the White House; he wasn't even the nominee; the election was a year and a half off.

359

Winters and Holloway and Brewer weren't privy to the arrangement that positioned them strategically. You might accuse me (and Orteig) of election tampering, but I never touched a ballot or a ballot box or paid someone to vote a certain way, and most of the refineries and pipelines through which I moved the cash lie outside U.S. jurisdiction. Besides, what Orteig and I got up to in 2007 was within only three years ratified as perfectly legal in *Citizens United*. As someone said to me once, the business of the Supreme Court is to discover law, not create it.

There's a risk of plunging the country into another "long national nightmare," which is how Gerald Ford described Watergate and associated commotions when he took over from Nixon. But the length of that nightmare was what? A couple of years, tops. The break-in was in August 1972, and within two years and a bit of change, Nixon was out of office. In a real crisis, with the right leadership, this country responds and heals quickly.

I plan to consult with Marina Hochster, who I hope will agree to be my Woodward and Bernstein combined. Over the past four years, thanks to B, I've gotten to know her. I respect her, and no present-day investigative journalist has the impact she has. Not that anything she's done has been a game-changer. Nothing she's ever written has made a real, practical difference. No politician or banker has gone to jail because of her. She recognizes this—and it drives her nuts, as she's told B and me.

It's the event written about, not the writing, that captures the public's imagination and stirs up its fury. It's *what* you have to write about, the creature you dig out of the muck, that grabs up the reader by his emotions; *how well* you report and write the story— dig up the dirt, come up with the right words and images—only enhances the effect. When Woodward and Bernstein tackled Watergate, there wasn't withal the static and suppression that there is now, and even then no one followed up on the story. The front page, the nightly network news: these were all you needed. The Internet didn't exist; neither did social media.

But if you have the right-size story—and what could be bigger than fixing a presidential election?—then the Internet and its off-spring can be unbelievably powerful when it comes to setting off a pandemic of anger and retribution.

So that's my scheme.

I realize this represents a 180-degree swivel from where I started, and you probably want to know how this has come about—this radical change of heart and intention.

To answer the question, I fear I'm going to have to give you some sense of what I've been up to since we parted company four years ago.

As I've said, the best part of the last few years has been my life with B and her family, but there have been some professional high points, too. None higher than the Shakespeare opera series under-written by my client Leonard King, who just sold his Zephyr fam-ily of hedge funds to a Qatari bank for a cool $10 billion. The series has been a huge success. I've attended the openings in Paris, Shanghai, New York, and Vienna, and all went well—especially Vienna, where the Adès *Tempest* was a huge success: ten curtain calls, standing ovations, and Leonard clapped onstage and pre-sented with a huge bouquet of roses.

He's setting up a foundation that he wants me to be the CEO of. I'm not sure how I'll respond. I relish my independence. My business is fine: I have all the clients I can possibly handle, and my senior people are taking on more of the workload—clients originally mine with whom they've worked are calling them first. I like my new offices off Columbus Circle, although I do miss the old gang at San Calisto (I've kept in touch with Scaramouche). Still, a salary of $3 million a year isn't to be sniffed at.

So everything was pretty hunky-dory until just ten days ago, when B called me from a chartered jet on her way to Boston. She had devastating news: while in London to see friends, her mother had been run over and killed. Looked left when she should have looked right while navigating Berkeley Square, and was struck by a lorry and killed instantly. Could I come up to help out, since her father is a wreck and her brother has gone to London to fetch his mother's ashes?

I rushed through the day's remaining business, threw together a suitcase, and headed for LaGuardia. B had invited me to stay at the family house in Brookline, but there are times when it's better to be nearby and available, but not underfoot. I checked in at the Hotel Charles, where I usually put up when I have business in Cambridge, and cabbed it to Brookline, arriving two hours after B.

It was weird being back in a house where, only a fortnight earlier, over Thanksgiving, I had stayed with the family under completely different emotional circumstances. But I swallowed my feelings and did my best to be helpful: ran errands, answered the phone, shook a great many hands, uttered the odd piety, and made myself useful—functionally and, I hope, spiritually.

Claudio returned from London on Thursday the 18th. The memorial service was held this past Saturday the 20th in Harvard's Memorial Church.

It was both moving and classy. The readings and music were well chosen and delivered with art and eloquence, and unlike most upper-class funerals, the eulogists didn't talk mostly about themselves. One felt this service was really about the Marjorie I'd known. The church felt truly suffused with love. After the instrumental interlude following the sermon—the slow movement of Beethoven's "Spring" sonata marked *Adagio molto espressivo*, performed by a violin-piano duo from the Harvard music school—I doubt there was a dry eye in the house.

The final reading was the zinger. After the final strains of "I

Was Glad," the congregation resumed its seats. A tall figure dressed in designer black appeared from behind the sanctuary, stopped at the front pew to embrace Thayer and his children, and made her way to the lectern. A rising murmur ran through the congregation as people realized who it was: the First Lady of the United States—FLOTUS, as the media and Secret Service shorthand her—Marjorie's devoted former law school pupil and mentee.

I couldn't help thinking immediately how tired Mrs. OG looked. What I saw in her face I've seen written in the features of other women, an expression peculiar to those married to men whom the world admires and praises and sucks up to, but men who are difficult to be married to, for any of a thousand reasons. When I reflect on OG's marriage, I always find myself thinking of the Clintons—and the FDRs. Couples whose marriages were more in the nature of the deal I'd cut with Orteig seven years ago than an exchange of sacred vows and a mutual true love. There are frames in the terrific Ken Burns documentary about FDR when Mrs. Roosevelt had that look. It must be terribly draining, to live with someone like that. And FDR was a great man. Destiny's jury is still out on OG.

It's almost as if the psychological history of her husband's presidency is written in her eyes and the corners of her mouth. I found myself wondering whether she too, like all those millions of other adherents, had been disappointed in her husband's conduct of his office. Was it Marjorie who once told me that that FLOTUS could have had a big public career on her own, but chose to put her own prospects to one side and commit her abilities 100 percent to her husband?

When the First Lady spoke, however, it was in a strong, clear voice that belied her drawn appearance. It surely left no one in the congregation in doubt that this is a very formidable person.

"I'm going to read a few passages from a book Marjorie held dear," she began. "The book is called *The American Democrat.* It's by James Fenimore Cooper. It was a favorite book of Marjorie's and she made it a favorite book of my husband's and mine. You might say Marjorie regarded it as a kind of secular catechism, but since the principles it enumerates are what any good Christian or person of faith—and certainly any good American—would hold dear, even though many of these seem lost to the present day, I have no hesitation in reading them here in church."

"The copy I'm reading from was Marjorie's own copy," FLOTUS continued. "She gave it to me when I graduated from law school, and I will cherish it forever. The passages I'll be reading are passages she marked. I've heard her quote one or two from memory; she obviously took to heart what she knew by heart.

"First, let me tell you just a bit about this book. *The American Democrat* was published in 1836, when Cooper had returned to his native land after seven years in Paris. It was written at the same time as de Tocqueville's *Democracy in America*, so it gives us the opportunity to compare what a long-descended American—these are the same Coopers who founded Cooperstown—thought of his country as opposed to a French aristocrat. Without going into too much background, I'll just say that Cooper didn't like much of what he saw when he returned to his native land. Much of what he complained of will seem especially resonant today.

"Now, let's start with this:

"Whenever the enlightened, wealthy, and spirited of an affluent and great country seriously conspire to subvert democratical institutions, their leisure, money, intelligence, and means of combining will be found too powerful for the ill-directed and conflicting efforts of the mass. It is therefore all important to enlist a portion of this class, at least, in the cause of freedom, since its power at all times renders it a dangerous enemy."

Hearing this, my first thought was, well, nothing changes, does it. "Leisure, money, intelligence, and means of combining." Hello, Dreck brothers.

The First Lady read for perhaps another ten minutes. I paid close attention. Cooper was a Yale man, and if Bones had been around when he was on the Old Campus, I like to think we'd have tapped him.

Clearly, Cooper favored what I guess you could call a "moral aristocracy." He was more than a bit of a snob, and yet at the end of the day his message is compelling, a point emphasized by the passage with which the First Lady concluded her reading:

> "It is peculiarly graceful in the American, whom the accidents of life have raised above the mass of the nation, to show himself conscious of his duties . . . (as a guardian of the liberties of his fellow citizens) . . . by asserting at all times the true principles of government, avoiding, equally, the cant of demagoguism with the impracticable theories of visionaries, and the narrow and selfish dogmas of those who would limit power by castes. They who do not see and feel the importance of possessing a class of such men in a community, to give it tone, a high and far sighted policy, and lofty views in general, can know little of history and have not reflected on the inevitable consequences of admitted causes."

With that, FLOTUS closed the book, looked out over the congregation for just a moment, as if to say, "You've heard what to do, now go do it," then bowed her head, murmured briefly to herself—presumably a prayer for Marjorie—and stepped down from the lectern. She paused again to embrace Thayer and the twins, and took a seat beside him in the family pew, with her bodyguards lingering discreetly off to one side.

I was impressed. Marjorie had often spoken to me of Cooper's book and had promised to get me a copy. About the only promise she hadn't kept. The passages that had been read reflected Marjorie right down to the last atom of DNA, I thought. True noblesse oblige—the real thing—mated to uncommon common sense; faith coupled with reason and spiced with decency. Courage. Moral knitting stuck to. Codes of behavior and consideration observed. Compassion.

There was one word in particular word that several of the speakers used to describe Marjorie, an adjective that they never would use to describe, say, the merely-although-obscenely-rich like the Dreck brothers, who are trying to buy the last remnants of civil democracy out from under its citizens, or a boastful loudmouth like Donald Trump. That word is "patrician." Marjorie was a perfect exemplar of the species. They're hard to find now, because the qualities that make up an authentic patriciate have effectively disappeared.

Ten minutes later, after a rousing rendition of "Oh God, Our Help in Ages Past" and a final benediction by the Harvard chaplain, the service ended.

The congregation walked across the Yard toward Quincy Street and the Faculty Club. The First Lady led the way arm-in-arm with Thayer and B. The rest of us trooped along behind.

It was then that I decided I needed to make my diary public.

Thinking back, I'm tempted to regard this short stroll as my personal road to Damascus. It was as if I heard a voice—Marjorie's voice—speaking to me out of a thunderclap heard only by me. I found myself thinking that I had somehow betrayed Marjorie. Ridiculous, I know. I had no idea she existed, she or her family, when I carried out my business with Orteig. And how responsible am I for what's happened? There have been shortcomings in OG's administration—serious, grievous shortcomings—and these have continued into his second term, when you'd think he'd be bidding hard and talking tough to reclaim his historical legacy. But would Hillary have been preferable, with her husband running wild peddling influence and access? Or John McCain? A legitimate hero, sure, but with Sarah Palin a heartbeat away? That the governance of this great nation has become even more of a moral cesspool than in 2007 can't be laid at my door; if you want to blame someone, blame Congress. Still, the feeling materialized and wouldn't go away—it was like a pebble lodged in a shoe—that I owed amends for my role in this state of affairs. Amends to the traditions I was raised in; amends to Marjorie and what she represented; amends for betraying so much of what I had been brought up to believe, values that I had allowed to slip away the deeper and further I ventured into fixing and manipulating.

But if amends were due from me or anyone, what form might they take? That's when I thought of making my diary public. It could change things. Change them big-time.

That's a great and probably completely unrealistic expectation, I told myself even as I probed the notion. What, realistically, are the chances of firing up an electorate self-disenfranchised by selfishness and greed and by an appalling ignorance of history and civics? How does one undo a political system totally corrupted by the wealth of plutocrats and the venality of legislators? Ask any rational observer and the answer has to be that the odds stink.

Still, you have to go with what you've got, and what I have still seems pretty potent, I thought as I entered the Faculty Club.

For the next hour I carried out the duties that go with being the designated boyfriend of the decedent's daughter: making sure elderly guests got seats and drinks and well-chosen plates from the buffet, rescuing So-and-So from You-Know-Who, trying to remember names and salutations. I did, briefly, get to shake hands with FLOTUS; the way she looked at me suggested she knew in a general way of my role in the Longstreth scheme of things and was inclined, at first sight, to tolerate me. How she might have felt had she known my role in putting her in the life she now led wasn't a matter I cared to conjecture.

She left after about an hour. B saw her out a side door and they chatted briefly before FLOTUS's limo took her to Soldier Field where her chopper awaited. When B came back, she led me off into a side parlor.

"You're going to kill me," she said.

"Really? Why, pray tell? At the moment I lack both means and motive."

"You know how I'm planning to get Daddy settled at Boca Grande and then come up to spend New Year's and most of the next week with you?"

I nodded. Boca Grande is an island off Florida's west coast, a sort of Leeward Harbor with palm trees. A lot of old Wilmington-Philadelphia-Baltimore money winters there, along with a sprinkling of Boston and Hartford. Marjorie and Thayer have been going there ever since the Brookline nest emptied and the big empty house became too much to deal with at Christmas. Boca's like most places of its kind: grown today to about three times the size that suited it best, everything bigger, fancier, faster, and more costly, but still shot through with agreeable reminders of the way upper-class Florida resort life used to be.

I thoroughly approved of the twins' plan to park their father in Boca for the winter: he'll be among solicitous friends, and there may even be an alluring widow or two to hold his hand. (In my view, men who've had blissful marriages tend to find new love pretty quickly. No scars to get in the way.) Just to make certain he's well taken care of, B and Claudio will do ten days on, ten days off through the winter. A week or two before Easter, whichever one of them is on duty will bring him back north and reinstall him in Brookline.

"Well," she said, sounding genuinely unhappy, "it seems I'm going to have to leave you the day after New Year's. Orders from on high." She went on to explain. FLOTUS has asked B to join her and the First Daughters at Camp David for New Year's and a few days afterward. "I think she's lonely, she wants company. Mother dying has hit her hard."

"It's hit all of us hard." I remarked, perhaps a little harshly. I'd been looking forward to our time together. "Where's the Great Man?" I added. "Off playing golf? Screwing up foreign policy?"

B ignored that. She remains a true believer, and OG's presidency is a matter she and I never discuss. "It's just not the sort of invitation I can refuse," she said. "You see that, don't you?"

Of course I had to. Being bid to hang out at Camp David is akin to an invitation from royalty or the pope. There was no point in arguing. Might as well surrender gracefully.

B nodded. "I'll make it up to you, I promise. I have to go to L.A. after Camp David to sign up this new production deal with Carousel, but I'm heading back to Boca for Martin Luther King weekend with Daddy. Why don't you join me then?"

The idea was appealing. Second-best but plenty good enough, so I assented. "But you *will* come up for New Year's Eve, even if it's only for the night?"

"Of course," she replied. "I'm really sorry about this, but . . ."

I could tell she had a lot on her mind. "Look, what will be will be," I said and made a small production of looking at my watch. "You know," I said, "I really need to get going if I'm going to make the 3:10 Acela. You and Claudio have a lot to do—and frankly so do I. The last thing you need underfoot is me."

She hugged me. I could sense her relief at getting rid of me. Even between couples who love each other desperately there are moments like these.

"Thanks for everything, darling. You've been a huge help. I'll see you on the thirty-first. I'll get to you by noon even if I have to charter something." We kissed and I rushed off to catch the train.

Which is where I am now, rattling south in an Amtrak "quiet car." I have with me the bound galleys of a book I've naturally been anxious to read: *Hope and Change: A Political Pilgrimage.* It's a memoir by Homer Orteig, to be published next March. I've skimmed the book rapidly, looking for names and dates that might jump out at me. So far I've only found this:

> I was livid when I found out that Holloway and Harley Winters had quietly lobbied against an amendment to the stimulus that would have restricted the payment of bonuses at firms that received bailout funds. Those bonuses had become a huge political sore point for the administration, but the finance guys argued that retroactive steps to claw back the money would have violated existing contracts.
>
> "This will be the end of capitalism as we know it," Holloway told me, to which I responded: "I hate to break the news, Mr. Secretary, but capitalism isn't trading very high right now."

He goes on to relate that the president's chief economic advisers often went directly against the expressed wishes of their boss.

My first, cynical reaction was: so this is what $75 million worth of "livid" looks like. Here was Orteig pretending to have been the victim of ideological forces he himself had conspired with me to unleash. Then an amusing thought struck me: how great my diary would look reposing next to Orteig's on a front table at Barnes & Noble. Possibly even packaged together at an attractive discount.

A bit later on, Orteig's memoir relates something that explains much. He admits that by late 2010, he had ceased to be considered a White House insider. He doesn't point the finger at Winters and

Holloway as principal agents in his fall from grace, but I can well imagine those two had a hand in it. What an irony! That November, OG took a bad hit in the midterm elections; not quite as bad as what befell him a month ago, but definitely a portent of bad political weather on the horizon. Would he have done better with Orteig still calling signals? Hard to say.

In this connection, let it be noted that Winters has definitively moved from Wall Street to Main Street and declared himself a man of the people. He's posted his notice of change of address, as it were, in a series of op-eds beginning two years ago that advocated more money for the common folk and heavier costs to the Street. As there's no more definitive and accurate a weathervane than Winters when it comes to charting shifts in direction of the winds of influence and opinion, this confirms my own sense that populism isn't dead—it's merely lying doggo, awaiting its day.

The train is now passing through New London. A while back, I put Orteig's book aside and did some serious thinking about how Marina might take my diary public. Not surprisingly, my thoughts keep returning to Watergate and the revelations that transfixed the nation back in 1973, toward the end of my first year at Groton. A bunch of us watched the hearings on a TV that belonged to my favorite American history teacher, and afterward we discussed them with the fervor of boys that age, before reality has frosted the rose. Our teacher would remark that he'd felt the same intensity twenty years earlier as a sophomore at Haverford watching the Army-McCarthy hearings.

It also occurred to me that I better look out for #1: no point in making a grand civic gesture that would land me in the hoosegow or get me assassinated by some raging OG voter. I ought to check with a lawyer about my legal exposure. Artie Han fits that bill—and he and Marina know each other through their mutual friendship with B. This could even be a three-way collaboration.

Before I do anything, of course, I'll want to reread the diary. Reread and maybe redact. It's been a couple of years since I looked at it, but I know there's stuff in there of no conceivable public interest, and that is not mine to disclose. Certain aspects of my relationship with Lucia, for example, and with B. There are other things that there'd be no purpose in making public. So on Monday, I'll go to the bank and get the flash drives I stashed there four years ago.

I've organized my immediate future. I'll spend Sunday at home clearing up my backlog. First thing Monday, I have a breakfast meeting in the Waldorf Towers, after which I'll fetch the diary from the bank. I have so much on my plate this coming week—office party, client conferences, and so on—that I probably won't get to it much before Christmas Eve. At that point I'll reread it, and decide whether to go ahead with this plan. I can tell you now that I'm 99 percent certain that I'm going to. If nothing else, I owe it to Marjorie.

Now I'm going to put my head back, close my eyes, and catch a nap. We'll be in Penn Station in a couple of hours.

# DECEMBER 21, 2014

A bad, bad day—especially for a Sunday.

My doorbell rang a little after 8:00 a.m. Pedro was standing there with a FedEx envelope.

"I'm sorry, Mr. Suydam," he said. "I was at my niece's birthday party yesterday, and we had a new kid covering the desk. He didn't know to put this inside your apartment."

I took the envelope, thanked him, wished his niece a happy life, and gave him $50 to add to her birthday haul. It's Christmas, after all.

I looked at the waybill. It was from Portland, Oregon, from someone named E. Morton. The name wasn't familiar to me, not right off, but I have a number of connections in Portland and usually have something going on out there.

Inside was an envelope with an engraved street address on the flap. It was paper-clipped to an ordinary 8-by-11 manila envelope.

The first envelope contained a handwritten covering letter dated December 19.

It read:

Dear Chauncey Suydam:

I am Clement Spear's daughter, and although this is a terrible first encounter between two people who've never met, I'm afraid I have very sad news. My father died this morning. He was diagnosed with pancreatic cancer just about the time he saw you in New York last spring, and the end came swiftly. He told no one, and we were sworn not to. He just retreated into the bosom of his family, reread and then had read to him some things that had meant a lot to him, and we took good care of him right up to his last breath. As you may be aware, Oregon law provides for physician-assisted termination of life for patients suffering from an incurable disease with a prognosis of less than six months remaining. Father considered that option but decided to let life and death take their course. In the end, he died without pain, almost as if he had willed his moment of departure. I was at his bedside when he left us.

Some weeks ago, not long before his condition obliged him to enter hospice care, he wrote you the attached letter, and instructed me to send it to you on his death. Do not take it badly that he never told you about his illness; he wanted to keep it secret from everyone except his immediate family.

He spoke of you often; I think he thought of you as the sort of son he had always wished for and you were certainly someone whose values he respected because they were the same as his.

"Antediluvian" was his favorite word when it came to the code of conduct he liked to think he lived by—and generally did.

I do hope we meet someday. It was Father's wish that there be no service marking his death and obviously we have honored his intentions. His ashes have been scattered (surreptitiously) at a park down by the Columbia River where he liked to go in the mornings to drink coffee, read the papers, and contemplate the dismal state of the world. I dare say there may be a fair amount about the latter in his letter to you.

Again, I repeat how unhappy I am that this should have to be the first communication between you and me, but as Father liked to say, death waits for no man.

With every good wish,
Emily Spear Morton

I read it again, then just sat there for a minute or so, trying to cope with this ugly news.

First Mankoff, then Marjorie, now Scaramouche! Is death some kind of sniper who has it in for me? Those were three of the fixed stars by which I've navigated. Now they're extinguished, all three.

When I had last seen Scaramouche back in the late spring, he seemed in decent fettle, and he sounded OK when I last spoke to him on the phone at the beginning of November. A bit short of breath, but that happens with men his age.

His letter was dated October 17, 2014, typed on plain computer paper. Written before he and I last spoke. So he knew. It's a long and eloquent letter, and I can't not include it here.

My dear Chauncey:

When you read this, you'll have had my bad news.

You've often heard me quote the great baseball executive Branch Rickey to the effect that "luck is the residue of design." Certainly in my case this has proven to be so. I moved here to be near my daughter Emily and her family and see more of them—as I recall we discussed this in New York when I saw you back in March—but I had no plans to die this soon. As it is, she and her husband and their children have been an ineffable source of comfort and care and this is a fine and caring little city in which to fall terminally ill.

I don't want you to be upset at being left out of the loop, as they say, but our last meeting in New York went so well, and was so happy an occasion for me, that I wanted to leave matters that way. It so happened that the very next morning a virtual sentence of death was pronounced on me by one of the "top men" (actually, in this case, a woman) at Sloan Kettering whom I had come east to consult. By then I was pretty sure what the verdict would be—I had already been

375

checked out by a slew of doctors at the Fred Hutchinson Center in Seattle—but you ain't cooked until you're right and properly done. Cancer seems to be a dish for which there can never be too many cooks.

I shall depart this mortal coil with few regrets. The accidents of history worked matters out so that my generation has to be about the most blessed in American history. We were born during the Depression; we just missed World War II; and we came of age in an era of unprecedented but—as it appears to have turned out—unlasting prosperity. Of course, I doubt if you'd say that had you been born black in the South in 1934, but if in that same year, as was my case, the stork handed you to well-off, white, well-connected Episcopal parents in Lake Forest, you couldn't have asked for better! The problem with being raised in such circumstances is that you are ill-equipped to deal with what I've concluded is the most vexing business in life: coming to terms with one's own insignificance.

Of course, back then we lived in fear of our parents, while today, parents seem to live in fear of their children, just another way the world of my boyhood seems to been turned inside out. That it has seems in no small part attributable to a gross dereliction on my generation's part with respect to the obligation to attend to the future, and to keep certain standards bright and polished the way a vintage car buff will tend to a 1940s Oldsmobile. If you want people to behave, you need to materially alter their perception of what they can get away with. In that, Wall Street's so-called "self-governance" has failed miserably.

Which brings me to the business in which I prospered for close to fifty years, since I went down to Wall Street at the invitation of Lembert Struthers, a fellow trustee at

Princeton with my father. That was in 1959, a world and time apart. The Street did what it did at the pleasure of the Federal Reserve, which behaved like a stern but fond parent. The Fed's job, its then-chairman William McChesney Martin liked to say, was to take away the punch bowl just as the party was getting going. By contrast, that pompous, bootlicking ass Greenspan's response was to keep pouring in more booze, with the result that Wall Street has behaved rather like a drunken rock band trashing a hotel room. My old friend Tom Hoenig, former president of the Kansas City branch of the Federal Reserve, once proposed that every four years we hold a sale in which we auction off the office of Secretary of the Treasury to Wall Street. It would appear that, of late, Struthers Strauss has always been winning the auctions.

Today's money people, whether in Wall Street, real estate, or any other rent-extracting, commission-driven business, will stick with you only so long as you are of use to them. When they decide you no longer are, they discard you with the same uncaring indifference with which they chuck away a used tissue. It was not always so. Messrs. Struthers and Strauss cared for and about their people. When I came to work there, there were older men kept on the payroll who were functionally useless except in terms of what they stood for and the honorable past they represented.

I must say that I was never as big a fan of Leon Mankoff as you were—Boola Boola, Skull & Bones, and all that— but it may be that when I finally cross that bourne from which no traveler returns I'll run into Mankoff and we can get to know each other better.

I don't know if there's decent champagne to be had in the hereafter, but I will drink a toast to that sly fox Merlin

Gerrett and the way he recently renegotiated his position in STST stock so as to end up with a bigger chunk at zero incremental outlay. When he and Leon made their deal back in 2008, it struck me as pretty pricey, although I have no doubt it had to be done for reasons of opportunity if not survival. Whether Mankoff would have gone for the recent revision of terms I can't say; when Gerrett found himself sitting across the table from Rosenweis, the sort of person who thinks "loud" means the same as "smart," he must have thought he'd died and gone to Trader Heaven.

Wall Street is the least of my worries, however. It is what it is, and 99.9 percent of the people who work there are honest folk like thee and me. Not above cutting a corner now and then, but who hasn't? What I fear for is the country.

It may be that I am just an Oxycodone-besotted Miniver Cheevy (look him up: poem of that name by Edward Arlington Robinson, America's great unrecognized poet) seeing chimeras in his old age, but I am not alone. I don't think I'm being paranoid when I agree with the opinion in some quarters that the present deplorable state of the union is the consequence of a multitentacled right-wing conspiracy to deliver the governance of the United States into the hands of a massive and collusive complex of the sort Eisenhower warned about—except that this version might better be described as "financial-corporate" instead of "military-industrial." One of the surest ways to achieve this is exactly what has been done: the wages of the mass of the population have been kept flat, thanks to such enabling forces as globalization and automation, while the difference between what people want and what they think they are entitled to has been puffed up and had to be filled in with debt.

The present occupant of the White House represents the

final piece of the puzzle. I wonder if his failures to deliver really aren't the result of an intransigent opposition party, as we have been told, but have been part of a larger scheme from the outset. He certainly came on as if sent by central casting: charismatic, articulate, just black enough, with a smart attractive wife and charming children: just the type the money men would have been looking for to bring their oligarchic scheme to final fruition.

I voted for him once, as I know you did, but in 2012—as we discussed at the time—I like you was unable to summon up so much as a grain of political conviction and stayed home on Election Day. I wonder now (and perhaps you do) whether the two GOP candidates he defeated in '08 and '12 were chosen because they were politically ridiculous and easily beaten. In the event, people voted for him in the expectation of a Grand Bargain; what we've gotten instead is a Grand Betrayal. This president's policies have delivered infinitely greater benefits to the 1 percent than to the rest; even his much-trumpeted health-care bill may drown the disadvantaged in a tsunami of paperwork, complexity being the preferred style of the white-collar fraudster and mega-swindler. And all the while the wicked and the reckless bankers who brought this mess down on the country's head not only go unpunished but have emerged as influential and well-rewarded as ever. Sadly, what this means is that I shall go to my grave without seeing one of my fondest dreams come to pass, which is to have seen at least one of the scoundrels, fools, and miscreants whose greed has led to the greatest depredations on the public purse in history led off in manacles.

You and I are, I suppose, in the so-called "1 percent." Could we—should we—have done more to arrest the way things have gone? I think we should have; but I doubt we could have. Seeing what the rest of the country is going through, I feel a bit ashamed, both for the advantages I enjoy, many of which were already mine in the cradle, and for not standing up for my fellow citizens. I fear I have done what my caste has always done: looked the other way and called for another martini.

Anyway, America is where it is, and how it all will end, God knows. If I had my health, and were confident of the financial future of Emily and her family, I would pledge my fortune and my sacred honor to this "Rediscovery Initiative" the Gerretts are rumored to be organizing. The Gerretts versus the Drecks. Billions versus billions. Good people versus bad people. That's a set-to I'd happily pay good money to see!

Well, now the end approaches. I flatter myself that I've fought the good fight, although perhaps with not enough determination, and lived a decent-enough life. Do I hear the sound of distant trumpets?

They say that Heaven and Hell consist in knowing through all eternity exactly what your children thought of you. I trust your father is content—and that I shall be, too. Neither of us subscribed to what has become Holy Writ among so many of my generation: that it is infinitely more important that the government get none of the family fortune than that the children get any. Of course, that now seems to be changing, as the nation is delivered with all deliberate speed by its legislators and judges to its inheritors.

That brings me to the subject of "class war," a phrase on many lips these days, but usually the lips of those who would have us believe they and their wealth are being targeted by the envious and impoverished. I find these claims of victimhood cowardly and unbecoming. I rather doubt

380

that someone struggling to put food on the table and keep a roof over his family's head has the energy or the inclination, let alone the resources, to bemoan that some plutocrat's yacht is a bit smaller than he'd prefer. Frankly, I wouldn't mind seeing a bit of the real thing—an anticapitalist jihad, if you will, a few heads cut off and castles burned to the ground—if only for the amusement value.

Have you read that silly fool Holloway's self-serving memoir? I had Emily get me the audiobook. Absolute tosh. I was delighted to see how terribly it sold on Amazon and elsewhere. I've either read or listened to a dozen of these things, and in none has the author admitted that he was asleep at the cash register.

Did you note how neatly he glides over that business a couple of years ago when he testified before Congress that as early as 2008 he suspected that LIBOR was being fixed by the big banks, notwithstanding that he and his fellow regulators and bailers-out used LIBOR to set the giveaway interest rates on the bailout loans? How you can commit the people's money using a pricing benchmark you believe to be a swindle confected by the very people to whom you're lending beats me. You can range far and wide before you'll find a better example of "crony capitalism"!

And so it goes, my dear friend. For me, it would seem that the *commedia*, as the clown sings, is almost *finita*. Let me just conclude with this thought. If one has to go, and it seems one must, this strikes me as about as good a time to take my leave as one could ask for. It seems to me that we have evolved a technocratic *nomenklatura* not so different from the old Soviet system in its effects. A massive tectonic shift has taken place, much more profound and devastating than even the gloomiest among us expected.

It's been brought on by technology, by the ascendancy of the money men, by the moral laziness of people of my age and background, by the decline of religion and the rise of fanaticism and many many other causes. Perhaps this is the stream Fitzgerald is speaking of at the conclusion of *Gatsby*, although as you and I have often discussed, he got it backward, and it is pell-mell into the dangerous future, not back into the ungrudging past, that our frail boats are ceaselessly swept.

Go well then, Chauncey, my dear friend. Godspeed and keep the faith. And as our old pal the Warrior would say: keep 'em flyin'.

As ever your chum,
Clem

PS: I trust you saw the article in the *WSJ* about how CDOs have risen like zombies from the grave and are back in vogue, being written to order by the big banks. How can this be allowed to happen?
PPS: Like most men of my generation, when young I was very taken by Spengler's *Decline of the West*. Does anyone read Spengler these days? I seem to recall Spengler saying that money will bring down Western democracy and that the power of money will then be conquered by force. Looking around the world, from Ukraine to Latin America to the Middle East to Bangkok, it's hard to disagree. Will it happen in America? It might.

After I finished reading, I took a deep breath, got up and walked around the room, then sat down and reread Scaramouche's letter, and then reread it again.

I was struck by the credence and impact he gives to memory. On Wall Street today, memory counts for nothing. Look how they skip from bubble to bubble. People die and take institutional memories with them into the tomb. STST as it was holds no present interest for anyone working there now, even less under Rosenweis than under Mankoff.

That's what I think I admire most about Scaramouche. He reached an age where enough of his contemporaries had died off to permit him a revisionist, boastful version of his own life and accomplishments, to claim to have said this or done that without anyone left to challenge him. But as far as I know, he never did. If anyone ever looked in a mirror and saw himself plain, it was Scaramouche.

Well, now he's one with the ages, asleep in Mammon's bosom. A month or so ago, just about the time Scaramouche would have been writing me this farewell letter, a book was published called *STST: The Death of an Ethos*, all about how STST had degraded ethically over the years. I'd read a couple of reviews, considered buying it, decided I just didn't care anymore. I sold my STST shares a long time ago. On the Street that's the ultimate separation. Don't look back. For a while, I was tempted to check the price daily, just to assure myself I hadn't bailed out too early, but after a while my interest faded, then disappeared. Before hitting the sack, something impelled me to go to the laptop and look up STST. Closed Friday at $185. Just about where I came in.

# DECEMBER 23, 2014

The past two days have been consumed with meetings, last-minute shopping, and must-attend Christmas parties. One thing on top of another. It's distracted me from thinking about Scaramouche, and I think I've recovered some emotional balance. I did call his daughter in Portland, and we had a nice conversation about her father. She sounds very pleasant; we agreed that if it seems our paths may cross, we'll look each other up.

I did get to the bank and picked up the flash drives that contain my diary, but haven't had a chance to go over it yet. Tomorrow the office is closed, and I'll have time to read it at my leisure. Then I'll FedEx it to Marina.

Today was the office party, lunch in a private room at Bar Boulud across from Lincoln Center. Everything was first class, and everyone seemed pleased with their bonus; the general jollification was gratifying; all went home happy. What with the business already on the books, and the topmost sector of the income distribution, where I do most of my work, never so flush, 2015 should be an even better year than 2014.

I called B when I got home. Thayer's setting in nicely at Boca, although she's going nuts: too many women in pearls and twinsets and men in pastel trousers with whales and frogs on them complaining about taxes. I can only imagine. Her current plan is to fly up here on New Year's Eve, arriving around midday, and stay at my place until the 1st or 2nd, depending on when she's expected at Camp David. That'll give me plenty of time to get the ball rolling with Marina about the diary. I can hardly bear all the excitement.

# DECEMBER 24, 2014

Woke up feeling very resolute and on top of things. I had budgeted five to six hours today for rereading the diary, and that's about how long it took, including a break for lunch and a bit of fresh air.

It's odd to reread something you haven't looked at in years. I fancy the diary shows me, on balance, to be a decent, patriotic, thoughtful American. That may sound immodest, and at odds with the facts, but there you have it. Sure, I pulled a fast one to get OG elected, but as disappointing as his presidency has been to many, I'm prepared to argue in my defense that he's done a hell of a lot better than any of those he beat out in the race to the White House—both times, in the 2008 election I fixed and in the 2012 election I had nothing to do with.

I know I'm taking a risk. When Marina breaks the story, I'll probably get hauled up before some Congressional committee, or worse. These are matters I need to discuss with Artie once Marina's on board. It seems possible that my political fix with Orteig may not even be illegal anymore, thanks to Citizens United, and if anyone wants exact info on where the money came from, the best I can do will be to give them the names of the feeders I used, all of which are located in jurisdictions where Congressional and other subpoenas have no standing. In any event, I expect Artie can negotiate immunity for me.

At the end of the day, here's the big question. The way the country is now, will this make the difference I think it might? The way the media work now, would even Watergate have stirred up the ruckus it did back in 1973? Earlier this year, the Federal Reserve released the record of its 2008 bailout deliberations, which you'd think would be a HUGE Wall Street story. And so it proved—for about ten minutes and one news cycle as everybody in the media hollered and danced about until they came to see that there was really nothing new there, certainly nothing like what I've recorded, what I was present at, what I heard and saw; nothing like the deals I cut. Nothing truly scandalous: just a bunch of buffoons making bad calls liberally sprinkled with favoritism.

After I finished reading, I took a walk around the block to clear my head and solidify my decision. When I got back, I took a few deep breaths and called Marina's cell phone.

Needless to say, she was surprised to hear from me. "Chauncey! What a pleasant surprise. Are you calling to wish me a happy Christmas?"

"Actually, I'm calling about a Christmas present I have for you." I thought of adding something like "the best present any journalist ever received from anyone," but held back.

"How sweet. I hope it's Ted Cruz's head. That's really all I want for my stocking."

"Alas, no—but it's still something I'm sure you're going to like. It's important that you get it ASAP. Where should I send it? I'm guessing you're out of town."

"You guess correctly. Actually, I'm in the Atlanta airport waiting to change planes. You say I need to get it ASAP."

"Before it spoils? Oh, goody—I hope it's caviar."

"My lips are sealed. Where should I send it?"

"I'll be back in New York Sunday afternoon. Can it wait until then?"

That didn't fit my psychological schedule *at all*. What does Macbeth say? "If 'twere done when 'tis done, 'twere well it were done quickly"? But I quickly got a grip, realizing the timing of this is entirely in our hands, Marina's and mine. There's no risk of anyone scooping us on this. I'm the one with all the cards.

"Sounds good. I'll drop it off at your place around lunchtime Sunday."

386

"Wonderful. I can't wait. How's our darling B?"

"In Florida getting her father settled. She's flying up on New Year's Eve." I didn't say anything about Camp David; that's B's affair; if she chooses to tell Marina about it, fine. I reconfirmed her address in the Flatiron District for the Sunday drop-off.

By 6:00 p.m., everything was in order. I went out to look in on some friends' annual Christmas Eve buffet over on Horatio Street but now I'm home. It's getting on for 10:30 p.m. I've briefly considered going to St. Thomas on Fifth Avenue for its famous midnight service. It's the church with the best music in the city, and the Christmas Eve service is conducted lovingly and reverently. I used to go with my father. He wasn't a religious type, but the beauty and the elegance of this particular occasion were irresistible to him. He even put on white tie, which people of his sort called "evening clothes" back then.

I decided instead to stay home and do what I've often done on Christmas Eve: watch a DVD of *A Christmas Carol*, starring Alastair Sim as Scrooge.

So here we are. The DVD player's cranked up, and the whiskey bottle's out. I feel the way I did all that time ago when Mankoff and I parted after that first meeting at Three Guys: on the brink of a huge adventure. Where this new stage will take me I can't yet know, but I've done all my homework, gotten everything organized. Funny, isn't it, how what goes around comes around. In February 2007, Mankoff had sent me off with his checkbook to put OG in the White House. Today—going on eight years later—I'm considering using the record of that mission to expel that same man from 1600 Pennsylvania.

So there it is: nothing left for the moment, then, but to bid you a merry Christmas, and God bless us, every one!

## DECEMBER 25, 2014

Call me Ebenezer Suydam.

Probably it's all Dickens's fault. And Alastair Sim's. And that last whiskey before turning in a bit before 1:00 a.m.

During the night, dreams came to me, and although they've since faded and fallen apart, they were hard to shake at first, they'd been so real. I vaguely remember something about Marjorie leading me somewhere, and Scaramouche—or was it my prep school squash coach?—along with flashes of my father and other vague figures and situations—jumbled and fragmentary, as if a church window had been shattered by a stone. And mixed up in all those scenes and images was the closing shot from *Three Days of the Condor*, when the Robert Redford character—except that I seem to recall it was me in the dream—is shown outside the old *New York Times* building, obviously getting ready to blow the whistle on the CIA.

I made myself a full and fulfilling breakfast, showered, shaved and got dressed. Took a call from a client at Lyford Cay (for some people, Mammon never takes a holiday) who wanted my estimate of how big an endowment gift to her alma mater would be required to produce an honorary degree. I told her $8 to $10 million ought to suffice. Could I get it done by the end of the year? I thought so—and would call her lawyer first thing tomorrow. Took another call from another old acquaintance, one of those rare college friendships still lively after thirty years, even though we see each other once a month at most, to make plans for our annual Christmas Day movie followed by dinner in Chinatown with enough friends to eat our way through a wide sampling of dishes. We decided there's nothing we really want to see this year, so it'll just be dinner. I'll meet him and the gang at Dumpling Circus on Mott Street at 6:30.

After sending out a bunch of "belated merry Christmas" e-mails, I called B in Florida, figuring this would be a good time to catch her, but my call went straight to her voicemail. Finally I turned to the business I dislike most about Christmas: opening presents. I'm a giver, not a taker—if you haven't already guessed. It was the usual mixed bag. Three copies of a book titled *Capital in the Twenty-First Century*, by a French economist with the funny name of Piketty who purports to have a logical explanation of why the 1 percent have ended up with everything. When the book came out early this year I read about a hundred reviews and have no need to parse the tome itself—but it'll look good on the office bookshelf.

There were a half-dozen bottles of wine and spirits, ranging from the really good to the merely overpriced; two pairs of cashmere gloves from my staff; and a rare first edition of Berenson's *Drawings of the Florentine Painters*, a book I'd long coveted, from a collector I'd helped get onto a top committee at the National Gallery in Washington.

Most of the stuff was, as I'd expected, high-end boilerplate corporate "gifting," chosen by administrative assistants and contract shopping consultants. When I finished opening the lot, I reckoned I was looking at around $5K in Madison Avenue store credit, sufficient to see Maecenas through a significant part of our own business-gift budget for 2015.

Just before it was time to go out, B returned my call. She sounds fine, if subdued, enjoying her time with her father and playing the role of mother hen. When we finished, we blew each other long-distance kisses, and thus my fifty-fifth Christmas went into the books. As the old Dodger fans used to say, "Wait 'til next year!"

# DECEMBER 28, 2014

Today's the big day, the day I drop off the diary at Marina's. It's been a pretty unexciting four days since Christmas. There've been the usual hassles to deal with. Clients having trouble finding a notary in Anguilla; last-minute changes in this or that subvention; client-requested billing adjustments; problems with naming rights. One client who wanted to know whether I think his decision to give up his U.S. citizenship for tax reasons will affect NYU's plan to give him an honorary degree this spring.

Every day, I keep asking myself: where does all this money come from? It seems to me that we've added one or two zeros to every new normal. Programs that ten years ago we would have budgeted at $1 million now start at $10 million. In 1971, the Met paid $5.5 million for its Velázquez *Juan de Pareja*; a dealer told me the other day at lunch that if he had it to sell today, he'd ask $250 million. People who used to be happy with a $500,000 annual income now sink into depression if it's less than $5 million. You hear billionaires complain that the more money you have, the less it seems to buy. If I'd told my old man that Park Avenue apartments like the one he raised me in would one day sell for upwards of $30 million, he'd've had me committed. And yet Washington assures us that inflation's long dead. But it's not as if I don't benefit: when the norms escalate like this, no one's likely to cavil if I bump my own meager fees by another 10 percent, as I'm planning to do next year.

Lucia called yesterday from London to wish me Happy New Year and to report that her concierge business is going great guns, with her Russian clients spending like crazy on property and furnishings now that Putin is sticking it to the oligarchs and they're shoveling their rubles out of the motherland as fast as they can. She's also seeing a decided uptick in her "sheik" trade. She attributes this to fear on the part of Saudi royals, UAE emirs, and other potentates that ISIS may be a real threat down the line, and they better be ready to bail the instant the bad guys in black appear within fifty miles of Riyadh or Doha. London's no longer as hospitable to these people as it was, and Nevada now seems to be emerging on as the escape hatch of choice, probably because it's mainly desert and, well, full of hookers.

"The royal 787 is on twenty-four-seven standby in in the capital," Lucia said, adding that preparations are advanced in a neighboring emirate to move close to a billion dollars' worth of Gauguin, Picasso, and Cézanne on short notice out of the country and into the ruling family's vaults in a Geneva report. She went on to report that a chum in MI6 tells her that ISIS agents are circulating in the Qatar slave labor camps where the Bangladeshis and others imported to build soccer stadiums and palaces are penned up. The terrorist enlistment teams are having no problem signing up recruits, so there's another powder keg ready to blow up.

It was after she told me that she'd just cashed a "rather handsome" STST bonus check for work done in 2008 that I recalled that I had a New Year's gift of my own for Lucia, a bit of gossip that would give her warm memories of Rosenweis an extra holiday glow. It's a tidbit I picked up from a client, a trust-fund glamour girl who's married to an editor at *Fortune*. It seems that the magazine's going to be releasing a poll that ranks how 100 highly visible publicly traded companies rate with the public.

"Guess who's right at the bottom?" I asked her.

"Citibank?"

It was a logical guess. Most people would pick a company that transacts a lot of face-to-face, voice-to-voice business with the public, and if you've ever wrestled with Citi's phone tree, you'll know why the big bank was Lucia's first choice. Besides, only two weeks ago, Sen. Elizabeth Warren, the Massachusetts Democrat who has turned out to be Wall Street's biggest Washington nemesis, got up on the Senate floor two weeks ago and really laid into Citi, urging the government to break it up.

"Not a bad guess," I said, "but no soap. Try again."

"One of the big airlines? Walmart?"

"Wrong on both counts."

I heard her hesitate, then, in a voice edged with happy anticipation, she said, "Don't tell me!"

I knew she'd gotten it. "Right the fourth time!" I exclaimed. "The mighty TARPworm, ruler of all it devours! They're top of the charts—and by a healthy margin. For the way they treat their first-year hires."

"How absolutely marvelous!" Then she paused. "Does Richard Rosenweis know this yet?"

"Don't know. STST's no longer a client, and I never speak to anyone over there. I'm surprised they haven't asked you to rush back and save the day."

"Fat chance!" And on that cheering note Lucia and I ended 2014.

B called late this morning, and I told her I have a table booked at Balthazar at 7:30 p.m. on the 31st. That'll get us home in time to watch a movie. None of that Times Square ball crap for us. A good dinner, a movie, bed: that's it. We alternate picks and don't let on until just before we sit down to watch. I'm no mind reader, but I have a strong hunch that this year B's chosen *The Dirty Dozen* because she's mentioned it a few times in recent months. I gather it relates to a new project she and Claudio have got going with Carousel, the big cable outfit.

The next two days should be terrific. Marina and the diary, then B for New Year's. One triumph after another.

This has been some day. Not at all what I expected. A total bummer.

You'll recall, Gentle Reader, that I left the diary at Marina's yesterday.

She called first thing this morning. Excited is hardly the word for how she sounded. Apparently she stayed up until three in the morning reading the damn thing and says she needs to talk to me soonest. Needless to say, her excitement is infectious. Like her, I can hardly wait to get going. But I had a lot on my plate today that had to be dealt with, so we made a date for 6:00 p.m. at my place to discuss strategy.

I got through the day OK, although I confess my mind was elsewhere a good deal of the time. In my business, you get pretty good at centering your thoughts on B while your face and small talk indicate absolute concentration on A. I made sure I got out of the office early in plenty of time for a pit stop to pick up some special cuvée Pol Roger with which to toast the salvation of this great republic—and Marina's future Pulitzer.

The bell rang promptly at six. When I flung open the door, a huge triumphant grin pasted on my face, I got a shock. Marina wasn't alone. Artie was with her, and I could see at once that this wasn't some fortuitous coincidence, their arriving together. They had the look of a tag team climbing into the ring. Something was up. I guessed that she'd shown Artie the diary.

Even as I was sorting that out, I took note of Marina's expression. Marina's not exactly a high-fiver, but I was still expecting something more exuberant and positive than what was on her face. At least the kind of smile you see when your team leaves the field at halftime up 45–0. What I was looking at was the reverse: down 0–45, and your quarterback's just been lugged off to the infirmary.

When we sat down, I decided to let them have the opening bid, and looked expectantly from one to the other. After a short pause, Marina reached into her handbag and took out the memory stick I'd dropped off just a day and a half earlier. She placed it carefully on the coffee table, then gave me a warm smile, and said: "Chauncey, you're right. This *is* potentially the greatest gift—the greatest scoop—any journalist has ever been offered. You make Deep Throat look like chopped liver." She paused, and I knew at once that bad news was on its way, and I could guess what it had to be. She was turning me down.

I'll give her credit. She looked uncomfortable when she told me that she feels she simply can't do this, that in her opinion it will tear the country apart, and she doesn't want to be the agent of its destruction. "Forty years ago," she said, "it was different. Watergate fell on differently tuned ears. The country still had a modicum of community left. There was a kind of civic pride that kept things together. A kind of common purpose, you might say; a consensus, an agreement—admittedly vague—about what this country is supposed to be like and who's entitled to what. Today there's none of that left."

She let that sink in. Artie just sat there, keeping a poker face, but his body language declared that he was on board with Marina's thinking. I didn't know what to say, so I just sat there, too. Now will come the conciliatory bit, I found myself thinking. And I was right.

"Chauncey, your diary is pure gold, journalistically speaking," she went on. "If anything can stand up to the money that's poisoned our politics, it could only be something like what you have. Your journal certainly clears up a number of things I've had trouble with. I could never understand how the candidate—what do you call him, 'OG?'—suddenly came by all that early money in

2007 and 2008. One minute his people were in the streets with tin cups, the next he had money coming out of his ears to the point that he could walk away from public financing. It looked legit, all those small contributions, but when you think about it, the final number—around $750 million, $25 for every person in the country—seems out of whack.

"The Winters and Holloway appointments never made any sense to me, either, and I couldn't for the life of me understand how someone like Brewer got her job in the Justice Department and then kept it. Everything she did and said about Wall Street prosecutions flew right in the face of what the president had talked about in his campaign. And I've often wondered how exactly Struthers Strauss got bailed out of its GIG trades. Or how Polton slipped the noose on that Protractor deal. Then there's Greece: why Struthers hasn't been punished for helping them pull a fast one on the EU, Zeus only knows. I don't suppose you have the answer to that?"

I shook my head. I still had no idea what to say.

"So I'm flattered that you think enough of me to give me first dibs. If I took your material to David Remnick, I'm sure *The New Yorker* would devote an entire issue to it. I think Graydon Carter would give his eyeteeth to publish it in *Vanity Fair*. You and I would be on every talk show you can think of, and you'll surely be asked to testify to Congress."

I hadn't thought of this. The idea of having to face a panel of the peckerwood troglodytes committed to put Wall Street's and the GOP's well-being ahead of the people made me shiver, even as I heard Marina finish: "You could probably get seven-figure bids from publishers for the book rights, Michael Lewis money. Bob Woodward would jump at this!"

"This isn't about the money, Marina. You know me better than that."

"Look," I said in a voice that didn't sound pleading. "I know there are great journalists out there. But as much as I admire people like Taibbi, I don't know them. This is an all-time hot potato, and I can only give it to someone I trust to cover my ass. I betrayed the voters when I cut the deal with Orteig, and now I'm proposing to betray the people in whose interest I acted. That's a shitload of betrayal for one little guy to be lugging around. Hell, it could get me killed. I need to feel comfortable with whoever I do this with, and with us WASPs, comfort begins and ends with old acquaintance."

This made her smile. I started to continue, but Artie stepped in and cut me off: "Chauncey, it isn't just generalities. There are specific practical, political reasons for not making this public. Right now the GOP is flailing about. They need a cause. They'd like nothing better than to impeach the president. Your diary will give them the ammunition they crave."

"Why should it?" I wanted to know. "Impeachment is for bad stuff that goes down in the White House. When I cut my deal, this guy wasn't even a nominee."

"You know what I mean."

She looked over to Artie, who took up the thread: "The truth is that OG hasn't been all that bad a president, considering the obstacles he's faced. But he needs—the country needs—to see him finish strong."

"He let Wall Street off the hook," I objected. "And what about health care? It's a mess." I was going to go down swinging. It's *my* diary after all, and maybe Marina had a point: these weren't the only two fish in the sea. At least that's what I told myself at that moment.

"Nobody can say whether the ACA's working or it isn't," Marina argued. "Health care's like Dodd-Frank. Once the lobbyists got through with it, no sentient human being could understand how it works, really. But people seem satisfied on the whole. Or at least, a great many people who didn't have insurance are now covered. The GOP claimed the costs would skyrocket, but that hasn't happened."

The fact was, I don't know enough about health care to argue one way or the other. "OK," I said, "give him the benefit of the doubt on health care. But what about foreign policy? You can't tell me that's not a total mess."

"You're talking about the Middle East," Artie said, "but that's a Gordian knot that Metternich, Bismarck, and Talleyrand combined couldn't have unscrambled. He who was our ally on Monday in Syria is fighting us to the death on Tuesday in Yemen. Mistakes have been made, no doubt, but you have to ask yourself: who could have done better?"

"What it comes down to," Marina interjected, "is this: your diary can cripple this administration, what little time it has left. But is that what we really want? Arthur's right; it's highly likely that releasing your journal will move the GOP to bring an impeachment bill. It'll be a straw man, but it will burn up vast amounts of political energy. And I will guarantee you that this president won't cave the way Nixon did. He's not a drinker, and he isn't exactly full of self-pity. He'll never agree to give in to people he holds in utter contempt. The government truly will grind to a halt. Nothing will get done."

"It seems me to that nothing gets done as it is," I responded. Weakly, honesty compels me to add.

Marina now took the debate in a whole other direction. I was having trouble keeping my thoughts organized. "Chauncey, you have to be pleased with yourself for what you accomplished," she told me. "You were given a job; you did it—and did it wonderfully well. But has it occurred to you that your dealings with Orteig may have been only one of a series negotiated with the 2008 campaign? Has it occurred to you that yours might not have been the only $75 million moved into the campaign in return for understandings concerning other spheres of business? He raised over $800 million overall.

"Just think about it," Marina continued. "Wall Street's just one of many hogs at the trough. Look at Big Pharma and the health insurance companies and what they stand to milk out of the Affordable Care Act. You can hear them licking their lips from here to Capitol Hill. You think they were handed that for nothing? Why do you think health-care stocks keep reaching new highs? And what about the trillions in untaxed profits the big companies and wealthy individuals have stashed overseas? The legislation that protects these would be worth a great deal more than $75 million to the 1 percent, wouldn't you think? There would have to have been fixes put in all over the place. You may have just been one— and not a very big one at that."

This is something that's bothered me from time to time since I carried out my mission for Mankoff. It might be flattering to consider myself the only game in town, the man who fixed the World Series. But how could I be sure? I frankly found the inference hard to take. Still, I had to concede that while the notion might be demeaning, it was also possible. Would Mankoff have done that to me?

Of course he would. That's why he was Mankoff.

"And think of what Fox News—people like O'Reilly and Hannity—will do with your diary," Artie now added.

I was starting to feel like the shuttlecock in a game of badminton. "Those people are liars," I said. "No one I know listens to them." Even to my own ears I didn't sound convincing.

Marina: "No one except half the country. The half the three of us don't know. The half I don't write for because I know they refuse to read me. The half with guns. Just imagine how they'll react, given the excuse. You think this will change their minds about anything? It'll only fan the flames. There could be blood in the streets. Is that what you want?"

"I'm not sure."

And I'm not. Or I wasn't—not at that moment. Tomorrow, when I've had a chance to think this all through, I may change my mind. One thing I'm sure of, though: Marina's not going to change hers. She's out. For reasons I would only learn about later from Artie, reasons I have to respect even if I think the hand I've offered her is stronger than the hand she's chosen to play.

Anyway, we wore out the subject for the next hour, arguing up one side and down the other. At one point we got into a circular discussion about how my disclosures would prompt some smart lawyers to bring a class-action suit, the way they did against BofA and Citi, collecting multibillion-dollar multiples of the piddling multimillion-dollar settlements Uncle Sam extracted. If they could figure out whom to sue, that is. The government, for inadequate vigilance with respect to the electoral process? Mankoff's estate? Me? I do well enough, but I'm not good for that kind of money.

In the end, they wore me down and I ran up the white flag. I know I've mentioned in this diary how I was trained in various schools to lose gracefully, a concept that's next to blasphemy in twenty-first-century America, so when I finally accepted that I might potentially be responsible for the destruction of a polity that had lasted for two centuries, I broke out the champagne and we drank to principle—another notion that's not exactly prospering in the way we live now.

When it came time to part, all that could be said having been said, Artie asked if he could stay behind. He had something else he wanted to discuss with me, he said. Marina gave him a suspicious look, but what could she do? We embraced at the door, and I promised to give B a big hug for her. We swore eternal fealty, that this would make no difference to our friendship, and I think the feeling is genuine on both sides.

"Well," I said when I returned to the living room, "that was a surprise. I was flabbergasted to see Marina chicken out like that. You don't get many chances in this life to do someone a favor that's a real game-changer, and here I thought I was doing just that. Handing Marina the keys to the kingdom, the goddamn gold of the Nibelungs and Aladdin's lamp all at once, not to mention a sure-thing Pulitzer Prize, and she turns me down flat." I eyed him suspiciously, then added, "Something's going on, isn't it? You going to tell me what that something is?"

"There is," Artie answered. "She's sworn me to secrecy, but I suspect she knows I'd tell you anyway, so here we go. Marina has a conflict of interest that she's not at liberty to disclose to you, but which I, as your friend, feel I should."

"Which is what?"

"Have you heard anything about something called the Rediscovery Initiative?"

"Only vaguely." Scaramouche had mentioned it in his final letter, but frankly, I hadn't understood the reference, and hadn't bothered to look it up.

"I'm not surprised. For the moment, it's very hush-hush. I trust you know who Merlin Gerrett is, but are you aware that he has a sister?"

"I didn't."

"Her name is Circe. Apparently their father had a thing for sorcerers and sorceresses. Anyway, it seems that Circe Gerrett is a kind of philosopher queen who lives a reclusive life in the Rockies. Somewhere in Montana. She has a big influence on her brother—she owns a huge position in his company through a series of trusts—and she's convinced him that the only way this country can be saved from itself is if enough *good* big money can be persuaded to go up against *bad* big money. Just like we discussed at lunch all those years ago."

"Bad big money, like the Dreck brothers?"

"Exactly. Hence the Rediscovery Initiative. 'Rediscovery' as in helping America rediscover its founding principles."

"In other words, a third party?"

"Not quite. Maybe, in time, but for the moment it's a bunch of ideas the Gerretts believe the electorate, from both sides of the aisle, can be convinced to buy into. It's a political philosophy that's the direct opposite of what the Drecks and people like them believe. They believe in top-down control of the political economy: by buying politicians, basically. The idea the Gerretts are backing argues that the way to go is through bottom-up reclamation. Brother and sister are committing $2 billion at first, and they've already signed up Bloomberg, along with some very big Seattle money, and a bunch of Silicon Valley heavy hitters."

I had to sound skeptical. "'Bottom-up reclamation'?" I responded. "Are you kidding? In this country? Now? When the 1 percent have everything nailed down and to their liking and the lower brackets are fighting each other for crusts."

Artie smiled. "Cynicism doesn't become you, Chauncey. Just hear me out. Have you heard of Benjamin Barber? He's a CUNY professor who wrote a book called *If Mayors Ruled the World*. Its thesis is that reform politics and sensible government must be local to really take hold, and that it should be built around mayors. Circe Gerrett read it, was impressed, and got her brother to read it; he was impressed, too, and when they decided to go ahead with this Rediscovery Initiative they also decided to make the "Barber plan" a core program. They're recruiting 200 mayors who represent a cross-section of America: high-tech, Rust Belt, college towns, dirt-road hamlets, urban sprawl, you name it. And Marina's writing the manifesto."

"How did she get involved?"

"It seems that Circe Gerrett's a big fan of her writing. She reached out to our friend to head up the Initiative's communications end.

As it happens, she caught her at just the right moment: Marina's decided to switch voltages. She's concluded that tearing-down journalism isn't doing any good. The bad guys are too entrenched; they just get up, dust themselves off, and go about their business."

This wasn't a surprise. Words rarely work: to do the job properly you need sticks and stones and they cost money.

"The way she puts it," Artie went on, "is that even before the Gerretts popped up on her radar, she'd decided to get out of the Chicken Little business. She was just plain tired of writing bad stuff about terrible people. And then like an answered prayer, Circe Gerrett calls and offers her this job."

"You know what they say about answered prayers?"

"I'm going to choose to ignore that. It's a job with tremendous access; I gather that the remuneration is terrific, not that money has ever mattered to Marina, and it jibes perfectly with her present state of mind. But for the Initiative to take hold, the country needs to be relatively calm—that is, in no more than its usual uproar, and certainly not in the hysterics your revelations are likely to set off."

"I see." And I think I did. And I had my doubts. You may think your boy Chauncey cynical when I say that the last thing the country needs right now is another one of those feel-good, do-good, save-the-nation causes with names like the Hamilton Project, which *bien-pensant* billionaires are always launching to show how imbued with civic and cultural virtue they are. On the other hand, $2 billion for openers? That's serious money. Of course, the better angels of our nature, if there are any such creatures left, had best be billionaires.

One other thing bothered me. Noble intentions tend to fall about when skeletons come rattling out of the closet. There's a factoid going round that Artie's worshipful attitude toward Merlin Gerrett conveniently omits. To be sure, Gerrett has created a lot of jobs, especially in and around his hometown, but he's also participated recently in a massive destruction of jobs and communities. Last year, Gerrett was a major participant in a multibillion-dollar buyout of a famous global home products company. The word in the financial pages is that since the buyout closed, the private-equity firm that put the deal together has eliminated product lines, shut down plants, and fired tens of thousands of workers in this country and overseas, all in the interest of jacking up the investors' rate of return.

Of course, I didn't point that out. I simply listened as Artie spelled out the Initiative's plans for an organizing convention patterned on Philadelphia in 1787, and we left it that.

Frankly, I'm at sixes and sevens. But what was I to do or say to Artie? I'm all for giving virtue and good intentions every chance, but what I possess is dynamite, and the targets I have in mind still seem well worth blowing up.

Is the nation really that fragile? I just don't know, and should that really deter me? Maybe we deserve to be blown up and let the next generation start over.

I need to do some heavy thinking.

# DECEMBER 30, 2014

I went to bed in a sulk and woke up in a sulk. It's hard to accept Marina's turndown. Still, what can I do? If I try to take the diary to a journalist I don't know, either I have to find someone to make the introduction or make a cold call myself. In both cases, there'll be some preliminary explaining to do, which risks tipping my hand. And suppose whoever I approach turns me down the way Marina has? Sees things the way she and Artie do, that everything provoked by the disclosure won't be so much a healing catharsis but a destructive convulsion? Frankly, I doubt there's much of a risk of rejection. Most journalists would sell their mother for a scoop of the magnitude I'm offering. So I'm inclined to see if I can find a discreet path to Matt Taibbi. He's right up there with Marina when it comes to high-grade muckraking; he calls 'em as he sees 'em; he's a really good, strong writer. But I want to think this over.

Anyway, nothing can get done until the New Year. B gets here tomorrow, and her visit will take up my time and energy for the next couple of days. She leaves the morning of the 2nd; by then, my sulks will have faded—I know myself well enough to be sure of that—and I'll be able to think clearly about what to do next. If anything.

# JANUARY 2, 2015

Two hours ago, I took B over to the heliport, where a presidential chopper was standing by to convey her to Camp David. She's probably arriving just about now.

I have a lot to report since my last entry. Let's begin at the beginning.

After the usual airline problems, B got to my apartment mid-afternoon on New Year's Eve. "Do you mind if we don't go out?" were practically the first words out of her mouth. "I've had enough of people in the last two weeks to last me five lifetimes. I need a bath and I desperately need a nap."

"I can well imagine." Her mother's sudden death, looking after her father, the memorial service, all the people to be thanked, welcomed, wheedled, air-kissed, chatted with. Wears me out just thinking about it. I wasn't particularly worried about canceling on Balthazar—I knew it would take them about five seconds to fill my slot from a waiting list that must stretch from Prince Street to Key West. So I persuaded her that there was plenty of time to bathe and then catch forty winks, and I left the plan in place.

Which is what we did. As we both knew it would be, dinner was just great, and we were back at my place by 9:30, wide-awake and raring to watch.

"So—what is it this year?" I asked. "My money's on *Dirty Dozen*."

She smiled delphically, went into the bedroom, and returned with a fistful of DVDs. "I thought you might like to see the first three episodes of *American Jihad*, the new show. These are a little rough, still; we need to refine them down and take out a couple of minutes across the board, but they'll give you an idea—and I'm dying to hear what you think."

In a way my *Dirty Dozen* guess wasn't so far off the mark. *American Jihad* is about a bloodless (!) terrorist campaign waged by a small group of disaffected Americans against the plutocracy that has taken over this country and appropriated its wealth and its governance. On one side, you have the usual mixed bag of types: the core group is led by an retired professor of political science and his wife, a medical scientist, and their daughter, a teenage computer prodigy; other members of the cadre are IT and weapons experts, a former Special Forces operative, a CIA agent, the retired CEO of a major bank, and an aggrieved veteran of Iraq and Afghanistan, along with various supporting characters with specialized skills. Most important, the Cadre, as it's called, has access to the same tools as its targets, from private jets to offshore banks; it has unlimited money, multifaceted expertise, and deep technology.

Their enemies list is made up of the types who are thrust into our awareness almost every day, thanks to their thirst for publicity and their (and their PR reps') genius for getting it as well as what they get away with, which varies from vulgar exhibitionism to breathtaking greed to a total lack of real talent. The specific characters are heavily disguised, yet somehow recognizable. The first of the three episodes B brought for us to watch involves a lavish party in a pretentious, architecturally mediocre beachfront mansion—the Hamptons presumably, but it could equally be Malibu or the Florida Gold Coast. It's the sort of vanity event dripping with self-proclaimed "socialites" that gets written up in glossy society magazines and websites. Everyone is strutting their stuff, posing for the camera, showing off how rich and important they are—until interrupted by a flight of three smallish crop-spraying drones that suddenly appear overhead. Earlier in the episode, we've learned about these drones; we've watched them being conveyed to the launching point by fake FedEx trucks, and we've watched them armed and launched. That we can figure out what's coming doesn't spoil our pleasure. Once overhead, instead of herbicides, they will discharge on the glitzy company a mist compounded of raw sewage and industrial adhesive.

The scene is very well done. The camera lingers lovingly on the hysterical faces and shit-smeared finery of the partygoers, as the drones disappear out to sea. B tells me they flipped a coin between leading with this episode, or one in which a bunch of shit-spewing IEDs are set off at Art Basel Miami. They're saving the latter for later in the season "because that way we'll give the viewer a double bang for the buck: mess up a lot of crap people and wreck a bunch of crap art."

The second episode also centers on a party, this time one of those huge charity affairs where a ticket costs $10K and everyone shows up in couture and other adornments calculated to outglitter everyone else. It's obvious that Claudio and his writing team had the Metropolitan Museum Fashion Gala in mind as a model, but here again, this kind of event takes place all over the world—it could easily be Venice or Newport. The weapon of choice in this episode is a strain of *novovirus*, the germ that not long ago incapacitated entire cruise ships with diarrhea and vomiting. In this instance, the jihadists, as they call themselves, infiltrate the catering brigade and dose the elaborate cuisine with the virus. I must say that I greatly enjoyed the spectacle of the crème de la crème puking and shitting all over each other's haute couture as they fight their way to the loos. The actress playing the alpha female English fashion editor—the event's big dog—gives an Emmy-worthy performance.

The final episode is the most dramatic of all, and comes closest to crossing a line I'll come to shortly. The opening shot is of a long shadow extending north into Central Park almost to Wollman Rink. The camera tracks the shadow southward to its source: one of the condo skyscrapers thrusting into the sky like enormous glass needles that have been built a few blocks south of the park, where Russians, Chinese, and other flight-capital investors are buying $20 to $100 million condos as investments.

The scene then cuts to the jihadists discussing a plan to launch a shoulder-fired Stinger missile into the building. The plan is to attack after dark from a boat in the East River, using a laser programmed to strike a darkened section of one the buildings, on the assumption that unlit equals unoccupied. The actual attack is a masterpiece of CGI. The follow-up, a montage of the building emptying out in a frenzy, purchasers calling from Beijing to cancel sales agreements and decorating contracts, moving vans halted in mid-journey, real estate brokers weeping into the telephone as panic spreads throughout the Manhattan luxury market, developers pleading with bankers for time, is very convincing.

I liked what I was shown. Of course I would, since it goes after the sort of targets I would go after if I knew how, and if some of them weren't among my clients. (I'm not unaware of my own hypocrisy.) The show was very carefully and cleverly edited to focus on what I've observed over time as the New Plutocracy's Achilles' heel: its overweening arrogance about how its great wealth empowers it, along with the class's utter lack of humor about itself. These people actually think they deserve to be liked because they are rich, but few have relationships based on anything except deference bought with money—from headwaiters, money managers, interior decorators, and the people who sell luxury cars and watches.

As entertaining as it is, a veritable feast of lighthearted schadenfreude, *American Jihad* has a serious—to my mind, perhaps deadly—political undertone. It tacitly endorses class welfare. As one character puts it in the first episode, "These rich cocksuckers are destroying civil society as we know it; civil society has to fight back and to make it so hot for the bastards they either behave or are driven back under whatever rotten log they crawled out from under."

"So what do you think?" B asked me after the third and final episode ended.

"I liked it. I think going nonviolent is a very smart choice. Still, you need to be careful. Even nonviolence could put bad ideas into people's heads. You don't want to find yourself under fire the way the video game makers were when that kid shot up that school in Connecticut."

B smiled. "I'm glad you say that. The nonviolence angle is my doing, and I had to fight Claudio tooth and nail on it. As originally scripted, that episode with the drones *did* use napalm, and people were horribly burned. The special effects and facial makeup were terrifying; they made your average cable-TV zombie look like George Clooney."

"Do you have an episode planned about your loathsome Uncle Wally? I'd think he'd fit the bill perfectly."

B laughed. "Don't think we didn't consider it."

As we talked, my mind kept returning to the notion that, nonviolent or not, *American Jihad* is loaded with stuff that will have an impact on impressionable minds, starting with whom to hate and moving on to how and where to get hold of certain weapons and how to modify them. For instance, how to buy a Stinger in Romania and fit it with a guidance system developed in Turkey. This is information that might be put to lethal use by some scrambled egg out there who's brimming with resentment and haunted by demons. I can see how, in the wrong hands, *Jihad* might exert a more dire influence than *Grand Theft Auto* times ten.

"No doubt about," I told B when we finally wrapped it up and got ready for bed, "you guys have a winner here. There's a lot of rage out there, and you're going to tap into it without directly inciting people to blow up Congress."

The next morning, New Year's Day, I woke up early, clear-eyed and clearheaded, as if I'd gone to bed at 10:00 p.m. instead of 2:00 a.m. An idea had taken possession of me. Somehow, somewhere in the night, I came to the decision that whatever else may happen to the diary, I must show it to B. Given how our relationship has developed, this is simply too big a secret to keep from her. There are risks in showing it to her, but worse risks in keeping it from her, especially if I go ahead and seek out Matt Taibbi or another journalist to work with.

I slid out of bed and left B sleeping. I got out my laptop and skimmed through the diary to make sure that I hadn't missed any potentially troublesome or indiscreet personal and intimate stuff. I set the text up on an iPad I had kicking around (I have a bunch, each engraved with a different corporate logo, from a couple of years back when iPads were the business gift of the year). Now I was ready to go.

I started the coffee machine, and soon the apartment was filled with the compelling aroma of an overpriced artisanal fair trade blend that I knew would arouse B. Sure enough, there soon came a few ladylike groans and snuffles from the bedroom, then the expected bathroom noises, and in due course B appeared, dressed in an old robe of mine, eyes still half-closed, following her nose like some classic goddess feeling her way through the Stygian underworld. She is a girl who just *has to have* her morning coffee; only then can life and awareness begin.

She went off with a cup, got dressed, and returned, and we sat down to breakfast. We didn't talk at first. I shuffled through the *Times* and the *Post*; B checked her cellphone for e-mail and read "the dailies," as Hollywood calls its trade papers. She called Thayer in Boca, wished him a Happy New Year, put me on and I did the same, then B spoke to Claudio and wished the same to him and Frederick. After she hung up, she sighed how much she missed her mother. "You know something about Mother?" she said. "She understood differences."

"Such as?" I asked.

"Such as that a 'right' isn't the same as an 'entitlement.' She understood what privilege entails." She paused. "I'm going to miss her horribly. I already do."

"We all will," I said. "In that connection, there's something I need to tell you about." I placed the loaded iPad on the kitchen island between us. She looked at it curiously, then at me.

"You need to read this," I said. "It'll take you a couple of hours, tops. Then we'll need to talk."

"This sounds very ominous!" she exclaimed.

"Fear not. You're going to find it interesting, I promise you."

I watched her start the diary. I have to say I didn't feel nauseously nervous the way my writer friends tell me they do when a wife or boyfriend is reading a manuscript of theirs a few feet away. After all, my stuff isn't literary; it's the facts that matter, not the style. I knew I was taking a chance, but I felt I had no choice. She could very easily decide that what I'd done was defraud her and millions like her, get up, and walk out the door and out of my life. On the other hand, without Mankoff and me, her candidate would probably never have gotten elected.

My estimate proved more or less on the money. It was just before 2:00 p.m. when she got up and came back to the end of the apartment where I was working.

"That was fast," I remarked. I looked at my watch. "Just under four hours for something around five hundred pages. Yeoman's work."

"I actually finished a half hour ago, but I needed to think this over," she said, handing me the iPad. "You astonish me. I thought I understood you body and soul, but it seems you have unexpected depths—as an evildoer, at least. You could use an editor, of course."

"Forget the grammar and my writing skills," I replied. "Evil-doer? *Moi?*" I was trying to keep it light.

"I've had to decide whether to walk out that door and never see or speak to you again. I'm not sure I'm suited to be the life's companion of a bagman for Wall Street. You know how I loathe those people." Pause. "Oh, don't look so hurt. I'm kidding. We all make mistakes. You must have been a different person then—at least compared to the Chauncey I fell in love with."

She got up, came around, and gave me a kiss. "What matters, darling, is the simple fact of your showing me this, and what that says about our relationship. How could I not stick around?"

"The latter would be preferable. There's some other background you need to know, things that aren't in there."

For the next half hour, I took her through what I've told you about in this coda, Gentle Reader. I started with her mother's death and memorial service and how it—and especially the First Lady's performance—had affected me, and the determination my time in Boston sparked in me to put the diary in the public service. Then I went through my session with Marina and Artie in great detail, point by counterpoint. I confess I made myself sound eloquent and penetrating in argument and valiant and graceful in surrender, like the famous Velázquez painting, but what the hell: aren't I entitled to some satisfaction? I didn't say anything about the possibility of offering what I've got to another top-notch journalist, because frankly I wasn't there yet.

"Are you trying to inveigle me into interceding with Marina?" she asked when I finished. "You can forget that."

"Frankly, I'd never considered that," I replied. This was true.

"What's more," B continued, "I happen to think she's right. I think what you have is a prescription for virtual anarchy and very likely violence."

"No more than that show of yours."

412

"That's not at all the same. The country's split down the middle. In a showdown, who's to say the radical right won't win?"

I couldn't disagree. "Marina thinks it will inspire the GOP to impeach the president," I told B, "which will *really* shut the country down. She doesn't want to have anything to do with that." I suppose I could have added something about Marina's involvement with this Rediscovery Initiative of the Gerretts', but I make it my business not to go around spilling other people's confidences. If and when Marina wants this association to be known, let her tell B herself.

"You seem to think the president has no idea of this?"

"At the time, I'm sure he didn't. Now: who knows?"

"What about his wife? I remember Mother telling me how close with Orteig the candidate's wife was during the campaign. Do you think she knew?"

I shrugged. "Maybe—but I really doubt it," I said. "Certainly there was no opportunity for Orteig to consult with her; I didn't broach Mankoff's offer until I got him on the plane, and by the time I dropped him off in Chicago, we had a done deal. If Orteig had taken her aside afterward and whispered in her ear, my guess is she'd've kicked her husband's butt and we'd've had a better president these past six years. Everyone says she's one tough cookie and that he's scared shitless of her."

"That was certainly Mother's feeling—although she'd never have used that word. But that has given me an idea. Suppose . . ."

It took about ten minutes for her to explain her thinking. My first reaction was: No way. But as B fleshed out her thinking, and I silently compared her plan to the alternatives, I began to come around.

What she wants to do is to take my diary and show it to FLOTUS, and let the First Lady make the running, in private, with her husband.

It seems that FLOTUS has been concerned practically from

413

year one of OG's administration that her husband was being undermined from within. That his policy and legislative difficulties weren't strictly attributable to the unholy Washington triad: K Street, its Wall Street and corporate clients, and the idiots and bought men on Capitol Hill.

"How do you know this?" I asked.

"Mother told me. She and I had no secrets. She and the First Lady spoke regularly—two or three times a week, at the end. The woman's desperate. The president refuses to accept what's going on, and if he doesn't, and doesn't do something about it in the next two years, his legacy will be no better than the Clintons'."

So what? That was my first thought. Legacy shmegacy. Is this administration all about ego? "A fate worse than death," I commented.

"Don't be silly. Mother used to say that the First Lady's literally seething at the way things have gone and what history's likely to make of her husband."

"And you think that the First Lady can use *this*"—I picked up the iPad and flourished it—"to light a fire under the president's ass? Get him to use these last two years to turn things around? At least as far as history's concerned?"

"I do. This is a president who likes to talk things to death. But shove *this* in his face, and there's no way around it. It's all here in black and white. But he's gradually come to realize that he's been made a fool of. And he would rather hand the country over to Putin than let the world see that."

No way to disagree with that.

"OK," I said. "Suppose I let you take my diary with you to Camp David and you show it to FLOTUS. I'm not worried about it leaking, because if it does, the GOP'll have a bill of impeachment on the floor within twenty-four hours, and nobody wants that. Do you think the First Lady can get the job done?

B nodded vigorously. "Absolutely! Mother always said that she thought the president is secretly terrified of his wife. Give her a weapon like this, and . . . well . . . Don't have to draw you any pictures, do I?"

People say about bankruptcy that it happens gradually, then all at once. Mind-changes can work that way, too. That's what happened to me.

There are great, great journalists and powerful writers out there, but they're pushing a boulder uphill, trying to pierce an impenetrable static of ignorance and partisanship. I was keen to give my diary to Marina because she's a friend, and I like to do things for my friends, and I trust her to get the max out of the diary's potential to stir things up. But now that she's turned me down, I'm starting to see things clearly. Willie Sutton robbed banks because that's where the money is; today, if you want to effect real change, you have to go where the power is, and that's not in the media. What real change did Jon Stewart ever effect? What policy was rejected because Paul Krugman said it should be? Would there have been a Watergate if Fox News and Limbaugh had been in business back in the '70s? I think we know the answer. Sure, it's a big gamble, but at times when so little in this country's civic life becomes us, why not take the shot?

Compared to what we might be, to the kind of exceptional country—the kind of exceptional people—we tell ourselves we are, America is in rotten shape. But it least it still works, sort of. We haven't turned into Egypt or Russia or Brazil. Not yet, at least. But we might.

"Why not?" I said, finally.

And that is how it came to be that when B climbed aboard the Air Force One chopper this morning, an iPad with my diary on it reposed in her shoulder bag. Matters are now out of my hands. *Che sarà, sarà.*

In its way, this is where I came in. Much has changed in the world and the nation since February 2007—one thinks of ISIS, of GOP nutcases controlling both houses of Congress, of *Citizens United* legitimizing practices I had to go to elaborate digital lengths to bring off—but on Wall Street little has: a few new games, "flash" trading, and a desperate chase after yield in the wake of the Fed's zero-interest-rate bailout. A few new names—the banks once ruled, it's the hedge funds and private-equity players now—but basically the same old extractive usuries, with the 1 percent capturing even more of what little is left. Rumors are circulating that the derivatives market is more attenuated and vulnerable than ever, thanks to a new clearing-house scheme and a bunch of credit "innovations."

Still, there's hope. Who can tell? Perhaps people like Elizabeth Warren are having a bigger reformist effect than we perceive. The wails and whines we hear from Wall Street may not simply be propaganda; they may have some basis in fact.

It's a brave new world, no doubt of that. Technology has taken over, from smartphones to stuff like Uber and Airbnb, and Silicon Valley, today the dominant force in the economy, seems as careless of the community life of the nation as Wall Street was in its greatest heyday. In 2007, *Forbes* listed 946 billionaires in the world; this year I'm told the number will exceed 1,800. If one expresses this increase in terms of social and moral productivity, it looks inflationary to me, no matter what the Fed tells us.

Any way you look at it, however, the next couple of years are going to be interesting. Of only two things am I certain: that the markets will fluctuate and that my beloved Mets will again finish at or near the bottom of the National League East.

It may be that the First Lady can use my diary to put some fury- or shame-driven backbone into her husband, as B thinks she will, and that the last two years of OG's presidency will finally put on parade the man people thought they were voting for in 2008. At the very least, I expect we'll see a big shakeup in the White House. Fortunately for Orteig, he's already out the door. Will Wall Street finally be led to the gallows? Will the SEC and other agencies finally begin criminal prosecutions for securities malefaction? We'll just have to see. I doubt it—but Washington will definitely make it tougher for the pinstripers. At some point, you do have to walk the walk.

It will be interesting to see if this Rediscovery Initiative that the Gerretts and other billionaires are funding, and that Marina's hooked up with, can gain traction. Can *good* Big Money take on *bad* Big Money and prevail? I think the country's ready for a legitimate third party—I know I am—and this may give the former mayor of New York the springboard he's looking for (or said to be looking for) to take a shot at 1600 Pennsylvania Avenue. It will take someone like him, with humongous personal resources, and self-confidence to match. People are saying that the next election will see upwards of $3 billion spent; the lousy $75 million I infused into OG's first campaign would hardly make a dent. I like the guy all right; he's smart and decent; my only concern is that he might do to the country what he did to New York City: turn it into a sandbox for real-estate developers.

So there we are. I realize that to end this way must seem a bit of a letdown. The story should end more dramatically, with assassinations and prosecutions. After all that's happened—all those years, months, days; all those schemes, plots, backroom dealing, and so on, you'd think I'd be able to supply a grander denouement. It looks as if T. S. Eliot got it right with his surmise that the world ends not with a bang but a whimper. On the other hand, I can't say I'm not a bit relieved. A smash ending often pulverizes everyone onstage. Look at the great Shakespearean tragedies, the Greeks—final curtains descending on stages littered with corpses.

And I'd be a liar if I didn't admit that now and then I've wondered whether taking the diary public might incite someone to take out a contract on me.

Time now to lower the curtain once and for all. These revels really are now ended and how and by what my little life will ultimately be rounded will be decided by fate and the woman I love. Who knows, maybe I'll pop the question.

So this is it for us, old soul. God knows when you'll be reading this. Anyway, I wish you well, I wish us well, I wish the republic well; in its best moments, this is a country very much worth saving from itself, if that's still possible and it might not be—so far have we fallen, so deeply have we been corrupted, so degraded are we intellectually. Still, there's always hope, but that will require forces more convincing and formidable than I could ever set in motion.

If I may rephrase the end of my favorite novel, here we are again then, boats against currents that drag us relentlessly into the future. There's nothing left to say, Gentle Reader, except what I think Tiny Tim would have said for all of us, to all of us, were he alive today:

God help us, every one!

# ACKNOWLEDGMENTS

A lot of research went into *Fixers*. My roll of honor of those who I honestly feel made a difference to the way this novel has turned out must start with Yves Smith, proprietor of the indispensable financial blog *Naked Capitalism*, and the journalists Matt Taibbi—whose reporting on Wall Street, crony capitalism, and the financial crisis hearkens back to the great muckraking journalists of Theodore Roosevelt's era—and William D. Cohan, one of the few journalists writing out of the same deep, skeptical experience of Wall Street as my own.

But at the end of the day, *Fixers* imagines connections between known sets of facts that add up to an alternative, plausible interpretation and explanation of the financial crisis and its aftermath. None of the central characters, the half dozen or so with speaking parts, is based on a real-life model.

This brings me to the people who deserve real credit for doing what editors and publishers are supposed to do: help an author wring the book he wishes to write out of the book he has written, and then help *that* book to find a readership. The first is Mark Krotov, whose arrival at Melville House solidified that relationship. I have every confidence that he and his colleague Julia Fleischaker will help this novel find the readership we feel it deserves. The same goes for the founders of Melville House—Dennis Johnson and Valerie Merians—with whom I have been working since they published my novel *Love and Money* in 2009. Indeed, it was a somewhat offhand suggestion by Dennis that prompted me to throw out hundreds of pages and rewrite *Fixers* entirely in the first person.

Finally, there is my girlfriend, now my wife, Tamara Glenny. In trying to list the ways in which she has made such a difference, I run out of nouns and adjectives. She is a fierce line editor, wielding a blue pencil like a scimitar; as a copy editor, she can pick nits with the best of 'em; as a taskmaster, she knows exactly when to wield the carrot and when the stick. She has been by turns supportive, critical, thoughtful, argumentative, sympathetic, intemperate, caustic, demanding, selfless, witty, and loving. Everything one craves in a wife and an editorial helpmeet.

I can't close without a shout-out to my children and stepchildren, their spouses and children, and certain old friends. Just knowing you're out there has kept me going.

# ABOUT THE AUTHOR

**MICHAEL M. THOMAS** is a former partner at Lehman Brothers, and the bestselling author of nine novels, including, most recently, *Love and Money*. His commentary and criticism have appeared in *The New York Times*, *The New Yorker*, *The Wall Street Journal*, and *The Washington Post*, and in a regular column for *The New York Observer*. He lives in Brooklyn, New York.

FEB 2 3 2016

GT Rot 3/17

PP 7/17

TRF MN 12/27